PETER'S CHOICE

✝

JOSEPH ORBI

ROM Publisher • New York

Peter's Choice ©1997 by Joseph Orbi

All rights reserved. No part of this book may be reproduced, stored in a retrieval system, or transmitted in any form or by any means, electronic, mechanical, photocopying, recording, or otherwise without prior written consent from the publisher, except in the case of brief quotations in critical articles and reviews.

ISBN 0-9661619-0-4

All inquiries should be addressed to:

ROM Publisher
340 East 64th Street
New York, NY 10021
(212) 759-0892

Printed in the United States of America

First Edition

Note from the Author

Peter's Choice is a work of fiction. Yet, in an effort to give it a ring of authenticity, I have kept the spelling of some of the proper names faithful to their origin. The "š" character in several words and names in the book is pronounced like the English "sh." The "ć" is pronounced like "ch."

Acknowledgments

A book like *Peter's Choice* is not possible without the help and moral support of many. Among them, Milan Stojanović went out of his way to make available important historical documentation when he should have been focusing on his studies at Harvard. And Patricia Woods, who unselfishly has invested many hours to bring *Peter's Choice* to fruition.

In particular, two extraordinary women must be singled out: Alicia Bibiloni and Jacqueline da Costa. Without them *Peter's Choice* would have turned into a very unrewarding expedition.

PETER'S CHOICE

I had most need of blessing, and 'Amen' stuck in my throat.

—Macbeth, in *Macbeth*

THE APPARITION

1

Louie the Fox scurried down the narrow and muddy country road, a road flanked by cow-less pastures. He pressed the large black duffel bag against his chest, trying to keep it dry—an almost impossible task. It was as miserable, as black and as blustery a winter night as one would not want to find anywhere, and the cold, torrential downpour soaked Louie's beat-up parka as he hopped and skipped from one side of the road to the other, trying to avoid the giant potholes of slush. The battle with the elements was an uneven one. Louie rubbed his hands continuously, when he wasn't wiping the flow from his nasal cavities with whichever shirtsleeve was less wet at the moment. He just wanted to get it over with, go home and drop dead, as long as he dropped dead in his dry bunk. He was a sorry-looking specimen—thin, old, twitchy and poor, though not as old, thin and twitchy as he was poor—and typical of the impoverished back roads of Louisiana. "The Fox" was quite an unsuitable nickname for Louie, but it had become attached to his name after he was caught trying to steal chickens from Bernie's ranch a few years back. The Fox was more a gerbil than a fox, and to label him "the Fox," with its implication of cunning and vigilance, was not to know him well—or not to know the difference between a gerbil and a fox. Even his protruding teeth (or what was left of them) and his look of hopelessness pointed to that domesticated rodent.

Louie arrived at the Miltedew's a half hour after leaving Father O'Malley hitting tennis balls inside the church. The Fox was in no mood for civility. He kicked open the dilapidated gate, scrambled the last three hundred feet across the yard, skipped up the five steps with an agility not commonly seen in a man of sixty, and arrived at the door of the run-down shack looking now like a gerbil who had been dunked in a fish tank by a fun-loving youngster.

The interior of the house was clean and neat, but also small, bleak and cold. A light bulb hung from the ceiling, trying unsuccessfully to keep the powers of the night at bay. An industrial carpet, green at one time, covered the floor. There were four windows, two on each side of the door that opened onto the front steps. One of the windows was taped over with a dark green plastic garbage bag, thanks to a large hailstone that fell from the heavens and, like an ill-fated meteorite, smashed through the glass, to end its life as a small pool of water in the middle of the living room. The consequence of that hailstone gone awry was that the shack looked like Moby Dick after getting his eye pierced with a harpoon. Inside, duct tape was put to good use keeping out the intemperate gales. The furnishings were meager and scattered: a couch concealed by a blanket, several worn chairs, two lamps without shades or bulbs, and a few family photos accompanied by two pictures of Elvis in a place of honor on the center wall, next to a large painted-on-velvet likeness of the Virgin Mary. To the side of the living area was a kitchen equipped with a microwave, a gas stove and small fridge, and further to the rear, off a narrow corridor, two small bedrooms and one bathroom. The only furniture in the bedrooms were the mattresses where every night Ray, Harriet, Teddy and sweet Alice Miltedew lay down to dream of a better life.

"Ray, where are ya?"

"Sunbathing." Ray sat hunched over like an invalid. Once tall and straight, he swayed back and forth in the rocking chair, bundled up to his thick eyebrows in a blanket, three pairs of pants, three shirts and every sweater and jacket he owned (though without, for no clear reason, the other perfectly warm blanket on the couch). His black hair reached to his shoulders and was filthy and matted. Wretched poverty had degraded not only his way of life but also his youth. His face was sallow, his stubble black and grey, his lips purple from the cold, and his big brown eyes sunk deep into their sockets, framed by black circles and clamped in place by the wide bridge of his long nose.

"Jeeessuuss, ol' buddy, ya look like shit." Then Louie got down to business. He apologized for being late—Father O'Malley had been a real pain in the ass, making him mop the kitchen of the rectory and sweep the hall before leaving for the night. Nevertheless, Louie had been able to stow away a few articles he proposed to peddle to his acquaintances, Ray among them. The Fox put down the duffel bag, unzipped it and began pulling out an assortment of electronic gadgets, placing them carefully on the floor before the master of the house. These included a Walkman with headphones; a blender; a juicer; and a small eight-millimeter movie projector with its own spool of film. As soon as the Fox finished with the display, he began to recite the retail value of each item: five dollars for the Walkman and headphones; five dollars for the blender; five dollars for the juicer; and five dollars for the projector. Louie plugged the projector into the wall to give Ray a demonstration of what the machine could do, while explaining several plans that could help even the most hard-up consumer afford the items offered. For instance, Ray could take three of the items for twelve dollars, three dollars off the original retail price. Or, if he wished, Ray could buy two items for eight-fifty, one dollar and fifty cents off; or Louie would consider selling all six items for twenty-two dollars even—a whole eight dollars below retail, a great opportunity for any discriminating customer.

"You're a thief," said Ray.

"I know that, ya know that—even the cops knows that—although not well enough, eh? He, he." The Fox grinned, one of his few remaining teeth making a quick showing. "Hey, buddy, what can I say, I am what I am, we are what we are—ya are what ya are—but, what's a feller to do? I'm splittin'—goin' and saying adios to this dead town, ol' buddy, and need some moolah to get outta here."

Ray stepped over the merchandise, brushed past the salesman, walked to the door, opened it, looked out, closed the door and turned to the Fox. "Know why I'm sittin' there—hour after hour, day after day, Louie? I'm sittin' there 'cause I can't find nothin' to do. No job, no *nothin*'. You know why it's so cold in here, Louie? 'Cause we have no oil for heat." Ray moved slowly toward the merchant. "Wanna know why we have no oil for heat? 'Cause I can't find nothin' to do to earn money so I can't pay for it, Louie. And you know what? Tomorrow they're shutting off the electricity, Louie."

"Easy, there ol' buddy." The Fox did not like the way his prospective client was looking him over.

"Life's a bitch, then the town goes belly-up. Mayor spits out a few fancy-pansy words—words like inflation, depression—as if they were chewed-up wads of tobacco. And then shits like me end up rocking back and forth day after day, staring and climbing the fuckin' walls!" Ray grabbed Louie by the neck and pulled him up a little, enough for the Fox to start looking like a fish out of water, with rolling and slightly bulging eyes. "So, let us here suppose," continued Ray, "let us here suppose I had a couple of bucks. You think I'd give 'em to a sorry-lookin', stinkin' rat like you for stolen shit? You're an asshole!"

There was a lot of fidgeting and sniveling before the Fox got away. He put his hand to his chest, and with a look that was meant to convey sincerity—but ended up as an unvarnished display of fear—cried out, "Hey, Ray, how come ya call me a rat? It's me, Louie! Remember? We go way back, man. *Way* back. Ya an' me! What's the matter with ya? *Ya*—" and here the Fox was quite emphatic "—ya call me a stinkin' rat—why?" The Fox continued to rant and walk in circles, flinging his arms in wild indignation. "Why ya threatening me, man? I was like yer very own daddy. When yer daddy cut loose, right? Who took care of ya, of yer old lady—even yer sister? Who? It was me, Ray, me! Louie Peps! I took ya huntin' when ya were this high!" The Fox attempted to show Ray's correct height during those sunnier times. "I gotcha yer first bike, yer first .22, showed ya how to kill lizards, ride a bike; then when ya fell off and broke yer arm, who hauled ya to the vet? And I woulda taken ya to a real doctor if I had a car, but I didn't and yer old lady didn't either, or Tony, yer uncle, he didn't do it—'course, he was probably stoned, like always. I ain't holdin' it 'gainst him, I swear I'm not!" And Louie shed a tear which had no sooner made its way down his cheek than it was lost in the other facial moisture accumulating on his upper lip. "Even—and as God's my witness I hate fishin'—I took ya fishing! Who gave ya yer first smoke, yer first grass? Me, that's who! Louie, the same Louie yer now calling a rat! Louie who showed ya how to use a rubber so ya could go fuck old man Puryear's wife! It ain't fair, Ray, if I have to say so myself. It just ain't fair! You calling me a stinkin' rat!"

"What the fuck are you talking about?"

"Talkin' about? Life, yers and mine, that's what I'm talkin' about! Yer gonna tell me now it never happened, right? Yer gonna turn 'gainst me, I know ya are, I see it in yer eyes! After everything I done for ya, I mean—yer like my very own!"

Ray was moved less than Louie had anticipated. The idea of anyone being related to Louie was enough to sink an evolutionist to despair. On the other hand, thought the master of the house, Louie could prove the fabled missing link. He was certainly out of his mind—probably taking acid again—since it had been less than a year since Ray had made the Fox's acquaintance. "You're a fuckin' fruitcake, Louie, you're brain dead."

The Fox reached into his parka and pulled out a wet and limp cigarette. "It ain't right, that's all I gotta say! It ain't!"

"Get the fuck out, you smell like shit." Ray turned away from the Fox, pulled the blanket over his shoulders and returned to his rocking chair.

"Ya know what yer problem is? Ya reached a time in life when being here, inside these fuckin' four walls, with yer fuckin' old lady on one side, the fuckin' kids on the other—is like—like fuckin' death! I know, I been there."

It was too much, even for Ray. He jumped up and seized the ranting Fox.

"Lemme go!" Louie shook himself loose, ran to opposite side of the room, tripped and fell backwards.

Ray looked down at Louie, and for a thousandth of a second felt sorry for him. In that thousandth of a second Ray saw, not Louie looking up, scared, saliva dribbling from his mouth, but himself. Is this what life had in store for losers after all was over and done with? But Ray was not Louie. Louie was a pitiful man, an oddball whom everyone shunned. Ray had a family and friends who loved him.

"Ray, goddamn it man, watch the coat!" the Fox screamed as Ray dragged him to the door. His protestations were enjoyed only by the elements, however, because by the time he yelled, "Yer fuckin' ungrateful, ya know that!" Louie the Fox was again being drenched by the icy and never-ending downpour.

Louie had once more ingratiated himself to the gate with a frontal assault when he remembered his merchandise. He jumped up and down and cursed. A little voice warned the wary Fox that perhaps, perhaps it would be better to wait and give Ray time to cool off; the Fox could always return for his goods later. "Fuckin' a, fuckin' ungrateful shit!" Louie muttered under his breath, then threw the parka over his head, hunched his shoulders forward and continued the long march to town.

Ray was back in his rocking chair when he realized the Fox had left his spoils behind. He threw off his blanket, ran to the door and yelled "Louie!" The Fox was nowhere in sight. Ray slammed the door and walked back to the chair. Suddenly, the wretched fellow was seized by an uncontrollable urge to bang his head against the wall, which he did—until he felt the warm blood oozing from his crown. Guilt was manifesting itself in due form. What would Harriet say if she came home and found property belonging to the church (stolen no less) all over the place? First a loser, then a thief! Ray dropped to the floor and screamed. "Why me!" He implored the gods as if the gods had singled him out from among the billions of people in the world. "Why me!!!" All the days he had sat rocking back and forth in the chair, the useless months, the thousands of worthless hours began to strangle his thoughts. There was no doubt whatsoever; as a husband, as a father, as a provider for his family he was a failure. Yes, his kids loved him and so did his Harriet, they all loved him and that made everything that much worse. The seething rage and indignation, the resentment and shame were suffocating him. He came up for air and started crashing and bouncing everything in the house off the walls; chairs, the table, the cans and everything else in the cupboard, the projector, the Walkman and the blender. Everything! He slammed them and smashed them until nothing was left in one piece. Ray howled, then stood silent in the middle of the room. There was only one thing left to do, something that would free him from anguish and liberate his family from a man paralyzed by failure. Stumbling about the freezing room, he took off his belt, grabbed a chair, climbed on top, tied the belt around a beam on the ceiling, wrapped the end around his neck, kicked off the chair and hung himself. He did not do so quietly, however. Human nature being what it is, Ray immediately changed his mind. He tried to tear off the belt encircling his neck while his legs lashed out in every direction, kicking the standing lamp and sending the room into total darkness. Ray's life did not flash in front of him, however; nor did he hear the voices of his grandparents who had passed away when he was a child and were now waiting for him in heaven (as Ray thought). He experienced none of that—thanks to a colony of hungry termites who had gobbled up most of the old beam to which the belt was fastened, leaving it unable to withstand Ray's weight, thin as he was. The beam came crashing down with a violent thud, foiling Ray's effort to kill himself but knocking him unconscious as it landed on his head.

He lay there for over an hour in the cold dark room, half conscious and with a great bump on his skull. He dreamed he heard the sweet voices of his children calling out to him, imagined his mother-in-law's Corolla grunting as it made its way to the house; he thought the car had finally given up in front of the house, flinging its door open and spitting out his little boy and girl. He heard Teddy and Alice cry out, "Bye, Grandma, bye!" and then the grandmother call back, "Get inside, don't you get wet, now! Tell your mother to come by tomorrow!"

"Yeah, okay!" cried Teddy.

"Okay!" echoed Alice.

Ray suspected that his children were climbing the steps as he had seen them do thousands of times and that the sick Corolla was trying in every way to drag itself off the property. He assumed that Teddy and Alice were tired; that Teddy was leading his younger sister to the door; that they were carrying their schoolbooks from that morning; that Alice was holding on to a very old and rather unglamorous Barbie whose hair looked like Don King's; that, although the family was terribly poor, Teddy and Alice were not burdened with a troubling sense of shame because most of the other children in the parish lived in like conditions; that except for the times when their daddy and their mommy argued, Teddy and Alice seemed happy; that Teddy, in his love for his little sister, would open the door and, if nobody was home, enter first, making sure it was safe for Alice; and that he would turn on the light and then let her in the room; that—that—

All of it went through Ray's mind while he lay on the floor, unable to move.

"Ma! Ma!"

"Ma! Ma!" Alice imitated her brother.

"Daddy!" This was Teddy.

"Daddy!" This was Alice.

There was a long and uncomfortable silence as the children stood outside. Teddy wondered if his parents had abandoned them forever. He had read the story of Hansel and Gretel and how they were left alone in the dark and terrifying woods. But Teddy knew it was only a silly book. Teddy knew he did not have an evil stepmother but a mother and daddy who loved him and his little sister very much and would never abandon them to the wicked witch. With that worry out of his head, Teddy shrugged, opened the door and walked into the house. "Get in," he ordered his little sister. "Hurry, you're getting wet!" Teddy pulled Alice into the room and shut the door.

"It's dark!" The little girl was not afraid of the dark, but given a choice, she would—like most children—invariably take a well-lit, cheerful room. While searching for some kind of light, however, Alice and Teddy were not ready for the dazzling eruption just above their heads. It was a brilliant kaleidoscopic universe with billions of twinkling stars, as lively as if the Creator had just finished setting them against the immensity of eternal black; as if He had ordered those same stars to perform for the heavens, led by angels swelling their exhilarated diaphragms and buffeting creation with such a glorious symphony that they beat down the night and routed the shack's bleakness to the borders of infinity. The children stood in complete, terrified and shivering awe as the Blessed Mother, the Virgin Mary, the mother of Jesus Christ, appeared dressed in crimson robes lined with silver, wearing a jeweled crown upon the gold veil studded with a galaxy of stars that covered her lustrous yellow hair. In one hand, as pale and delicate as the finest porcelain, Mary held a silver scepter encrusted with diamonds and rubies. In the other, she carried a small sphere made of gold, emeralds and sapphires. She hovered a few feet off the ground opposite the children while the lofty choir of a million angels sang praises to Jesus.

What else is there to say? Teddy and Alice were struck with a mix of all-encompassing love, abject fear and total confusion. They looked at each other as "Hallelujah!" thundered in their ears. They dropped to their knees at once, crossed themselves three times, brought up their hands in fervent prayer, looked at each other one last time, turned again to stare at the blazing Virgin and fainted.

LEGACY OF MADNESS

2

In early 1941, long before little Teddy and sweet Alice were born, Hitler, it could be said, was not a happy man. Operation Barbarossa had to be postponed when a British-backed coup toppled the pro-German government in Belgrade. As the Germans were venting their wrath on Yugoslavia and blitzing the capital in retribution, a black Mercedes with a red cross on each door and diplomatic plates approached the entrance to the camp. It had traveled all night from Banja Luka, winding up and down the hills and valleys of the Croatian landscape.

A flag with a large checkerboard *U,* symbol of the Ustaše, stood high above the massive brick entrance. Attached to its façade was a sign that greeted all those ill-fated souls who passed through the iron gate: "Work Service of the Ustaše Defense Assembly Camp III." The word *Ustaše* means rebel in Serbo-Croatian, but by this time Ustaše had become synonymous with the Croatian fascists that in 1941 set up, with a little help from their friends, the Independent Nation of Croatia.

Two rail-thin peasant youths sporting dark green military jackets and wool caps, and lugging Maricić carbines examined the automobile before letting it continue inside. It was late afternoon in late spring, and the flood waters from the river had yet to subside. The glint of the sun bounced off the windshield as the sentinels respectfully requested the priest at the wheel to get out and open the trunk. They were not to take anything for granted; the enemy looked just like they did.

The concentration camp was east of the Jasenovac plain, on the banks of the river Sava, between the Croatian cities of Zagreb and Banja Luka. It was a large compound, with dozens of barracks running parallel from one end to the other, and was divided into five distinct zones, each one specializing in a different mode of extermination. Two tall, electrified fences encircled the complex, and watch towers rose from the ground at intervals—sinister, dark, wooden and square, like coffins with rectangular slits for machine guns, from where the ever-vigilant Ustaše sentries scanned the horizon. Father Draganović was impressed with the no-nonsense look of the place. He did not mind letting the guards look inside the trunk; the only thing in it was his spare tire. Draganović was relieved to have finally arrived at the camp. At one point in his trip he doubted he would make it at all, because maps were out of the question in case he was stopped by partisans—those insurgents backed financially and politically by Stalin who were fighting the Ustaše and the Germans for control of Yugoslavia. The priest had been obliged to rely entirely on the directions he memorized before leaving Zagreb. Unfortunately, directions most of the time rely on road signs and topography, and war has a way of doing away with both. Once the inspection of the car was finished, Draganović drove a little way into the camp and stopped beside a low flat building with a loudspeaker on the roof and a crudely lettered sign that read "Commandant." Father Draganović turned off the engine and stepped out of the car. He heard a boisterous cheer coming from the north end of the camp. For a moment Draganović thought the guards might be engaged in some form of recreation—playing soccer, perhaps—to alleviate the pressures of their disagreeable but necessary duties. He himself could not understand, however, how anyone could waste precious time in such impractical pursuits in the middle of a war. But while war is many things, it is hardly ever practical. The priest turned to a heavyset guard walking by. "Filipović?"

The man did not reply but pointed instead in the direction of the applause and the bravos. A funnel of dust enveloped Draganović as he walked in search of the friar. Father Krunoslav Draganović was thirty-two, and looked more like a rugby player than a priest. He was tall, with a large, tanned frame and a strong build. His dark brown hair was cut fastidiously close, his lips were razor thin, and his eyes were grey and determined. They revealed an unbridled conviction that stemmed from the father's inexhaustible faith, a faith anchored in his righteous and fanatic crusade for Croatian independence. Here was a man who loved precision and detail, a man who did not idly spend time contemplating action. If action was called for, contemplation was beside the point.

"Filipović!" called out the priest. He spotted the friar watching a group of guards and prisoners assembled at the edge of the embankment. Brother Miroslav Filipović was dressed, not in the garb of his order, but in full Ustaše uniform, with a pistol on his hip and a wooden mallet stuck through his belt. The friar was a plain-looking man with dark complexion, about twenty-eight years old. He was tall and stocky with a broad forehead on a small square head. His features included a very small mouth with thin lips, hardly improved by a pair of black eyes, puffy cheeks, a flimsy mustache and slick, combed-back hair. Brother Miroslav was so professional in his role of camp commandant that he was known, affectionately, as Brother Satan. "Father," Filipović said with a frown, "I thought you were coming tonight."

"What is this?" asked Draganović pointing to the spectacle taking place before them. The camp guards had lined up the prisoners in four rows, one behind the other, that extended for two hundred meters along the edge of the embankment. There were thousands of men, women and children, most of them on their knees, with their hands tied behind their backs, while others were already floating below on the red waters of the Sava. Not far away, at the other end of the camp, Father Draganović noticed seven tall crosses with seven prisoners who were being crucified.

"Oh, just a bit of fun. The guards have bets on who can do more prisoners in a day," replied Brother Satan. "Life here is dull, we have to make sure the guards don't get bored. The last thing I need is a bunch of mad Croat peasants running around with guns and knives and nothing to do."

"Charming," Draganović remarked dryly. He saw that the prisoners were not being shot, but were having their throats slit; others were bludgeoned to death with mallets. "Why don't you shoot them?"

The priest remembered what Mile Budak, the minister of religion and education, replied when the British envoy inquired as to how the new government of Croatia would deal with its ethnic minorities: *"For them, we have three million bullets."*

"No, no. The rules of the contest are clear. Each participant kills in medieval fashion, with a knife or hammer," explained Filipović. "That man over there is winning." The brother pointed to a fair, stumpy fellow moving with incredible grace from one inmate to the next. Each time he moved on, the body of the previous prisoner would stiffen, then slump forward while his head fell back. "His name is Braciko, way ahead of the rest. He has a special knife, you see, and so far he's cut the throats of over one thousand three hundred and sixty of them in a little over five hours. That's two hundred and seventy-two an hour. He is absolutely amazing and very shrewd. He concentrates mostly on children. Their throats are more pliable and tender, easier on the blade, you understand. I have never seen anything like it in my life. And you know, he stopped to take lunch. But, who cares, nothing but Serbian trash here, Jews, and yes, we have Gypsies too."

"War," sighed Father Draganović.

"It's a strain," joined Filipović. "Would you like some coffee?"

"Coffee? Not that Turkish mud that tastes like—"

"No, no, no. I have just received a box from Rome. It's Puerto Rican coffee—delicious, trust me."

"I don't have much time."

"You're always in a hurry, Father. Look, see those two men over there? They are the ones I told you about." Filipović pointed at two friars keeping count of the competition. "They are conscientious and hard working, just what you need." He cupped his hands to his mouth and called, "Petronović. You and Radonić, come here!"

Hearing they were being called by the commandant, the friars turned to look at Filipović and lost count of the bodies falling into the Sava; this was not appreciated by those participating in the competition. Brother Silov Petronović was very short, very stout and in his late twenties. He was a simple man who had lived all his life among the brothers of his order. He had a quick step that invariably outpaced whoever was with him, and made him lean forward as he walked, indicating a sense of mission and purpose. His tonsure scalp, combined with premature baldness, made it difficult to judge whether his lack of hair was due to that particular Catholic hairstyle, nerves (which caused his hair to fall out) or both. Petronović had black eyes, red eyebrows and extremely pale skin tinged ever so slightly with yellow, due to a troublesome liver. He wore the standard Franciscan habit, a holster with a Walther P-38 strapped to his side, and sandals (which were deep in mud). His friend, Brother Borna Radonić, was taller, older, thinner and far more restrained than his colleague. He had thick, black hair full of tiny tight curls, green eyes, thick black bushy eyebrows, a small nose and long fingers. Unlike Petronović, Brother Borna took as much time doing everything as he could get away with, and his particular, and peculiar, pedestrian custom included keeping his bony frame at a slight backward pitch, impressing the onlooker with confident resolve (it was, in fact, camouflaged procrastination). Seeing Petronović and Radonić walking together at a distance, it was as if the letter *V* had suddenly sprung to life and was gliding along the way, accompanied by flowing skirts. As the two friars approached the priest and the camp director, a loud cheer was heard. "Braciko, he's the one to beat!" remarked Petronović.

"Brother, this is Father Draganović. He's come from Zagreb and has something to tell you. Come, let's go inside, please." Brother Miroslav took Father Draganović by the arm and led the group to his barracks.

"Excuse me, Brother, what is Puerto Rican coffee? You get it from Rome?" Father Draganović was understandably surprised.

"You're not the only one with connections in the Holy See, Father," responded Filipović as they entered the barracks. "I get a pound of Puerto Rican coffee every two months. Don't we, Silov?" The good brother turned to his subordinates and began to prepare the coffee. "Don't you know that most of the Puerto Rican coffee is bought by the Vatican?"

"What is—Puerto Rican?"

"From Puerto Rico, an island in the tropics, I think." There was a long pause while the friars and the priest imagined where the blessed tropical island that grew such Catholic coffee might be located.

"The coffee is delicious," volunteered Radonić.

The room they were in had one cot, three wooden chairs, a woodstove and an old microphone wired to the loudspeaker on the roof. A large bucket stood on the floor in place of a sink and lavatory. Two windows on the room's south side provided a fine view of the outhouse as well as adequate light during the day. One light bulb provided adequate light during the evening. Every once in a while a light breeze would glide in from outside and a sweet, acrid aroma would mingle with that of the brewing coffee.

"What's that smell?" inquired Father Draganović from the window.

Brother Satan darted a look at the friars before answering Draganović. "It's from the pottery shed. Yes, it smells sometimes, but only when the wind is from the south."

The pottery shed was a large room in a different part of the compound that accommodated about forty prisoners at once. The victims were brought in and, before they knew what was happening, the doors would lock and flames spew out from the walls, turning the pottery shed into a crematorium.

"Silov, you and Borna are going back with Father Draganović," said Brother Satan.

"Back?" asked Petronović.

"Where?" said Radonić.

"Banja Luka," Draganović replied. "I need your help. I don't have enough men to help with our new laws of conversion; we are overwhelmed."

The friars looked at each other, then at the priest, and smiled. "You've come—for us?" It was nine months since they had arrived in Jasenovac, nine months filled with misgivings, hard work and intense emotions—time they would have preferred to spend elsewhere. There were some very good and dedicated men in the camp, true patriots, true Catholics, and the two would miss them; but then again, maybe not.

As Filipović prepared the Puerto Rican brew, it dawned on Father Draganović that there was no running water in the room, and the water used to prepare the coffee was probably taken from the river, the same river where bodies were even now being dumped.

"You know, I have changed my mind. I do not want coffee, thank you."

"No coffee? How can that be?" Brother Satan noticed the ever so slight look of concern and disappointment in the priest's eyes. "Oh, don't worry, Father, I don't use water from the Sava. We have our own well. It is fresh, pure water, I assure you. No one takes water from the river—well, except those that do not matter," Filipović finally smiled.

"In that case, I will have coffee after all. Then we have to get going."

By now the delicious aroma of the coffee was filling the room. Filipović served the black Puerto Rican brew in Croatian tin cups; he apologized for not serving sugar or anything to eat, but had no doubt Draganović would understand. A louder than usual roar came from the riverbank, and before too long, the survivors of the contest were being dragged back to their barracks. At the same time a group of guards carried their champion on their shoulders. Petar Braciko was a happy man, brandishing his deadly and victorious instrument for all to see.

"I take it you two know how to drive?" said the priest to the friars.

"I do," said Petronović.

"I don't," said Radonić.

The priest put the cup down. "Filipović, you were right; the coffee's delicious. Thank you."

"Most welcome," returned the hospitable friar.

"Let's go. Oh—take off your weapons," directed Draganović.

"Why?" Petronović had gotten used to his Walther.

"No guns." Draganović was firm. All three would be shot on the spot if the insurgents caught them carrying weapons; friars were not supposed to be armed.

Brothers Silov and Borna took off their gun belts, handed them over to Filipović, and joined Father Draganović in the car. The priest had noticed earlier that both friars had a strong odor akin to raw onion. But they were engaged in a war and allowances had to be made.

"May God be with you!" Brother Satan cried, waving. Before the brothers had time to wave back at their former commandant, the car was driving through the gates. Soon they would be in Banja Luka. In the morning Draganović would be face to face with the poglavnik, Ante Pavelić. Or rather he would have been, if not for a band of partisans who had other things in mind.

Father Draganović had turned off the main road at Bosanska Dubica to avoid an ambush, so common along the main routes. The detour led him to Mrakovica, where once again the road joined the main thoroughfare to Banja Luka. Back roads were difficult in the day but doubly so at night. They had not driven for more than an hour up a mountain pass when, at the far end of a particularly difficult turn, a roadblock appeared, forcing the priest to slam on the brakes and downshift in a desperate effort to avoid a collision. Even before the car stopped, a group of men thrust their flashlights and guns through the windows and roughly tried to drag the occupants of the car outside. They were clearly partisans, which meant they were communists, which meant they probably hated priests and friars. Father Draganović and the brothers kept their composure as a thin and gaunt-looking fellow, sporting a large scar on one side of his forehead, shone a light in their faces.

"And what do we have here? A priest and a couple of brothers?" The man swept the light from one face to another, always ending on the priest. "Is this possible? You seem to have lost your flock. And where is your Christ leading you tonight?"

Father Draganović ignored the blasphemous remark and assumed the most benign expression, while the friars kept their heads high, proud and challenging. "I am the Vatican attaché to the Red Cross in Yugoslavia. I am on a mission of mercy. Brothers Silov and Borna are my aides. You will find my papers indicate as much."

"Your papers, priest. What about them?" The fellow pointed his light at Silov and Borna.

"They are mendicant friars, my son. They never carry papers."

"I am not your son, and you're a spy, priest."

Draganović observed that if they were indeed spies, they were traveling in the most conspicuous disguise of all. The partisan countered that if the priest and the friars were not spies, then they were couriers for the Ustaše. He turned to a couple of men inspecting the car. "Find anything?"

"No!" replied one man with a strip of brown leather in his hand.

By now the seats had been pulled inside out, and the rich interior of the car slashed with bayonets as the partisans looked for clues to the identity of the men they were holding, their mission and destination.

"Under the car, look under the car!"

But the men did not need further instructions. They ripped everything out of the trunk and explored every cavity in the engine. The search took twenty minutes, twenty minutes that seemed an eternity.

"Too clean," said one of the inspectors.

"I really don't know what you're looking for," ventured Radonić, accentuating every syllable with contempt.

"For a reason to shoot you," returned the partisan leader, then waved his flashlight and began walking briskly into the woods. Three of his men followed and forced Draganović and the friars, at the point of machine guns and bayonets, to do likewise. They walked for nearly half an hour and emerged from the dense web of shadows and monstrous black silhouettes of the forest into a clearing on the side of a hill, bright with moonlight but desolate and scorched. The stars and a full moon gave Father Draganović the sense of being caught in the mouth of a slumbering volcano, with only the light beaming down from the heavens giving evidence that he was still alive.

Not far from the walls of the volcano, a very square and solid two-story structure with a few faded tiles left on its roof emerged among the mortar craters and dead stumps of trees ravaged by bullets. The once proud summer villa had fallen on terrible times, not unlike a woman marred by ungrateful lovers; its lovely lines and ornaments pocked by cannon fire; its many windows and doors boarded up or missing; its once elegant and colorful gardens now a cemetery where dead machines were laid to rest. The partisans led the prisoners into the house and down a dark corridor, to a back room as sinister as it was barren. A plain wooden chair rested in a corner; two windows that at one time must have held a grand view of the surrounding hills were boarded up and impenetrable; three oil lamps lit up the room.

Father Draganović and the brothers were each placed in a different corner of the room and ordered to strip under the watchful eyes of two hungry-looking partisans, who did not find it particularly interesting that, of the three clerics, Father Draganović was the best specimen, his body strong and muscular, while the friars were sagging and malleable. Every seam in their clothes and every orifice in their bodies was searched. After the partisans were convinced their guests were not hiding anything on their persons, they bound the naked friars with coarse rope and forced them to kneel on the cold cement floor. Draganović, his hands tied behind his back, was left standing against the wall.

Two other men then entered the room. They wore what at one time must have been olive green uniforms of some army or another. They looked very much of the land, with dark hair, deep black eyes and faces full of crusty lines. They did not carry guns and looked both less hungry and far more friendly than their colleagues standing guard. The new arrivals flanked the priest: a short thin fellow about fifty-five years old, with a large and apparently expanding bald spot, greying sideburns and a very black thin mustache that would have better suited a foppish matinee idol than a partisan; and a younger man in his twenties, broad and tall, with thick black hair, big bones and the uncanny profile of a bear. Their comrades stood by with sunken eyes and crossed arms, looking tired and somewhat bored, leering at the friars. "Well, priest, and what were you doing in Jasenovac?" inquired the older man.

"And traveling in a German car heading south, eh, priest? That's what I'd like to know," added the bear picking his teeth with a hunting knife.

The inquisitor looked carefully at Draganović but the priest showed no signs of distress. What the man should have done was feel the priest's pulse, which accelerated quickly, the heart pumping streams of blood into Draganović's brain, causing a throbbing headache of anger and fear. It clear was clear to him that he and the friars had been betrayed. "I am on my way to Sarajevo on a mission for the Red Cross. It is, I can assure you, a mission of peace, a mission of love."

As *love* would have it, the bear turned aside for but an instant to put his knife away, then whipped around and smashed the right side of the priest's face with his huge fist. The back of Father Draganović's head slammed against the cement wall and he felt blood gush from the lacerated cheekbone as the sound of crushing bones reverberated across the room. The priest was feeling he had to lie down, when the excited bear landed a powerful uppercut to his groin. Draganović's body bent over sharply and black bile spewed from his mouth and nose, as his legs yielded to the pain.

Brother Silov closed his eyes and prayed. After hearing the name Jasenovac, he had resigned himself to death. Radonić, on the other hand, shrieked, protesting the abuse of the priest and damning the partisans to everlasting hell. He made such a ruckus that the partisan guarding him pulled out a hunting knife and ordered the friar to stand. When Radonić refused, the man took the knife and placed it firmly against the brother's cheek, pushing upward, compelling Radonić to get to his feet or risk losing half his face. Once on his feet, Radonić thrust his head forward, defiant, leaving the partisan no choice but to grab the brother's penis, stretch it as far out as possible and put the cold steel against it. "You are going to be quiet."

And indeed, Radonić became perfectly still. He was unable to take his bulging eyes from the sharp edge indenting his defenseless organ. He remembered rumors of unspeakable atrocities committed by the partisans, where prisoners were forced to bite off other prisoner's testicles and then be castrated themselves.

In the meantime, at the other end of the room, Draganović was being savagely beaten by the bear, while question after question, peppered with irreverent obscenities, were shouted in his ear. The only thing the inquisitors were able to get from of the priest, however, was blood from his head, nose, eyes and ears every time a kick or punch landed in his body. And, yes, several of Draganović's teeth were knocked out and his eyes swollen shut. Still, Father Draganović did not lose consciousness, though he would have welcomed this gladly. In the back of his battered mind, he felt that if he could only hold up, all would be well. This last thought had just crystallized when one of the two men working him over (he could not tell which) grabbed Draganović's left arm and carved the likeness of a sickle just below the elbow. Draganović felt nothing as he finally wandered off into the soothing void of near death.

"Wake him up," said the mustachioed partisan to the bear.

The latter, whose green uniform was now much splattered with the priest's blood, tried to persuade Father Draganović to get up off the floor by gently prodding him with the tip of his boot. Unable to inspire the priest to play Lazarus, the inventive fellow thought that maybe a little water would do the trick, and began to relieve himself upon Draganović. This action roused the most curious response from the other two guards in the room. They seized the friars and savagely raped them. First, they introduced the chill, irregular steel barrels of their rifles into the friars' anal cavities, then forced the brothers to perform oral copulation, while continually slapping and punching Petronović and Radonić in the face.

And there they were: the Croatian priest lying on the floor in a pool of his own blood but showing signs of life, sputtering out communist piss; and the good friars prostrate on the floor, bleeding and gagging on partisan semen. Then, another member of the communist resistance entered the room. His name was Milan.

"Seen them before?" inquired the bear.

"I don't know this one, never saw him before," and Milan pointed at Draganović. "But those two—yes!" Milan had gained considerable weight as well as facial hair since Brothers Borna and Silov had last seem him. Yet the friars recognized the young man at once. They remembered the boy (for he had been no more than that) as the only prisoner to have escaped the death camp at Jasenovac.

"They worked for Filipović," said Milan. "That one," he pointed at Petronović, "he pinned down my little brother so Brother Satan could beat his brains out with a hammer!" If Milan had not been told that the trio was going to be shot, he would have killed the friars and the priest on the spot. "They are animals! They are not human, they are fiends!" Milan sank to his knees and pleaded, "Please, I want to kill them with my own hands, please!"

The older, mustachioed partisan walked over to Milan and helped him up off the floor. "I'll bring them outside. You do anything you want to, but make sure when you finish they are dead." He signaled the bear to take the sobbing young man out of the room. Just as the bear was about to open the door, however, a bullet tore open his head, Milan's green shirt filled up with small red holes, and thousands more rounds pierced the walls; the partisans were under fire. The other partisans in the room fared no better. Before they realized what was happening, they were dead, their bodies riddled by gunfire they never heard. A Ustaše artillery round blew off the roof of the building, leaving Father Draganović and his friends in the open, under a heap of dead partisans.

The attack lasted ten minutes, after which everything in that once proud villa was dead. Or, almost dead. Fortunately for the friars and Draganović, they were on the floor when the onslaught began, and—except for the abuse they suffered at the hands of the insurgents and a few new bruises attributable to falling bricks and stucco—they remained alive, though barely conscious. After a short while, Brother Silov thought he heard voices. Not knowing who the voices belonged to, he kept silent, waiting for the voices to go away. A few moments later, two Ustaše soldiers kicked down what was left of the door and lit up the room with a powerful flashlight.

"Got them all," stated one of the soldiers.

"Sons of whores," added the other.

"Help us! In the name of God, help us!" screamed Brother Borna, crawling out from under his tormentors.

3

It was a feat of modern architecture. The top floor of the seven-story ministry building had been eviscerated, and fifteen different offices, rooms, chambers, antechambers and suites combined to make one colossal parlor worthy of Dr. Ante Pavelić, the *poglavnik,* or leader of the Independent Nation of Croatia. It was strikingly different from the three-room flat he had shared with his family in exile. His office was not only large but extravagant beyond the grotesque. Thick and heavy tapestries concealed the north, south and west walls, while three wide doors led to the secretarial pool and the poglavnik's adjutants. Two windows on the east wall reached from the carefully polished, black marble floors to the ceiling, and an enormous chandelier indicated to anyone interested the precise center of the cavernous room.

"I am so pleased that the Holy Father approves of our policy." Pavelić held a dainty teacup and saucer. He leaned against his immense oak desk, which, for all its size, had only an inkstand on top, nothing more. On the wall behind the desk hung a Renaissance painting of the Madonna and Child, a gift from Artuković, point man in the assassination of King Alexander and Pavelić's minister of internal affairs. To the right of the desk, standing all by itself in a corner, was a flagpole with an imposing checkerboard flag.

Pavelić was a middle-aged man with a long and rectangular head, thick black hair kept tapered and short, a rough, leathery face and lips that almost never cracked a smile. He rarely raised his voice, though that does not mean he was soft-spoken, as indeed he was not. His uniform was always crisp and smart; his black shirt and matching tie, khaki trousers, and a chest full of decorations complemented each other with fascist elegance. Tucked neatly inside his right-hand pocket the poglavnik kept a small Walther PP-K. The pistol was a gift from the ranking Nazi general in Croatia, Austrian General Edmund Glaise von Horstenau.

"He is quite gratified," returned His Excellency, Josip Ramiro Marcone, abbot of the Benedictine order and legate of the Holy See to the Independent State of Croatia. The monk was sixty-five years old. He had a tuft of white hair on a round head that matched the robes of the Dominican order he wore that day (the reason for this unusual preference for the Dominican habit over that of the Benedictines was never made clear). Marcone was of average height but not of average proportions, being quite a lumpy fellow, with a fleshy face, a protruding stomach (which often served as a platform for his clasped hands) and a bulbous nose. Sometimes, when people looked at His Excellency, they thought of a white owl perched on a limb, pondering whether to swoop down on his prey or merely enjoy the art of intimidation.

"More tea?"

His Excellency shook his head and put down his cup. "I understand you are meeting with the führer—soon?"

"Yes," replied Pavelić.

Marcone smile. It was a matter of debate in the Holy See as to whether Pavelić was more loyal to Hitler and Mussolini, who put him in power, or to his Christ, the source of his inspiration. But Pius XII liked Pavelić, considered the Croat head of state a good Catholic and appreciated his fervent defense of the faith. His less attractive qualities were seen as minor blemishes in the face of a Central Europe threatened by Orthodox Christianity and Bolshevist atheism.

"And where is Stepinac? What is he up to these days? I have not seen him for some time." The abbot got up, indicating the meeting was over and only formalities remained.

"Up north converting the heretic masses," answered Pavelić with a smile. "Stepinac is working closely with Father Draganović."

"Who?"

"Father Draganović. He is responsible for implementing the policy of conversion." Pavelić turned and pulled a silver rope to summon an escort for the abbot. "You must have run into him sometime. Draganović was secretary at the Institute of Saint Jerome." The Institute of Saint Jerome was a Croatian nationalist organization attached to the Vatican; its goal was to further Croatian autonomy.

"Ah—" Abbot Marcone vaguely recalled an intense priest running up and down Vatican City, holding conferences with one cardinal or another, always seeking support for an independent and Roman Catholic Croatia.

"His Excellency is leaving," announced Pavelić when a soldier appeared in the room. The man, dressed in the same *Fascista* uniform as his leader, stood by the door awaiting instructions. "Please escort him to his car." The leader of the Ustaše thanked the abbot for the extraordinary help the Holy See had rendered his nation and swore eternal gratitude. The abbot nodded and walked out the door, followed by the Ustaše blackshirt.

Pavelić was once again left alone to ponder how to further the interests of his new nation. He returned to his desk, opened a drawer and pulled out two secret communiqués. Both were from Minister Artuković. The first paper showed a number and nothing else—*425,534*. To another person, it could have meant almost anything: the young nation's deficit; the figure for bribes paid to foreign dignitaries; the cost of Hitler's birthday gift; the price for a new bridge; the number of guns bought from Italy; or even the sum total of a loan received from the Holy See. Few would have equated *425,534* with Pavelić's success in cleansing Croatia of Serbs, Jews and Gypsies.

The second note was more detailed. The minister was concerned that the German SS was exercising undue influence over their Ustaše counterparts. Pavelić did not share his friend's anxieties. He was more concerned about the Italians than the Germans. The poglavnik had a long-standing debt to Mussolini. The Italian dictator had given Pavelić shelter for seven years and refused to deport him to France when the Croat leader was charged with the assassination of Alexander I of Yugoslavia and the French foreign minister Louis Barthou in 1934.

Also, Il Duce allowed Dalmatia, long in Italy's sphere of influence, to join Bosnia-Herzegovina and other Yugoslav provinces in becoming part of the new Independent State of Croatia.

Pavelić sighed and looked at his watch. He put away the secret memorandums, picked up a small notebook bound in rich leather and decorated with the checkerboard flag embossed in gold, flipped a couple of the pages, put the book down and summoned his secretary by way of the intercom. "Where is Draganović?"

There was some hissing and crackling before he received an answer. "N-not here, Excellency," stammered the voice at the other end of intercom.

"I know he's not there, but he's supposed to be, yes? So where is the priest?" called out the president to his secretary. There was nothing except more crackling and hissing. "Well?" Pavelić was not getting an answer, he was getting annoyed. He thought the crackling and hissing from the intercom irritating, and the lack of a response deliberate. "Come in here."

Two seconds later, Nikola, Ante Pavelić's very humble, exceptionally small, extremely narrow, unduly frail, inordinately nervous and awfully pale secretary was struggling with one of the heavy side doors. The little man was not considered by anyone, let alone himself, one of the important secretaries working in the ministry. He was not of high enough standing to be trusted with the secret papers going from Pavelić to his ministers, nor was he sufficiently influential to sit and record the many meetings between the poglavnik and his cabinet. Indeed, Nikola would probably never have been given the opportunity to work for Ante Pavelić had it not been for the secretary's extraordinary talent for fast typing. The speed at which Nikola hammered (with phenomenal accuracy at that) the keys of his cumbersome Italian iron typewriter was legendary in the corridors of the Croatian bureaucracy. Whenever there was an oversized manuscript to be typed, the sort of trite, voluminous handbook that governments thrive on, it was invariably dumped on the little man's desk.

Nikola stood waiting, as he always did, in a perfect ballet position number one—his right foot slightly in front of the left, both almost touching at the heels and pointing in opposite directions. Three overlapping layers of wrinkles hung beneath each red eye (worried and frightened eyes), while a cloud of cigarette smoke and the accompanying stench of nicotine followed him everywhere.

"Here!" Pavelić pointed his index finger at the far end of his desk. This meant, of course, that Nikola was obliged to make his way across to the other side of the room, a distance of at least twenty-five meters and one that Nikola did not navigate without pain. He was not a young man, though his age was as undecipherable as a Mongolian dialect, with estimates varying between forty and sixty-five years old. He did not walk like most people but hobbled, shifting his weight from one leg, debilitated by a youthful bout with poliomyelitis, to the other. In addition, his stamina was suspect and his voice hardly audible because of a slight case of emphysema.

"Where is Draganović?" inquired Pavelić for a second time.

Nikola put up his hands, shrugged and said the priest went to Jasenovac the previous day, but had expected to return to Banja Luka the following morning. Father Draganović had failed, however, to send word or to telephone that he would be late for his meeting with the poglavnik.

"Not like Draganović," observed Pavelić. The father was known for his punctuality. "And what is he doing in Jasenovac?"

Nikola did not know what had motivated the priest to wander off into the hinterland, but recalled that Father Draganović had voiced concern that the program of forced conversion was understaffed and that he needed one or two additional souls to help manage it successfully. Nikola reminded Pavelić that it was the poglavnik himself who had suggested the Franciscans as possible candidates, since the order had accumulated much praise for running internment camps like the one at Jasenovac.

"Well, if Draganović's gone off to look for help, I am certainly not going to stay here and wait for him to get back. You're stinking up the place—go."

Nikola turned quickly, limped back to the door, opened it and vanished. Pavelić walked to the window and opened it a crack to get rid of the smell of stale cigarettes. He had tried several times to have the secretary give up the annoying vice, even to threatening the man with "Hitler abhors smoking," followed by "In our Croatian Catholic utopia smoking cripples will be exterminated." Nikola had made two or three attempts to give up smoking, but the experience was an excruciating ordeal not only for him but Pavelić as well, because the secretary's nerves would unravel and the sweet and temperate man would turn into an obnoxious, cocky and impudent monster; the incredibly efficient aide would become a sloth, spending his hours meandering about the ministry with a dazed look. The only alternative was to dismiss Nikola, but Ante's children were very fond of the little man.

Pavelić stood looking out the ministry windows, at the tree-lined avenue and the ornate park across the way, with its fountains, almond trees, benches and old men, when Nikola reappeared carrying one of two little Pavelićs in his arms, while the second little Pavelić followed close behind. The Pavelić children were beautiful indeed, which was curious because Ante was an extremely ordinary looking man and his wife, Marija, though a woman of style, was no raving beauty.

"Papa!" called out little Katarina from the arms of the secretary. Nikola laughed as he put the six-year-old on the floor. He was strong enough to carry her into the room but no further. Although Pavelić had warned Katarina not to kiss the little man because she ended up smelling like a rose that had been dumped in an ashtray, the little girl did anyway, and then ran to her father. Pavelić got on one knee and received his daughter with open arms. Katarina was a happy, beautiful child with a lively and ever-present smile who was constantly bouncing about; her long hair fell to her waist like an exquisite cascade of honey. Her eyes were the color of almonds and her skin without a blemish, perfectly white and perfectly soft. She was dressed in an exquisite blue velvet dress—just brought in from Rome—adorned with white lace and satin, over white silk stockings and a pair of shiny black shoes with a blue velvet buckle trimmed with gold thread. The child smothered her father with kisses, which he reciprocated with as much tenderness and love.

"Kati wanted to show you her new dress." Marija walked in behind the children, and prompted her daughter to model for her father. She was a head taller than her husband, with a certain elegance and charm, long brown hair neatly coifed in the latest Paris style, dark brown eyes and a face that, if not beautiful, was pleasant to look at.

"It is simply the most beautiful dress I have ever seen! Are you sure you're not a princess?" The poglavnik was beaming with delight.

"I am, I am!" answered the little girl with a giggle.

It was Didi's turn. Ante got off the floor and greeted Damir, his son, nine years old, whom his sister had taken to calling Didi. The boy was dressed in breeches and a brown tweed jacket over a light brown shirt and tie. Didi was a quiet boy who, when spoken to, preferred to answer in Italian, the language he had learned living five of his nine years in Italy. He had eyes that reflected a meditative and inquisitive yearning, and possessed an ethereal quality that often—after one had spent time with him—made it seem as if the child had not been present at all. Damir was tall for his age, slender, his skin pure alabaster; his wide hazel eyes were framed by the most extraordinary dark blond brows, and his thick lashes and the dark circles under his eyes gave the impression that makeup had been applied. His flawless features and dark blond hair underscored an astonishingly beautiful face.

Ante shook his son's hand in a formal greeting, then picked him up and dispensed as many kisses and hugs to the boy as he had to little Kati.

"Papa, I want to go outside—to play. Mama won't let me," complained the little boy. "Why not? The other boys do, and they don't get in trouble."

Ante took Damir and sat him on the desk. He took off the boy's hat and kissed him on the cheek. "We've been through this already, haven't we?"

The boy nodded.

"It is too dangerous for you to go outside."

"Why? Why is it dangerous?" Damir got down from his father's lap.

"Because I am the poglavnik. As leader and president of the country a lot of people like me and look up to me, but a lot of people do not and would like for me—for us to go away. Those people are very dangerous and will do anything to hurt me and those I love the most—and that's your mama, your sister and you."

"But we haven't done anything!" cried out an indignant Didi.

Few people had ever seen the poglavnik's family. They lived on the north side of ministry in a twenty-room flat provided by the state. Marija and the children never wandered outside except with a security detail as massive as her husband's. Damir and Kati were barred from playing anywhere but in their apartments or in the courtyard of the ministry with one or two other children whose parents were thoroughly vetted and always under the watchful eyes of their Ustaše bodyguards. Pavelić understood how difficult and unnatural it was, particularly for Damir, and longed for the day when he could make it up to the boy. "Why don't you stay here—today, eh? I was thinking of going to the country; you'll come along."

The boy leaped into his father's arms and kissed him. Didi was happy and eager to share an afternoon with his papa, something he rarely had a chance to do. Still, even at his young age the boy understood the outing was his father's way of talking about something else so the poglavnik need not explain who wanted to see them go away.

Marija was grateful the question of Damir's going out to play was laid to rest, although she was not thrilled that her husband and son were leaving the capital, regardless of the security detail and the troops that would accompany them. The president went over to his wife and gave her a kiss. He had confidence in his army.

A fleet of four armed troop carriers, equipped to take on a small army, and three Citroëns with Ustaše secret police escorted Dr. Ante Pavelić and his son to Glina, a Serbian village nestled halfway between the capital and Zagreb. The motorcade sped out of Banja Luka, running down anything that ventured into its path. Its victims included seven chickens, a dog, two cats, and almost little Amela. Amela was a seven-year-old girl who decided to cross the dusty road at the same time the thundering convoy turned the corner. Amela panicked and became confused about whether to run forward or retreat. The lead troop carrier would have struck sweet Amela like a wave of steel had it not been for her older sister, Zehida, who placed her own life in jeopardy as she ran after her little sister, grabbed her by the scruff of the neck and dragged her to the side of the road in time to avoid a double tragedy.

Damir had been kneeling on the back seat of the limousine looking out the rear window when he locked eyes with little Amela. He saw that the dust and dirt raised by the motorcade had already dried the child's tears into a thin layer of caked mud. Damir recognized the girl as a Muslim. He had heard Nikola and even his father talk about the Muslims many times. Muslims did not believe in Jesus, they were evil, dirty and never to be trusted. Yet Damir felt sorry for the little girl. She did not look evil, but very scared. Then again, he was just a little boy and his father was never wrong.

Archbishop Aloysius Stepinac was a member of parliament in the Independent Nation of Croatia, and vicar to the army of the Ustaše. He was holding mass in Glina's village square, part of the government's continuing effort to enlighten its Serbian citizens. The archbishop had entered the village in the company of four priests, a hundred Croatian regulars and a dozen or so Ustaše secret police. The army assisted the reverend fathers to set up a platform while loudspeakers summoned the townsfolk (all Serbs) to assemble and convert. In this ritual Stepinac never failed to employ the symbol of the Ustaše government—a cross made up of a gun, a dagger and a grenade.

Stepinac was an unremarkable looking man, thin, with a lean, rigid face and a bald crown. Yet his charismatic personality, powerful voice and pious eloquence inspired even skeptics with the promise of salvation. He was a zealous missionary striving to increase the size of his Catholic flock. "My children!" boomed Stepinac over the loudspeakers, "Gather, gather and come forward! Let the everlasting glory of Christ the Lord grace your lives through his messenger of love and peace—our Holy Father!"

The town buzzed with cries of joy. Everyone was attending the mass, all twenty-five hundred; tears flowed from almost every face, old and young alike, though few young men could be spotted because most had gone to war (those at hand were either crippled or retarded). Children, too—all were crying, grateful to the army and especially the secret police for making them see the path to salvation.

"Holy Father, in your hands we place our sinful hearts so that in your divine wisdom we may seek the majesty of Christ the Son! *In nomine Patris, et Filii, et Spiritus Sancti*—" and the people of Glina lined up in front of the makeshift stage while the archbishop and his four attending priests ministered Holy Communion, the Eucharist improvised with peasant bread and wine provided by the soon to be Catholic villagers. They carefully crossed themselves and echoed "Amen!" *Carefully,* because the Orthodox go from the forehead to the breast, then touch first their right shoulder, then their left. When Catholics cross themselves they go from the forehead to the breast, then touch their left shoulder first and finish by crossing over to the right.

The sun was a perfect ball of fire, the skies were unclouded and the air was dry, making it possible to see into infinity, which was precisely what Stepinac was doing as he raised his head for an instant and invoked a blessing for an old Serbian grandmother who had just opened her toothless mouth to its fullest, expecting His Reverend Excellency to drop a morsel of the Host inside.

Pavelić's motorcade arrived outside the village and stopped. The poglavnik ordered the troops to stay back while he took Damir by the hand and went to meet Stepinac. Antu Moškova, Pavelić's large, debonair and deadly bodyguard walked alongside the president and his son while five other security men trailed close behind. As they reached an alley opposite the green where Stepinac was holding mass, a twinkling and playful beam of sunlight bounced off one of the many decorations Pavelić sported on his chest and found its way to the ever-attentive eyes of the archbishop. The archbishop leaped down from the platform in an instant, leaving the attendant priests to fend for themselves. He shoved, pushed and dug his way through thousands of peasants, surfacing finally next to—

"Dr. Pavelić, Dr. Pavelić! What an honor! What brings you here?"

"I could not stay away, I wanted to see this—had to see it for myself," replied Pavelić. "It's amazing!"

The archbishop's eyes drifted from the president of Croatia to the child at his side.

"My son, Damir," said Ante Pavelić.

"Well, hello young man." Stepinac put out his hand and smiled. Didi did not reply but presented his customary curious frown. He was about to kiss His Excellency's ring (as he had seen his father do many times with bishops and the like) when Stepinac pulled back the hand, patted Didi on the side of the face with much tenderness and made the mistake of looking the boy in the eyes. The experience upset the archbishop, for, in an instant, his soul was scrutinized and judged. Stepinac immediately turned his eyes from Damir and focused attention on the boy's father. He seized the president and led him arm in arm around the edge of the maze of people who up until a few minutes before had been loyal Orthodox Christians. Moškova, the bodyguard, flanked the priest while Damir took his father's hand and looked straight ahead at the old men, women and children waiting in line to take the Eucharist.

"Glina is small," said Stepinac, raising his arms to heaven and describing the accomplishments of the Catholic Church of Croatia. "It is smaller than average, if truth be told. But there are other towns where if we did not convert twenty thousand in one afternoon, we did not convert one."

Conversion. Didi did not understand what it meant, but he had a sense that it was a very good thing because his father was extremely pleased and kept thanking the archbishop over and over.

"It's my duty—to my Church, to my country," replied His Excellency.

The group had reached a space next to the platform where the priests continued to hold mass when four soldiers appeared with a man and boy in custody. The shepherd (for that was his vocation) was emaciated, with droopy eyes, a crinkled face, a lump of tangled hair. He begged the soldiers for mercy, explaining that he had not been hiding but was looking after his three sheep, unaware that anything was going on in the town.

Pavelić could not help comparing Damir to the shepherd's son. They were about the same age but Damir was probably the most privileged child in the country. He was healthy, beautiful, well-fed, well-dressed and clean. The other boy was filthy, in rags, barefoot, with his head shaven to fight off lice. He was scared out of his wits, hungry and holding a *svirala*—a shepherd's flute that caught Didi's attention.

"Papa," said Damir softly, tugging at his father's sleeve, "can I play with the little boy?"

"I don't think so," Pavelić answered his son, then turned his attention to the peasant boy. "What is your name?"

The boy looked to his father for help, but the man was unable to offer much of that because he was forced to lie face down in the dirt. And so the boy fixed his eyes on Damir, who was curious to find out why the little shepherd looked as terrified as the girl he had seen on the side of the road.

"Hello? Did you understand what I said?" asked the poglavnik when the boy did not answer him right away. "What is your name?"

"A-lek-s-sandar," stammered the little boy at last.

"Aleksandar, your name is Aleksandar?"

The boy gave a nod.

Then Pavelić addressed the boy but looked at Stepinac. "And—I bet, Aleksandar, that they call you Saša, eh? Is that what your papa calls you? Saša?"

Saša tried to look up, but the sun was behind the man and Saša could only blink at the towering, black silhouette asking questions.

"Of course he does, of course he does," continued Pavelić in a warm, friendly tone. "Do you know how to cross yourself, boy?"

Again, Saša looked to his father. The man was allowed to get on his knees but was so frightened he wrung his hands and began to utter what sounded like a hysterical giggle.

"Come, boy, cross yourself," directed the poglavnik.

Saša lowered his eyes, gave a deep sigh and began the ritual learned as a toddler from his grandmother. His thin, bony right hand moved slowly across the chest. First, he touched his forehead, then brought the hand down to his breast, and was about to touch his right shoulder when Pavelić pulled out his PP-K and shot him in the head, the report from the small-caliber pistol going undetected except by those standing close by.

Little Saša fell in a puddle of his own blood. He let go of the svirala he had been holding in his other hand. The little flute rolled on the ground until it stopped next to Didi. Saša's father grabbed at his dead boy and cradled the body quietly, not even daring to look up at the man who had murdered his son, not even daring to utter a sound or display the pain he felt bursting from his broken heart.

Moškova waited for orders from his president, and the soldiers held themselves on alert in case the incident caused any disruption in the proceedings. Stepinac immediately administered to the boy the last rites; Pavelić put the gun back in his holster; and Didi—he let go his father's hand and never held it again.

"Beast," muttered Pavelić, and quickly made his way back to his car, leaving Stepinac and the soldiers to tie up the loose ends. Didi did not follow his father because he could not move; he could not move because he could not take his eyes off the dead boy. Then, as in a trance, little Damir picked up the svirala and put it in his pocket.

"Damir!" called his father. But it was up to Moškova to take the president's son in his arms and carry the boy back to the car, while one soldier stabbed Saša's father through the eye and another crushed the dead boy's skull with his boot.

The presidential escort was standing about, smoking and chatting, waiting for orders to return to the capital. At the sight of the poglavnik, the soldiers snapped to attention and prepared to leave. Didi sat facing his father.

"What's the matter, why are you crying?" asked the poglavnik.

But Didi did not answer. Instead, he looked at his father with the same penetrating stare he used to reserve for strangers, and what he saw frightened him more than anything he had seen that day; he looked at his father and saw a man he did not know. The man who sat across from him was not the man who used to hold him at night before the fireplace, who told him stories of his own childhood in Bradina; he was not the man who played with Didi and his little sister on the floor, tickled them and made them laugh with silly clownish faces; the man who made a point to see them to bed each night and who spent hours reading to them until they fell asleep; the man who each morning would softly walk into their room, pull aside the curtains and gently wake them up, even help them out of bed and to dress; the man who, when time and duty allowed, took his little boy to the park and taught him to play soccer. That man who Didi now recalled with so much longing, that man who used to reassure his young son with loving words and hugs, that man ceased to exist. In one clear summer afternoon, a Serbian peasant had lost his little boy, and Damir had lost his father.

"Come, sit next to me."

Didi shook his head and refused to move.

"Didi, those people are the enemy, can you understand that?" Pavelić pointed to the village. "I dare say, if those people out there were in power, if they ruled the army, they would have us murdered. Would you like that to happen?"

Didi shook his head.

"They are not Catholics like us, that's why the archbishop was trying to convert them. Only when our country is rid of the Orthodox, the Jews and those filthy, ungodly Gypsies, only then will we be proud of our Croatia, only then will we have a nation pure and strong. Do you understand what I'm saying?"

Again Didi shook his head.

"The Holy Father has given his personal blessing, he urged me to bring the true religion of Christ to these people. It has to be done, you know!"

Didi closed his eyes to keep from looking at death.

"You're just a boy. Some day you will understand and be proud of what I've done here today."

Yes, Damir was a boy—but Ante Pavelić's prophecy remained forever unfulfilled.

4

The motorcade was returning to Banja Luka when, a few kilometers south of Glina, it ran into a broken-down jalopy that appeared suddenly out of nowhere and nearly rammed the president's car. The soldiers immediately took positions to safeguard the poglavnik and his son from a possible ambush. They were about to shoot the passengers of the insolent, attacking wreck when it was discovered that the three men inside the car were already half dead, their faces lacerated and bloody. One of the men—unconscious in the back seat—was beyond recognition. His head was a bloated mass of black and blue, with the nose, ears and mouth held in place by patches of dried blood.

The poglavnik stayed in his automobile until the soldiers secured the area, then, leaving Damir in the care of Moškova and five additional bodyguards (with instructions to shoot anyone approaching whom they did not recognize), he went with pistol in hand to investigate what the commotion was all about. "Who are they?" asked Pavelić of a lieutenant.

The soldiers had dragged the men from the car. "I don't know, Excellency," answered the soldier, "but they were roughed up pretty bad, wouldn't you say? That one doesn't have much left." He pointed at Father Draganović.

At first, Pavelić did not recognize the priest, but as he stepped back, he noticed the red cross barely visible under a thick layer of grime on the passenger door. "Let me see his face!" commanded the poglavnik. The soldiers rolled the priest on his back. "Father Draganović?"

"Yes, yes, it's Draganović—Draganović!" screamed Brother Borna, as indeed it was, though it almost was not.

"Water! Get water, now!" Pavelić took charge of the welfare of the priest.

It was a full hour before the friars settled down and another half hour before they were able to describe their ordeal at the hands of the communist guerrillas. Pavelić was indignant, not because of what had happened to the friars and the priest but because partisan troops were operating so close to Banja Luka. "Damir!" Pavelić summoned his little boy, who quickly appeared behind a wall of Ustaše bodyguards. Pavelić knelt beside the boy and pointed to the comatose priest. "You know that man. That is Father Draganović. He has been at the house several times, remember? Do you see what those beasts have done to him? This is why we cannot take pity, this is why we must be ruthless. Look what they do to a priest, Damir, to a man of Christ, look!"

Damir looked at Draganović, then at the friars. He felt sorry for them too.

Pavelić arranged for the priest and friars to be driven without delay to the hospital in Banja Luka. Brothers Silov and Borna showered the president with grateful blessings as they and the still unconscious priest were placed in one of the Citroëns and taken away by two Ustaše secret police. Once the wounded clergy were on their way, Pavelić ordered a return to Glina. This time the convoy made its way into the center of the village, where they found Stepinac, the attending priests and the accompanying troops getting ready to move on. The archbishop was surprised to see Pavelić back in town and was appalled when he heard what had befallen Father Draganović. But Pavelić was not going to accept the treatment of the priest as an unfortunate and unavoidable consequence of war. Those who mocked the authority of the Catholic state by assaulting the clergy would pay with their lives.

Pavelić summoned the chief of his Ustaše detail and withdrew with the man for a private tête-à-tête. By the time Pavelić returned to the company of the archbishop, the Croat regulars had fanned out and were going house to house, seizing every man, woman and child and leading them inside the Orthodox church in the center of town—over two thousand souls, pressed so tight it was suffocating. Damir looked out from the car, fearful for all the little boys and girls being dragged off. "Run, run—get away!" his bodyguard heard him scream. Then, Damir did what any terrified child does when living a nightmare, he fell to the floor, shut his eyes tight and covered his ears. He sobbed uncontrollably because there was nothing he could do to stop the screaming outside.

When Ante returned to the car (in the company of Archbishop Stepinac) he was not amused to find Damir huddled on the floor. In fact, he was not pleased at all with the way things had turned out—a simple outing had become an irritating imbroglio. Pavelić ordered Damir off the floor and apologized to Stepinac—who was returning with them to the capital—for his son's lack of common sense and civility.

In the choking madness of the moment, a sturdy old peasant woman who never ceased to look on the bright side of things stood in the very center of the house of worship, underneath the enormous chandelier that hung from the dark, majestic vaulted ceiling. A thousand candles lit in the name of a thousand divinities tendered their white and grey smoke to the heavens; a hundred saints and an Orthodox Christ and Mary watched from their gold-embellished perch above the mass of screaming women, children and old men crushing one another from all sides. The old woman thought that Catholic rituals were simply very odd: first you convert and swear loyalty to the pope, then your sins are washed away in your own blood. She smiled at the irony and raised her eyes to catch a glimpse of Christ as the Son stretched out his arms and pointed an accusing finger at the vultures poised at the windows overhead, faceless black shapes against the dazzling sunlight carving out their contours. It was bliss looking upon the face of Christ—as a grenade bopped her on the head and exploded, followed by an interminable volley of machine-gun fire that slaughtered the population of a small town called Glina.

The drive back to Banja Luka was as uneventful as it was quiet. It is true the archbishop tried several times to engage the Pavelićs in conversation on a wide range of subjects. He asked Dr. Pavelić, for instance, his thoughts on how long the British could hold out before capitulating to the German blitz, but the president was in no mood to be social.

"Not long," was the curt reply from the taciturn head of state.

Having failed on the field of global conflict, Stepinac turned to the son and asked if he preferred Banja Luka to Zagreb, if he had met other children his age in the new capital and if, before leaving Zagreb, the boy had had the chance to see the Gypsy Circus from Hungary, with its clowns, acrobats and even one or two wild animals. Damir shook his head once in answer to all three questions, and retreated into the relative privacy of his inner self. Afterwards, Stepinac thought that perhaps his question about the circus might have been slightly inappropriate, since the boy's father hated Gypsies as much as any other ethnic group and would probably have had the entire company torched inside the ring.

Once in Banja Luka, Stepinac went to look after Father Draganović. Ante and his son went home.

The car had barely stopped in back of the ministry when Damir jumped out, dashed past the security men, ran up the stairs, flung open the door to his mother's room and threw himself into the reassuring arms and sweet kisses of his mother and sister. "My sweet boy, what is the matter? Why are you crying?" Marija and Katarina were playing checkers.

"That boy has done nothing but embarrass me all day—in front of the archbishop, no less! I am completely ashamed of him!" Ante stood at the door, his face full of contempt as he pointed an accusing finger at his son. The outburst stunned Marija, who could not remember the last time her husband shouted at her. "Talk to him," added the poglavnik. "He is to behave like the son of the president and not like a whimpering buffoon. I will not tolerate it, I absolutely won't!" Pavelić slammed the door, leaving Marija to caress her son's face while Katarina, in sympathy with her brother, also cried. Their moment of commiseration did not last long because as quickly as he had left, Pavelić returned and stood in the doorway again, with his arms akimbo, his head thrown back and his jaw sticking out—a regular Croatian Duce. "He should be proud, you understand, proud! What—what is the matter with him!" And as suddenly as he had reappeared the great dictator slammed the door on his family for a second time and vanished into the secret and forbidding halls of the ministry.

"What happened, tell me, my darling." Marija kissed Damir's wet cheeks and stroked back his hair.

"Saša—Saša—" repeated Didi over and over, never letting go of the little flute.

☦

For four days Damir refused to get out of bed, refused to eat and just stared at the ceiling. He placed Saša's flute under the pillow and did not allow anyone to touch it—not even his beloved Kati. Marija was so concerned about the boy's declining health that doctors were summoned from Switzerland. All the medicines in the world—half of which were administered to little Damir—proved unsuccessful in bringing about a change. Even Nikola—under the strictest orders not to smoke anywhere near the boy—even Nikola tried to cheer him up. The secretary brought along a box of toy soldiers, toy planes, toy battleships, toy cars, a puppet show (which he and Kati put on in style) and a small spaniel. After hours of aiming to please and entertain, Damir looked at Nikola, pointed at the toy soldiers and said in a weak voice, "They kill children."

Well, it was enough for the secretary to lose his composure, not because Nikola was unaware of the unhealthy repercussions of war upon children, but because Damir's blunt observation brought back a hundred ghosts of an unhappy and forlorn childhood; all because years before, during another big war, a Serb officer decided he could afford not to shoot the crippled boy, but could ill afford not to hang his brothers. So vivid was the onslaught of spooks upon the flustered little man's memory that Nikola quickly gathered his toy armada, left the ministry, dumped the lot in the garbage, went home, smoked four packs of cigarettes, downed two bottles of brandy, and wept.

The ritual passing of time turned days into months; Damir ate only enough to stay alive, and the child, who was never stout to begin with, became emaciated to the point that Dr. Hansmann, a psychologist from Bern, advised Marija to prepare herself for the worst. In his opinion, Damir suffered from acute depression and was willing himself to die. Suddenly, the wife and mother who was known to raise her voice only to shower her family with love became angry and insubordinate. She threw the doctor out, burst into Ante's office (the president was meeting with Artuković) and confronted her husband. She demanded an explanation as to why Damir had come home so troubled after venturing into the country with his father. The minister begged to be excused, and left the Pavelićs to smooth out the waters of their matrimony, waters that became so tempestuous and foul that anyone attempting to navigate them risked drowning. Ante listened carefully to his wife's concerns and for a moment the storm clouds dispersed and the sun made a feeble attempt to spread happiness and warmth—until Pavelić told his wife what had happened in Glina. It was obvious that the moment of seeming tranquility was only the eye of an incredibly violent hurricane that now rained down discord and fury upon the couple, driving away forever any possibility of reconciliation in the Pavelić household.

But Marija was not the only one worried about Damir. Kati cried and cried, and prayed and prayed to the Blessed Mother for her brother's life. And Ante? He was anxious for the boy as well. He visited his son each night and spent hours sitting at the bedside, talking of the things they would do and share once Damir recuperated. They would go mountain climbing; maybe take a trip abroad—to Switzerland, where the whole family, even little Kati, could learn to ski and sled. So many plans, so many hopes if only Damir would get well.

One night, when the summer rain rattled the windowpanes, and the warm breeze from the garden flirted with the feather-like white curtains, Ante buried his face in his hands and begged his Lord Jesus Christ and innumerable saints to spare the little boy. Pavelić even asked forgiveness for misdeeds that may have triggered the divine wrath bearing down on Damir. Damir never heard his father's lamentations because every time Ante came into his room the boy turned away, closed his eyes and held Saša's flute to his cheek.

Damir's refusal to acknowledge his father wounded the poglavnik's pride more than he cared to admit, and the visits to his son's room became less and less frequent until one day they stopped altogether, leaving Marija and Kati to look after Damir. Sometimes Marija spent the night in a rocking chair beside the bed, humming softly, hoping it would comfort her boy. Other times she knelt by the bed and begged him not to let go, to put aside the sadness and the loneliness that had overtaken his life. Then, Marija prayed, because there was nothing else to do.

Late one evening, after Marija retired to her rooms, Damir's bedroom was filled with an exquisite fragrance—just before someone called his name.

"*Damir!*"

It was the voice of a child.

"*Damir! Damir!*"

It was a few minutes before "*Damir!*" found its way through the seemingly impenetrable mist of the boy's subconscious, pushed aside the beginnings of a dream and caused Didi to open his eyes. The fireplace was still lively and the room warm and comfortable but—he was alone.

"*Damir!*"

He turned slowly and lay on his back.

"*Damir!*"

He thought perhaps there might be someone under the bed, so he leaned over the side, stuck his head under the bed frame and saw his slippers.

"*Damir! Damir!*"

The little boy had no recourse but to gather his strength and sit up on the bed.

"*Damir!*" he was called again.

Suddenly, a gust blew open the French windows. Damir looked out into the night and saw stars like sparklers on New Year's dancing against the black sky. The sly moon, not wanting to be outdone, decided not to shine on the world that night, but fixed its glow only on little Damir's room.

"*Damir!*"

Didi decided the voice was calling from the garden. He boldly cast aside the plump goose feather comforter and the silk sheets, and carefully got out of bed. He walked barefoot across the room in his nightshirt and propped himself upon the windowsill. And there he saw—saw and was dazzled by a magnificent blaze of colors, and a collection of flowers the likes of which he could not believe: thousands upon thousands of cowslips, marigolds, red and yellow and white roses, assorted colored tulips, hellebore, violets, purple lilacs, dogwood, hibiscus, lilies, rhododendron, narcissus, daisies and forget-me-nots—each one brighter and taller than the next—all blooming spectacularly that late autumn night; and hundreds of thousands of yellow birds and blue butterflies that were chasing each other about the garden as if it were spring.

"Damir, Damir, Damir, come and stay,
Not in bed but out to play!"
"Damir, Damir, Damir, come and stay,
Not in bed but out to play!"

The flowers beckoned the boy with their stems and smiles.

"You woke me up!" said Damir with a frown. "Why are you calling me? I can't go out, I don't feel well. And besides, it's the middle of the night!"

"Damir, Damir, Damir, come and stay,
Not in bed but out to play!"

"You're all very beautiful," said Damir, "but I can't, I really can't." No sooner had Damir finished speaking, that Saša appeared from behind the flowers. There, surrounded by the towering, colorful flora, stood the little shepherd. His head was not shaven, no. As a matter of fact, his light brown hair twirled and tossed in the playful breeze. His brown eyes were as happy as ever and even his clothes were enchanting, for Saša was not dressed in tattered rags but in a brand new holiday suit that included a white, long sleeve woolen shirt, an embroidered vest with intricate patterns of silver and gold silk braid, and a fine pair of sturdy woolen pants that were held in place by the traditional sash; a sash that matched in every way the variety of blooms in the garden. Oh, yes, Saša also sported a brand new pair of yellow opanci, shoes with pointed, curved toes and all.

"Damir," said Saša, "you have my flute!"

Damir was so startled he fell backward. Well, you should have heard the flowers laughing and making fun of Damir as the little boy rubbed his behind.

"Damir," Saša called again, "you have my flute!"

"I know, I know! Do you want it?"

"Yes, of course I want it!"

Damir was more than happy to return the flute to its rightful owner. "Wait, I'll be right back!" But just as he pulled the svirala from under his pillow, Damir felt a tap on the shoulder and turned to find Saša beside him.

"You must be rich!" exclaimed Saša, throwing his arms in the air, looking around and laughing.

"Damir, Damir, Damir, come and stay,
Not in bed but out to play!"

Damir ran quickly to the window. "I can't come out, Saša is here with me!" And Damir turned to Saša (who by now was making himself quite at home) and said, "I thought you were dead."

That certainly changed the mood in the room. Although he did not seem too concerned, Saša pondered for a moment before he broke out in a laugh that brightened up the room. "I can't be dead, you won't let me die!"

"Me!"

"You!" And Saša ran up and down picking up first a kite, then a ball, and even climbed on the wooden horse. "Oh, this is—heaven!" said the shepherd leaping off the horse and throwing himself on the wide, sumptuous bed, and covering himself with the comforter (his yellow opancis sticking out at the end).

Damir thought the remark interesting and probably quite well-informed, since the peasant boy was surely to have had a good idea what heaven was like. "Hey, does this mean I'm dead, too?"

"Nooo—not really."

The truth is, Damir expected a different answer. He expected to be told that either, yes, he had indeed died from his long illness, or no, he was not dead, which of course meant he was alive. Damir did not expect *not really,* which could only mean that he was not alive, and yet, not dead.

"I don't understand something." Saša jumped out of bed, again climbed onto the wooden horse and set off on a wild race. "Why do you want to die?"

Damir stood in the middle of the room watching his friend playing with the toys.

"You can't, you know. I don't want you to!"

"Why not?"

"Because," Saša dismounted and ran to Damir, "if you die," and the boy playfully poked Didi in the stomach, "I won't be able to play with you anymore."

"Can't we play—over there?" Damir joined Saša, who sat on the floor examining a red kite.

"Over where?"

"In heaven," replied Damir.

"In heaven? We? Us? You and me, playing in heaven?" Saša laughed, he laughed so hard he rocked back and forth. Then just as suddenly, he stopped laughing. "I guess we could, but we can't because—because you're not dead!" Even if Damir were dead, Saša explained, getting to heaven was not as simple or as sure a thing as one might expect. Saša picked up a large ball, bounced it up and down a few times and threw it across the room. And so the two boys spent the next couple of hours, playing catch, playing checkers (Damir had to teach Saša how to play) and talking, laughing, running and chasing each other around the room. After an exhausting wrestling bout where Damir and Saša rolled on the floor for a good ten minutes, Damir's poor health got the better of him.

"Do you want me to go?" asked Saša looking concerned.

"No! Don't go! I'll be fine, it's just—I'm a little out of breath, that's all. Please don't go!"

"I won't, then!"

"Promise?"

"Promise!" And Saša picked up a picture book from the floor and threw himself on the bed next to Damir (this time he took off his yellow shoes). Didi closed his eyes and fell asleep.

It was six in the morning when Marija returned to her son's room and was alarmed to find the windows wide open and all the toys scattered on the floor. She could not imagine Damir having the strength to leave his bed to open the windows, let alone to make such a mess of his room. So, Marija blamed the servants. "Who did this? Who!?"

"Mama, shhhh! You're making too much noise!" said Didi from his bed. "You're going to wake him up!"

Marija looked at her son, who did not look any worse for having slept with the window open all night. With one quick wave of her hand, Marija dismissed the maids and went to Damir. "What is the matter, darling?"

"Shhhh!"

"What's wrong, my love?"

"Shhhh!!!"

"What—what is it?" Marija thought Damir was hallucinating.

"Saša! He stayed up all night looking at pictures. He's very tired," Damir nodded to the right side of the bed where Saša was resting, his head under the picture book.

"Saša?"

Damir nodded and smiled. Marija remembered that Dr. Hansmann predicted delusions before the inevitable end. "Oh, my poor, poor child!" Marija tried to take the boy in her arms, but she did so by reaching over Saša.

"Mama, please stop it!" Damir jumped out of bed with a degree of energy Marija had not seen in months, took his mother by the arm and gently led her to the door. "Do you think I can have breakfast? I'm very hungry, and I'm sure if he ever gets out of bed—" Damir meant Saša. He grinned, shrugged and gave his mother a look as if to say, "What do you want me to do? I can't very well ask him to leave, now, can I?"

Marija stood outside the bedroom door for a minute before she regained her composure. It appeared her son had acquired an imaginary friend and his name was Saša. Marija thought she had heard the name before but could not remember when or where.

Suddenly Damir popped his head into the hall and gave his mother a start. "Ham, eggs, toast, strawberries and a big glass of milk!" Then, his tone changed and he added, "Make that two orders of ham, eggs, toast, strawberries and milk. I don't know what he likes for breakfast, I guess we can send for goat's cheese as well? Isn't that what they eat in the country? I mean, I don't know—" And Damir went back into his room, closing the door behind him.

Indeed, the first thing Marija did when she got back to her room was send for her son's breakfast. She had to repeat the order three times to the cook, a middle-aged matron who had worked for the Pavelićs longer than Damir's lifetime and was so happy to hear of the change in the little boy that she kept dropping to her knees to give thanks. Then, Marija woke up her daughter with the news that her beloved brother was hungry! Throwing good manners and modesty aside, Katarina ran out of her room and barged into Damir's without so much as knocking on the door first. She found him sitting on the bed, half dressed and trying to tie his boots. "Didi!" The little girl threw herself on her brother and kissed him. Damir fell back and almost out of the bed. "Didi, you're not sick anymore!"

"What's the matter with you? Can't you see he's sleeping! You're acting just like Mama! Now, really!"

The little girl paused in her unrestrained show of love, not because Damir was cross, but because she didn't know what he was talking about.

"Saša! He's right here!"

And as Didi was trying to tell his sister about his friend, Saša yawned, stretched out on the bed, opened his eyes, looked at Damir and said, "I'm hungry."

"I already sent for breakfast. Ham, eggs—"

"Oh, I love ham and eggs." Kati thought Damir was talking to her.

"I'm talking to Saša." Didi led his sister over to the shepherd. "This is Saša, my friend. Saša, this is my sister, Katarina."

Saša waved. "Hello."

"He said 'hello,' Katarina," explained Damir.

"H-hello—"

"Can she see you?" Damir suddenly realized that perhaps no one else was able to see his friend, the little shepherd boy who up until the night before Damir believed was dead.

"Sure she can—if she wants to," and Saša started jumping up and down on the bed.

"You *can* see him, yes?" Didi asked his sister. "He's my best friend!"

"Why is he making faces at me?" asked Kati.

"He's showing off."

Marija, the cook and two maids carrying the breakfast tray were halfway up the stairs when they heard the children laughing and a noise that sounded like a ball bouncing off the wall. Marija opened the door to the bedroom and found her son fully dressed, her daughter still in her nightshirt—and both of them on the floor playing marbles and having a wonderful time.

"Mama, Damir is not going to die, he's not going to die!"

"Of course he's not," joined Saša. "He has to play with me!"

Marija could not understand why Damir and Katarina started giggling. It could only mean that her little boy had recover—just in time. "Get dressed," Marija ordered her daughter. "Come, come!" Katarina was so determined to stay with Damir and Saša that Marija had to order her out of the room. "Remember you are a lady, always a lady—and ladies dress for breakfast."

"Hurry up!" Didi called out. "We're hungry!"

The change in Damir was nothing short of a miracle but Marija was still scared; Damir could suffer a relapse and die. None of the doctors (and there were dozens of them) who examined Damir had been able to effect a change for the better. On the contrary, as time went by Damir's health had deteriorated. But that day, that morning, Damir was hungry!

Now dressed, Katarina dashed past her mother into her brother's room. "I'm back! I'm back!" she screamed. "Save some for me!" She had put on her favorite blue dress hoping to impress Saša.

Marija closed the door to her son's room and left him to enjoy his breakfast in the company of angels.

Damir grew stronger and happier each day. He and Saša became inseparable and Kati embraced the little shepherd as a brother. On the other hand, the arrival of the Serbian boy unsettled the servants for a number of reasons. First among the complaints was the boy's religion; second was that the maids and nannies now had three children to care for, one of them invisible. But, everyone did what they could to humor Damir and his fascination—everyone that is, except his father, who thought Damir's behavior an affront and assumed the boy had lost his mind.

Late one night, almost a month to the day after Saša first appeared, while Marija was in her room reading and little Kati dreamed of fairies and enchanted lands, Damir and Saša sat quietly on the floor of their bedroom (Damir's was now the *boys' room*) playing checkers. Damir noticed that Saša was unusually quiet. "What's the matter?"

"Oh—nothing, and a lot," answered Saša, getting up from the floor and walking to the window.

"Saša?"

Saša did not answer. He looked outside, his back to Damir.

"Are you all right?" Damir got up and joined Saša. He saw his friend was crying. "What's wrong? Did I do something—oh, please, I'm sorry, please don't be angry with me!"

"Who said I'm angry?"

"Are you sick, then?"

"No, I'm sad."

"Why? Is there something you want? Can I get it for you?"

Saša shook his head. "I have to go. I don't want to, but I must. There's nothing to do, that's it."

"W-why? When?"

"I won't be here when you wake up."

"Please—"

"You cannot come with me, Didi. You have to stay here and take care of your mama and your sister."

Damir began to cry. And the beautiful, colorful garden that every night joined the boys in song and play turned grey and cold; raindrops fell on the flowers and they too, seemed to be weeping; the moon became dull and looked terribly sad.

"Are—are—" It was almost impossible for Damir to get the words out. "Are you going to heaven? Are you?"

"I don't know." Saša wiped off his tears with his shirtsleeve. "Here, keep it." Saša placed the svirala in Damir's hand. "Keep it until I come back."

"You're coming back?" The flowers stopped crying and paid close attention to the conversation.

"Yes," answered Saša. "I'll be back."

"When? Where? I'll have a car pick you up! I'll have Nikola–"

"No, no, no. You can't."

"Why not?"

"I'll be Peter."

It was strange news indeed. "Peter? Not Saša?"

The little shepherd shook his head. Then, he shrugged, gave Damir a shove and said, "Now teach me some more checkers—before I go!"

And he heard the flowers in the garden singing—

"Saša, Saša, Saša, come to play,
"Saša, Saša, Saša, come and stay,
"Saša, Saša, Saša, come and play—"

5

"I don't understand why he's coming here," said Hitler to Ribbentrop. They waited for Pavelić's train to arrive. "I don't like the man. He never smiles; he's too somber for my taste."

The meeting between the führer and the poglavnik was to take place at the train station, in the picturesque Bavarian village of Berchtesgaden. The German SS had set up the passenger lounge with posh leather chairs around a long rectangular table supplied with an assortment of soft drinks, coffee, tea, Viennese pastry, strudels, fruit tarts and other delicacies that would appeal to any sweet tooth. In the middle of the lounge—which could at any given time contain two thousand souls, regardless of where they were going to or coming from—there was a clock that from its squat base reached halfway to the ceiling. The large, fat-faced clock, to the chagrin of the station master, always ran a little late. High above the floor, just below the cornice, rows of windows let the sparkling Bavarian sunlight shine in on the German swastika and Croatia's checkerboard flag, displayed side by side on the south wall with equal prominence.

"Glum, that's what he is, plain glum," offered Reich Marshall Göring as the locomotive from Salzburg, with the Croatian delegation aboard, sounded its Bavarian whistle, and hissed to a stop exactly when and where it was scheduled to.

"Serbs and Croats, they are the same to me—Slavs," added Hitler.

Ribbentrop grinned. The steely-eyed foreign minister knew the führer, as the ditty went, "had a little list," and the Croats were somewhere at the top.

"Mr. President, wonderful to see you—again," declared Hitler, standing just outside the door to the station and two steps above the poglavnik. He raised his right arm in fascist salute, then shook hands with Pavelić, who in his enthusiasm raised his arm a little too high and squeezed Hitler's hand a little too tightly. It was all in the name of camaraderie and one-sided admiration, however. A moment later Hitler led Pavelić inside, among a flurry of flashing cameras sent to Berchtesgaden by Goebbels, Hitler's minister of propaganda, to record the meeting between the German leader and the president of the newly established Independent Nation of Croatia. Once everybody was behind closed doors, sitting on their comfortable chairs, the smiles turned to frowns, nods and delicately worded phrases indicating mutual understanding if not agreement.

"I think," began Hitler, "now that you're in control, my dear Dr. Pavelić, you should establish a fifty-year policy of national intolerance, much like ours." The führer darted a look at Ribbentrop.

"We already have such a plan," answered Pavelić, holding a piece of strudel between his fingers. "What's more, we have solved the Jewish question. I tell you, you will be pressed to find a live Jew in Croatia."

Hitler looked from Ribbentrop to Göring, then back at Pavelić. "Then you are to be commended."

Ante Pavelić stretched out in his chair, delighted to have been praised by the most distinguished and powerful man in the world.

"However, I must warn you," continued the führer, "Jews are like cockroaches; they hide in the most unusual places, have an incredible facility to adapt, even in the harshest environments, and can disguise themselves as something they are not. Isn't it true, Reich Marshall?"

Göring was having a difficult time keeping his eyes open. "Indeed, yes," he blurted. "Jews—humph, they're regular actors."

Hitler found the analogy amusing and waited to see if Pavelić thought likewise.

The führer was not disappointed; Pavelić actually broke into a laugh. "You're right, we have accomplished many great things in a short time but we must remain vigilant. I can assure you, my führer, Croatia will be cleansed of Slavs and Jews, make no mistake."

The foreign minister applauded, Hitler nodded, and the Reich Marshall yawned. "I beg your pardon, Mr. President," said Göring, "but I thought that Croats were also—Slavs. Am I mistaken?"

Pavelić, it should be noted, did not flinch. "Yes, you are," he answered, finishing off his strudel. "You see, Croats are descendants of the Ostrogoths, who as you know can be traced back to the third century, to the Greuthingi. They are identified as a distinct tribe of Germans."

It should also be noted that Göring's eyes widened, his brows lifted, his medals got heavier, and his pulse accelerated as he listened to the history of the Croats according to Ante Pavelić.

"Around the fifth century the Ostrogoths joined—reluctantly, from what I understand—Attila the Hun, even occupied the highest levels of government in the Hunnic empire. In the year 455 the majority of the Goths left the merciless and disintegrating Hunnic domination and were received as settlers on Roman soil in what is today Croatia. Later, in 485, a struggle developed between the Eastern Empire and the Goths, each trying to secure the Balkans for themselves, with the difference that we—meaning the Goths—were trying to gain control of the Balkans in the name of Rome; that's why we are Roman Catholics. I must add that many Serbs are not Slavs at all, but are also descendants of the Goths. Unfortunately, they were converted by the Eastern Church, but their blood—that remains Gothic in every way." Pavelić smiled condescendingly at Göring, hoping his explanation put an end to the generally held view that Croats were subhuman Slavs. But the Reich Marshall had already decided he was not at all interested in the history of Croatia, and had given himself to the soft enveloping grace of his chair.

Hitler slapped both hands on his knees and sprang to his feet. "Extraordinary!" He looked at Göring. "Live and learn, I say, live and learn, most extraordinary, quite illuminating. So, what else can we do for you? Is there something you need to help your country–"

Ante Pavelić did not let Hitler continue. "As a matter of fact, there is." He was feeling bold. "We would like guaranteed autonomy, full independence. If you could see to it that Il Duce does not do anything—rash. As you know, he is upset because our governments established commercial ties, which I feel is in our best national interest. But Mussolini has threatened to take back Dalmatia."

The führer nodded, took hold of Pavelić's arm and led him to the door. "Don't worry about Benito; he is, how shall I say, he is so—Italian. Throws his arms in the air, shouts and bangs his fist, but he will not do anything, I promise."

An SS guard opened the door and the two leaders walked outside to face the German press. As Hitler escorted Pavelić to the boarding platform he announced that it was—"With joy and satisfaction that Germany embraces the new state of Croatia and its people, after they so valiantly helped the Axis powers demolish the artificial nation that was once Yugoslavia and won the struggle for their independence!"

In exchange for the lavish praise, the poglavnik presented the führer with a flag from the Seven Year's War and a chess set, both of which had once belonged to Frederick the Great.

Ante Pavelić waved good-bye to Adolf Hitler. He was overwhelmed by a deep feeling of confidence. In a few hours he had put the oaf Göring in his place and received personal assurances from Hitler that Italy would not meddle in the affairs of Croatia. Adolf Hitler waved good-bye to the poglavnik and wondered how Ante Pavelić, the leader of a nation artificially created by Germany, had been able to get his hands on two such glorious icons from Germany's past. He also thought that perhaps it had been a mistake to postpone invading the Soviet Union just to set things straight in Yugoslavia, a country inhabited by cretins inclined to fratricide. To think he put off the definitive German conquest for a group of savages. "Let's get back to work, please!" And Hitler turned away from the platform.

A few months later, with the Nazi armies fully engaged in Russia, Mussolini sent two divisions and occupied Dalmatia, saying it had to protect Italy's coast from insurgents. Il Duce blitzed Hitler with letters and communiqués demanding the partition of Croatia, a state the Italian dictator viewed as being governed by lackeys of the Germans. Soon after, Ante Pavelić broke with the Ustaše in part due to the dissension promoted by German agents within the group, who were furious that Pavelić had been unable to stop Mussolini from taking back the coveted Dalmatian coast. By that time the partisans were in control of a sizeable portion of the country, and their activities made life impossible for the Quisling government. It did not come as a surprise, thus, when German radio announced that the Pavelić cabinet had resigned and a new government had been sworn in—"according to Ustaše principles." Ante Pavelić had no choice. He and his family went into hiding.

☩

On the surface, Father Draganović had a far quieter time during his four months in the hospital. At first, the priest was under the expert medical care of the Sisters of Providence, who were under the exacting supervision of Archbishop Stepinac. Slowly, Draganović regained much of his strength, if not all of his features. Two surgeons were flown in from Budapest to rearrange his broken jaw and shattered nose. All in all, the mending of the wounds was a slow and painful process that compared with his beating at the hands of the partisans. The day the communists launched their first attack on Banja Luka, Archbishop Stepinac helped Father Draganović into a wheelchair, placed him carefully in the back seat of a grey Citroën, and sent him to his mother's farm in the mountains above the small town of Travnik. Ana Draganović was to smother her son with enough old home remedies, love and care to nurse him back to health. For Father Krunoslav Draganović, the Second World War had come to an end.

The friars Silov and Borna spent less than two days mending their lacerated bodies in a hospital, then armed themselves and became couriers between the Catholic convents and monasteries around Croatia that had become intelligence cells for the Ustaše. The brothers enjoyed this clandestine work and were often praised for their zeal. Everything was going well for the two until they heard that the war in Europe was over, that Mussolini and his mistress had been shot—their bodies displayed for the masses in Milan—and that Hitler was missing and presumed to be as dead as Il Duce. In the meantime, the communists took control of Croatia, Serbia, Slovenia, Bosnia-Herzegovina, Dalmatia and Macedonia. They did so using every means available or necessary, including the outright extermination of whole villages, regardless of ethnicity. The Catholic clergy became a favorite target of the new government and thousands of priests, monks and friars were hunted down, imprisoned or executed, especially those who had collaborated with the Nazis during the war. It is not surprising then, that after very little pondering Brothers Silov and Borna decided to seek refuge in a monastery. They still had the revolvers given to them by the Ustaše and they kept the weapons tucked inside their habits, although by then the garments were so full of holes it would have been anyone's guess what the friars' religious persuasion was. For over a year and a half after the end of the war the brothers roamed the countryside in search of sanctuary. They mingled with the lucky survivors of the war—hordes of displaced and emaciated men, women and children; Serbs, Croats and Muslims making their way to the refugee camps set up by the Red Cross throughout the country; hundreds of thousands of people carrying nothing with them but defeat, crushed hopes and despair; every single one marching, in his turn, to the different measures of Tito's drumbeat. To Silov and Borna's dismay, every monastery they came to was occupied by troops from the Federal People's Republic of Yugoslavia, and every soldier, as far as the friars were concerned, was an ex-partisan. Finding something to eat became very difficult, and begging for food was pointless, since everyone else was just as hungry as they were. And so, late one wet summer night, feeling as despondent and as unhappy as two men who had been without food for days had a right to feel, the brothers traveled to the one place in the whole country they thought was still under the control of their brethren, the abbey of Toranjmost, not far from Komar in the heart of Bosnia.

The monastery was a four-level, fourteenth-century impossibility set atop an extremely inhospitable, exceedingly high and unduly rocky cliff top. It was always blanketed with a dark, ominous mist and was cut off from the rest of the world by a dense forest crisscrossed with innumerable hidden crevasses—deep black chasms camouflaged by thickets of poisonous thorns where, at any given time, a passerby could drop away and disappear. This charming resort was accessible only by crossing a slender wooden plank, a crude railing that extended for ten meters over a dizzying three-hundred-meter plunge. Reaching the cloister was an even more difficult (and dangerous) rite because of the swirling midday winds that could knock devotees off the side unless they fastened themselves with ropes and crawled on their bellies from end to end. Yet, no matter how fraught with uncertainty an expedition was in daylight, at night it was an adventure few dared to undertake and even fewer survived. This was precisely what Brothers Silov and Borna set out to do, not because it was their intention to challenge fate, but because they were so hungry they could not wait until daylight.

It was after sundown when they embarked on a slow and exhausting climb that defied their senses. The only way the brothers knew they were heading up the cliff in the absolutely black and fetid air was by the subtle incline of their bodies. Silov and Borna were swallowed whole by the voracious gods defending the woods. Giant spider webs clung to their hair, faces and bodies, and the dank thicket of branches, cones, pine needles and leaves formed a barrier that could be breached only by plunging through it, sending thousands of industrious night crawlers up their habits, making the trip even more unsettling. Three and a half hours later the two friars reached a clearing. They knew it was a clearing because they could not feel anything ahead—nothing except a drop of thirty meters onto a bed of razor sharp rocks and spikes. The companions hugged the edge of the precipice and walked for another half an hour until they came upon the narrow span leading to the abbey. As usual, the bridge was covered by haze, making it difficult for them to pick out three ferocious Dobermans racing toward them from the massive gates of the abbey. The dogs, part of an army patrol, were less than ten meters away before the friars realized what was happening. Silov and Borna turned on their heels and ran hysterically for their lives in the opposite direction. As luck would have it, one of the dogs lost its footing and fell off the bridge, distracting the others and allowing the friars a few, precious extra seconds to reach the other side of the platform, drop into a sinkhole, and vanish.

Silov and Borna tumbled violently down a ravine, and avoided death only when their fall was cushioned by the entire population of the monastery, which lay in heaps of decomposing bodies at the bottom of the ditch. It was impossible to see but quite possible to touch, feel and smell the rotting flesh and the cold, stiff joints, the hair, teeth and eyeballs, all unmistakable to a pair of Franciscan brothers out for a stroll on a balmy summer eve. The brothers wanted to scream, so intense was their horror and disgust. But their fear was worse. They remained in the mass grave for almost an hour, scared even to breathe. Finally, but only when they were positive the soldiers had given up finding them alive, Silov and Borna made it out of the ditch. Silov found he had a large gash on his forehead and Borna's left knee was bleeding from a wound that cut deep into the bone. The friars were doing everything possible to hold out against the awful pain and wretchedness of their despair, when a northerly squall let loose and soaked the hapless duo. If anything, the rain was a relief. The brothers gasped for air, pulled off their habits and scrubbed themselves in the downpour, Radonić doing it with such force that he seemed to be trying to purify his body from any contamination acquired in the grave. He retched, but his stomach had nothing in it to throw up. "This is not human!" he screamed. He was standing in the middle of the road sobbing, saliva and bile foaming from his mouth. "I can't take this, I can't!" Borna tore the rags he had just taken off.

Silov ignored his friend's wounds and calmly nursed his own. "Get a hold of yourself." He understood these were not the best of times; he understood that if they ran into the army they would be shot; he understood they had not eaten a good meal in months and had been sleeping outside for just as long; yes, he understood all of that. But they had to keep faith; God would look after them.

"God?" Borna's tears mingled with the raindrops that pelted his face. "What makes you think God is looking after us any better than He's looking after anyone else!?" Every so often lightning outlined the brother's haggard face. "Forget the Serbs, forget the Muslims; our people! Croats, Catholics, priests, friars! God is not looking after them at all, is He now? And they kept their faith, didn't they? Haven't we? We have been forsaken!" Borna cursed and cried until he was so exhausted his knees buckled and he fell to the ground, shivering, his naked body lashed by the torrential rains.

"Look, it's obvious we can't continue this way. Let's do something else," said Silov matter-of-factly. The other started to say something but was not given a chance. "I'm serious; if this is all we have left, let's use it." Brother Silov took out the gun that was still at his side. "Why not? We have no choice but to become ban—bandoleros."

"What?" Borna had never heard the word before.

"Bandolero. It was in a movie. It means bandit."

Borna started to laugh, though it was unclear what he found funny—the idea, which was absurd, or the expression (quite earnest) on Silov's face, or both.

"We have spent our lives learning scriptures and doing the dirty work for others," said Silov. "Well, if we don't do something for ourselves, we'll die. We have to use our wits, get food, clothes, money and a way out of this miserable place."

Borna ripped off a piece of his habit and wrapped it tightly around his leg just above the knee. Then, he got up and threw what was left over his head, tying the torn habit at the waist as best he could. "Rob who? The peasants? They have less than we do."

"I don't know about that. I lost my sandals in the fall; now I'm barefoot."

"Me too," declared Borna.

"No, nobody has less than we do," returned his friend. "I'm telling you, we have nothing, nothing, except this!" Silov brandished the revolver in Borna's face.

"But, who are you going to rob?"

"Anyone, and we take what we can." Silov walked around in circles, trying to remember what you were supposed to do and say in a robbery. Precision in such matters was very important; bandoleros had to use strong language to make people fear them right away, thus avoiding an uncooperative victim, or worse a confrontation that could result in someone getting hurt. "I don't mean we take it on as a vocation, you know, just a few stickups so we get a little cash—not much, we don't need much."

"What if they object?"

"Who?"

"Those you try to rob. They're likely to protest."

"I would too, I guess," confessed Silov.

"Are you going to shoot them?"

"Not unless they make trouble." Silov stared into the night. "Are you ready? We have work to do." The weapon in his hand was an instrument of fear, granting him the powers of life or death, as the life of an outlaw awaited them.

Borna raised himself with great difficulty, his swollen knee shooting a disturbing degree of pain up and down his leg.

"Come, we don't have all night."

"It hurts, damn you!" cried out Borna as he hobbled to catch up with his friend.

Silov stopped. "Let me see," and he raised the other's habit to examine the damaged knee. "Mmm, I can't see a thing. But, try to walk a little faster, or it's going to take us a week to get out of here." He meant out of the hills and into the valley. And Silov was off again, Borna trailing his most impatient colleague.

It did not take them a week to reach Komar, just a few hours, in fact. By falling into the sinkhole the two friars had found a very direct, though painful shortcut to the base of the cliff, just five kilometers from the edge of town.

As the clouds dispersed and another morning tested their resolve, the brothers met a tall, hefty Muhammadan driving a horse-drawn wagon, empty but for a large black dog curled up in the back, a few strands of hay and a very sharp-looking sickle next to the driver, that, along with the man's sturdy constitution, made further speculation of a robbery unnecessary. It would be another hour before the brothers ran into another possible victim, or rather victims: three shifty-eyed men who looked like deserters from one army or another, unshaven, unclean, all of them eyeing the brothers with the look of a cat about to pounce on a nervous canary. Even though the three renegades were on the other side of the road, Silov felt a need to hold his gun at the ready lest he and his companion become victims themselves. Luckily for the friars, the three men felt just as Silov and Borna had felt earlier that afternoon when encountering the Muslim farmer: it was not worth the trouble.

After hours walking aimlessly without knowing if they would ever see another human being, the pain, the hunger, the weariness, the doubt and the smell of rain once again demoralized Brother Silov and Brother Borna.

"I have to rest. The knee's acting up again," complained Borna.

It was already afternoon. "It's just as well," said his friend. "I mean, I can't believe it, where is everybody? Maybe, maybe we ought to find another road. This one's going nowhere." Brother Silov threw his arms in the air, frustrated and angry with the world.

Borna sat down and slowly stretched out the leg with the wounded knee. He closed his eyes and prayed for courage to go on and patience to deal with Silov.

Suddenly, Silov picked out a black dot in the distance. His senses sharpened. His eyes fixed on the dot, his ears pricked up, his nostrils flared and his concentration became absolute. Borna noticed the change in his friend's demeanor when the other suddenly stood up, oblivious to a honking flight of geese and two large mosquitos sucking blood from the bald spot on his head. The tall friar scrambled to keep pace with his companion, who was already on his way. Ten minutes later they slowed down as the dot transformed itself into an extremely hunched Muslim woman, shrouded in black. Only her hands and eyes were visible. One hand held a thick stick marred by deep gashes in the wood; the other gripped a black sack hung over her shoulder. Her tired green eyes, which seemed weary of suffering, were sunk deep in her face, hidden in part by thick, tawny brows. Those same eyes, eyes that were like emeralds set on black granite and left to blister in the sun, locked onto the brothers as they walked by.

"Old woman," called out Silov.

She stopped, turned ever so slowly and screamed in a croaking, powerful voice—obviously the product of a thousand pleas. "Old? And how do you know I am old?"

"You look bent enough and walk with a stick," returned the friar with a chuckle.

"And you're ugly enough and smell like dog shit!"

"Feisty, isn't she?" Borna whispered aside to his friend.

"Mother!" Silov called out with contempt.

"I'm not your mother! I spit on your mother!" She raised her veil, spat on the ground and lifted the stick high in the air, leaving no doubt it would come crashing on his head if Brother Silov got within reach.

"And I spit on you, you Muslim whore!" The little friar was flushed. He bounced up and down, pulled out his gun and took aim. "What do you have there, money, jewels, eh, witch?" The good brother thought it would be an easy undertaking to rob a woman alone in an out-of-the-way place. He ranted and swore he would fill her with bullets unless she relinquished everything of value. His performance was meant to frighten his victim, an assumption—one in a string of many—that proved wrong and left Silov confused, forcing the friar to rethink, review and improvise. The woman outscreamed and outcursed the brother scream for scream and profanity for profanity, always aiming her stick at his head. She grew so loud and violent that Silov kept to his side of the road.

"Swine!" she shouted. "You murdered my son! You murdered my children! The wrath of the Prophet will avenge the martyrs!"

"Leave her be, she's mad," said Borna.

"Yeah, I know she's a crazy hag. What if I shoot her in the head?"

"A bit extreme, wouldn't you say?" argued his partner.

Silov pretended to pull the trigger, and made a sound to imitate the shot that would put an end to the old woman's hysterics. It did no good; her verbal assault not only continued but intensified. The scalding, acrimonious tongue-lashing—which kept the brothers confounded (and nervous because someone might come along to interfere)—lasted three minutes. Then, the woman dropped her stick, clenched her chest, let out one last virulent howl and fell to the ground.

All was quiet; only the rustling of the leaves was heard as the wind picked up.

"What happened?"

"I don't know what happened any more than you do," said Silov with an impatient smirk.

Borna looked away. He was getting tired of Silov's condescending attitude.

It was another minute before Silov decided the woman had suffered a heart attack or some kind of seizure (in which case, she was still alive). He took great care as he walked over to the heap of black fluttering robes. It was just as well, thought the brother because he did not have to waste a single bullet (he had six left). Moving with the swift grace of a scavenger rat, he knelt by the body and looked for anything worth taking. As he was about to turn the body on its side—

"Borna," he called in a hushed voice.

"What is it now?" Borna had stayed where he was, thinking, with good reason, that the woman's behavior had been so bizarre that she was, perhaps, faking death, laying a trap and just waiting for the brother to come near so she could crack him on the knee.

"Will you come here?" insisted his companion as he straightened up and tapped his impatient foot on the ground. "Tell me, what are we going to do now?" Silov pointed to the sack the woman had been carrying where a baby, not more than six months old, wearing loose diapers and a colorful paisley shawl to protect him from the cold, smiled up at the brothers. It is true the thought of having the baby join the woman crossed Brother Silov's mind, but when Christ said, "Suffer the little children to come unto me," He certainly did not mean to go and make it easy for them. "Any ideas?"

Borna picked up the baby, carried him to the side of the road, removed the wrappings and confirmed his gender. "We can't leave him here; it could be days, maybe weeks before he's found. He'll die for sure."

"So?" Silov turned the woman's body on its side and removed her veil. She had been old, to be sure, seventy-five years old at least, with long deep furrows all over her face and a mane of white hair under her shawl.

"We have to find his kin," said Borna.

"Didn't you hear what she said?" Brother Silov aimed an accusing finger at the mound of black in front of him. "That kid's family's wiped out!"

"Maybe, maybe not. He's sure to have other relatives," reasoned Borna, looking at the baby in his arms.

Silov walked quickly to the tall friar, got up on his tip-toes, and brought a finger to Borna's nose. "You are not Saint Christopher! Besides, even if you were that burdened saint you would not bear a Muslim devil on your back!"

Borna was just as stubborn and refused to abandon the baby to be eaten by the hungry wolves that, as everyone knew, roamed the countryside in search of defenseless prey. That allusion to wolves was a conscious effort on the part of Brother Borna to get the patron saint of the Franciscans involved in the debate.

Silov eyed him with suspicion. "We drop him off at the next town, got that? Otherwise you're on your own because I—me, Silov Petronović—I am going to—to Rome!"

"Don't be an ass. See if she's carrying papers," directed the other, and walked away, cradling the baby.

Silov cursed at the old woman for not providing anything but trouble; not money, not jewels, not food, only a copy of the Koran and a sniveling, fiendish Muhammadan whelp. The brother made such a scene that the baby got frightened and began to cry. He was a bit thin but had a beautiful round little face, a wisp of dark blond hair, matching brows, brown eyes and pale cheeks.

"You know what I was thinking?" asked Borna.

"I don't care! Do you hear me, I don't give a damn! As if we didn't have enough to worry about!" Brother Silov walked over to his friend, placed the old woman's volume on top of the baby and walked away. "Christ is weeping this day, Borna; he can see you carrying that little demon with the book of Satan on his chest! Look at you, just look at you! How Christ weeps this day!" screamed Silov. "You're a disgrace, a traitor to the faith!" he yelled, then turned, walked backwards and pointed at the baby. "Remember that his kind have tortured and murdered our brothers for ages! They are worse than Serbs; at least Serbs believe in Christ who died on the cross!"

Borna did not answer or looked at Silov. He tucked away the Koran, held the baby close to him, and thought about finding a place where they could take shelter once it began to rain.

6

"He's much maligned," said the pope, with a slight emphasis on *much*. He held a Chesterfield loosely between his lips. The Blessed Father walked two steps in front of Archbishop Giovanni Montini, pro-secretary of state for humanitarian affairs, and Abbot Marcone, who had left Croatia just days before Ante Pavelić became another fallen star.

Towering rows of age-old Roman cypress and thick ivy hid the high, surrounding walls and provided privacy and shade for the midday stroll. A small pond made of granite tiles shaped like water lilies was the centerpiece of the peaceful garden behind Castel Gandolfo, the pope's summer residence overlooking Lake Albano. Four shrubs marked the perimeter of the pond; they had been trimmed by Father Gratale to look like round green buttons. Two narrow paths of the same grey stone led to a heavy, rusty iron gate that connected with the papal apartments, and, in the opposite direction, to a white marble Madonna in an ivy-covered niche. The Madonna watched the water lilies and offered guidance to *this* pope, the former Eugenio Pacelli, known to Catholics around the world as Pius XII. The pope was in his mid-sixties. He was about five feet seven, with dark eyes, a nose that was perhaps a bit too wide, lips that were perhaps a bit too full and a demeanor that was perhaps a bit too stern. The little hair he had left (he never had much to begin with) was tucked under a white zucchetto that matched his pontifical robes. Behind the wire glasses (with shades) was the steadfast determination that made Pius XII someone to be reckoned with.

Pacelli had become pope in 1939, at the outset of Hitler's invasion of Poland. He kept the Vatican indirectly involved in the war through an intricate network of emissaries and secret agents, while at the same time making sure that Vatican City remained neutral territory, thus avoiding the anarchy and destruction happening in most of the continent at the time. "Dr. Pavelić was a bastion against Orthodoxy, he did everything we asked for, even declared the Independent Nation of Croatia—by constitutional mandate—a Catholic state." The pontiff put out the last of his cigarette on a modern standing ashtray placed inconspicuously behind the Madonna of the Water Lilies. "Has he been told of our plans?"

"No, Holiness. We—we thought the information might be better received if it came from you," said His Excellency Marcone.

"So, where has he been all this time?"

Archbishop Montini flipped through his notepad where he kept meticulous notations of everything he said, did, was told or was instructed to do. The notepad would have been a rich source of intelligence for anyone inquiring into the official business of Archbishop Giovanni Montini. He was a mousy little fellow that looked older than his forty-five years. He had olive complexion, a small, plain face with large circles under his brown eyes and his stamina was legendary; one could spot Montini day and night crisscrossing the halls of the Vatican even when someone else would have been glad to do his bidding. "At the end of the war, Dr. Pavelić crossed over to British-held territory at Maribor, where he was protected by British Field Marshall Alexander for several months. Then Father Draganović arranged for him to come to Rome—to live at the Institute of Saint Jerome." Montini flipped a page and went on. "Oh, yes. Just this month the American CIC—CIC stands for Counter-Intelligence Corps—ordered his arrest. We were lucky that Father Draganović has a man inside the CIC and was able to get word to us in time. The order to arrest Dr. Pavelić has since been rescinded."

"Where is his family?" asked the pope.

"Still in Yugoslavia, Holiness. Father Draganović is looking out for them."

"Father Draganović is certainly keeping busy these days," observed Pius XII.

"Unfortunately, the situation with Dr. Pavelić has become more complicated since Tito demanded his extradition. And of course, now we have reports of—" Montini was about to allude to the atrocities perpetrated by the Croatian government during the war when the pope turned around, faced the archbishop and ordered him to stop. Montini put away his notepad.

"I don't want to hear about *reports*," said the pope. "Every day I am deluged and puzzled by *reports*—reports of death camps in Poland, reports of millions murdered by Stalin—his own people no less—reports of hundreds of thousands slaughtered by Tito's partisans! So, let's not talk about reports and let's get this man safely out of Europe so he can start his life over again." Both Excellencies nodded humbly. "Communist propaganda, that's what I call what you call *reports*! First Orthodoxy, now Bolshevism! Where will it end?" The pope reached for another Chesterfield and his Zippo.

The creaking of the iron gate meant that Father Zanini had entered the garden. The old priest had spent all his life in the service of popes. He never aspired to anything else, so while other priests ascended or descended around him, depending on this or that pope's whims and prejudices, Father Zanini was a veritable icon of stability in the papal household. He walked carefully (he had tripped one morning on a tile protruding sightly from its base and broken his wrist) and straight to the Holy Father. "He has arrived."

Neither the pope, the archbishop nor the abbot turned to acknowledge Zanini. "He has arrived" could have been announced from a loudspeaker, called in on the telephone, sent by telegram, broadcast by wireless, delivered by post, scrawled on the blue Roman skies by an adventure-seeking aviator, or even pronounced in a deep resonant voice from above. They knew *who* had arrived, and that *he* had arrived in secret.

"Mr. President, wonderful to see you—again," said Pius XII softly. He put out his hand to be graced by the lips of Ante Pavelić. The poglavnik was reluctant to kiss the ring because he knew Pius XII enjoyed a cigarette now and then. The thought of the Blessed Father yielding to such a worldly vice, along with the faint aroma of nicotine and the yellow stain on the pontiff's ring finger, made the exiled Croat leader queasy. Nevertheless, as the two clerics looked on from the side, Ante Pavelić took the sacred hand of the pope and planted a Croatian kiss upon the pious ring of Pius XII. A moment later Pavelić and the pope were arm in arm, taking laps around the water lilies, with Montini and Marcone trailing a few steps behind.

Pavelić was dressed in a conservative dark grey suit tailored by the house of Personeni, in Bergamo. Although the double-breasted jacket made him look like an international financier instead of a deposed tyrant, Pavelić—if you had asked him—would have preferred the fascist military uniform to the suit.

"My son, you know how grateful we are for your struggle in Croatia, a struggle that even if set back for the time, continues and will continue until communism is dead," said the pope softly as he completed the first lap around the pond. "Unfortunately, we have been placed in a most awkward position. As outrageous as it seems, you know, of course, that the present government of Yugoslavia is demanding your capture."

Pavelić kept his eyes turned downward, as if asking the grass what to reply.

"The Reds in your country suspect we are helping you in some way, as well we should." The pope stopped for a moment and looked straight at Pavelić. "We will continue to do so, of course." The pope, Pavelić, the archbishop and the abbot had now completed the second lap around the pond. "May I suggest, however, we help you somewhere else?"

"Somewhere else?"

"Argentina."

"Argentina!"

"South America," added the pope in case Pavelić had failed geography. "Oh, you will be well received. We have many friends there. Why, Perón himself inquired as to your willingness to—" and here the Holy Father sighed, "—give him a few pointers on matters of state security; on how to combat communism." This statement from Pius XII meant one of two things. Either Perón was unaware of Pavelić's history as a failed dictator—if not, why seek advice from a man who could not keep insurgents out of his own backyard—or the Argentinean ruler was doing the Holy See a favor, one that sooner or later would have to be repaid.

"President Perón is a very good Catholic," joined Marcone.

"We will get you safely out of Italy and your family out of Yugoslavia. His Excellency," and the pontiff turned to Montini, "has the details." As the third lap around the water lilies was now over, the pontiff took a rosary from his pocket, gave it to Pavelić, put out his hand and bid Pavelić a safe trip to South America.

The poglavnik kissed the pontifical ring again, put away the rosary, and after his obeisance, watched Pius XII return to the house accompanied by Marcone.

"Mr. President, we have to be practical. There's an army of assassins looking for you. You can't stay in Rome. Besides, it would not be fair to compromise the Holy See," said Montini.

"What of my family?"

"You will soon be together again. Come, everything is taken care of." Montini led Pavelić out of the garden to the gleaming black Mercedes-Benz waiting at the front of the building. "I dare say," added the archbishop with a hint of regret, "I do not think we will meet again. God be with you." Montini graciously stood to one side as the chauffeur—a tall, wide swarthy Croat about twenty-two years old, with a no-nonsense air, a thick neck, a deep raspy voice, small black eyes and short black hair who answered to the name of Rostas—opened the back door for the poglavnik.

"Is everything all right, Mr. President? You look a bit pale," said Father Draganović as Pavelić plopped his body next to him in the back seat.

The poglavnik looked at the priest and shook his head in disbelief. "I'm going to Argentina! Argentina! Did you know they were sending me to Argentina?"

Father Draganović did not answer, giving Pavelić to understand that indeed, the priest had known everything.

Pavelić crossed his arms and shook his head. Even before he had gone into exile, he had made a list of places where he and his family might want to relocate; Argentina was not on the list.

Montini waved and Pius XII watched from his second-story window as the car turned a corner and was gone. "He's much maligned, much maligned." The pope took out the Chesterfields, put another cigarette in his mouth and stared out the window. Regardless of what happened, thought Pius XII, he was declaring war on communism, and he intended to win; after all, the Latin church had a two-thousand-year head start on manipulation, intrigue and repression. Bolshevism did not stand a chance.

Ante Pavelić knew almost nothing about Argentina. He had had two impromptu chats with Juan Perón and members of his delegation during the induction of Croatia into the Rome-Berlin-Tokyo military alliance and had concluded that the Argentineans, beside speaking Spanish (a language Pavelić found inexplicably dull), were so bombastic it reminded him of peasants who have suddenly come into money. The Argentineans also were determined to imitate the Germans in everything but courage. It was the poglavnik's opinion the Argentineans were riddled with the inferiority complex of a people who thought of themselves as something they were not. It did not occur to the poglavnik that many Croats too, himself included, saw themselves as something they were not—as he clearly pointed out to Hitler during their meeting at Berchtesgaden.

The limousine sped north, heading back to Rome. It swept through the cramped and busy Roman streets and serpentine boulevards, avoiding by the narrowest of margins pedestrians and vehicles alike. The car did manage to clip the cassock of a priest who dared step in front of it, as if to warn him, "You belong to us, look sharp!"

Pavelić never looked out the window. He closed his eyes and let his mind drift back to better times when his word meant life or death, when he was a man respected, feared by his people and revered by his family. Now his options were two: go to Buenos Aires or face an assassin's bullet. The more Pavelić thought about it, the more he was tempted to gamble on the killer's expertise.

An hour later the car drove past Vatican City, turned right on Ponte Margherita, kept to the right of the Piazza del Popolo, made another right on Via della Ripetta and continued until it reached the Institute of Saint Jerome, almost on the corner of Via Tomacelli. The institute was made up of a little church and a priest's college attached to the church. Although, by Roman standards, the church was quite modest, the college was not. It was a two-story building honeycombed with rooms that looked like cells; some bigger and more comfortable than others. The halls were guarded by armed youths in civilian clothes. Each of the young men wore a pin with an emblem of a checkerboard *U*.

As soon as the car pulled up to the back door, three men immediately came out of the building and surrounded the car. Once they made sure it was safe, the driver got out, opened the door for Pavelić and escorted the poglavnik into the building; Draganović remained in the car.

Pavelić was met inside by Draganović's lieutenant, one Father Artemus (Pavelić was convinced this was not the priest's real name). Father Artemus was a thin man with red hair and freckles left over from his youth. He could talk forever without taking a breath, spewing out words like machine-gun fire, but thanks to the priest, the Institute of Saint Jerome ran with military efficiency and Father Artemus was careful to provide his guests with maximum comfort and security. For instance, there was never more than one important guest staying at the Institute at any given time. The Institute was a transit point where visitors would come and stay before going somewhere else. After the war, *somewhere else* meant, for the most part, South America, which in turn meant, in general, a one-way ticket to Argentina, Chile or Bolivia.

"You must change—in case you are stopped by the Americans," said Father Artemus, meaning the American Fourth Army, which patrolled up and down the coast to prevent smugglers from smuggling and war criminals from getting away. "You will find your disguise on the bed." They walked through the dark, narrow hall to Pavelić's room, where the poglavnik found the full dress of a cardinal on top of the bed, including an impressive ring, a gold cross on a chain, a rosary and the distinguished-looking plumed red hat. "What is this?" asked Pavelić in a tone that showed he already knew the answer; Artemus, accordingly, did not reply but quickly closed the door.

Pavelić sat on the bed for a moment. For the first time since he was a child, the poglavnik felt like weeping; he was being abandoned. Still, he did not cry or yield to self-pity; a common trait among despots is their inability to feel compassion, even for themselves.

Twenty minutes later, Ante Pavelić was again sitting in the limousine across from Father Draganović. If the clothes did not make him look like a man at odds with life, the expression on his face did. "Where are we going now?"

"Genoa. Your boat leaves at one in the morning. We'll make it just in time. You will find Argentina a nice change; don't worry." Draganović reached for a small basket covered with a red and white checkered cloth, placed it on his lap, and began taking out one item at a time. "Are you hungry? I brought along bread, prosciutto, cheese and butter—" and Draganović looked in the basket. "Ah, there's also chocolate, and to drink, let's see, a very fine, even if I say so myself, a very fine Chianti and the most delicious coffee in the world." Draganović pulled out a large thermos.

"I don't want to eat," returned Pavelić.

"Mr. President, we're going to be on the road for a long time, then you'll be at sea for two weeks and I don't think cabin service is going to be all that great." Draganović took out a knife from the basket and cut a piece of cheese. Then, he brought out two napkins, two glasses, uncorked the bottle of wine and offered the poglavnik a drink. After a slight pause, Pavelić accepted the glass, and even a piece of bread and chocolate. "Your suitcases—actually, one suitcase—is in the trunk. It is filled mostly with food and three shirts. These minor inconveniences are unavoidable, of course, until you reach Argentina." The car had left behind the city limits and was speeding north along the coast. Pavelić was tempted to look out the window and savor the rolling hills, the small villages and the Italian skies—all, perhaps, for the last time.

"Try the coffee, it's quite delicious—if you like coffee," said Draganović. He wiped off his glass with the red and white checkered cloth, opened the thermos and poured some coffee for himself.

"What will happen to my family?"

"I am personally taking care of your family. They will be fine," assured Draganović. "Mr. President," Draganović fixed his eyes on Pavelić and his voice took on a less official and much warmer tone, "with everything that's been going on, I—I haven't had time to thank you." The poglavnik looked carefully at the priest and for a moment did not know what Draganović was talking about. "If it hadn't been for you," continued Draganović, "I would have died by the roadside like an animal. I will never forget what you did for me—and my companions."

Pavelić did not say anything. For some reason he blamed the unraveling of his world to the afternoon trip to Glina.

"Look," Draganović moved the flannel curtain and looked out the window, "the Holy See is determined—we need a reserve of Croatian leaders in exile to help defeat Bolshevism."

They were five kilometers from Genoa when Pavelić was asked again to change clothes. The driver reached under the seat and pulled out a bundle of clothes tied together with a thin brown belt, which he passed across the divider to Father Draganović, who gave them to Ante Pavelić.

"Change?"

"I don't think it would be a good idea to get on the boat dressed the way you are." Draganović put aside the food, opened a briefcase and took out a set of documents. He made sure they were the right ones, before giving them to Pavelić. "You will be traveling as Pedro Gómez, a Portuguese national. This is your passport. These papers—please study them carefully—include a background of your new identity. One can never be too careful about these things, although I am sure you will not have any trouble reaching Argentina."

"Pedro Gómez!" called out a large man wearing a seafaring uniform who stood at the base of the ramp leading to the *Philippi*. The boat was large and very old, possibly dating back to the turn of the century. It was used to haul everything across the seas, including war refugees, exiles, war criminals and their victims—all, now, in the same boat.

Gómez stepped forward and the man stamped his passport several times. "Go on, go!" Pedro Gómez climbed the ramp slowly and boarded the ship. He did not look back. There was no one to wave good-bye. Draganović was already on his way back to Rome.

Once aboard, Pedro showed his papers to a scruffy-looking ship's mate, then followed the young man down three levels to the large, rusty ballast tank. "Pedro Gómez? I remember you!" said the sailor.

A group of stragglers were already there, most of them wearing their caps just above their eyes, hiding their anxious expressions and carrying nothing with them but the clothes on their backs. The ship's mate stopped next to a low bunk set against the cold, steel wall of the ship. "Ah, there's your pal!" He nodded to a drab-looking man huddled in another bunk. "That's Esquivel, Jorge Esquivel. You two have made this trip seven times already, seven times since April. Faces—I could care less for faces, but names, I never forget a name, especially those making their way through the Ratlines."

Pedro looked puzzled.

"We're called the Ratlines," explained the mate. "In fact, that's what we do, help rats get away." The man sneered, turned and disappeared up the ladder.

Pedro Gómez and Jorge Esquivel. It would not be their last trip together, either. They would meet again in the same dark hole of the same old ship, traveling to the same far-off ports. Pedro Gómez—Ante Pavelić, Klaus Barbie; Jorge Esquivel—Andrija Artuković, Josef Mengele, Adolf Eichmann.

7

While Pedro Gómez suffered the indignities of an Atlantic storm four days after leaving port, a Citroën was making a run in the dead of night. It dashed up and down the narrow and dangerous mountain roads; its headlights were painted over except for two thin slits in the center to avoid detection from a distance. The sound of heavy rain made it difficult for anyone to hear the approaching automobile. In the back seat were Marija Pavelić and her children, dressed not in their usual finery but in the rough, everyday clothes of peasants. At the wheel was Nikola, the poglavnik's secretary, who had been chosen to accompany Marija and the children because he knew how to drive and because Marija trusted him.

Marija did not look any worse, considering that the last four years had been spent bouncing from one dark cellar to another and relying on strangers for protection. Although he had grown tall, Damir was still just a boy of fifteen and Katarina a little girl barely twelve years old. The family had left Zagreb with instructions not to stop for anything or anyone, but to drive until they reached Travnik. Everything needed for the trip had been provided for; there were enough cans of petrol in the trunk to deal with any unforeseen detours, and enough food to feed them for a week. Tito had placed Ante Pavelić first in a long list of enemies of the state to be killed on sight; his family was fair game for mercenaries and others seeking retribution, which made Marija's and the children's flight from Zagreb necessary and very dangerous.

No one in the car had said a word for a long time. Marija kept her eyes closed and prayed they could make it safely to the mountain. Katarina did not speak for fear her words might wake-up some horrible monster lurking outside. Damir reflected on the many turns their lives had taken in the past four years; and Nikola concentrated on the delicate job of maneuvering the motorcar.

Suddenly, the road turned sharply and the Citroën skidded. Nikola spun the wheel quickly, piling the Pavelićs into the right side of the car.

"Nikola!"

"What?" The secretary was relieved and thankful that he had kept the car on the road.

"Do you have to go so fast!"

"Yes!" Nikola's patience had run out about the same time as his cigarettes.

"Mama—" Katarina wanted to say more but was too frightened.

"Soon, we'll be there soon," was the only comfort Marija gave her daughter.

"Where is Father?" Damir asked. The question was not one of concern. It was simple curiosity; Marija and the children had not seen Pavelić in over six months.

"I don't know," answered his mother. "I don't know."

Another ten minutes went by before Damir continued. "Is he alive?"

Marija looked at her son. "I am sure, yes." Ante Pavelić was still her husband, still her children's father, but there were too many ghosts between them. She would never forgive him for making their lives hell. She was and would remain Ante Pavelić's wife; he was and would remain unloved.

Damir looked out into the dismal, sopping night. The rain buffeted the window as the black silhouettes of trees raced by. The boy was puzzled why he so often found himself thinking of Ante Pavelić, the poglavnik; Ante Pavelić the murderer; Ante Pavelić, his father. He wanted to hate Ante Pavelić, wanted to convince himself that his kinship to Ante Pavelić was an accident, an obscene aberration impossible to explain. He often wished he would wake up one morning and be told that, in truth, Ante Pavelić was not his father, but that he had been switched at birth and that his real father was a peasant, a teacher, a scientist, a baker, a musician—anyone but Ante Pavelić. So the boy would try to be everything his father was not.

Suddenly, the car hit—well, Nikola thought he might have hit a deer that had challenged the car's right-of-way, though deer were hard to find due to the starving populace. The truth is the impact was such that the little man became disoriented and lost control of the car. He slammed on the brakes and stopped the car less than a meter from a tree.

"God protect us!" screamed Marija.

"Mama!" cried Katarina.

While his mother and sister were terrified, Damir felt a bewildering anticipation.

Nikola quickly got out of the car. Searching the area with the help of several matches and his dim headlights, he was not ready to find the remnants of Brother Silov's clothing hanging from the front fender and the late brother's twisted and broken body about seven meters away. Across the road, in the general direction of Komar, Nikola found another man, less battered than the first but just as dead. By gravitational coincidence, Brother Borna had managed to land sitting down, with his legs crossed, his head propped up and his eyes opened as if to say, "Where on earth did you learn to drive?" It was enough to make the excitable Nikola hysterical. That is not to say his behavior was less than responsible or his bearing not full of courage—given the circumstances. The first thing he did was to pop his head inside the car to make sure the family was all right.

"What happened?" screamed Marija, pressing her children close to her.

"We-we h-hit s-something," stammered Nikola. The secretary felt everyone should take responsibility for the accident; after all, he was forced to drive a car he had never driven before, to a place he had never been to in his life.

"What did you hit?" Marija was not about to let Nikola place the blame for his driving on her, let alone her children.

While his mother and the secretary argued, Damir opened the door and went to look for himself.

"Damir! Come back here! Damir!"

"Damir!" Katarina feared for her brother.

"Hush!" Damir was looking at the front fender when Nikola showed him Borna. The heavy rain stopped and was replaced by an annoying drizzle, as the secretary and the boy looked down on the cross-legged corpse.

"Two of them, the other one is—he's all over the place! I have murdered two men!" Nikola started shaking, sobbing and crossing himself.

"It was an accident; you murdered no one," said Didi, unable to take his eyes from the body. As the boy stood on the side of the road, on this moonless and rainy night, he did not recognize the man through the distorted features, dirty face and long beard; Damir did not remember that once before, under rather livelier conditions, he had gazed upon the same face. "What is that?" asked Damir with a sudden snap of his head.

"What? What do you mean? Do you hear something? Oh, my God, Reds, we'll get caught!"

"Shhhh—" Between the rustling of leaves, Damir heard the faint cry. "Sounds like, like a baby."

"A w-what? W-where?"

Nikola tried to stop him, and his mother and sister implored him to get back in the car, but Damir could not hear them; he only heard the sorrowful cry of the infant boy who, on impact, had been thrown from Borna's arms and landed in a wet thicket that cushioned his fall. The baby was lying on his back, covered with the same shawl (now stained with blood) in which the friars had found him.

"Saša!" There, in the middle of a lonely road, under a black, thankless and troubled sky the Croat boy held in his arms an infant born to Muslims.

"What is it? What do you have there?" Marija opened the door for her son.

"A baby!?" cried Katarina.

"A what? Oh, God have mercy! Damir, where is his mama? Nikola, my God, don't tell me you ran over his mama! Nikola, where is—"

"It wasn't his mama," returned Damir.

"What are you saying, eh? Are you telling me that child was by himself? Nikola, I order you to tell me now!"

The secretary was so shaken, he had trouble getting back in the car. Even his teeth chattered like castanets. His mind was a labyrinth full of devils and fiends, as he imagined burning in hell forever for taking the lives of the two men.

"Nikola, I am talking to you!"

"There is nothing we can do, Mama, they're dead," said Damir, examining the baby for injuries.

"Who is dead?"

"The men!" screamed Nikola as he backed up, changed gears and stepped on the gas.

"Men? Men! You hit a man? You hit more than one? How many? Keep your eyes on the road, damn you!" Marija was frantic.

"Stop screaming, please, you're frightening Saša."

"What? 'Saša!' Don't start that again, Damir, my nerves can't take it, they can't! We have to—Nikola, go back!"

"Mama, it's too dangerous; besides, they're dead," said the boy.

"You cannot keep him, Damir."

"Saša stays with me."

"That is not Saša!"

"Yes, he is!"

Marija stopped arguing with her son and complained that the secretary should not have left the scene of the accident without something that could have shed light on the identity of the baby.

She was rebuffed: it was Nikola's custom to respect the solemn privacy of the dead and no one was more dead than the fellows they had left behind.

"Yes, fine, but this makes it all the more difficult to find out who he is, where he comes from!"

"Mama, listen to me. Saša is back and I will not let anyone take him from me."

"That baby has a family somewhere, we have to—"

Marija could just as well been talking to the late Brother Borna.

"He is beautiful. Do you think he's hungry?" Katarina fed the baby a little cheese, then gave him some juice.

"Oh, Lord, he does not look well," said Marija. She touched the baby's forehead, feeling for the tell-tale signs of fever. "He has a temperature. Any bruises, broken bones? Take off those dirty things. Here—" Marija helped Damir remove the soiled and stained cloth and replace it with a blanket they had brought along.

There was no sign of injury on the baby except a bump on his forehead. Damir took out the svirala and began to softly play a folk tune he had learned on his own—a shepherd's song, one shepherd boys played when the night stole upon the herd and the lads lay down to rest under the stars. As soon as Damir stopped playing, the baby placed his hand upon Didi's face.

"He likes you," said Katarina.

"He is my friend." Damir embraced the baby. "Here, take it." And Didi offered the little flute to the baby. "It's yours."

They reached the outskirts of Travnik at one in the morning, coming upon Mount Vlašić from the west.

"Look!" Nikola pointed to the shadowy outline of the town half a kilometer below their vantage point. At that hour no sign of life was apparent; the citizens of Travnik were resting, getting ready for whatever the next day might bring.

"Drive on, please," pleaded Marija.

Nikola stepped gently on the accelerator and the unwieldy Citroën continued on its way. He had been told to drive east along the north side of the town, crossing a mountain road that cut north to south, and to continue until he came to a woodcutter's cart at the corner of a narrow lane. "There it is!" The secretary turned left and headed up the mountain. It took another half hour before it looked like the car could go no further. "And now, are we supposed to—"

Suddenly, from behind a tree about five meters away a powerful light blazed, blinding everyone in the car for a moment as a heavyset, well-armed man in a dark green rubber cape, hat and boots, rushed the vehicle, flung open the door to the driver's side, and shoved Nikola aside. It was all over in a matter of seconds, giving no one time to scream.

"Who are you?" Marija found the courage to ask, though her tone was full of misgivings.

"Don't say anything," whispered Damir to his mother.

By then, the car was bouncing up and down and sideways over a tight, muddy and steep mountain path with a drop of a hundred meters on the right. "C-can y-you c-c-carry me o-on y-your back?" Nikola could hardly get the words out. This was the agreed-upon password for the rendezvous.

"It's a little late, for that, don't you think?" replied the man at the wheel. "I am not Saint Christopher," answered the driver, darting an unfriendly glance at the secretary. "You are two hours late."

Nikola turned, propped himself up, and looked back at Marija with a nervous, but gratified and self-conscious grin; mission accomplished. "I'm sorry, but we had a little t-trouble on the way."

The man did not answer. Indeed, no one said anything else for forty-five minutes, until the Citroën—after climbing a winding dirt road along a sharp, rising cliff—reached the farm.

Ana Draganović was waiting for her guests. She was sitting in the parlor reading her prayer book and toying with her rosary when she heard the car pull up. "It's about time!" she said, and ran to the door. Time, that unkind undoer of man, had treated Ana Draganović with a certain gentleness. Her eyes were large, brown and serious. She was in her late sixties, but except for white hair—always combed straight back, with a tight knot that held every strand firmly in place—four lines crisscrossing her forehead, and a small wart on her left cheek, she could have passed for a woman ten years younger. Hard work around the farm had kept Father Draganović's mother strong and fit. "Come, come! Inside, all of you, inside!" Ana was pulling and shoving everyone into the house when she saw the baby. "Hello. No one said there was a baby. No one said anything about a baby! Kruno, what is this baby doing here?"

Father Draganović stood in the middle of the room, drinking coffee. He was in a pair of work pants and a peasant shirt. "Mother, please," said the priest, then turned to the man who had denied being Saint Christopher. "Rostas?" But Rostas shrugged and shook his head, indicating he did not have a clue. Finally, Draganović set down his cup and turned to Marija. "I am glad to see you made it safely."

"Oh, Father, oh, Father!" Marija swooned, forcing Draganović to take hold of her while Ana slipped a chair underneath. "We are being hunted like savages!"

Father Draganović looked at Damir, then shifted his eyes to the baby. "Who is that?"

"His name is Aleksandar but he's called Saša," answered the boy.

"Aleksandar?"

"Oh, God, oh, God!" cried the secretary. "Oh, Father, I have sinned!" Since his arrival, Nikola had not stopped getting up and down on his tiptoes.

"Stop that, please, it's very annoying," said Father Draganović to the secretary.

"You wouldn't happen to have a cigarette, would you, Father?"

"No."

Nikola buried his face in his hands.

"Kruno, you didn't tell me about a baby," whispered Ana to her son.

"I know, Mother, don't let it worry you." Again, Father Draganović turned to Damir. "Who is he?"

Damir explained what had happened on the way.

"What makes you think his name is Aleksandar?"

Damir looked at Father Draganović and simply said, "It is."

"The poor thing was just—wrapped in filthy rags," added Marija.

"Where are they—the rags, I mean?"

"In the car."

"You will tell me about it later, won't you?" said Draganović to Damir.

Damir did not answer. He turned his attention to Saša and left the priest to assume what he liked.

"Father, where's my husband?"

Father Draganović sat next to Marija and took her hand.

"How is he?"

Father Draganović would not say.

"When was the last time you saw my husband?"

Father Draganović could not say.

"Is he still in the country?"

Father Draganović did not say. In fact, he said nothing.

"Oh, God!" cried Marija. Katarina knelt beside her mother, took her other hand and kissed it.

"Madame," said Draganović finally, "you and your children are safe." Draganović looked in turn at each of his guests, particularly the children, and his voice became even more grave. "Remember, absolutely no one, but no one must know who you are. This place is isolated, no one ever comes up here, but we cannot be too careful."

"I should say not!" interjected Ana.

"There's an old man who's been with us for some time, a shepherd. He sleeps in the barn, does odd jobs and looks after the animals. As far as he's concerned you are cousins from Banja Luka and your last name is Draganović, do you understand? Draganović. Please, it is for everyone's safety. I cannot stress the point enough."

"Oh, they will be careful, won't you my darlings, won't you?" Marija begged her children. "I warned them, Father, I did."

"Now, I am sure you are very tired. I think you'd better get some rest. We will talk later." Father Draganović gently helped Marija out of the chair.

"But the baby, Kruno, what are we going to do with the baby?" Ana pointed emphatically at Saša.

"I will take care of him," said Damir.

Ana looked from her son to Damir and from Damir to her son.

"You heard him, Mother, he will take care of the baby."

"How can he? He's just a boy!" protested Ana. "Oh, come with me, then, come, come," she added with a sigh of resignation.

Damir cradled the baby and followed Ana up the stairs to the second floor. Old as she was, Ana skipped two steps at a time and showed Damir to the end of the hall, and to a door so small it should have belonged in a doll's house.

"He looks about six or seven months," said Ana.

"Oh, no, he's really about my age," countered Damir.

Ana frowned and looked mystified but went on. "He'll cry all night, pee and make poo-poo. You will learn, you will learn!" Ana mumbled something under her breath about boys not knowing a thing about babies, opened the little door, and climbed in two strides the six steps to the upper room. "Watch your head!" Ana touched the ceiling with her hand. "When Kruno—Father Draganović was a boy he sat there, at the window, and read for hours and hours and hours. He liked it up here; I do not know why so do not ask me. It is a very small room but maybe he felt closer to God, up in this room. He used to bang his head all the time." Ana began to walk away. "You know, I have a little crib; it was Kruno's, has to be in the cellar. I'll bring it up, yes, and—old diapers, even baby clothes. I never throw anything away. You never know, you just never know."

Before Damir was able to thank Ana for her concern, she flew down the stairs and left him and the baby in the little attic room they would call their own. The room was a triangular niche with a latched window that opened to a grand view of the surrounding cliffs and the mountains beyond. It had a bed, a night table an oil lamp and one shelf of books, all about religion. Damir put the baby on the bed and opened the window. The rain had stopped and a chilly wind from the north gently nudged the thunderclouds away, revealing the stars and the biggest, fullest moon Damir had ever seen. "Saša, look!" Damir picked up the baby and held him up so he too could look out the window. "See the moon? It's smiling again!" As he stood looking out, Damir saw Father Draganović, the man known as Rostas and Nikola get in the car and drive away.

It was almost five in the morning by the time everyone settled down. Nikola was given a cot in the cellar, right next to the furnace, where, curiously enough, a small dust-covered crib had stood for thirty-odd years. The secretary was unhappy, not because the room was damp and chilly, or because he was an ungrateful lout, but because the fiery metal monster reminded the secretary of the hell he had earned for himself that day.

8

By any standard the Draganović two-story farmhouse reflected antiquated prosperity. It was set at the top of a hill against an immense cliff, and faced a lush valley that until recently—say, thirty-five years before—had been part of a dense forest full of many wild animals, in particular wolves. Ivo Draganović cleared many trees and killed many wolves to build his house on the hill, and have a place for his sheep and goats to graze. He planted fruit trees, and flowers around the house and made the inside as comfortable as possible for his bride, who, after all, paid for most of the furnishings with her dowry.

The house was of brick and mortar with a thatched roof. Turkish tapestries covered the walls downstairs and the floors were of glazed earthenware tiles. Plumbing, a luxury in any mountain dwelling, provided water from a well. A living room, a small library, a dining room and a kitchen occupied the downstairs. The kitchen was outfitted with a wood-stove, a breakfast table, a one-faucet sink and a large pantry. Upstairs were four bedrooms, the little attic that Damir and Saša now occupied, and one bathroom—the latter the most elegant and European of all the rooms in the farm, with Italian fixtures, including a bidet.

Of course, none of the decorations, furniture, or anything else at Ana Draganović's reflected anything else but her piety. Indoor lighting took the form of candles and ornate oil lamps. Heating for the winter months and nippy evenings year-round was provided by a fireplace in the main rooms and a maze of steam pipes that crawled like metal snakes throughout the house. They were fed by the wood furnace in the cellar.

Not more than twenty meters to from the house was a modest barn where a hundred or so chickens, two cows, ten pigs, seventy-five sheep, fifteen goats, innumerable rabbits, one sheep-dog, seven or eight cats (to fend off the mice), one old horse and Pero Bojić all lived. The animals helped sustain the farm by providing enough wool, cheese, ham, milk, eggs, rabbits and poultry for Pero to sell in Travnik's open market every month, just as he had done since the turn of the century.

The night the Pavelićs arrived, Pero was sleeping in his perch after a long and tiring day in the fields. His thin, frail body was wrapped in three thick woolen blankets, while dreams of his youth summoned the shepherd. The unrelenting tyranny of age had afflicted Pero with a partial shrinking of the limbs. Still, after celebrating his eighty-third birthday, he was the tallest among the old men in Travnik. He had very round and large eyes under a set of bushy, droopy eyebrows that gave him an air of melancholy, though he was rarely in that frame of mind. Pero had kept most of his teeth and some hair, which the years had turned white as the wool of his sheep. He also possessed a sense of humor that, when put together with his blunt views about everything, seemed almost rude, though it was said that only Pero's sheep were more gentle than the old shepherd.

As a young man, these qualities, in addition to an air of vulnerability and a handsome face, made Pero a favorite with the ladies, though no reputable father would allow his daughter to contemplate wedding Pero because, well, he was just an illiterate sheepherder and not interested in being anything else. Still, whenever Pero ventured into town, the girls offered themselves to him in clandestine trysts. Because Pero was short on pride and not remotely interested in himself, he was, likewise, not concerned with what anyone else thought of him, not at all and not ever. He was unmoved by flattery or praise, untouched by lasting romantic sentiments, and embarrassed when his friends teased him about having crushed the aspirations of a certain maiden. Instead, Pero was most preoccupied with, as it were, *concerns of truth,* concepts that his restless, curious mind was always trying to decipher through one metaphysical exploration after another, giving Pero a look long identified with dreamers and men who are about to get shot. For instance, there were times when he would lie on the grassy hill and ponder: "Why is it people can't be like plants and make oxygen every time they take a dump?" or "What was God thinking when he created the flea?"

The morning the cousins from Banja Luka arrived, Pero was up as usual, at daybreak. He stretched his old limbs and blinked twenty-five times to provide his eyes with exercise, because that particular activity helped promote good vision. Then, the shepherd donned a pair of crusty pants and shirt, put on the only pair of boots he owned, dragged himself to a washstand on the other side of the barn, scrubbed his face with a wet rag, grabbed his walking stick that was as bent and full of knobs as its master, put on his hat and went to feed the animals.

Pero felt—no, he did not feel—he knew someone was watching him as he stood outside the barn sprinkling chicken feed to a swirl of cackling hens. You learn to know if you are being watched after spending your life looking out for and being looked to by wolves. But this time Pero did not care that he was being watched because it was not a wolf looking down from the attic, but a boy, a boy holding a baby.

"Hello," called out the shepherd without looking up at Damir.
"Hello." Damir wondered if Pero was talking to him.
"Who is that, your brother?"
"No."
"Your sister?"
"No."
"Your uncle?"
Damir laughed.
"Why do you laugh? I had a baby for an uncle once."
"He is my friend," said Damir.
"Your friend? What is his name, this friend of yours?" Pero continued feeding the chickens.
"Aleksandar," answered Damir.

"Me—I am Pero. And you?"

"Damir."

"I bet you want to come down and help me feed the pigs."

"The pigs?"

"You can bring Aleksandar; he can feed the pigs too." Pero went into the barn and left Damir to ponder whether or not to help feed the pigs.

The boy closed the window, put Saša on the bed, and was trying his best to change the baby's diapers when Ana came into the room followed by Marija and Katarina. "Do not tell him your name!" warned Ana.

"I only said—"

"I heard, and you said enough. No more! Pero is an old man, he is a good man, but he is a Serb."

"Yes, madame," said the boy.

"What are you doing?" Katarina laughed.

"What does it look like I'm doing?"

"You will be a good papa some day," Ana said to Damir.

"Did he give you trouble last night? Did he cry?" asked his mother.

Damir shook his head. In fact, Damir had spent half the night staring at the ceiling and half the night on his side, his chin cupped in his hands, watching the baby sleep in the old crib. Between one and the other was a little shepherd boy surrounded by the Ustaše, his eyes agonizing, sad and fearful, an instant before a bullet slammed into his head and the lifeless emaciated child dropped to the ground. Between one and the other was a shepherd boy saying, "I will be Peter." Between one and the other was Saša. "He cried a little." Damir looked at the baby lying on his back in the crib and nibbling on the svirala. "I think he's hungry."

"Bring him downstairs." Ana turned and left the room with her customary lively step, expecting her guests to follow. She had only allowed herself to sleep a few hours because she wanted to make sure Marija and her children were well looked after. She set a bountiful breakfast table of hard-boiled eggs, hams, cheeses, loaves of bread, milk, fruits and tea to which every creature at the farm must have contributed its share.

"Madame, we are so very grateful to you and Father Draganović," said Marija.

"We are doing our Christian duty, my dear, our Christian duty. Now, please, sit down—eat!"

"Where's Nikola?" asked Katarina.

"He went with my son—to town I think. They'll be back tonight."

Ana buzzed around the kitchen, committed to making the Pavelićs feel secure and welcome. Every once in a while she would take out her rosary and hold it between her fingers as she sat sipping tea in the company of her guests, only to bounce from her chair, tuck away the rosary, pick up the baby and feed him his bottle so that Damir could enjoy his breakfast in peace. Even with the baby in her arms, sometimes munching on a hard-boiled egg and making a mess of everything, Ana would go get a jar of preserves from the pantry she thought the children might enjoy. Her kindness and generosity never, never wavered, because Ana Draganović understood that it was much harder for the Pavelićs to be dependent on the Draganovićs than it was for the Draganovićs to show compassion for the Pavelićs.

The first couple of weeks were the most difficult for the cousins from Banja Luka. Father Draganović believed that even in their remote sanctuary it was important for them to remain inconspicuous, particularly in their dress, that it was crucial they be transformed from the wife and children of the poglavnik, from sophisticated and privileged urbanites, to sophisticated and privileged country cousins. In addition to the fear of being found out, the tedium of the simple, uncomplicated country life took its toll. To avoid sudden and unnecessary displays of impatience, sulking, pouting, fretting and exasperation that invariably led to griping, grumbling, whining and self-pity, which ended always in tears, Marija and the children were each given a task to do for the indefinite duration of their stay. In the opinion of the priest, the worst thing for the Pavelićs to do was to do nothing at all. Ana undertook the herculean task of teaching Marija and Katarina to spin, weave and sew their own clothes.

Fancy hats, elaborate frills and ruffles, fine gloves and delicate Parisian fashions in blue, green, red, silver and gold silks were not in vogue; rather, it was black and white, plain, sturdy and austere skirts, blouses, shirts and aprons of wool and linen. Rouge, mascara, lipstick and perfume—all those exquisite feminine decorations—were strictly avoided, thus allowing Marija and Katarina's natural beauty to manifest itself. Ana also decided to enlighten the Pavelić women about a few rudimentary household duties, for instance how to prepare a meal, how to make a bed, how to sweep and dust—routines as unfamiliar to them as taking a cat for a walk on the moon.

It could be said then that, besides Nikola—who was relegated to odd jobs around the house that required limited physical exertion, such as chopping wood and lugging it on his back down a precipitous flight of stairs leading to the cellar in order to feed the fiery and ever-hungry dragon—Damir had the easiest time adjusting to the change in lifestyle. He had the good fortune to inherit some of Father Draganović's old clothes, obviating any need to learn to spin, weave and sew. Marija, Katarina and Nikola indulged Damir as they had throughout his life, and even the stern Ana, who was greatly impressed with the boy's behavior and tender nature, favored him over the others. Only Father Draganović regarded Damir with a certain amount of polite disinterest, although courtesy was always observed; after all, the boy was the heir-apparent to the poglavnik. Whereas the women regarded the boy's devotion to the baby as an amusing curiosity, the priest thought it reflected the obstinacy of a spoiled adolescent and complicated an already difficult situation. Regardless, Damir continued to take care of Saša.

Thanks to the love and care that Damir and everyone else lavished on him—in addition to plenty of good, nourishing food and the healthy mountain air—Saša went in the space of seven months from a thin, frail baby to a healthy, rugged and playful little fellow. He learned to walk faster than anyone thought possible, and by the time he was a year and a half Saša was already sputtering long sentences of baby talk that drove everybody to distraction. He amused the household with creative compressions of their names. "Maja" was for Marija. "Ina" stood for Katarina. "Nana" meant Ana. "Ola" implied Nikola, "Tata" represented Father Draganović, and "Pu" indicated the old shepherd. The only names Saša pronounced accurately, both the proper name and the nickname, were "Damir" and "Didi."

By then it was impossible to pick up Saša against his will. Katarina continued to try to feed him his bottle, cradling him as she used to do just a few months earlier, insisting he remain a baby, but Saša would have none of it and would spit out the bottle, sit up, point and demand in incomprehensible gibberish a piece of—"t'at 'ake 'able" (cake on the table). Then he would fidget, kick and cry unless he was released, sometimes in diapers, sometimes naked—and allowed to run loose.

Pero shook his head and complained more than once, "This Aleksandar is a pain in the ass!"

"Saša, did you hear that?" Damir laughed, hugging and kissing the baby. "You're a pain in the ass!"

In addition to his many accomplishments, Saša soon learned that you could get from point A to point B much faster if you ran. He acquired the nerve-racking tendency of dashing in and out of the house without opening and closing doors quietly. He simply rammed them with his stout little body, expecting the doors to yield. When, for some reason, they did not, Saša bounced off and landed on his rear. One day, in a fine display of confidence, the baby bolted down the slope outside the front door, only to trip and tumble past a group of grazing sheep that were astonished to see a tot rolling by. A large black rock finally stopped his descent, and, fortunately, only Saša's pride needed mending. "Damir! Damir!" he cried, waiting to be rescued by his friend.

That same afternoon, the baby took advantage of Damir's being busy—he was arguing with his mother, who was scolding him for acquiring the manners and language of a peasant as indicated by one or two florid expressions he had picked up from Pero—and Saša, dressed in sagging diapers, ran off to chase the chickens, the rabbits and the cat. The feline, a large striped warrior, used to clashing with wolves, turned on Saša, and—well, let's just say the tot never went after the cat again. But not contented with scaring the animals half to death, Saša grabbed a piglet, made his way to a fat, indolent sheep, and tried to climb on top of the beast as if it were a pony. At the sight of the piglet-carrying toddler, the animal panicked, baaed loudly, bucked and called to her sisters to stampede.

"The—They're out!" Pero ran from the well pounding the ground with his stick, cursing aloud and calling out to his faithful cur to chase after the sheep making their wobbly and angry way down the hill. Damir was not as worried about the sheep as he was about Saša. He found the little angel in the pigpen trying to hold on to the piglet, while a large, fat sow (its mommy) jabbed Saša with her snout. The cries, the oinks and the baas brought everyone from the house. Thank goodness Father Draganović was away. Marija and Ana shrieked; Nikola hopped and hobbled to help the shepherd chase his deserting flock, stumbled, banged his head and had to be attended to by Ana. Katarina rushed to give her brother a hand. "Tell me what to do!" she shouted, being as unacquainted with irate pigs as her brother was.

"I don't know! Just get her off!" Damir tried to hold on to Saša, but the baby would not give up the slippery little pig. Katarina was laughing so hard that when she grabbed and yanked the sow's tail to pull it away, she lost her footing and slipped under the pig's belly, just as Didi, who by then was holding Saša upside down, stumbled and fell backward.

It was a few minutes before the children walked out of the pigpen covered in mud and other less agreeable stuff. Marija ran to Damir, yelling at him for not keeping an eye on the baby, and immediately sent him to help Pero with the sheep. Katarina rushed the baby to the well and in a voice that pretended to be angry ordered him not to move, not to twitch, not to breathe, while she took off his diapers and poured bucket after bucket of water over his head, rinsing off the mud and dung. Then, she hauled him into the house, placed the baby in her mother's care and went to take a bath herself.

By the time Pero and Damir rounded up the sheep (still upset and vowing with loud baas to stomp on little Saša if they ever got a chance) it was nightfall. "See!? I told you." said Pero. "That Aleksandar is a pain in the ass!"

By then, the Pavelićs looked (and sometimes behaved) very much the part of common country folks. Damir even shaved his head to simulate the traditional rural remedy for fighting lice, something that was visually effective though unnecessary.

Father Draganović spent less and less time at the farm, leaving his guests in the care of his mother. He traveled from one refugee camp to another as part of the *Commissione d'Assistenza Pontifica,* the Pontifical Commission for Assistance, supposed to help refugees seek repatriation in postwar Yugoslavia. It was a wonderful cover for Father Draganović, who was busy securing phony Red Cross identification papers and passports for notorious ex-Ustaše war criminals so they could be shipped safely across the Ratlines. Some days the black Mercedes marked with the red cross appeared parked in the space between the house and the barn, and, like a long lost relative, the priest resurfaced without warning. One night, Saša was brought out to show off a dainty new shirt and trousers Katarina had fixed up for him, using the priest's old baby clothes. Damir paraded the baby around the room, then, let him go. Everyone clapped, cheered and called out, "What a handsome boy!"

Quite unexpectedly, little Saša walked over to Father Draganović, put out his arms and beckoned the priest to pick him up. Damir was about to intervene, perhaps because he did not want to inconvenience Father Draganović, possibly because he was jealous. To everyone's surprise, Draganović took the baby in his arms and sat him on his lap.

"Ah!" was the sentiment heard in unison from Marija and Ana.

"Damir," said Father Draganović, "don't you think it would be a good idea to have this child baptized?"

"Oh, that is indeed a wonderful idea, Father!" interjected Marija.

"Indeed!" agreed Ana.

"I-t-it s-should have been d-done m-months ago," said Nikola with his customary trepidation.

"No," said Damir. "I'm sorry, but it's not a good idea at all."

"What are you saying?" asked Marija after a very, very brief pause.

Father Draganović regretted at once having brought up the subject, and decided to let the women argue the point.

"He has to be baptized," said Ana once again. "He just has to!"

"What if Saša is already baptized?" Katarina thought that it was possible, since the baby was at least half a year old when he was found.

"But how can you be sure?" observed Ana. "And what if he was? There is nothing wrong with doing it again." As far as she was concerned, the more you were baptized, the better your chances of making it to heaven.

"Saša cannot be baptized," insisted Damir.

"Why not?" Ana darted confused looks from one end of the room to the other. "What on earth could be wrong with having the baby—"

"No!"

"Damir, you are being rude," said Marija.

Father Draganović got up and handed the baby to Damir, who was, by then, standing in the middle of the room feeling quite ill at ease. "If Damir does not want the baby baptized he must have a very good reason, one that, unfortunately, he is keeping to himself. I know Damir to be responsible and honest, and there is no doubt how much he loves this child."

"Well, yes, that is all true," admitted Ana.

"So, let us respect his wishes. In the end, it will be up to Damir whether the little one attains salvation or not. I am sure Damir will do what is right." The evening went on without further talk of baptisms or anything else, except one or two trivial references to sheep, the weather, the coming winter and some passing allusions to life in Zagreb, Belgrade, Rome and Berlin. As the cold mountain winds howled like hungry wolves, Ana brought out her knitting implements, Marija glanced at a fashion magazine Father Draganović had brought back from Rome for her diversion, Nikola waited for someone to talk to him (and fantasized having an American cigarette), Father Draganović tended the fire, and Damir settled down to play a game of chess with his sister.

Katarina was white and Damir was black. They played on the floor, while Saša tried to entertain himself. The baby sat for a few minutes with Ana, who immediately put him to work holding up the yarn. As soon as he was liberated, he wandered in Marija's direction, but found her reading matter very dull, so he continued to roam aimlessly up and down the room, until it occurred to the tot to try his luck with the secretary. Saša pulled Nikola by the arm, trying to get the little man to go outside with him and search for a small yellow striped kitten that had recently surfaced in the barn—the son, no doubt, of the large striped warrior. Since Nikola had an aversion to cold howling winds and felines of any sort, he courteously declined and tried to follow the old line, "Ignore them and they will go away." For Saša, the next logical stop was the priest, who was working the fire and, therefore, gently asked Saša to stay back, lest the baby get hurt, or worse, do something to produce a conflagration. Saša gave up. He was tired of rejection and decided to deposit his little self next to Damir and Katarina, who were by then quite involved in their match. He sat quietly with his legs crossed, toying with the vanquished pawns, rooks and bishops given to him by the players. Perhaps it was the serenity in the room, perhaps it was the dreary slowness of the game. Whatever the cause, it was apparent that sleep, the archenemy of infants worldwide, was gaining quickly and without mercy on Saša. His head would wobble and fall off to one side, startling him and making him sit up and look around to make sure no one had seen him doze off. Of course, everyone was betting on how long it would take for him to yield to slumber. Not long, as it happened. The child lined up all his black and white pieces on the side of the board, lay down, put his head against Damir and fell asleep.

"Well, well," said Katarina, stroking the baby's hair.

"Half an hour later than y-yesterday!" observed Nikola with a cough.

"I guess," said Damir standing up, "I'd better put him to bed."

"Checkmate," said Katarina as her brother picked up the baby.

"What do you mean 'checkmate'? You can't!" protested the boy.

"Katarina, why don't you let him win once in a while; after all, he is older than you are," said Marija with a chuckle.

"W-when was the last time he beat you?" asked the secretary.

"Oh, never, he's too impatient," laughed Katarina.

Damir was going to say something quite impolite but caught his mother's eye just in time.

"Goodnight, Damir."

"Goodnight, Mama." Damir knew everybody was watching as he carried the baby up the stairs.

As the evening wore on, Ana, Katarina and Nikola retired one after the other, leaving Marija and Father Draganović by themselves. They stayed behind not because they were not tired or because they were particularly fond of each other's company, but because each had something to say to the other.

"More coffee, madame?" offered Father Draganović.

"Oh, yes, that would be nice. You know, Father, I never drank coffee until I came here. Tea, I drank tea. But your coffee is positively delicious."

"It's very special; it's grown in a tropical island, you know, and I bring it from Rome."

"How interesting." Marija did not really care to know what an immense distance the coffee traveled before ending up in her cup; instead, she wanted to ask Father Draganović—

"It's absolutely fascinating," the priest interrupted her thoughts and denied Marija the chance to continue, as her tone and gesture indicated she wanted to do. As with most things in his life, Father Draganović had become fanatical about Puerto Rican. "I discovered that in the mid-1840s a Puerto Rican bishop went to Rome and ingratiated himself to the pope—Pius VII—by providing His Holiness with a kilo of coffee, as a small token of devotion on the part of his diocese, the island of Puerto Rico."

"Puerto what?"

"Puer-r-r-to R-r-r-ico," Father Draganović rolled the *r's,* further proof he had studied the subject in detail. "It's an American colony—though how a people with the taste and culture to produce this delicacy can subordinate themselves to others, I don't really understand. Anyway, the coffee caused such a sensation that when the bishop complained that his country did not have a relic, Pius VII acted immediately, offering the bishop his choice of martyrs from a whole collection of saints resting in the catacombs—in exchange, of course, for a yearly supply of coffee."

"A saint?" Marija frowned.

"Yes. The Puerto Rican bishop claimed Saint Pius, a first-century martyr whose remains are in the island of Puerto Rico to this day, thanks to Pope Pius VII's love for a cup of good coffee."

"Trading coffee for a saint, isn't that sacrilegious, Father?"
"Depends."
"Depends?"
"On the prominence of the saint and the quality of the coffee."
Marija smiled politely and looked at her cup.

"I was thinking that maybe, since the Holy See has so many martyrs everywhere, perhaps it could trade a few for—"

"Father," the word shot out of Marija like an arrow dipped in grief, "when are we going home? It's been almost two years!"

Father Draganović slowly put the cup to his lips, took a sip of coffee, put the cup down, took a deep breath and said, "First we must determine where 'home' is going to be, yes?" The priest picked up a spoon, scooped up a teaspoon of sugar from a small silver bowl resting on the coffee tray, and poured it into his coffee.

"Where can we go?"

"Far, far away."

"England? France?" Marija's fear showed in the trouble she was having getting the words out.

"Madame, you know I cannot tell you anything else. Please, trust me. Everything that can be done, is being done." Draganović could not help but feel sorry for Marija. "There are many, many people working very hard to bring this—" and he made a little flourish with his hand as he searched for just the right words "—your predicament to a happy ending."

"I hope so, I really do. We are so very, very grateful. Madame Draganović has been so kind and we will never forget your many attentions, Father, but it is such a burden on you and your mother. Besides," Marija was afraid she might start crying, "I think it is time we started building our lives again. My children need to be in school." She did not cry, but wiped her eyes with a handkerchief. "I mean, when is it going to end? What is to become of us? I'm so scared!"

"I must tell you that Damir worries me," said the priest, although "worries" was not the word he really wanted to use. He was, in fact, he was not worried as much as he was dismayed with the rebellious nature of the boy. "I know how painful the separation from his father has been for Damir. I am sure he idolizes the poglavnik, as well he should, but I don't understand his infatuation with the baby. Is he thinking of taking that child with him when you leave here?"

"I don't know." Marija thought it would be best to keep the family nightmares in the family.

They sat quietly for a few minutes. Father Draganović focused on a small spider making its painstaking journey down from the ceiling; Marija closed her eyes and shook her head. "Years ago," she began, "Didi fell very ill, Father. All the doctors said he would die." Marija opened her eyes and saw the priest standing by the fireplace, looking to catch the spider. She waited until Draganović snapped the slender silk thread with his fingers, and tossed everything, including the crawling acrobat, into the flames. "One morning," she continued, "after Didi had been bedridden for months and had withered down to nothing, he woke up, suddenly regained his appetite, his strength and acquired an imaginary friend. Damir said his friend was a Serbian boy, a shepherd called Saša."

An imaginary friend, reflected Father Draganović. Of course he had to be a Serb. "Saša," nickname for "Aleksandar." The name was identified with the dynasty of Serbian kings, the last of them assassinated by Pavelić's henchmen in 1934. A good Croat would never name his son Aleksandar. The priest turned, grabbed the poker, jabbed the red-hot cinders, stirred the fire, straightened up, leaned against the mantelpiece and looked at Marija. "Interesting."

Father Draganović, however, remained unaware of the bond he shared with Saša, the shepherd boy, thanks to Ante Pavelić's messianic flair for taking and granting of life.

9

It was not a Parisian, a Roman or even a Berlin café; it was not a bistro found along the Champs Élysées and it was certainly not a trattoria nestled between elegant boutiques in the shade of Il Duomo. It was a simple kavana, a smoke-filled little room set up in the front of a house in the least friendly neighborhood in the otherwise picturesque town of Travnik. Up until the end of the war, the tavern was an irritating hangout serving a dull crowd of cronies dating back to the First World War. Then, a government bureaucrat decided to establish the headquarters for the local militia in a rundown hotel across the street from the kavana. Young conscripts—mostly Serbs and Muslims, a few Croats, and even fewer Jews—found shelter from the oppressive military discipline by wandering in and out of the tavern day and night, sometimes staying long enough to flirt with the owner, a thirty-year-old woman named Olga, who was married to Rostas, the same Rostas who drove Pedro Gómez to catch a boat and later refused to be mistaken for Saint Christopher.

Shortly after, the regulars of the watering hole—like Vidak the barber, a fellow who for years made a habit of stopping by for a beer after being on his feet all day—found every chair in the tavern occupied by the neighbors from across the street. The tavern had never been so popular. When possible, Rostas did his best to loosen the tongues of the militiamen with free drinks and cigarettes. In this manner he obtained up-to-the-minute information on military and police operations that otherwise would have remained confidential.

It was intelligence indispensable if one was pursuing a different political agenda to the government. It was intelligence necessary if one intended to stay one step ahead of the enemy.

While Rostas collected intelligence in town, high up in the mountains Damir felt an inner peace that had eluded him for a long time. Even so, he was restricted, unable to enjoy the liberties and carefree life most boys took for granted. He wanted to roam the countryside, go hiking, see the cave Pero said was in the hills. To his disappointment, the most Damir was allowed to do was join the shepherd when the old man took out the herd.

They left before sunrise, and after forty-five minutes reached a grassy slope where the sheep grazed. Pero and Damir made themselves as comfortable as the elements allowed.

The shepherd untied a red and black checkered blanket he carried rolled-up on his back, wrapped himself in a thick quilt a lady friend had made for him years back, took out a tarnished tin flask of raki (a clear but potent brandy), lay back, closed his eyes and mused. Damir also spent the day wrapped in a quilt, one, perhaps, not as historic as Pero's loving memento, but thick enough to keep him warm.

Saša was sent out in so many layers of sweaters and jackets, along with mittens, two mufflers and a red woolen hat tied under his chin, that he looked like a bipedal member of the flock with a crest on top. He spent the day running after the dog who drove the sheep who were sick and tired of not being allowed to graze in peace. Damir kept an eye on Saša while he listened to Pero reflect on just about everything: from sheep to salvation and hell; from women to boats and the crucifixion.

"If you were on a boat," said Pero, "and that boat smashed against the rocks and you almost drowned, you wouldn't be so quick to go in a boat again, I mean, you'd be scared of boats, right? Or—or if you were caught in a fire and got burned, you'd be scared of fires, yes?" Damir knew that sooner or later Pero would get to the point. "Well?" continued Pero, "Can you see Jesus on His Second Coming finding crosses everywhere?"

Damir thought he was unqualified to respond, so instead, the boy opened his eyes, lifted his brows, shrugged and picked his teeth with a straw.

"Damir! Damir!" Saša called from the field where he was chasing the sheep. "Comeeeer—Comeeeer, Damir!"

"Saša leave them be! I'm warning you!" The baby laughed and ignored the warning.

"How come he's not afraid of animals?" The behavior of humans, large and small, sometimes puzzled the shepherd.

"Saša's never been afraid of sheep," returned Damir.

Pero thought for a long time. "Never?"

"Never," confirmed the boy.

"You had sheep in—Banja Luka?"

Damir did not answer.

By midday the sun dismissed the morning chill and the shepherd, the boy and the baby enjoyed a lunch of cold meats, cheese, hard-boiled eggs, fruit, bread and goat's milk.

"Pero," said Damir with a mouthful, "were you in the war?"

"All my life there's been war. I don't remember when someone wasn't shooting at someone else."

"But, did you fight in the war?"

"Fight who? The sheep? The goats?"

It was perfectly clear to Damir that in a war you fought "The enemy."

But who was the enemy? The Croats? "You're a Croat," said Pero. "You my enemy?"

"No!"

Pero swallowed, wiped his mouth with the quilt, took out his pipe and let his mind drift back sixty years, to the time when he worked for Ivo Draganović (Krunoslav's father), a man who called for the extermination of all who were not Croats, only to buy drinks for everybody in the kavana twenty minutes later—vodka for the Serb, wine for the Jew, and coffee for the Muhammadan. Many were the nights when Pero the Serbian shepherd and his Croat master drank and winked at the ladies together; many were the nights when the Serb carried home the drunken Croat smelling of cheap perfume.

Pero laughed and a cloud of smoke shot from his mouth. He glanced sideways at the sheep. "I don't have enemies, do you?"

Again, Damir did not answer. He sat quietly for a moment, then threw off his blankets and ran after Saša, who was sitting next to the dog imitating the bleat of the sheep (and humiliating the flock, which thought Saša was making fun of them). When Saša saw Damir running after him, he bolted. Didi was forced to chase him down, around and in between the sheep and goats. Finally, one of the sheep stuck out its leg and tripped Saša. (The story could not be corroborated in any way but Damir maintained it happened.) Damir tackled and tickled the baby, threw the screaming, laughing tot over his shoulder and hauled him away as he baaed at the mortified sheep.

Pero aimed his pipe at Saša and extemporized—

"Such a little pain in the ass,
and what a strange friend he has,
a boy with big eyes,
little hair and no lice."

Damir grinned, rubbed his head and wiped off Saša's runny nose. Pero threw a blanket on Saša. "Where's his papa?"

"He's an orphan," explained Damir.

"Ah—" Pero smoked for two minutes. "And you, you orphaned too?"

Fear took hold of Damir, and he turned very red. "M-my father—"

Pero put out his hand and shook his head. "Don't lie because you can't tell me something I have no business knowing in the first place." Pero stuck his nose in the brandy flask. "You know, I have known the Draganovićs for a long time—longer, I think, than I ever wanted to. If I had known I'd lived this long, I would have done something to avoid it." Damir knew what Pero said had nothing to do with the Draganovićs. "I guess you can say—he was a good kid," added Pero.

"He is a good kid," corrected Damir.

"I meant Krunoslav the priest, not your Aleksandar," said the old man. "Your Father Draganović was ten or eleven when I showed him the cave. Once the little shit tried to find it on his own. He was lost for a whole day, ha! Ana—Ana was furious! She hit me, can you believe that? She hit me with a broom and threw me out of the house!" Pero looked at the clouds and tapped the side of his head with the flask. "I remember everything—it's all here, in this head."

It was a few minutes before anyone said anything else. Saša took off his mittens, stuck his thumb in his mouth, lay down beside Damir and fell asleep.

"Pero, what do you think—do you think God exists?"

"What kind of a question is that coming from a Catholic boy like you? God—exist? Of course!"

"How do you know? How do you know there is a God?"

"Because!" Pero swept his right arm, taking in the landscape as far as the eye could see. "He is all around. He is in the trees, in the grass, in the clouds, in the sheep—in this child." Pero pointed at Saša. "He is in you, in me–"

"God is not in heaven?"

"Heaven is here," and Pero poked Damir in the chest, then, lit his pipe and puffed away, pleased that he was able to share some of his wisdom with the boy.

"Inside? But I thought—"

"Yes, and hell is too—in you, in me, heaven, hell!"

Damir frowned.

"You don't think God's got a looooong white beard, sits on a throne and rules the universe like a grandad, now—do you?"

Damir had never thought about the white beard.

"God is—let's see," and the shepherd rubbed his forehead, "God is All."

"All? But, if God is All, He is good and He is evil!"

"Well, to have one," Pero pointed his finger to the west, "you must have the other." Then he pointed to the east. "The other side of right, is wrong, like daylight is to night, like hot is to cold and ugly to beautiful."

"Opposites!" said Damir with a smile.

"And out of that struggle springs life," added Pero.

"If that's true, then half the people in the world are evil," said Damir.

Pero shook his head. "No, no. Everyone in the world is a little of both." And yet, the shepherd went on, human beings intuitively choose good over evil as they prefer beauty over ugliness. For instance, what if all the people in the world were in a room and in that room were two pictures: one, a picture of a crystalline mountain stream surrounded by a lush forest of evergreens covered with glistening, pure snow under a perfectly blue sky; the other, a picture of a dead rat rotting in a sewer, its mouth stuffed with stinking blood, bile, garbage and shit. Which picture would the people prefer? "I bet most would opt for the nice picture—the one that is obviously beautiful, don't you think?" said Pero. "Yet, there is always some horse's ass with a liking for rats!"

"That's right," agreed Damir.

"But that's because they are stupid and ignorant. Ignorance blinds men so they can't see—or know the difference between beauty and ugliness, between right and wrong—good and evil."

Damir sat up and said in a loud whisper, "So, then, how's a person punished when they've sinned and died. If they don't go to hell, where do they go?"

"Here!" said Pero without hesitation.

"Here? You mean we're in hell?" Damir's brows got closer and closer.

"Seems that way, no?" said Pero with a sober face. "I think when someone's been evil in a past life, they have to make up for it somehow when they are reborn."

Damir's jaw dropped. "Reborn?" It was the first time he had heard someone talk about what he always knew was much more than a possibility.

"It depends how much harm, pain and suffering they caused back when they were before," finished the shepherd with his unusual logic.

"A lot, a real lot!" Damir raised his voice a little.

"One could be born blind, deaf, retarded, poor, miserable, stupid, sick, armless, fingerless, faceless—you name it! That way, they're destined to stay out of trouble next time around. It's one way to pay what's due, to gain a balance, harmony between the soul and God the All!"

"What else can happen to a man that's evil?" Damir did not have any trouble imagining the fate waiting for his father.

Pero pondered, then began laughing so hard he bounced up and down. "He spends his life working for the Draganovićs! Oh, I must have been very wicked!"

"Very!" Damir also laughed and made such a ruckus that Saša woke up and pouted because he thought Didi was making fun of him. It was not until Damir picked him up, hugged and tickled him that Saša began to laugh as well. "How did you learn all that?" Damir was awed at the shepherd's grasp of mountain metaphysics.

"Living in the midst of God."

Damir's mind raced with a thousand more questions he needed answers to, questions that he would, in time, bring to Pero the shepherd, who in a matter of a few hours had become the wisest man the boy had ever known.

"Damir from Banja Luka, how old are you?"

"Seventeen."

"Tell me something, Damir from Banja Luka, do you have a girl waiting for you in Banja Luka? You did not break her heart when you left?"

Damir rolled his eyes and shook his head, pretending he was bored. It was not the question that confounded Damir as much as the concept of *being in love*. "Have you ever been married?" he asked the shepherd.

"Married?" cried out the shepherd, and broke into verse—

"Marriage was invented
by the Devil himself
for torturing humans
before they go to hell."

No, he was never married, but he did fall in love with a girl called Rosalinda.

"Who's Rosalinda?" asked Damir.

Pero put the pipe in his mouth, closed his eyes and smiled.

Rosalinda was a Gypsy, all of fourteen years old, who owed her name, which meant "Beautiful Rose" in Spanish, to the memory of her papa, a handsome bullfighter who'd been gored to death by a bull just after her conception. Rosalinda's mother, a luscious Gypsy flower herself, was traveling across the Iberian Peninsula when she met the dashing toreador. Rosalinda's lips were red, like wet, wild cherries resting in the morning dew; her hair rolled down her back to her waist like a waterfall of polished brass; her eyes shone with the deep green of a perfect emerald; and her skin was as white and flawless as a Botticelli Madonna. The only imperfection in her otherwise flawless features was the larger-than-usual, though very neatly arranged, top row of teeth in her tiny and delectable mouth—a row that had one front tooth missing, the result of an altercation with Micha, her very short, hairy and extremely violent lover. However, the sting of that missing pearl never robbed Rosalinda of the spirit to be merry or to laugh aloud without reservations—sweet, happy girl that she was. No, Rosalinda continued to play girlish pranks on her brothers (all seventeen of them), and she still danced wildly and with feverish sensuality around the late evening fire, as the elders enjoyed the call for love from her tambourine and the writhing, undulating rhythms of her naked body—a rose-colored veil shrouding the lower part of her face in mystery.

Pero met Rosalinda when the princess and her subjects (one hundred and twenty of them) wandered into the district from Romania and to their dismay ran out of food. It was the luck of the Gypsies that brought them down a mountain pass where they encountered the shepherd's bounty grazing peacefully in the hills. There, with fiddles, zithers, mandolins, tambourines and drums the court encamped, hidden deep in the woods yet within a skip and a jump of their next meal, waiting for the shepherd to take a snooze. But Pero never lay down to enjoy the pastoral scene after lunch. Instead, he chose to smoke his pipe and finish a small wood rendering of two lambs and a baby goat he had been working on for weeks.

The morning turned into afternoon and afternoon into evening, and the fiddles, zithers, mandolins, tambourines and drums grew weaker and weaker. The Gypsy children who were always happy and carefree began to cry from hunger; the women harangued the men for allowing the caravan to run out of provisions; and the men debated whether a direct or indirect assault on the unsuspecting sheep was justified. After pondering for what seemed an interminable amount of time and after a candid exchange of insults, the elders decided not to risk failure and instead sent Rosalinda, their sweetest, most ravishing love siren as bait to entertain the shepherd while a group of six men, their heads decorated with colorful handkerchiefs and their faces with stubble, whisked away the young, plump and wooly members of Pero's flock.

Rosalinda emerged from the forest dressed in the thin mist of early evening and her flimsy veil. At first, Pero thought she was a *vali*, a nymph of the woods, until the girl lay down at his side and her delicate fingers crept up his shirt. No one could have foreseen what followed. That night, Pero the shepherd made continuous, tender but passionate love to the Gypsy girl, employing every organ and orifice. At one time Pero and Rosalinda held each other for over two hours, their bodies as one underneath the shepherd's thick, warm quilt. Rosalinda had never experienced such pleasure before, never had her entire body been so thoroughly and exquisitely alive, so that the slightest touch from Pero—even on her hair—caused her to moan and whimper with desire. No one could have imagined what followed the night Pero Bojić peeked under Rosalinda's veil below a starlit summer sky. That night, when three lambs vanished from the hill, Rosalinda, the Gypsy princess, to her astonishment and delight, became victim of her own exploits and fell madly in love with Pero the shepherd.

Pero stopped daydreaming, stopped venturing to town on Thursdays and stopped taking the flock back to the farm at night. Instead, he waited for the girl to appear between the rays of the moon, like a sensuous fairy.

Unfortunately, as in most fairy tales, Pero and Rosalinda's love was just one step ahead of disaster. Ivo Draganović hated Gypsies. He wanted to dismiss Pero, but Ana (practical as always) insisted the shepherd work without pay until he paid them back for the rustled sheep. Not that Ana viewed the affair with less concern than her husband. In fact, she was outraged, but not so much because she thought Pero was deceived—after all, deception was to a Gypsy what singing was to choirboys—or because he would wander aimlessly through the woods waiting for his love. No, Ana was peeved because Pero kept telling everyone that Rosalinda was a princess. Ana thought Gypsies had no business assuming aristocratic airs.

Pero took the ridicule as he did everything else, with a shrug and a grin. He viewed the incident as preordained by gods, who must have decided to toss a morsel of divinity in his path. He was so infatuated with Rosalinda that at one point he thought of quitting the pastoral life to join the youthful vixen and her clan in a life of singing, dancing and stealing. And indeed, this would have been the case if not for the epidemic disappearance of a sheep here and a chicken there, all which the citizens of Travnik, incited by Ivo, attributed to the Gypsies, who were even blamed for the emergence of a nasty strain of influenza that befell the town. The mayor was forced to name a delegation whose mission was to go up to the mountain, find the wandering tribe and respectfully explain to the elders that unless they packed their fiddles, zithers, mandolins, tambourines and drums and left the area at once, every Gypsy man, woman and child would be shot, hung, or set on fire—perhaps all three—depending on the mood of the townsfolk at the time. When Pero heard the news he packed his few belongings and dashed off to join Rosalinda. He searched up and down the mountain for seven hours but the only thing he found at the Gypsy campsite were three balls of white wool being tossed about by the wind.

It took the shepherd two years before he recovered. Only then was he able to sit outside and wonder, "Why everything we say has been said before and will be said again?"

Many years later, a toothless Gypsy hag, prematurely aged from suffering showed up in Travnik, dazed and sick. She was accompanied by two tall young men who looked remarkably alike. These were her boys, she announced to anyone that would listen, twins. Could someone, she asked, tell her where she could find Pero the shepherd? No one did, and the woman died shortly after. The twins quickly cremated the body and, with a bit of prodding from the authorities, left town, never to be heard of again.

"It is sad to lose someone you love so much," said Damir.

"You never lose them," whispered Pero with his eyes closed. "You never do." For Pero Bojić, the essence of life and death, love and pain was locked in timeless memories as eternal as the spirit of the universe, memories that followed the thread of a being from one life cycle to the next. To experience those same memories with the same intensity as before, all one had to do was remember. For the old shepherd the soft embrace of Rosalinda was as real as the warming rays of the sun.

The moon was showing half its face over the range when Pero, Didi and Saša trekked back to the house. Pero led the herd and Saša ran around like a sheepdog's assistant. At one point, he followed the dog into the woods. The dog, wise animal that he was, ran back to Pero; Saša did not.
"Better get him—wolves, you know."
"Wolves? I feel sorry for them!" said Didi.
It did not take him long to find the baby hiding behind a tree. "How can you run so fast? You have a diaper between your legs! Come on, you!" Damir picked up the little trouble maker and had begun the walk back to Pero when he stopped, put Saša down, took out his pocketknife and carved his name on the bark of a tree. Then, he turned and said, "Your turn!" Damir held Saša's hand and next to "Damir" wrote "Saša."
It was half past seven when Pero retired to the barn. Damir and Saša went into the house hoping they were in time for supper. Saša was full of life after his afternoon nap and ran around telling this one and that one every piece of mischief he had gotten into that day, although he never mentioned that he had been tripped by a sheep. That bit of gossip was told by Damir to those at the dinner table. Everyone laughed at the thought of Saša finally getting his due from the tormented animals.
Dinner that night was courtesy of Katarina, who had labored the whole afternoon in the kitchen determined to impress them with a dish of rabbit with tomatoes, onions, garlic and potatoes, seasoned with generous amounts of paprika. Everyone was enjoying the meal (it was quite tasty if a bit rubbery) when a sudden, urgent pounding at the front door reverberated through the house.
"Father Draganović!" someone called from outside.
It was Rostas and he was armed with a revolver and a shotgun. He was shaken, perspiring as if it were the middle of a summer afternoon instead of a chill autumn night. Just behind Rostas was

his transportation, a black horse outlined against the night. The fog enveloped the animal, leaving only its head to shimmer as the lights from the house reflected off its sweaty hide. A coil of mist swirled every time the horse whipped its tail right or left.

"Get them out, now, no time to lose!" Rostas kept looking at the road below.

"What is it?"

"Militia! Six, or seven of them, armed—in two cars. They will be here in fifteen minutes—they're just down the road!"

Here was the payoff for good intelligence. "Wake up Pero," ordered the priest.

"Hide—take the horse and go into the woods. I will signal from upstairs when they leave." The priest hurried to the dining room and announced to the party that they were—

"Leaving? What is happening, what is it?" asked Marija.

"Soldiers are on the way. You have to get out of here now. There's no time to take anything. Damir, the baby stays."

"No!" Damir grabbed Saša and held him tight.

"Listen to me! You have to go hide in the mountains. Pero is going to take you where no one will find you, but it's a dangerous hike, especially at night and in this fog. You can't afford to get held up and that's exactly what will happen if you take the baby. It would mean the end for all of us. Now, put him down and go!"

"Damir, my darling, think of your sister!" Marija held on to Katarina, who was very scared.

Saša sensed something was wrong and he darted frightened looks left and right. Damir tried to calm him down, but the baby began to cry.

"Damir!" Marija was losing patience.

"I'm not leaving Saša!" Damir backed up against the wall.

Father Draganović raised his voice slightly. "If you take him, you will be caught, if you stay you will be caught. Either way you will certainly never see him again!"

The boy glared at the priest. He hugged and kissed Saša then slowly turned him over to Father Draganović.

"Damir! Damir!" cried Saša.

"I'll be back, Saša, I swear I'll be back, you'll see!" Tears streamed down Damir's face as the baby reached out for him.

Ana gathered jackets, sweaters, blankets and two lamps for the Pavelićs to take with them.

"Nikola, you too."

The little man had remained in a corner looking around and not knowing what to do, and wishing someone would tell him. "I-I-will not s-s-stay for a-anything!" stammered the secretary. He hopped nervously around the table a few times (like a top winding itself) before rushing out the door.

Pero was already waiting for them. "The cave," said Father Draganović, holding Saša in his arms. "Wait there until I send for you." The old man never asked why the cousins from Banja Luka had to go hide in the mountains like thieves. He wanted to, but never did.

Father Draganović watched as the group grabbed on to a rope (to avoid getting lost) and seconds later vanished, swallowed by the almost impenetrable fog. With luck—Pero had to find his way through a score of hidden mountain paths—they would reach the cave in an hour.

10

The police and soldiers arrived in two black, nondescript automobiles which almost did not make it up the mountain.

"Hello," said Comrade Durković getting out of the first car. Father Draganović held the door open and the policeman entered the house, followed by six soldiers and a fat little red fellow wearing a long, brown leather coat.

Durković was an ordinary pale-looking man of thirty-five, who needed to shave at least twice a day to avoid the dark shadows that appeared on his face around four in the afternoon. He had a widow's peak, a large bald spot on his crown, brown eyes, grey teeth, hunched shoulders and a tired look. The policeman was wearing a brown jacket that did not match his pants and a tie that was ten years old. "I am sorry to disturb you," said Durković. "I need to ask you a few questions. Do you mind? Are you very busy? Would you like for us to come back some other time, perhaps?"

Father Draganović minded very much, he was very busy, and would have preferred for Comrade Durković and his men to go away and not come back.

"I have been told that you are good friends with Aloysius Stepinac? Is my information correct?"

"I know His Excellency."

Durković looked at Ana, who was sitting in a corner whispering soothing nothings to Saša, praying he did not call out for Damir.

"And—please tell me, when was the last time you saw Stepinac?" asked Comrade Durković to the priest.

"A few months ago."

"Before he was arrested?"

"Yes."

"Would you mind if we looked around, Father?"

"Look for what?"

With a wave of his hand the policeman signaled his men to search the house. Then, he took out a pack of cigarettes, offered one to the fat little red man beside him, and sat in the chair usually occupied by Nikola. "You don't mind if I smoke, do you?"

Ana could hear the men going through the upstairs rooms. A short time later three of them marched down into the cellar, where it became evident they were leaving no stone, or piece of furniture, unturned.

"Nice place you have here, madame," said Comrade Durković to Ana. "It must be very expensive to maintain, yes?"

"The farm has been in my family for generations. We are self-sufficient and make a little on what we sell in town, that is all," intervened Draganović.

"Father, the records show Ivo Draganović—your father—bought the farm in nineteen hundred and seven. That's not that long ago, is it?"

"What do you want from us? We do not bother anyone. I am an old woman, my son is a man of God, what is it you want?"

"Is that your grandson, madame?" Comrade Durković knew that Ana was, as she said, an old woman. He also was aware that her son was a priest, and since Father Draganović was an only son, who then, was the child in the old woman's arms?

"My great nephew," said Ana softly.

Comrade Durković looked at Ana in a way that made her think he thought she was lying when the loud ring of crashing metal and breaking glass was heard from upstairs. Comrade Durković jumped out of his seat, ran to the staircase and scolded the soldiers, demanding they be more careful. "I am sorry," he said. "We try our best; still, accidents happen. What can we do? I will be more than happy to file a report, not that it will make any difference, I'm afraid."

"What is it you want?"

Durković beckoned the fat little red man, who produced a piece of paper and gave it to Comrade Durković, who in turn passed it along to Father Draganović. It was a copy of an official document. The letterhead was from the foreign ministry of the Independent State of Croatia in Zagreb and read:

Confirmation of Receipt. Hereby the receipt of the archives of the Foreign Ministry of the Independent State of Croatia is confirmed, specifically:

1. a chest covered with tin and marked with <u>AB-I</u>, sealed with two locks,
2. a wooden chest marked with <u>AB-II</u>, sealed with two locks,
3. three wooden chests marked with <u>PAV-I-III</u>, sealed with one lock,
4. a wooden chest marked with <u>OL-I</u>, sealed with two locks,
5. a wooden chest marked with <u>OL-II</u> sealed with one lock,
6. a small wooden chest covered with tin and marked <u>RZ</u>, sealed with one lock.

For all of the locks the keys are simultaneously transferred, one for each lock.

Zagreb 6 May 1945

On orders of the poglavnik to transfer 8 chests.

Received a total of 8 chests

A. Stepinac
Archbishop

Father Draganović glanced at the paper, shrugged and gave it back. "What is it?"

"Come, Father, you can read, can't you? It is a receipt signed by your friend Stepinac for the war booty hoarded by the Ustaše."

Father Draganović showed no emotion other than a little indignation. "I don't understand what it has to do with us."

"Not 'us' Father Draganović, you." Comrade Durković pointed his nicotine-stained finger at the priest. "Your relationship with Stepinac is documented. This house is almost inaccessible, a perfect place to hide the spoils of defeat."

"I am afraid you are wasting your time," replied Father Draganović softly.

"I am afraid we have to look anyway," returned the comrade, smiling.

The search went on for almost an hour. Draganović remained standing in the middle of the room. Ana put Saša to bed and Comrade Durković and the fat little red man smoked one pack of cigarettes between them.

"Nothing," said one of the soldiers climbing out of the cellar. "But—"

"What?" Durković flipped his cigarette butt into the fireplace.

"Well, down there—I don't know, it's too neat."

"Explain," ordered his superior.

The soldier was a tall dark-haired man about twenty-three years old, with a bushy mustache, black eyes and a long nose, which he seemed to put to good use. "My mother's basement is full of dust and cobwebs, full of junk that no one wants but nobody wants to throw away. This place here, well—there's no dust, no cobwebs, looks like someone's been sleeping there."

"Any visitors, father?" asked Durković suspiciously.

"Pero, our farm hand, we let him sleep inside when it gets too cold."

"Of course," said Durković. "And where is Pero now?"

"I don't know. I called him before sundown but he did not answer. He's probably in town getting drunk. Pero is a good man but has always been morally reprehensible."

Comrade Durković stared at Father Draganović for a second, then turned to the tall soldier. "Very good. You should be a policeman. Come, let's go."

Casually, the soldiers and the fat little red man filed out of the house, got in their cars and waited for Durković. "Sorry for the inconvenience, Father," said the comrade turning to the priest before he went outside. "Keep in mind that we are watching you. We know when you go away, we know when you come back, we know where you go, and we know who you meet with. In short, Father Draganović, we are very interested in everything you do. Good night."

Thirty seconds later, there was no trace of the policeman or the soldiers as the cars turned around and disappeared in the fog.

Father Draganović waited five minutes before he went outside and called Rostas with a very loud and shrill whistle.

"Do you think they'll be back?" Ana was upset.

"Yes, maybe not tonight, but they'll be back."

"What are we going to do?" asked Ana.

Just then, Rostas tapped on the kitchen window. He was holding the shotgun ready in case it was a trap.

"Listen to me," said Draganović. "Take the baby home with you."

"The baby?" said Ana. "Why? Kruno, you can't, you just can't!"

"Mother!"

"You promised Damir!"

"It has to be done."

"He's going to be heartbroken, Saša adores him!" Ana began to cry.

"Look," said Father Draganović gently, "Damir cannot have a say. He has to think the militia took the baby." The priest decided the Pavelićs had to leave the mountain as soon as possible and they could not afford to take the Saša. He also could not allow Damir to challenge his authority, which would happen once Damir found out Saša had to stay behind. It was to be a fait accompli. "Once I get them out of the country and they're safe, then, maybe, who knows. If nobody claims the kid, I'll wrap him up in a Sunday suit and put him on a boat to Damir. Right now, I don't have time for arguments or temper tantrums."

"Oh, Kruno!" As sad as it was, Ana understood her son was right. She immediately went up upstairs for the child.

"Olga won't mind?" asked the priest to Rostas.

"Mind? Why, she loves children—as long as they belong to someone else."

"It's only for a day or two, but keep him out of sight." Draganović added, "Our friends—they must leave at first light; better if this time they travel during the day; they'll blend right in with the rest of the refugees."

Ana bundled Saša in warm, heavy clothes that included the little red woolen hat, then wrapped two mufflers around his neck, kissed and caressed him over and over again, trying to keep the baby from crying. Rostas sat Saša in front of him on the horse, tied a rope around himself and the child, and soon became a galloping storyteller, all the way to Travnik.

No sooner had Rostas left with Saša that Father Draganović put on a pair of hiking boots, a heavy jacket and left to fetch the Pavelićs.

They were sitting around a small fire, courtesy of Pero, about three meters from the mouth of the cave, after a hazard-filled expedition that relied on the eyes and recollections of an eighty-three-year-old shepherd, who was able to find his way—on a moonless night—up the side of a mountain cloaked in fog and drizzle. Pero had last visited the cave over ten years ago, when he had sought protection during a nasty hailstorm that pummeled him mercilessly with hail the size of oranges. The cave was hidden behind trees, bushes and a large boulder. The only way to reach it was by climbing a ridge twenty-five meters high. Inside, the cave was approximately six meters wide and four meters to the ceiling. Pero held that it was possible to reach the other side of the mountain by walking through the long interconnecting tunnels that made up the cave.

Marija and Katarina were still frightened, and Nikola was not feeling well; his frail body was in pain after hopping up and down the mountain in the cold. Damir sat brooding, angry with himself for letting the priest keep Saša. The only one that was indifferent to the climb and the weather was Pero who, after forty-five minutes of sitting by the fire, in the company of four sulking and silent bodies, decided to take a nap and wait.

Damir was overanxious and restless. Since he could not go outside, he decided to explore the cave. He got up, picked up one of the lamps and was on his way—

"Where are you going?" asked Marija.

"For a walk."

"Stay where you are, it's dangerous. Heaven knows what's in—"

"To you everything is dangerous," said Damir. "I can't do anything that you don't think is dangerous. I have never been able to do anything that you didn't think was dangerous." Quickly, Damir's complaint grew louder and more vehement. "I never had friends because you said it was dangerous; I couldn't play outside because you thought it was dangerous! I'm sick and tired of being told that everything, everything is dangerous! Leave me alone! I don't care! I hope I find a great bat that sucks my blood and kills me! I don't care anymore! Just leave me alone!"

Well, it was the first adolescent outburst to escape Damir and it caused tremendous anxiety in his mother. Even the secretary, who was dozing on and off, was so rattled he rebuked the boy for his insolence.

"Bonk!"

Katarina wondered what would happen to her brother after his lack of consideration and respect.

Pero looked from one player to another, chewing his unlit pipe.

Marija placed her hands on her waist and faced her son. "Don't you ever, ever use that tone of voice with me! Do you understand? Don't think for an instant you're too big to get whipped, because you're not! Now, sit down and don't even think of going anywhere! All I need is for you to get lost in this—in this—" Marija could not find words to describe where she and her children were hiding.

"With all the things I have to worry about. Sit down!"

"No!"

It seemed to Damir that the angrier his mother became, the taller she grew.

"Sit down, I said!"

"I am not going to sit down! I'm tired of sitting down, tired of not having a life, tired of—"

"Stop!" screamed Marija. For the first time in her life she did not have a clue how to deal with her son.

"Didi, you should not talk to your mama that way!" The secretary felt obliged to intervene on behalf of his mistress. "You are taking advantage that your papa's not here. The—"

Nikola did not finish. His eyes locked with Marija's and the word "poglavnik," which was next in line to sally forth, was tackled, captured and thrashed before it even made it to his lips. The secretary fell as silent as the stalactite perched over his head. If Marija had been able to control matter with her mind, the sharp icicle-shaped deposit of carbonate of lime would have dropped from the roof of the cave and sliced the secretary in half.

"Bonk!" was all Nikola got for his troubles, and Damir walked off into the dark recesses of the mountain.

"Damir!" called his mother.

"Damir!" yelled his sister.

Damir did not answer and did not come back. Marija sank to her knees and sobbed.

Damir walked for about five minutes, dazzled by the strange environment of the cave. His anger subsided but was replaced by guilt, guilt for having yelled at his mother and hurt the secretary's feelings. But Damir's dignity and his sense of adventure—an unlikely alliance made to justify the exploration of the cave—compelled him to go on. He found that the farther he walked inside the cave, the narrower the hole became. He scanned the walls with the lamp hoping to find one or two prehistoric paintings or hieroglyphics never seen by modern man. Instead, what he did was disturb the sleep of the upside-down residents of the cavern, who took flight toward a more secluded and definitely darker corner of their lair; some actually bumped into Damir as a sign of their irritation. Soon, Damir came to a sharp right turn where the trail continued for about thirty meters before it split. To the left was a rivulet that trickled from an unseen tributary and led to a grotto guarded by a huge rock—the depository for one tin chest marked <u>AB-I</u>, sealed and locked; a wooden chest marked <u>AB-II</u>, sealed and locked; three wooden chests marked <u>PAV-I-III</u>, sealed and locked; a wooden chest marked <u>OL-I</u>, sealed and locked; a wooden chest marked <u>OL-II</u>, sealed and locked; and a small wooden chest covered with tin, marked <u>RZ</u>, sealed and locked.

The boy thought he had come upon a lost treasure left there by marauding pirates, though he never stopped to think that Travnik was a little out of the way for any pirate, marauding or not. As Damir tried to pry open one of the chests with his fingers, Pero appeared from behind. The shepherd was not able to see the treasure because the rock hid the chests from view.

"There you are! Come on, your mother's very upset."

"Wait! Look what I found! Where's your knife?" Damir was so excited he grabbed the old man by the arm and showed him the chests.

"What do you make of this?"

Pero brought his lamp to the surface of one chest, brushed away the dust with his hand.

"Do you think, do you think it's a pirate treasure?" Damir was so excited his voice cracked and his arms were like two swords executing wild flourishes.

"I don't think so." The old man moved from one chest to another.

"Wait till Saša hears about this! Open it, go ahead!"

"I left my knife in the sack."

"Let's get it!"

"Hold on, just hold on a second." Pero looked for a nice hard rock to break open the locks.

"Do you think we could get in trouble?" asked Damir, realizing that perhaps the owners of the chests would not take kindly to the intrusion.

"People my age don't get in trouble." Pero smiled. He soon found exactly what he was looking for. It was black, it was smooth, it was hard, and it had been lying against the back wall of the cave for a millennium. He chose the chest marked <u>PAV-I</u> and before Damir could say anything else, Pero landed such a swift and powerful blow to the lock, it cracked down the middle. Pero lifted the cover and Damir thought the contents of the chest looked like gold, but was not sure.

"It's gold, all right, but—but these nuggets have a strange shape." Pero picked one up, looked at it carefully, then showed it to Damir. "It looks like a tooth; wouldn't you say it has the shape of a gold tooth?"

Almost out of sight in a corner of the chest there was a paper folded in two. Its letterhead was from the foreign ministry of the

Independent State of Croatia. The note read: *From the Work Service of the Ustaše Defense Assembly Camp III—on orders from the poglavnik...*

Pero handed the paper to Damir. "What does it say?"

The boy read it and began to tremble. Although Damir did not realize the extent of his find, and did not know what the words "Defense Assembly Camp III" meant, the word "poglavnik" was enough.

"What's the matter? What is it? What does it say? Read it, come, come!"

Haltingly, his voice hardly audible, Damir read the note, then tore it to pieces.

"What are you doing?" It was a moment before Pero understood the meaning of the note Damir had just read. The old man scratched his stubble and repeated aloud, "Ustaše Defense Assembly Camp III?" before the mystery of the chest unraveled. "Jasenovac! These are gold teeth, yes, from the victims of Jasenovac! The poglavnik, the Ustaše, yes, it is! My God!" He dropped the gold tooth back in the chest. The last phrase was uttered with such contempt Damir buried his face in his hands and began to cry. "My father!"

"Damir, what is it?"

"My father! He did this."

"Your—father? I don't—"

"Ante Pavelić is my father." Damir wiped off the tears with his hand.

Pero's body went numb, he was paralyzed; his blood settled at his feet and his brain was unable to command his body. His one-time eloquence left him. The only sign that Pero was still among the living was his eyes, eyes that could not stop staring at the boy, eyes that could not believe for one moment the child he thought to be the most compassionate, caring, giving and loving of all the people he had ever met could be the son of a murderer like Ante Pavelić.

Damir saw the disappointment and pain in the old man's eyes.

"Pero—"

"P-Pavelić, you, you—"

"Pero." The boy knelt beside the shepherd. "You asked me if I was an orphan. I am, we all are—we have been made orphans by Ante Pavelić."

The old shepherd did not move as Damir told him everything, including about the time he went with his father to Glina, where he saw for the first time a poor little Serbian shepherd boy named Saša. The old man watched the boy's handsome features become distorted by his grief. "Oh God, I'm sorry!" cried Damir.

It was a good two minutes before Pero regained control of himself. Slowly, in a voice quivering with sadness and pity—sadness for the innocent victims of a senseless massacre and pity for the burden Damir had to bear the rest of his life—he held out his tremulous hand. "You have nothing to do with this."

Damir embraced the old man.

Pero even forced a smile from the boy when he said, "No wonder that little pain in the ass is not afraid of sheep!"

Pero took the boy back to his family. He realized that Marija and Katarina were the wife and daughter of Ante Pavelić. And who was Nikola? A bodyguard? Not likely; probably a servant. And what were those boxes doing in the cave? No one else knew about the cave, no one except for—

"Where were you?" Father Draganović had arrived at the cave just as Damir and the shepherd rejoined the others. Marija and Katarina were still very upset with Damir, and Damir's nightmares slowly began to gather once more.

"Where is Saša?"

"Where have you been?" repeated the priest.

"I—I went to see the cave," Damir was not going to let the priest in on his secret.

"Pero?" Draganović looked hard at the old man.

"Like the boy said." Pero nodded toward Damir.

"Is everything all right, Father? Are we going back to the house?" Marija was getting ready to leave.

"Everything is not all right. You have to leave the mountain. It's too dangerous for you to stay here any longer. Damir, I am afraid I have bad news. The army—"

"Where is Saša? Where is Saša!?"

"The soldiers took him."

"What have you done with Saša?" screamed Damir.

"Damir—" Father Draganović held his temper.

"Why are you doing this? Why are you lying to me!"

Damir was almost hysterical.

"They took the baby! Oh, my God! Oh, my God! Poor little Saša!" cried Marija.

Katarina held on to her mother and also began to cry.

Nikola denounced the militia and Pero was enraged. Why, he asked himself, why would they take the baby? What could the army possibly want with the baby?

Marija took her son in her arms. "I am so, so terribly sorry!" Saša had become one of them, they had come to love the little fellow. Damir fell on his knees and wept. He wept for the infant he found on a wet, dismal night; wept for the baby he nurtured back to health with selfless devotion; wept for the little Serbian shepherd boy who shared his dreams, his hopes and his nightmares; wept for the little friend who years back returned to save him from death; wept for the child who was all joy, laughter and unabashed affection; wept for Saša who, once again, was lost! Damir could do nothing else—he wept.

The sun was already master of the skies when the group returned to the farm. Pero went to feed the animals while the Pavelićs were dispatched with hugs, kisses, tears from Ana, plenty of food in three baskets, and reassurances from Father Draganović that in a few weeks they would be safe from their enemies—whoever they happened to be. Then the Pavelićs were supplied with passports that described them as Spanish nationals, and sent on their way. Nikola stayed behind. He remained at the farm until Father Draganović thought it was safe for the secretary to return to Zagreb. There was nothing for him to do in Argentina; Nikola had become "unnecessary."

Marija kissed him, thanked him and told him that she thought and would continue to think of him as a member of the family. Katarina also kissed the secretary and extended her affectionate farewell with a heartfelt hug. She promised Nikola she would write as soon as it was possible and made him promise to write back in his fastest possible typing. Didi embraced the little man he always thought of as his friend. "I'm sorry I yelled at you," said Damir with tears in his eyes.

The parting proved almost too much for Nikola, setting off a coughing fit that shook him to the bone. Then, Damir looked for Pero and found the shepherd doing the same thing he had been doing that first day when Damir, with Saša in his arms, first saw him from the attic.

"I'll write," said Damir.

"I can't read," said Pero.

"Will—will I see you again?" asked the boy, putting out his hand.

"Every time you think of me."

"If—if you see Saša, tell him not to forget me, tell him I love him and—and I'll be back for him!" Damir embraced his friend and could not stop crying. "Good-bye, Pero."

"Good-bye, Damir."

Marija called her son. She and Katarina were already in the car, the same car in which they had driven to Travnik almost two years before, and that reappeared now with a new coat of paint.

Pero let go of the boy and resumed scattering chicken feed. Damir walked slowly to the car, he was feeling the weight of the farewell. He turned around only once, to wave good-bye, but Pero was already in the barn. The boy would perhaps have been surprised to see Pero sitting on his cot, his face buried in his hands, staring at the ground and making his old boots wet with his tears.

Later that week, Father Draganović stood by the window in the library and watched as the first, wet snows of the year trickled softly to the ground, laying down a fine coat of silvery ice on which a good half meter of the white, cold stuff would be piled. One of the good things about the monotony of life in the mountains, he thought, was its constancy—constant tedium—something that could always be relied upon. The priest knew the Pavelićs were already on their way to South America, that Nikola was back in Zagreb, and that Pero would be going around the back to the kitchen door where Ana was waiting with his supper. Pero would then take it back to the little corner in the barn he shared with the animals, and there he would sit amongst the brothers and sisters of his stew—with a generous amount of wine—and the day for the shepherd would finally end. The priest knew that much.

Pero scooped his last bit of potato, soaked his last piece of bread in the sauce and chased it down with one last drink. All throughout the meal he thought of Damir and his last name—Pavelić. Pero grunted, smashed the metal bowl and spoon to the ground (the dog licked them clean), threw his hat against the wall and let the wine transport him to happier, sunnier days, when he would sit on top of the hill and watch his lover walk out of the forest dressed in loose colorful silks trimmed with gold and silver, her garments and her long red hair rippling to the jubilant rhythm of the summer wind.

Rosalinda approached softly, so softly in fact she seemed to glide across the lush mountain grass into the arms of her lover. Six songbirds wrapped them in the most exquisite melody as the pastoral scene played to idyllic measures. Gently, Pero drew Rosalinda closer and let his fingers feel the softness of her back. A passionate, yet delicate embrace finally brought them together, Rosalinda's lips ever so inviting. It was ecstasy. The kiss, the clasped bodies exchanging lives, the voracious hunger of the princess sucking the soul from her lover. Pero felt the tightness in his chest, his lungs gasping for air. He tried to open his eyes, but could not; he tried to lift the thick, heavy blanket from his face but, in the end, Pero looked deep into Rosalinda's eyes—her passion was insatiable—dropped his arms and surrendered to the eternal embrace of love.

THE TENOR & HIS DAUGHTER

11

Hidden behind a tall, massive wall and no-nonsense iron gate, in Fincas (an area known for its large farming interests and adjoining the suburb of Caseros, outside Buenos Aires), *el jefe*, as he was called, paced up and down the living room, pulled on the telephone wire and shot questions to a subordinate at the other end. "Press? What press! What is going on?" He did not scream but his pulse quickened, his blood pressure rose and his face showed his anger. *La Prensa* the largest daily in the country, had sent reporters and photographers, even dispatched a movie crew aboard the *Afortunato* to cover the arrival of an opera singer in Buenos Aires. "Listen to me!" said el jefe, his voice becoming lower and softer as his rage increased. "Make sure that there are no photographers on the docks when they get off! I don't care what you do! Do not, I repeat, do not leave anything to chance!" He slammed the phone down and stood staring at the wall. He was not only angry, but he was frustrated as well. Someone should have said something about the famous person aboard the same boat as Marija and the children. It was an intelligence lapse and Ante Pavelić was going to make sure somebody was held responsible.

Ante had not seen his family in almost three years. Even before he went into exile his wife and children had become distant and indifferent. He was not convinced that bringing them to Argentina made sense, but in the telegram Ante received from Father Draganović, the priest had not given him a choice: *Dávilas arrive*

Buenos Aires on the third. Stop. Buona fortuna. Stop. KD. Stop. Secrets, codes and lies. Some things never changed.

When he first arrived in Argentina, Pavelić was provided with a small apartment inside an army base twenty kilometers north of the capital. His only visitor was a priest who brought news from Father Draganović. Once a month a car picked him up and took him to meet with his hosts; otherwise, Pavelić was left alone. He had spent the best part of a year and a half at the barracks, but secured roomier lodgings when he learned of the arrival of his family. Pavelić moved to a large, comfortable two-story Spanish colonial house that had been the residence on terra firma of an Argentinean admiral who fell from grace with Perón.

The concrete house was painted a light yellow. It had red tiles on the roof and a frieze of leaves and vines in relief that went around the building—a demarcation line between the lower and upper levels. The ground floor included a set of French doors that opened to a marble terrace with a view of the front yard. An identical pair of French doors opened to a second-floor balcony poised right above the main door from where a Juliet could, if called upon, wave to her Romeo outside the property, though her Romeo would have needed to be either very tall, be standing on top of a ladder, or have already climbed the three-meter-high and half-meter-thick protective wall that enclosed the grounds. The front yard, with its unimpressive rose garden, suffered from neglect and was kept forever in the shade of a grand ombu tree and two royal palms. A massive iron gate led to a narrow driveway to the right of the lawn and into the carport that adjoined the main house. The carport was equipped with an electric steel door that opened automatically when the car approached, and shut and locked just as instinctively when the car was inside. All the windows in the house were encased in wrought iron, and the front and back doors were covered by iron grills. A shed behind the house was converted into living quarters for the live-in help, which at the time was made up of a driver and bodyguard, both in the person of a short but corpulent Italian man named Rubén (the Tito government had captured Pavelić's former bodyguard, Antu Moškova, after the war and had him shot). As an added measure of safety, Ante Pavelić employed neither a cook nor a cleaning woman. He preferred to divide those chores between the bodyguard and himself, with most of the cleaning going to the bodyguard.

The kitchen was decorated with wallpaper patterned after the god of grain and vegetation. It was a large and modern kitchen because the Admiral's mistress had enjoyed experimenting with classics from the Cordon Bleu. A double door of red quebracho opened to the formal dining room where a long, ornate table with thick sculpted legs could sit fifty-two at any time. The next room was the library. It had shelves that reached as high as the ceiling, filled with books dealing with the political philosophy of the high seas. It had ample leather chairs, a number of hunting and fishing victims mounted on the paneled walls, a wonderful collection of music with thousands of records, a phonograph and various decanters of Spanish brandy, cognac and whiskey. Marble floors were the rule throughout the house. Sometimes a rug or two warmed a particular room—the library, for instance—but most of the floors remained hard, lovely and bare. A marble staircase with a polished mahogany balustrade led upstairs. The master bedroom, like the kitchen, was furnished with every modern gadget and then some. It included a radio and a contraption that made the bed vibrate (Ante never turned them on). The adjoining bathroom was decorated in aquamarine tiles and had a shower, a bathtub and a bidet. There were three smaller bedrooms across the hall and they shared a bathroom whose yellow tiles were decorated with daisies and sunflowers.

To Ante's surprise, he found the politics and practicality of the Argentines much like his own. He needed to improve his Spanish, but since most of the Argentineans he dealt with—colonels, generals and thugs—spoke German or Italian, communicating with his colleagues was not a problem. For all of his initial trepidations, Ante Pavelić settled down and tried to make the best of his irrevocable condition. He kept an office in an out-of-the-way and shabby little building connected to the presidential palace, an office that was not supposed to exist.

About the same time that Ante was arranging for his family's arrival, his daughter was jumping up and down, tugging at her brother's sleeve and pointing to a thin strip of brown in the distance, the first glimpse of the Argentinean coastline. "Look!" cried Katarina. "We're here!"

Not yet. The *Afortunato* did not dock for another six hours. Still, the promise of a new life, new friends and school were enough to make the girl as delirious as if she had been opening red, green and yellow gift-wrapped bundles on Christmas morn.

After leaving Travnik, the Pavelićs spent two days in a safe house in Mostar, traveled south to the inconspicuous coastal village of Baška Voda, changed clothes, made a covert and uneventful dash across the Adriatic in a small ferry, landed just south of the Italian seaport of Pescara on a star-riddled midnight, received one last set of instructions from Father Draganović by way of Rostas, traveled by car to Naples, boarded the *Afortunato* and journeyed safely and in second class to the Americas.

The war had been over for two years and traveling across the Atlantic in the *Afortunato* was almost as safe as going to the corner for bread unless the steamer bumped into a leftover mine bobbling on the surface. The not-so-luxury liner, initially commissioned as *Titano di Mare*, was re-christened *Afortunato* after the war because it had carried troops and supplies for the Mussolini government hundreds of times during the war without coming under fire. The ship had three enormous stacks spewing black smoke that revealed its location long before the boat itself came into view. It was five decks tall with the top three levels going only halfway to stern. The first class compartments were, properly so, at the top and the measure of passenger comfort and service diminished the closer one got to the waters below. Two tall masts, one bow and one stern, were used to hang radio and telegraph antennae in addition to banners of vibrant colors encrypted with geometric maritime symbols that, although totally incomprehensible to those not familiar with protocol on the high seas, were still imposing and interesting to look at, if for no other reason than that a person could spend the day staring at the flags and never decipher their meanings. Six lifeboats, three on each side and each equipped with a variety of lifesavers, hung from gigantic iron pulleys, and were held in place by massive twisting ropes.

Travel to South America was a lark for the Dávilas, Spaniards from Majorca in search of a new and better life. Even so, the tension and the tantrums increased each day they got closer to Argentina because no one knew what to expect in the land of che and tango. Marija would have preferred to live somewhere in Europe, alone with the children, away from Ante Pavelić, his cronies, the intrigues and the inescapable hazards such a life brought on the family; Damir and Katarina felt the same way.

Father Draganović had counseled Marija against fraternizing with the other passengers, as custom called for during long transatlantic jaunts, so, she and the children stayed clear of homesick Spanish nationals on board with a yen for conversation and Yugoslavian assassins traveling on business.

It was not easy. Katarina wanted to go outside to play with the other children but was not allowed, making the girl impossible. And although Marija felt sorry for Katarina and knew how difficult it was for her to be sequestered in a small cabin room playing cards day and night, Marija was more fearful of the change that had overtaken her son. Damir had scarcely said two words since leaving Travnik. His mother trembled at the thought of Didi falling ill as he had as a small boy in Banja Luka. Then Marija had the best doctors and nurses available, and still the boy almost willed himself to die. It was of serious concern that they were at sea and that in an emergency she could only depend on the power of prayer and the limited medical resources on board.

Marija and Katarina tried as hard as they could to distract Didi with games and conversation, but when they did they inevitably talked of Saša and Didi's eyes filled with tears and his mind wandered to the mountain, to the happy recollections of the baby and the old shepherd.

It was no problem keeping Didi in his room. He refused to go out except at night when he took long brooding walks around the decks, despite the weather or the swaying of the ship. Sometimes Katarina accompanied her brother; once in a while Marija accompanied her son; a few times they both joined Damir; but usually Damir insisted on being left alone. He should have challenged the priest! The nightmares, those awful dreams that had lessened during the family's stay at the farm, returned. The little shepherd boy was again surrounded by the Ustaše, his eyes agonizing and sad, but this time he cried out for "Didi!"

Twelve days after the Dávilas went to sea, while Marija and Katarina played (what else?) cards in their cabin; during a rather misty twilight and following a leisurely, hour-long walk that had taken Damir back and forth and up and down the ship dressed in a pair of green corduroys that were too short, a light brown shirt that was too tight, tall rubber boots and a black rubber cape that flapped like the wings of an anxious bat trying to overcome the ocean spray; in this haze of early evening Didi found himself in the lower decks of the big boat, separated from the water only by the metal hull, surrounded by hordes of sweating, stinking, impoverished peasants: Bohemian Gypsies, a cacophony of screaming filthy children, knots of old men smoking pipes and cigarettes, young men who eyed the young women and talked of money and sex, young women who teased the young men with tantalizing eyes, and beldams praying continuously to Providence to help them survive the two-and-a-half-week crossing of the ocean.

One of these women sat in a makeshift, yellowish-brown tent surrounded by twigs of burning incense, four cigarillos and six candles. The crone was covered in layers of glittering reds, pinks and greens. She beckoned Damir and offered to tell him his fortune. Didi tried to ignore the hag; the stench of incense, the formidable damp heat and the woman's face were enough to make the boy nauseous, but her words "You have lost someone very dear more than once and I have much to tell you," caught his attention. Her voice was a croaking monotone and her Italian was as disjointed as her features. She pointed with her crooked finger to an empty spot just in front of her. "Let me look at you," she added. Before Didi could make himself comfortable—which was impossible given the state of his nerves—the old woman began to describe to him not his fortune but his past. "Give me your hand." The sorceress intended for Damir to lay his hand on top of hers—something he was reluctant to do, but did anyway.

"Are you—are you a Gypsy?" he asked, thinking that perhaps the old woman could be kin to Pero's princess.

"I could be a cobbler and still see you are grieving." It was his aura, she added, the grey and dark green all around him, revealing discouragement and forewarning doom.

Damir sat cross-legged on the floor and the sorceress busied herself peering into his soul. The boy listened as she described his melancholy with magical accuracy. A cool and soothing breeze, like that which beckons the moon and the stars in fall, fell upon the tent. The old woman begged Damir to cast aside the sadness, the anger and the dastardly idea of killing himself. "You are born of evil, yet you are compassionate and just," she said. "Such contradictions are never resolved without suffering." The hag let go of Didi's hand, picked up a cigarillo and lit up with the help of a candle. She drew long and hard, trails of smoke seeping out her nostrils and the sides of her mouth. "You are blessed by two, you'll be blessed by three. Now go, you are wasting time!" she said aloud. "Climb and find the sovereign that will give you comfort and cheer your days."

Before Damir was able to get to his feet, before he was able to blurt out, "What?" the old woman staggered out of the tent and vanished. It took Didi a few minutes to shake off the feeling that it was all an illusion, at which point he found himself on the next deck up. The elder of the Bohemian Gypsies below had paid extra to settle his large family, a dozen chickens and three goats in six rooms with cots and portholes from where they could, if they had not by then grown sick and tired of it, look out to sea.

"*Climb!*"

The next deck was set aside for that brand of political refugee who had money left over after paying out bribes to innumerable officials and doling out cash to scores of underlings just to be let out of a one country and into another.

"*Find the sovereign!*"

The boy ran along the side of the ship until he reached the ladder that would take him to the main deck. He raced up the rungs, two and three at a time until he could go no further without heading for the bridge. Didi looked around, took a deep breath and grabbed the railing. He felt the sticky, wet salt from the sea on the polished, wooden railing. Damir closed his eyes and fell, fell, fell—

He passed second class, right on by the porthole to his mother's cabin and even thought he caught a glimpse of Katarina waving back. Down he went, by the political refugees with money left over; by the Bohemian Gypsy with the large family, a dozen chickens and three goats; and even going by the witch who warned him against doing anything so cowardly as suicide—he flew right by the mass of peasants and stinking old men and hit the water without a splash, without a sound, and was seen no more.

Blackness. He felt nothing but cold and wet as he sank down, down, down until Damir heard what he thought was God singing a lullaby to the sleeping cherubs in heaven. He opened his eyes, shook off his vision of death and was quickly drawn to the stateroom where a sweet, impassioned voice caressed a gloriously romantic melody.

Now, music is the divine expression of the soul. Tyrants—or men who at one time were tyrants, or would be tyrants—lack a conscience and their souls are corrupt. One might speculate, then, that a man with a corrupt soul cannot but feel that music is irrelevant, a waste of time. Many tyrants have used music in the past as a tool, as propaganda, provoking and riling the masses with patriotic marches and hymns. But it would be difficult to imagine a tyrant sitting in the comfort of his living room listening to a minuet, a symphony or cantata, and allowing it to fill his soul with transcending love. Not *love* in the sense of a temporal infatuation or lust, but love in its purest form, love as the worship of life.

Damir grew up in a home where music was as alien as a book on Serbian folklore. His father did not care for it except during a military parade or in church, and Marija—well, she subjected her pastimes, her likes and dislikes to her husband's. Of course Damir had heard music before, in the streets of Florence, Zagreb and even in Banja Luka. He had heard Nikola whistle all kinds of tunes at one time or another. Also, just before they sought sanctuary in Travnik, the family stayed with friends whose youngest son played jazz records from America. All that was very well, but it did not affect Damir one way or the other. But the sounds coming out of the musical cabin sent a shiver up and down his spine, every nerve in his body became a tingling wire, his heart came almost to a stop, he gasped, tears swelled up in his eyes, emotion choked him, his brain was unable to put together one thought and his whole body shook. How was Damir supposed to know he was listening to love?

He approached the room where the music was coming from. The door was ajar and Damir looked inside. The room was enormous and easily the most luxurious cabin in the *Afortunato*, with walls paneled in rich, dark mahogany, a large chandelier, supple leather chairs, thick Persian rugs, ornate lamps and a grand piano in the center. Standing next to the piano, accompanied by a tall, brown woman with thin fingers that resembled spider's legs, was a chunky little man somewhere in his mid-fifties, with a swarthy complexion and black, slicked-down hair. He was dressed in a dinner jacket of crimson silk, black velvet loafers stamped with a gold crest, and a bright red ascot; the man also had a very broad neck and a mouth that could not have opened wider.

Damir turned around, leaned against the outside wall and began to cry. The anger and melancholy that he had kept buried beneath layers of remorse poured out like a stream of sorrow when the tenor reached for one of those high notes that makes legends of fat little men.

"*Scusi—*"

The singing stopped. Didi was shaken from his reverie by another, equally beautiful sound. This time it was a girl's voice speaking Italian, a girl about his age, quite adorable, with the softest yellow hair and large sparkling blue eyes that seemed to laugh aloud even when she did not. She was dressed in a delicate flowing white gown adorned with ruffles and pink trim that matched her soft, rose-colored cheeks, and the daintiest pair of white satin slippers Didi had ever seen.

"Isabella—" crooned the little man from inside.

"I'm coming, Papa!" returned the girl before she turned once more to Damir. "Well? What are you doing? What is your name?"

It was to be a night of magnificent disparities. Damir was so flustered he was unable to remember his real or assumed Spanish name. Instead, he wiped away the tears, stared at Isabella for the longest time before he summoned enough courage to point to the wide throat in the red ascot and ask "Who is that?"

"That is the greatest tenor since Caruso," claimed Isabella. "The magnificent Beniamino Gigli, my papa."

Didi was going to say something else but did not have time. Isabella took him by the hand and led him to Gigli. "Papa, this boy will not give me his name but I think it's because he's overwhelmed by your 'Nessun Dorma'—" Isabella stopped, took a short breath and added, "as well he should." Isabella left Didi standing in the middle of the room and walked to the great Gigli. "Is he not gorgeous, Papa? I think I am in love with him," she declared to her father.

Damir's brows made such a deep furrow and his eyes opened to such a degree that Gigli was forced to explain, "Please, don't be concerned. Isabella is a romantic, and it's my fault. It's what I get for singing Puccini, Verdi, Bellini day and night." And just as Gigli was beginning to ease the boy's mind somewhat, the tenor turned to his daughter and said, "You will make a beautiful couple."

"What is your name?" Isabella persisted.

"Damir."

"Da-mir." Isabella gave each syllable its own musical note. "I am Isabella Gigli and this is Elvira Pucci, my father's personal secretary and accompanist."

"How do you do," said Elvira in a deep, resonant voice.

It was a wonder that such an elegant, impeccable young miss like Isabella never thought that Damir looked like a peasant, that his hair was far too short and very much out of style. In fact, Damir could have been a bald scarecrow; it would not have made a difference.

"Damir?" joined Gigli. "Where are you from?"

"Cr—Spain."

"Crspain? Is that in Spain? I have been to almost every corner of that country, that fine, fine country," said the tenor.

"He speaks perfect Italian," observed Isabella.

Too perfect for a Spaniard, thought Gigli.

Damir admitted that he had lived in Florence as a boy where he learned to speak the language of Boccaccio, Dante and—Isabella. No one, though, forced Gigli to admit that his repertoire included works that he sang all over the world—in French in Paris, in German in Berlin (before the war, alas) and in Spanish in Madrid—and that he could therefore oblige the boy in perfect Castilian.

Confronted by the absolute courtesy of the great tenor and the adoring eyes of his daughter Isabella, Damir had no alternative but to bolt out of the room, leap down a slippery flight of steps and lock himself in his mother's room.

"Didi!" Katarina yelled when her brother ran in and the wind from outside sent the playing cards flying off the table. "What's the matter with you?"

"Shhhh!" Didi quickly locked the door to the room and peeked under the brown curtains covering the porthole to make sure he had not been followed. He sat on the bed, terrified and out of breath for a moment, then jumped to his feet and turned off the lights. Sweat streamed down his forehead, and his eyes had become two tennis balls.

"What's wrong?" asked Marija alarmed. She was about to scream because the rooms in second class did not have telephones to call for help, when a light *tap-tap-tap* at the door forced her to lay her right hand on her breast and hold her breath.

Katarina grabbed the lamp on the night table and firmly held it at the ready but another light *tap-tap-tap* was heard, this time, followed by the sweetest nightingale calling *"Da-mir—"*

"Who is that?" Kati asked her brother in the dark.

"Da-mir, are you in there?"
"Maybe this is not his room."
"I saw him go inside, Papa!"

Marija had heard enough. She turned on the lights only to have Damir quickly try to turn them off again only to have his mother slap his hand away with a warning. Marija composed herself and opened the door. "May I help you?" She was surprised at the sight of Isabella and her short, rotund father.

"Buona sera, signora, my name is Isabella Gigli. This is my father, the great Beniamino Gigli. Where is Da-mir?"

"I think," Marija turned and saw Didi sneaking into the water closet, "he's looking for a place to hide."

The boy was mortified. Marija introduced herself as Madame Dávila, then moved to the side and did the same with Katarina, who was still holding the lamp in her hand. The great Gigli bowed and apologized that it had not been his idea to burst in unannounced; he was forced to run after his daughter—his impulsive daughter—who thought she had said something to offend young Damir because the boy had fled their room suddenly and without explanation. That was all Gigli or anyone else said for ten minutes. Isabella went from one end of the room to the other praising her new friends. She said that Marija was far too young to have a boy Damir's age and claimed that Katarina possessed the most beautiful skin she ever saw. Then, standing between Damir's mother and younger sister, Isabella announced her intentions to marry "Da-mir" as soon as he was willing, which caused the boy to swallow hard, Marija to cough, Kati to scratch her head and Gigli to explain again that it was all his fault for singing Puccini, Verdi and Bellini.

Next, Isabella invited the Dávilas to dinner as she spun and practically did pirouettes around the room. Marija enjoyed the moment more than anyone could possibly imagine. Her polite smile did not express her pleasure in seeing how Damir's eyes—eyes that a few hours before had been depressed and lonely—had taken on a special gleam; they expressed now not fear for his life, or sadness because he missed Saša, but misgivings about the unusual predicament of being pursued, not by murderers and kidnappers, but by an enchanting girl.

Unbeknownst to her children, Marija was delighted to meet Beniamino Gigli. She had witnessed one of his triumphs at La Scala while the Pavelićs lived in Italy. Marija had gone to the opera as the guest of an Italian general's wife and though she did not care much for opera, could not even recall what played that night so long ago, Marija remembered the amazing voice and the ovations every time the great Gigli capped an aria or stepped in front of the curtain. But, the danger to her family had not diminished despite the fact that they were so far from Croatia; Marija had to think about that before she said anything else. "Signorina, Maestro, you do us great honor," she said, "but, really, we could not impose."

"Oh, of course you can," replied Gigli.

Marija smiled and said nothing else.

Later, as Beniamino and Isabella walked back to their cabin, the great Gigli advised his daughter not to speak Spanish to the Dávilas, counseled the girl not to ask Damir or Katarina things like "Where did you go to school," or "What does your papa do?" but keep the conversation in the general areas of what the Dávilas, and not Isabella, liked to talk about. Gigli was not a stupid man.

Not surprisingly, Isabella, Katarina and Damir became inseparable for the remainder of the trip, due both to Isabella's persistence and Beniamino's pledge that the Dávila children would not associate with anyone but his daughter. Marija was pleased because it allowed Katarina and Damir to be like other children, in spite of Gigli's fame, and if only until they reached Buenos Aires. The friendship also relieved some of tediousness and the tension, even if it came almost too late. Katarina and Isabella would have become confidants if not for Beniamino's warning to his daughter about trying to learn too much about the Dávilas. This inhibited his daughter's predisposition to think that everyone was as straightforward as she was.

Kati knew that Isabella genuinely liked her, and she thought the world of Isabella, but she also understood their rapport was based on self-interest. For Isabella, it meant being close to and being able to look at, or talk to, or talk about—Damir. For Kati it was the opportunity to be free from the restrictions set upon her and Damir. Kati was determined to make the best of it.

And Damir? He was allowed to watch the great Gigli at work. The boy sat in a corner of the stateroom, most of the time with his eyes closed, listening to nothing else, seeing nothing else, feeling nothing else but the music and the voice, caressing each other like lovers in an intimate, slow dance. He still thought of Saša, of course. Always. The baby's eyes followed him everywhere, tormenting him with guilt. But that was old news. Now Damir had another thing to worry about. He could not understand why Isabella made a fuss over him. Her uninhibitedness made him wary, and her interest in him made him—nervous. For a while Didi tried to stay back, watch and listen, study Isabella from a distance, but the afternoon following their encounter on the top deck, Didi summoned up his nerve and looked Isabella in the eyes. What he saw surprised him, though it should not have. He saw the perfect goodness of innocence and two sparkling crystal bells that chimed, "I love you."

✥

"But you must, you absolutely must!" laughed Isabella. She was determined to have Katarina at her side while Damir led her off the *Afortunato* in front of hundreds of reporters and important dignitaries, all there to welcome the great Gigli to Argentina.

"My dear," said Beniamino to Isabella, "maybe Madame Dávila, Kati and Damir do not like being tormented by the press or like being blinded by flashbulbs. For us, well, it's part of what we do, but—"

Marija nodded gratefully at the little tenor with the big voice.

"Oh, you will come and stay with me, won't you?" Isabella said to Katarina. "And you will call me, yes?" she entreated Damir.

It was three o'clock in the afternoon. The Giglis and the Dávilas had spent together their last day aboard the *Afortunato*. First, they had breakfast; then, went for a stroll on a gorgeous, cloudless morning. The breeze from the sea was crisp but the waters were calm. Gigli, Elvira and Marija walked in front, Gigli sporting an elegant cape, red ascot and fedora; Marija wearing an out-of-fashion blue dress, a trench coat and hat; and Elvira wearing an expensive, luxurious fur that had cost several little creatures dearly. Their conversation centered on the children. Isabella and Katarina trailed behind talking about everything girls their age shared in common, and Damir brought up the rear to avoid being dragged into his sister's conversation.

Katarina was the first to spot land. Everyone said how happy they were that the long and trip was coming to an end. In fact everyone was sad. Gigli because it was time to deal with the press, interviews, stage directors, more interviews, conductors, more press, artistic directors, receptions for government officials, and worse— other singers; the children because their time together had been such an unusual and fun affair that they wanted to extend it and not to have the normality of everyday life set in; Marija because for two weeks she had avoided thinking about the inevitable, and now the inevitable was about to happen.

After spotting land, Gigli invited the Dávilas to an extravagant buffet for lunch, then decided to treat them to a rare show indeed. He asked Isabella to sing the romantic "Vissi d'arte" for her guests.

Isabella refused. She had studied voice but for a couple of years and felt unworthy of her father's praise. Gigli insisted. In the end, his daughter walked to an empty chair across the room, sat down, set her eyes on Damir and waited for Elvira to play the first notes.

A frown marked Isabella's brow and softly, ever so softly she extended the sad pianissimo *"Vissi d'arte, vissi d'amore–"*

The voice was like a silver thread, each delicious musical passage kept aloft by the most delicate modulations. It was vibrant, dynamic, every phrase expressing the passion and anguish of the betrayed. The voice became suppliant, then challenging. Isabella reached out to heaven, and, just as it began, the pianissimo faded and the lament claimed a love that could not be denied, not even by death.

"Bravo! Bravo!" Gigli rushed from his seat to kiss his daughter. The Dávilas joined the tenor with no less enthusiasm, Marija and Katarina crying out "Magnificent! Fantastic!" Their applause almost drowned their cheers. Only Damir remained in his seat, staring at Isabella, dumbfounded in open-mouthed reverence.

There was a knock at the door. Gigli, still clapping, rushed to answer while the Dávilas congratulated his daughter. Beniamino found the captain of the *Afortunato*—hat at his side—the first officer, and two men dressed in long, dark leather coats, hats and sunglasses who had made their way from shore in a dinghy. They carried a message for Madame Dávila. Gigli invited them to step inside but the two men declined, asking instead to speak with Madame Dávila in private.

"Yes?" asked Marija.

A minute later Marija was gathering Katarina and Damir. "We must go," she said in a way that made them understand they had to. Marija thanked Gigli and Isabella for their countless attentions and an incredibly lovely day. It was time to say good-bye. Beniamino bowed and remarked that it had been a pleasure for the Giglis to have met the Dávilas. Katarina and Isabella kissed and embraced. Damir stood aside for a moment, before walking to Isabella and doing the only thing he thought was correct. He took the girl's hand and brought it to his lips.

"Oh, please, give her a kiss," urged Katarina. "She's not going to bite you."

Isabella looked up at Damir and waited. Didi looked at Isabella for what seemed a lifetime, then leaned forward and gave Isabella what could be described as a stiff kiss on the cheek, stiffness in this case the result of anxiety and lack of air in his lungs due to the accelerated beating of his heart.

In formal greetings and farewells, the kiss is nothing more than a mechanical convention. Many times, the cheeks of the participants simply brush one against the other and the lips are excluded from the exercise. In this case Damir did give Isabella a kiss, even if its execution was feeble and wan. Fortunately for Damir, Isabella gently seized his face and kissed him firmly and lovingly on the cheeks. "Da-mir," she said in the same musical way she first pronounced his name. As she stood looking up at Damir, Isabella took out a paper from a little pocket in her dress. It was a piece of personal stationery with *Isabella Gigli* embossed delicately at the top and sprinkled with her favorite cologne. Inside, Isabella had written the name, telephone number and the address of the Alvear Palace Hotel. Isabella folded the small piece of paper with much care, took Damir's hand and placed the note inside. She looked at Damir and her eyes glistened. They were so sad and fair Damir had no choice but to look away.

"Stop this, you're going to make me cry," said Gigli to his daughter. "I'm sure Damir and Katarina will call you as soon as they can."

It was all over quickly—the good-byes, the kisses and embraces—much faster than anyone thought possible. The Dávilas were escorted back to their room where they remained for two hours after the boat docked. The Giglis went ashore and were engulfed in a mass of adoring fans—and the press. "*Gigli! Gigli!*" Every few seconds Isabella looked up at the *Afortunato* hoping to see Damir. She did not.

On the way to the hotel, Beniamino remarked that as they disembarked, another limousine—its windows draped with black curtains—was parked at the opposite side of the pier, while a man, much like those who had escorted the Dávilas back to their rooms, stood leaning against the car looking sullen and unfriendly.

Perhaps, thought Isabella, the Dávilas were members of a royal family traveling incognito.

"The possibility," answered Beniamino, "is quite remote."

12

It was dark when the Dávilas walked off the ship. Rubén crammed the luggage in the trunk of the car. "Welcome to Buenos Aires, señora," he said in Italian. "El jefe is waiting for you at the house."

"Who?" asked Marija, looking at Didi.

"Il capo," clarified Rubén.

"Who is that?" asked Didi.

"Your father—I think?" Rubén slammed the door to the trunk. The bodyguard was as tall as Katarina, which meant he was tall for a girl but short for a man. He was thirty-four years old with a face that did not require to shave every day. His skin was fair and his hair light brown. His eyes were black and very round, while his mouth was very small and featured a protruding lower jaw and wide cheeks that gave Rubén the look of an imbecile. A scar swooped down from his left earlobe halfway across his cheek and gave the impression that Rubén was a man of extremes, likely to bash someone's brains in with a hammer, or stab or shoot them in the heart, all of which of course he would gladly carry out as long as he was paid. Rubén was not the type of man the government security services employ; those sorts are thugs with political affiliations. Rubén was best described as a *babysitter*, a goon without political views. In any case, the scar was not a wound acquired in the line of duty but was a result of childhood neglect. He was dressed in brown pants, a cream-colored shirt, a white tie, patent leather shoes, a hat, a medium-length brown leather coat, and a shoulder holster with a Colt .45 automatic pistol tucked snugly under his arm—an enormous weapon for such a small man to be lugging around.

Once the Dávilas were secure in the big, black American car, they raced through the boulevards of Buenos Aires heading for Caseros. Didi remarked that Argentina was cold though it was the middle of summer. Marija explained that the country was far south of the equator; when it was summer in Europe it was winter in Argentina.

"Like Australia," observed Didi.

"Like Argentina," clarified Rubén, who was very proud of his country.

They entered the city limits and cruised the streets as the city got ready for its nightlife, which held as much promise as its day life, which left the in-between an afterthought. Buenos Aires was bigger than Zagreb and far more colorful and modern than Florence, thought Damir; at least it looked that way at night. The boy wondered what the city would be like in the daytime. Didi looked out the window on the left side of the car as Katarina looked out the window on the right. Marija did not care to look out either to the left or the right, but stared straight ahead, her face taut and serious.

"This is the Avenida 9 de julio, named for our day of independence. It is the largest city boulevard in the whole world, much bigger than Park Avenue in New York," said Rubén turning his head toward the back just enough so his passengers could hear him.

"You are taking us home, yes?" asked Marija.

"Si, si. We will be there in about fifteen minutes." Fifteen minutes that went by with the speed of the *Afortunato*. No one except Rubén said a word. "Have you ever been in Argentina, madame?"

"No."

"It's a great, beautiful and vast country," announced the bodyguard with patriotic fervor.

"Excuse me, sir—" said Marija, leaning over to make sure Rubén did not miss a word of what she was going to say.

"Please, call me Rubén."

"Rubén, as you probably know, we have had a very long and tiring two weeks on a boat. I do not mean to be rude but I am not in the mood for conversation. Please, get us wherever you are taking us, to meet whoever—"

"Your husband. You're going to—"

"Let me finish!" Marija raised her voice enough to make sure the little bodyguard would not interrupt again. "Just drive, please—quietly."

If someone had asked Rubén at that moment to name the worst sin in the heavens and the earth, he would have removed his hat, scratched his scarred cheek and without another moment's thought said, "Ingratitude." Ingratitude after he had been friendly when he did not have to be, after he was helpful when it was not expected of him, even when he had driven out of the way (his passengers did not know this) to enchant the new arrivals with the marvels of the most magnificent city in the world. To be ungrateful was worse than to be unfaithful and el jefe was obviously married to a stuck-up, ungrateful German bitch, which forced Rubén to swear never again to display his friendly disposition or to play tour guide. Her loss to be sure, *pendeja*.

"I think we should go to the opera," remarked Damir, still looking out the window.

It was past nine o'clock when the gate to the house opened to allow the Pontiac inside. Ante turned on the perimeter lights from the study and the grounds turned bright as day. Rubén drove the limousine into the garage, turned off the engine, climbed out and waited for everyone to get out of the car.

"Where is my husband?" asked Marija, straightening her dress.

Rubén took off his hat, turned around and walked into the house. Marija and the children followed through the garage door that led into the hall.

Ante pretended to be looking at an atlas when Marija entered. Then Damir came in, followed by Katarina.

To the husband it seemed much longer than three years since he had seen his wife and children. The wife, he thought, had put on weight; the wife thought her husband looked old and tired. Damir thought his father's eyes were dead; the poglavnik was surprised at how tall Damir had become; Katarina remembered her father as being a much bigger man; Ante Pavelić thought his daughter had turned into a lovely young woman.

"At last," said Ante. "Rubén, please take the luggage upstairs." The bodyguard nodded, tweaked his nose and left, closing the door behind him. If Ante had been an optimist, he would have expected that after so long his family would rush into his arms. But he was not an optimist and his arms were not stretched out to receive anyone, even if in a surge of feeling and blinded by the moment anyone had dared to do so. Marija," Ante beckoned his wife.

Marija approached slowly and kissed her husband on the cheek, then stepped to the side waiting for the children to do the same. Katarina approached her father with a daughterly, though quite formal kiss, but Damir stood his ground and simply nodded to acknowledge his father was in the room. Ante followed with the only thing that came to mind. "You are hungry, yes?"

The family sat around the kitchen table as Rubén emptied the contents of the refrigerator and laid everything in front of them: a ham, boiled potatoes, a few bottles of soda and a leftover bottle of white wine. It was not a banquet but it did not have to be. Though they had every reason to be hungry, Marija, Damir and Katarina did not feel like eating. "Things are different here," said Ante. It was probably the understatement of his life. He asked Rubén to let out the dogs, which meant the bodyguard was dismissed for the night. Ante Pavelić wanted to be alone with his family.

Rubén grabbed his jacket and hat from the counter, opened the door and went outside.

"Is he going to be here long?" asked Marija.

"Rubén? Yes." Ante told his family that the bodyguard only knew the family was not Italian, nothing else. Rubén could not tell a Hungarian from a Bulgarian, or an Albanian from a Rumanian, or a Greek from a Croat; therefore, it did not matter whether the family spoke Serbo-Croatian in his presence or addressed each other by their real names. "And yes, I'm afraid Rubén is—necessary, as are the dogs." He turned to Damir and Katarina. "Two Dobermans. They're not pets, they are necessary," emphasized Ante. "Now—" It was going to be a long night.

The briefing that began in the kitchen moved to the living room after an hour. The family sat listening to their husband and father and watching each other's reactions as Ante explained what life in Argentina would be like. Everyone would have his own bedroom. The rooms were located on the second floor and to avoid arguments as to who got what and why, the bedrooms were already assigned. Their surname was not Dávila anymore but Bianchi. There were many Argentineans and Italians in Buenos Aires with that name. "Bianchi," said Ante Pavelić, was as common and insignificant a family name as anyone in his position or with his special needs would want. To go along with Bianchi, Marija would be Maria, Damir would be Miguel, Katarina would be called Sara.

"Sara! What a ghastly name!" Katarina did not want to be called anything but Katarina and certainly not *Sara*.

"It's a biblical name," explained her father with the most negligible, the faintest, the most imperceptible trace of a smile.

Unfortunately for the girl, the names were already recorded with the immigration authorities, and their identification papers carried the names of Daniel, Maria, Miguel and Sara Bianchi. Miguel and Sara would start school in September, at the start of the next term, because schools in Argentina began in March and it was already mid-July. They were enrolled in a private academy where most of the students were American, English and German. Contact with Croatian or Yugoslavian nationals was prohibited in person, by telephone and most definitely by post.

"You mean I cannot write to Father Draganović?" Damir was determined to bombard the priest with letters asking about Saša.

"Particularly to Father Draganović," Ante replied quickly.

"But—" Damir was not going to give up so easily.

"My sweet, the point is that nobody back home must know where we are, it's that simple," joined Marija.

"You are not little children anymore. I am sure you know that the time you spent at the farm was not for you to learn how to be farmers or sheepherders but because it was necessary for your safety. The government in Yugoslavia has Father Draganović under surveillance. Any attempt to get in touch with the priest would be intercepted by the secret police, and as a consequence we would all be in great, I repeat, great danger," added Ante, looking at his son.

Damir sank in his chair.

"You are not to speak anything but Italian outside the house, or in the presence of strangers. In time you should learn Spanish. That is all I have to say, unless Marija—unless you have something to add."

"What about—" Katarina began to speak but stopped halfway and looked at her brother. "What about friends?"

"Friends?" Ante looked at his wife. He understood what the girl said but not its implications.

"Are they allowed to have friends? I think that is what Kati—"

"Sara," interposed Ante.

"—what she means," added his wife.

Ante looked around the room, got up and walked to the windows draped with dark, green fabric, windows that otherwise would have given him a splendid view of the trees, the lawn and the wall. "What kind of friends?"

Neither Didi nor Katarina had any idea what kind of friends. They supposed that "friends" meant children in school, playing outside, or someone like Isabella. Since neither had ever attended school—they were taught at home by friars and tutors—and since they were never allowed to play on the street, what Didi and Katarina really wanted to know was if they would be allowed to associate with people other than the family and staff, or continue to live in secret and in fear.

"It cannot be helped," replied Ante.

"Nothing's changed! We came halfway around the world and nothing's changed! We shouldn't have come here!" Didi was on his feet.

"Didi—" Marija put out her hand trying to keep her son from becoming too insolent.

It had been a long time since the poglavnik had seen his son. The boy's lack of respect was something he did not expect.

Damir threw his arms in the air, looked at his mother, pointed to his father and repeated matter-of-factly, "Nothing's changed."

"It is time you went to bed," Marija told her children; she wanted to be alone with her estranged husband.

Damir immediately left the room, showing great insensitivity and the kind of manners he had picked up at the farm. He did not say "Goodnight, Father, goodnight, Mother," or "I'm happy to be home at last," or "Until tomorrow." Nothing. He did not even give his mother a goodnight kiss. Katarina, being much younger and having lower expectations was not as frustrated as her brother. She thought that at the least her parents, especially her mother, deserved a kiss.

"I will take the children and go back to Europe. I will not torture them anymore!" Marija said bluntly to her husband.

"That is not your decision. You are my wife and they are my children. You will do as I say."

"No, I will not!" Marija wanted to look out the window, distract her eyes for a second, perhaps find a little comfort for the loneliness and the sadness she felt. But she knew that her husband would object if she tried to open the curtains. "Don't expect us to live like rats hiding in dark cellars or to run away to the mountains again—not again, not ever! It's not worth it." Marija wept. Except for the children, she did not have anyone in the world (and certainly not in Argentina, a country as alien to her as another planet), not a friend, not a brother or sister, no one she could turn to for help. She had married a man who was an embarrassment to his people, and even his Church was keeping its distance. Marija and her children had become irrelevant and had been abandoned.

"What is the matter with you?" Ante was losing patience with his wife. "You obviously have forgotten who I am!"

"I'm afraid that is impossible!" Marija shot back.

It would not do. Insubordination was intolerable, from his wife and certainly from his children. He had enough troubles as it was. Generals were as whimsical as popes and the Pavelićs' stay in Argentina was dependent on that fine, fine line with secrecy, self-interest and profit on one side and international pressure on the other. He could wire Father Draganović and ask the priest to send Marija and the children back, but to where? It did not matter what country in Europe they went to, they would still be exposed to Belgrade's thirst for revenge. America, perhaps? Even so, it would be humiliating if word got out to Croatians around the world that their poglavnik could not control his wife and children. "Fine. What do you have in mind?" asked Ante. It was time to compromise.

Didi's room was bigger than the niche he had shared with Saša in Travnik. He sat on the spacious bed and thought of his little friend. He got up and went to the large window that looked out to the back of the house. He saw the shed the bodyguard lived in and two shadows patrolling the grounds, silent, vigilant, deadly. Didi looked at the sky and there was the moon, an Argentinean moon, one that spoke Spanish and did not share his secrets. "Tell your cousin back home that nothing's changed." He opened the window but a crack and paced back and forth. The bedroom was devoid of charm, without pictures on the walls or books on the shelves. Didi threw himself on the bed. He wished to wake up in Travnik with Saša and Pero, and it took him a few seconds before he began humming "Vissi d'arte." "Da-mir," he said aloud, imitating Saša. "Da-mir," he said in a sing-song, imitating Isabella. "Da-mir." Welcome to Argentina.

Next morning, the Bianchi family woke for the first time to the stunning brilliance of a perfect Argentine sunrise, which as every Argentinean will tell you, outglows every sunrise in the world, so much so that the *Sol de mayo* (the sun of May) has center stage in the Argentinean flag, symbolizing Argentina's bursting through the clouds when it proclaimed its independence from Spain in July of 1816 (that the sun of May is bursting through clouds in July does not seem to bother Argentineans).

Daniel Bianchi left the house at seven, not because he had pressing business to attend to but because he preferred to let his wife and children familiarize themselves with the house and the grounds as they began another period of adjustment. Damir was first to rise. As a matter of fact, he was up long before his father, since the steady bed and the absence of waves crashing against the sides of his room prevented him from sleeping most of the night. The boy was going to wait until his mother called him to breakfast, but decided to go downstairs when he heard his father drive off in the company of the bodyguard. Didi put on a pair of pants but did not bother to put on a shirt or shoes before he walked out of his room and down the cold marble steps. First, he stopped in the kitchen, opened the icebox, did not find anything worth munching, so he continued the exploration of the house through the dining room and by way of the living room, which took him into the library. In another place and time the door to Ante Pavelić's private study would have been locked and under guard by the Ustaše and Damir would never have contemplated going in. The study was Ante's sanctum sanctorum and not even Marija dared violate its privacy. Only Ante Pavelić and God knew what terrible secrets were locked behind the little gold knobs that pulled the delicately sculpted drawers of the dark wooden desk, and only Ante Pavelić and God would continue to hold the secrets because Damir was not interested in secrets, terrible or not. He was not interested in anything that had to do with his father. Damir *was* interested in the brown square box sitting on a small table, next to a floor lamp on the other side of the room. Slowly, cautiously, as if the room were a sacred archeological find with trap doors ready to spring death upon the intruder, the boy walked to the phonograph and lifted its cover. He tilted the bulky metallic arm, held it for a second and put it back in place. Then, Damir took his finger and carefully turned the turntable around and around. As the boy entertained himself he noticed that the wall behind the phonograph was full of record albums stacked one on top of and next to the other, from a few centimeters off the ground to a few centimeters below the ceiling, all in alphabetical order and classified by type of music: ballads, zarzuelas, jazz, symphonies, concertos and, in particular, opera.

Kati thought she was dreaming. Like her brother, the girl had trouble sleeping without the rocking of the sea. After hours of thinking, worrying about what had happened between Damir and their father, she tossed around in bed until one or two in the morning and finally succumbed to fatigue. It was almost nine o'clock next day when the booming tenor was heard throughout the house.

"*Ridi pagliaccio!*"

Kati opened her eyes, disoriented. But she quickly regained her bearings, jumped out of bed, dashed out of the room and ran into her mother in the hall. Marija looked just as puzzled as her daughter and far worse for lack of sleep. They rushed downstairs and into the library where they found Damir with a wide grin on his face. "Gigli!" said the boy proudly, showing off a 78 rpm disc with Beniamino's picture on the cover.

"Get out! Get out, I said! Now!" It took a scolding and threats of all kinds to get Damir out of the room. The boy argued, he stomped, he pouted, he supplicated, he reasoned, he beseeched and in the end, whined so his mother would allow him to stay in the room to listen to the music. Marija was firm; Didi had no business being in his father's study, which he knew perfectly well was forbidden.

"Would you ask him for me, then, please, if I can listen to music when he's not home?"

"Ask him yourself!" Marija shoved Damir out of the study.

"I don't want to talk to him!"

"Then, I guess you won't listen to music!" Marija shut the door to the library and returned upstairs with Katarina, leaving Damir standing in the hall. It was not that she was afraid to ask Ante to let Damir use the phonograph; no, it was not that at all. Marija felt it was essential for everyone's peace of mind that Damir become more conciliatory toward his father. Forcing father and son to communicate on any level could prove useful.

Damir remained by the door to the library for ten minutes; barefooted, shirtless, bewildered and angry Damir. Finally, he marched off to his room and did not come out until his father returned home at two that afternoon. As soon as Ante had sat down in his study, Damir knocked on the door, waited for the "Come in," and entered to talk to his father for the first time—in a manner of speaking—in three years.

"Sir, I need to talk to you."

Ante was taken back by his son's assertiveness. "Yes?"

"I would like, sir—"

As Ante looked at listened to his son, he imagined a thousand different reasons why Damir wanted to talk to him. Did Damir want to go back to Croatia? Did Damir want to move out and live on his own? It was not unthinkable; the boy was certainly old enough. How old was he, anyway? Ante tried to remember his son's age. Damir was already taller than his father. Did Damir want to go to work and not go to school? Did Damir want to be sent to school in another country? What was it Damir had in mind?

"To listen to music."

"What was that?"

"I said, sir, I would like to listen to music," repeated the boy. What is this boy talking about, thought Ante. "Music?"

"Yes, sir."

"Where? What music? Explain yourself, please." In the seven months Ante had lived in the house he never noticed the brown box until that moment, when Damir pointed it out to him. "What is that?"

"A phonograph. I would like your permission to sit here and listen to records," added Didi. He was ready to argue his case as forcefully as he had done with his mother, maybe more—by threatening to run away.

"Yes, of course," said the poglavnik without hesitation. "Certainly you can listen to music, if that's what you want."

"It is what I want, with your permission, sir," added Damir.

"Fine." Ante was relieved that the request from his son had not been unreasonable.

"Thank you," Damir inclined his head and was about to walk out when—

"Damir—"

"Yes, sir?" The boy did not turn to face his father, but closed his eyes, his hopes dashed; Damir was convinced that in the brief moment it took him to walk to the door, Ante had changed his mind.

"I have a better idea. Why don't you wait until I leave—I'll be leaving soon. Why don't you wait and take that machine, and all the records if you want, up to your room?"

This time Damir did turn around. "To my room, sir?"

"Well, that way you can listen to music anytime. I don't care much for music these days."

Damir nodded, quickly closed the door, let his broad smile and pounding heart lead him to the kitchen, fixed himself something to eat, finished his meal in five minutes and waited for his father to leave the house.

Marija and Katarina spent their day working around the house cleaning, arranging furniture, taking trophies off the walls and for the most part, adding what the house had lacked ever since the old mariner was cast off, the charming touch of a female that often transforms four walls into a home. It took Damir two days to move the twenty-odd thousand records from the study to his bedroom. He spent all his time, day and night, listening to opera. Sometimes his mother knocked on the door and ordered him to turn the volume down. Many times the request was accompanied with a threat. Damir sat on his bed, lay on his bed, walked around the room and sat by the window following the music with the accompanying libretto (in Italian). Sometimes, he also tried to sing along, something Katarina did everything to discourage. Damir was slowly creating a world for himself where the only sounds were operatic highs and lows, sounds that for very brief moments made him forget who he was, where he was, why he was there, his love for a child in a distant land, and the confusion that a delicate name embossed on a perfumed piece of stationery provoked. Isabella. It had been almost a week since he last saw Isabella. Did he dare give her a call?

"Mother—" Damir had waited all morning and afternoon; waited until his mother had taken a short nap and was rested; waited until she sat down in the kitchen for a cup of tea, which was when Marija was in her best humor. The boy also made sure Kati was in the room. He knew his sister would help to explain that it was a matter of honor for them to call Isabella.

"Honor?" Marija smiled at her daughter, not daring to smile at Damir so as not to embarrass him.

"I told her I would call her, Mama," said Kati.

"God knows what she's going to think of us," added Damir.

"We can't say we're going to do something and not follow through," continued Katarina. "It's not proper."

"Not at all," seconded Damir.

Marija looked from Damir to Katarina, then turned her eyes to the cup of tea. She sipped her drink and thought how generous the Giglis had been to her children.

"We gave our word, Mother." Damir thought Marija was taking too long in giving her answer.

Marija looked up at her son but remained quiet. She realized that Damir was not calling her "Mama" anymore. She tried to think back to when the change from "Mama" to "Mother" had taken place. She liked it better when he called her "Mama." There was a sweetness about the word, an innocence that was lost in the way he said—

"Mother!"

"I'm sorry, I was distracted."

"Did you hear me?"

"As I remember, I never heard either of you tell Isabella you were going to call her," said Marija with an expression far too serious to be sincere.

"Of course we—" Katarina began to protest while Damir tried to think if that had actually been the case.

"I heard Isabella tell you to call her. I saw Isabella give Damir the note with the telephone and the rest. But, *you* tell her you were going to call? No, sir, I did not hear that. I'm quite positive I did not."

"Well—" Damir was fishing not only for words but for a reason to call Isabella. "Don't you think we should?"

"Ah, that is something else altogether," observed his mother as Rubén entered the kitchen with a newspaper in his hand.

"El jefe wants to talk to you, señora," he said, then turned around and left.

Marija finished her tea, rinsed the teacup in the sink, dried it with a clean rag and put it away in the cupboard. "I'll ask your father." She was about to leave the room—

"Mother—"

"Yes, Damir?"

"It's a matter of honor," said the boy seriously. Then, he looked at his sister and waited for his mother to leave the kitchen before cracking a smile.

Marija found the door to the study open and Ante writing in a small notebook while the bodyguard sat close by reading the newspaper—all about a soccer game between Córdoba and Rosario. "Marija—" said the poglavnik without looking up; he continued to write for a moment, then turned to the bodyguard. "Rubén, will you please—" The bodyguard folded the newspaper, placed it under his arm and left the room. "Marija, we should employ a servant." Ante did not feel it was appropriate for the wife of the poglavnik to be sweeping, dusting and cleaning like a housemaid.

"I did that and more at the farm," said his wife.

"Yes, well, this is not the farm. Do you have any objections to a servant?"

Marija had no objections. The only problem was that she did not speak Spanish and could not, therefore, interview the candidates herself. Ante had anticipated that and already had an applicant in mind. It was a woman recommended by a friend at the foreign ministry, someone with excellent references, hardworking, wonderful cook, humble and of a quiet disposition. "And she speaks some Italian."

"No one related to your friend outside, I hope?" said Marija, referring to the bodyguard. "The last thing we need is a little female brute making soup."

"No," said Ante softly.

"And she's not kin to any other thug that works for you?"

Ante stared at his wife for a moment, then he almost laughed. "You are more insolent than ever, Marija," he said before returning to his writing. "I'll have the woman come by. You can talk to her. As I said, she speaks Italian. You can make up your mind yes or no. One more thing—" Again, Ante stopped his note-taking and this time put down his pen alongside the notebook and leaned back in his chair. "The children look like peasants." Ante did not mean that his son and daughter's refined features had become crude or that his heirs had been transformed into country bumpkins by the mountains of Travnik. What he meant was that Damir and Kati's dress was unacceptable.

"It's been years since I bought them new clothes."

"We're living in very cosmopolitan, extremely fashion-conscious and sophisticated city," said Ante. He took a small envelope from the desk and handed it to his wife. "Money for clothes. If you need more, tell me." Although the envelope was small, the bills were not. The envelope also had a piece of paper with the name of a store where she should go. "Rubén will take you there when you are ready." Ante assumed the discussion was over. It was not.

"Damir needs a haircut and both children need to go to a dentist and have a medical examination. It has been too long, far too long."

"Yes, of course—very important. I'll get a few names of doctors and dentists. As far as a haircut, well, I have a man who comes to the house to cut my hair. I'll have him drop by day after tomorrow—at noon. Anything else?"

"I think we need a gardener. The front of the house is beginning to look like a jungle and jungles breed vermin."

Ante picked up his pen and made a note to that effect.

"And the children want to call on a friend."

Ante continued to write until he came to the end of the page. He slowly closed the notebook, clasped his hands, placed them on the desk and gave his attention to his wife. "Say again?"

"The children want to call on a friend," repeated Marija.

"Friend? What friend? Who?" asked Ante. "And where did they make the acquaintance of this friend? How long have they known this friend and what do you mean they want to call on the friend?"

Marija related the story of Isabella Gigli and her father, how they met on the *Afortunato* and how much the children enjoyed each other's company. Isabella and her father were going to be in Buenos Aires only a few weeks and were kind enough to ask the children to call on them.

"Gigli! Gigli! Gigli! Gigli!" thought Ante. "He is a singer," he said softly, which, as Marija knew only too well, meant the poglavnik was upset.

"An opera singer," Marija clarified.

Ante did not care for the distinction. The singer was followed everywhere by photographers and the press.

"And a daughter who was quite taken by your son." Marija could not repress a smile.

Ante pushed back his chair, stood up, walked around his desk and made his way to the window. He drew open the curtains, allowing a flood of light into the room—not because he thought it was dark in the room, but to symbolize how vulnerable the family would become if he allowed Damir and Katarina to call on their "friend." Ante went on to say that he could also have the protective wall around the house removed, dismiss the bodyguard, get rid of the dogs and have his picture displayed on one of the many billboards around the city. But, he added, why go through the trouble? All he had to do was go to the opera, have his picture taken with Beniamino Gigli and be murdered at the end of the week!

The lecture lasted fifteen minutes and only when he talked of being murdered did Ante's voice became nearly inaudible.

"No one will take pictures of my children." Marija was indignant. She was not a fool, she knew precisely what to do, and as she said before she was not going to allow Damir and Katarina to become reclusive paranoids. The children needed to enjoy what was left of their youth.

Why not choose someone less inclined to get themselves on the cover of every magazine and newspaper in the world? Why not the daughter of a mason? Why not the children of a bookkeeper? Why not the son of a clerk? Why did it have to be a singer, and why did it have to be Gigli!

The point was irrelevant because Damir and Katarina did not choose Gigli, Isabella chose Damir and Katarina was going along for the ride.

The poglavnik stood at the window for the longest time, his eyes staring out into space. He was debating ten alternatives at once. Since he did not like any of the ten, Ante chose number eleven. "Do as you please," he said, and left the room.

Marija heard Ante's footsteps as he walked to the end of the hall, heard him tell the bodyguard to put away the newspaper, heard Ante go out by the side door, heard him get in the car and shut the door, heard Rubén start the car, heard the door of the garage swing open and the rusting iron hinges of the front gate creak, and finally Marija heard the limousine drive out into the street and into the afternoon traffic.

13

Isabella and Beniamino Gigli were in their apartments on the top floor of the Alvear Palace Hotel. The rooms were the most opulent, the most comfortable, the most unreasonably expensive the hotel could provide the great Gigli, who insisted on nothing but the best for himself, his daughter and his secretary, each room providing a degree of luxury and elegance befitting the opera luminary. The hotel, along with most of its decor, was reminiscent of a French chateau—a chateau in the Recoleta, an upper-class section of Buenos Aires. Each room had exquisite lace curtains on the windows, a classic collection of works of art on the walls, sparkling chandeliers, luxurious sofas and beautiful Persian rugs covering shiny hardwood floors. For the entertainment of its guests, the management of the Alvear Palace provided a radio and a phonograph, both imported from the United States. In case Maestro Gigli was not satisfied with the excellent international cuisine served in one of three restaurants that indulged the hotel's guests to the point of absurdity—such as the time a local movie star demanded to be served broiled pheasant with poached eggs resting on two rings of Hawaiian pineapple—his accommodations included a full kitchen and a chef was on call day and night. In addition to everything else, the hotel provided a grand piano so the maestro could rehearse and vocalize in comfort.

If someone happened to ask Manolo Ortiz, the general manager of the Alvear Palace Hotel, why Beniamino Gigli received such extraordinary courtesies, the manager would simply have answered that it was nothing special, because all guests at the Alvear Palace Hotel were treated with similar graciousness.

At that moment, however, Isabella's mind was not on the amenities of her quarters. "Papa, do you think he lost the paper?" The Dávilas—or rather, Damir—had not called Isabella.

"No, my darling, I don't think he lost anything," answered the tenor putting on his overcoat while Elvira called for the car. "And if he did, either his sister or his mother would remember the name of the hotel. It is the most famous hotel in the country. All Damir has to do is look up the telephone number in the local directory."

"But what if he does not have a directory? Or a telephone, Papa?" Isabella walked to the window and looked up at the Argentinean sky, which had lost its haughtiness and become despondent.

"Then it does not matter whether he has lost the number or not, my darling."

"But Papa!" cried Isabella.

"Elvira, my love, wait for me in the car. We'll be right down." Beniamino handed his libretto to the tall brown woman with spider-leg fingers, indicating that he needed to be alone with his daughter.

Isabella had not been the same since getting off the *Afortunato*. Every day she asked at the front desk for messages and every day she was disappointed. When Gigli and Isabella went out, the girl seemed listless and worried. Although she tried to be cheerful around her father, she missed Damir—or whatever the boy's real name was. "My sweet, what is it with Damir? Why are you so—" Beniamino did not want to use the word "smitten" or "infatuated" but, truth be told, the girl was showing all the signs of being in love for the first time and first loves are always quite unsettling.

"He needs me, Papa!"

"Ahhhh." Beniamino did not ask his daughter why she felt that Damir needed her. "Isabella, I have never lied to you in my life and I never will. It is possible you may never see Damir again."

"Why! Oh, Papa, don't say that, please don't!" Isabella threw herself on the sofa and wept.

"Not because he may not want to see you, my lovely, but because he may not be able to. We don't know anything about him or his family. The war just ended. There are a lot of people leaving

Europe for many different reasons, some not quite honorable. Damir is not a Spanish name, neither is Kati nor what was their mother's name—" Beniamino tapped his forehead.

"Marija," said Isabella between sniffles.

"Right. If they are Spanish I'm a goat. Heaven knows why they came to Argentina. I hope there's nothing to it and they're just being—eccentric. But, remember how the mother did not allow Damir and Kati to meet with anyone else on the boat? In other words, my love, I think that their name is not Dávila, and God knows what it really is. I hope it is not Bormann or any such thing. That would create untold difficulties."

"Who is Bormann?" asked Isabella, wiping off her tears.

"Martin Bormann, Hitler's secretary."

Not too far away, but far enough in other ways that physical proximity was irrelevant, Damir indeed wanted to call, but would not; Marija said it had nothing to do with her and refused; but Katarina was more than happy to call Isabella. She called the hotel from the telephone in the downstairs hall.

"Alvear Palace Hotel, good afternoon," answered the operator.

"Isabella Gigli," said Katarina to the operator.

"Isabella Gigli? *Un momento, por favor*," returned the operator, and Katarina was able to understand everything she said—well, all except *por favor*, because *un momento* meant exactly the same in Spanish as it did in Italian.

"Lo siento, pero no contestan. ¿Quiere dejar un mensaje?"

Katarina looked at her mother and shrugged. It was as far as she could go with the hotel operator.

"Scusi, ma non—"

"Ah, parla Italiano?" Nothing like an operator at a first class international hotel.

"Si, si—Italiano!"

"Non ce risposta da la habitazione de la signorina Gigli. Vuole lasciare un messagio?" Which meant that no one was picking up in Isabella's room.

"Si, grazie. Communicarli a la signorina Gigli che la ha chiamato Kati e Damir. La chiameró piú tarde." Kati and Damir

had tried calling her and would call later. Marija did not allow Kati to leave the telephone number to the house.

"She's with her father," explained Marija. "Just keep trying."

They did. Katarina called five times between four and six in the afternoon. Isabella was still not back. By then, it was too late.

Two hours after Damir and Katarina tried to call the hotel the first time, Supi, an affectionate nickname for Supencio Martinez del Arrollo, was looking at the guest book while his staff of several clerks, ten bellboys, and three telephone operators busied themselves registering guests, signing out others, carrying luggage, delivering flowers or a bottle of champagne, answering telephones and, as a matter of course, simply running the Alvear Palace Hotel with the efficiency worthy of its fame. Supi was a short fellow about fifty years old, had a dignified bald spot on the front of his head, and the grey hair on his temples was perfectly coifed—as was his thin, grey mustache. As usual Supi was dressed in tails, with a white carnation attached to his lapel and a watch chain hanging from his vest pocket. He was the quintessential, ever-efficient hotel whip, one who at the moment was trying to find a way to bump a guest from his suite in order to accommodate an American movie director arriving that night. The guest about to be thus inconvenienced was not an important guest, just one who should have gone elsewhere during his brief stop in Buenos Aires; he was not important enough (as evidenced by his meager gratuities) to be a guest at the Alvear Palace Hotel. All the same, switching guests from one room to another was not a practice Supi approved of, and it was one he thought especially unwise for an institution such as the Alvear Palace Hotel. Besides, the situation had now become more complicated than it should have been, thanks to the arrival of Beniamino Gigli. Bumping guests was a procedure that required special handling. That meant extra effort and extra time, time Supi could not spare. The lobby had turned into a mob scene, with dozens of reporters wandering about, dignitaries coming in and out at all hours of the day, and, what was worse, crowds of other artists and singers, some of them quite well known, marching through the vestibule accompanied by their retinues—all paying homage in one way or another to the great Gigli.

As Supi focused on *Suite 315*, he failed to notice two men approach his green marble station. They were dressed in long black leather coats, wore black hats tilted to the right, and hid their expressions behind dark glasses. The two tried to gain Supi's attention with a very friendly and eloquent "Psst!"

Supi turned slowly, raised his left eyebrow, looked the men over—he thought they resembled a pair of apes—and said in a voice that sounded like an upper-class Englishman's, though he spoke Spanish, "Yes?"

The men pulled out badges identifying them as members of a government security branch, the sort of government security branch that demanded Supi's attention. "You're the front desk manager," said the shorter primate.

"I am," conceded Supi.

"Gigli," said the big baboon in two syllabic bursts.

"The maestro?" Supi raised his right brow to match his left.

The orangutans exchanged looks. They did not know if they meant the maestro or not. They thought Gigli was a singer and since *maestro* meant "teacher" they were confused. Perhaps the front desk manager was talking about someone else. "The singer."

"The same man," assured Supi.

The security chimps wanted to know if Gigli received a lot of telephone calls during the course of a day. Supi replied that indeed, that was the case but that as a service to the great Gigli, all calls, including those made to anyone attached to the star, were personally screened by Supi to keep opera devotees from pestering their idol. "Is there something wrong, gentlemen?" The idea of calling them *gentlemen* was a nice touch, thought the manager, one that indicated his unmistakable superior breeding.

The tall gorilla took out a piece of paper and slipped it across the green marble. It was a list of names, he told the front desk manager, and if anyone whose name was on the list called Gigli or anyone in Gigli's group, the call was not to be put through, under any circumstance, at any time, regardless. "Do you understand what I am saying?"

Supi read one of the names. *Damir*. What kind of name was that? But, Supi understood very well. He remembered his brother-in-law, who did not want to understand when two apes like the ones standing across from Supi dropped by his store with a simple request. The brother-in-law ended up in the hospital with both his knees shattered. *Katarina*. Where did these fellows get these names? Yes, Supi always made a point to help the authorities, always. *Marija*. Clearly, the names were foreign. All Supi had to do was paste the names on the switchboard, give the operators their instructions and *"finito."*

"We will know if a call gets through," said one of the gibbons, although Supi did not catch which one because he was still looking at the paper with the foreign names when they vanished in the crowd.

Supi rang for a bellboy, and a short thin lad of about thirteen, with red hair and a face full of freckles, immediately appeared at the marble station. He stood at attention in front of the manager just as he had been trained. "Very good, Mr. Ferrín, sir, excellent. Please put out your chest a little more if you can; otherwise, it is excellent," declared the manager.

"Yes, sir!" Young Mr. Ferrín pulled in his stomach and expanded his chest as far as he could and inadvertently held his breath for too long.

"Breathe, Mr. Ferrín, please take in air or you will collapse and wouldn't that be a pretty sight." Mr. Ferrín exhaled and regained his color. "Now, sir," continued Supi. "Will you be so kind as to ask Doña Inés to give you any and all messages she may be holding for Maestro Gigli or for any member of his troupe. Please do so quickly and bring them here at once, sir." Supi nodded to indicate that the boy could fly to the head switchboard operator. "Keep your chest out sir!"

The boy was gone and back in a minute with a fistful of small rectangular slips of paper that Supi recognized as being from the hotel's message pads. "Thank you, Mr. Ferrín, back to your post, thank you," said Supi, waving the boy away. The manager looked over the messages intended for Gigli, reading the names of the callers carefully to himself. "My, this *Kati* has been busy! There must be a dozen *Katis* here. I wonder how the name's pronounced. What *is* a Kati, anyway, is it a man or woman?" Supi smiled as he separated the *Kati* messages from the others. "We will never know, I guess." Supi then took all the messages that said "From Kati," tore them up, threw them in the wastepaper basket and made his way to the telephone room to have a chat with the operators.

Katarina tried calling the hotel another six or seven times, until eleven o'clock that night. "Try again tomorrow," said Marija to her son and daughter, and kissed them goodnight.

Next morning Damir was up at five and woke up his sister at seven. At seven-fifteen brother and sister were calling the hotel.

"Who may I say is calling? One moment, please. I'm sorry. Line's busy. Would you care to leave a message?"

"Who may I say is calling? One moment, please. I'm sorry. No answer. Would you care to leave a message?"

"It's Damir and Kati. Two names. Damir, D-a-m-i-r; Kati, K-a-t-i. We'll call later."

"Maybe they don't speak Italian," suggested Damir after his sister had put down the receiver.

"Sure they do!"

"Do you think—" Damir began but could not finish the thought. The possibility of Isabella not wanting to talk to them was so painful, the boy could not even put it into words.

"One way to find out," said Katarina reading his mind.

"How?"

"I'll tell them I'm someone else," answered Kati with a smile.

Except that if Isabella was really trying to avoid them, getting through by lying might make things worse. Isabella's anger at the deception would be even more bitter than her disinterest. "No, it's not right," concluded Damir. "Besides, they know your voice by now."

"Then you call and tell them you're her uncle."

"Uncle!"

At that moment their father came downstairs. Damir and Katarina said a perfunctory good morning and retired to Damir's room to try and make sense of what was happening. It was inconceivable for Damir and Katarina that Isabella's friendliness would have been a pretense. Impossible! Unfortunately or fortunately, depending on one's point of view, because of their sheltered life, Damir and Katarina had never experienced the duplicity of human nature as expressed in hypocrisy. Evil, yes; but evil is not hypocrisy. Hypocrisy, simply stated, is the practice of insincerity and although most evil people are hypocrites, it is also true that there are many evil people who are perfectly sincere. Even their father, whom Damir thought was the most horrible person in the world, was not a hypocrite. Perhaps, thought Damir, Isabella had decided she did not care to be friends with him or Katarina. That was not hypocrisy but a change of heart. Everyone has the right to a change of heart, even though they may break someone else's along the way. And last, it was possible that Isabella was uncomfortable with the inconsistencies and doubts surrounding the Dávilas. In that case, who could blame the girl for not wanting to get involved with people who had so little to offer and so much to hide?

Late that morning—after Katarina was told for the eleventh time that the Giglis had gone out and would not return any time soon—Marija took the children shopping for clothes. They went to a store in a narrow lane off Avenida Diagonal Norte, in the heart of Buenos Aires. They spent three hours at the clothing emporium, known for its small but distinguished clientele and its discreet proprietor, Señora Almirón. The señora was a Portuguese woman who had lived in Sicily for a number of years before the war and had left the increasingly belligerent atmosphere of Palermo in '39 to move with her family to the more peaceful Buenos Aires. She was small and stout, about sixty-four years old, with a friendly, unfading smile. She had established herself as a merchant of high fashion for upper-crust Argentineans; all the merchandise in her store was imported from New York, Paris and Milan (all, that is, except the leather goods).

The outing to Señora Almirón's marked the first time Marija had taken Damir and Katarina to buy clothes. Between "That's ghastly!" and "I'll never put that on!" or "I'd look like a fireman!" (remark from Damir after his mother suggested a red shirt), in addition to "Can't we go somewhere else?" and "I'm hungry!" it was an experience Marija was not likely to repeat soon. In the end, she dismissed her children's objections, suggestions and comments and bought them enough clothes and shoes to last them through the year. Señora Almirón escorted the group back to the limousine and encouraged Marija to drop by again anytime.

On the way back to the house, Katarina asked her mother if they could "drop in" at the hotel and see if Isabella had arrived.

"People like us do not 'drop in' on people like the Giglis. Remember they are not here on vacation, but to work on the show."

"Opera," corrected Damir, who was thinking of Isabella.

They drove through Plaza de Mayo and the Casa Rosada, the official residence of the Argentine president. Of course, they did not know it was the Casa Rosada because Rubén refused to tell them. "They're nothing but a bunch of Russian assholes anyway," thought the bodyguard.

It was six o'clock when they arrived at the house. Katarina and Damir called the hotel several more times without success and continued to do so until they went to bed at eleven-thirty. But Damir was not tired and it was impossible for him to do anything else but conjure up reasons why Isabella did not want to talk to them. How could he sleep, how could anyone even think of doing so? Impossible! He spent an hour by the window playing "Vissi d'arte," thinking how much better was Isabella's singing of the famed aria. Didi stared at the moon. Could it be that Isabella was looking at the moon at the same time?

It was two o'clock in the morning when he tiptoed downstairs in the dark and dialed the telephone number he had memorized. He waited for almost a minute before the night operator picked up.

"Alvear Palace Hotel, good evening," said Hortensia in a tired voice. It was obvious she had been taking a snooze.

"Buona sera," said Damir to let the operator know he spoke Italian, not Spanish.

"Buona sera."

"Isabella Gigli," continued Damir.

"Gigli. Ehh—" the operator hesitated for a second. "It is very late. Is she expecting your call?" asked the operator.

Damir had to lie. There was no way around it. To find out if Isabella was a fraud or the loveliest creature he had ever seen in his life, Damir had to say, "Yes."

"What is your name, please?" the operator followed every protocol.

"Eduardo." Two lies in less than one minute.

And the operator put Damir on hold while she took the last precaution—she called the room.

Isabella had been asleep for two hours, although her sleep was not a comfortable one because she had been thinking of Damir. Had she frightened him off? Maybe he did not like her. Maybe he did not exist. Who was Damir? And so Isabella cried herself to sleep. The telephone rang, startling her. "Yes?" she said, half asleep.

"Señorita, Eduardo is on the line."

Damir stood barefooted in the cold room but he could feel the perspiration trickling down his neck. He knew the operator did not believe his name was Eduardo.

"Eduardo," began Isabella, "I don't—" In less than a second Isabella might have cut off all possibility of ever seeing Damir again, except that, from deep in her memories—memories of a lost boy she met on a ship called *Afortunato*—Isabella had a hunch that this was not a mistake or a prank call. "Put him through!"

"Go ahead, sir," said the operator.

"This is Isabella—"

"Isabella!" Damir's throat was as tight as could be without a halter.

"Is it you!" Isabella sat up in bed. "I've been waiting for you to call! Why didn't you?"

"But we have! We've called and called, left all kinds of messages!"

"Oh, dear, sweet Damir, where are you?"

Click. The line went dead. At the sound of "Damir," the operator—the very conscientious telephone operator—disconnected Damir from Isabella. Hortensia had stayed on the line to make sure the call was legitimate. Too late. She knew that as soon as Don Supi found out she had put the call through she would be discharged, in spite of her tenure, in spite of her seven children.

"Damir!" called Isabella from her end. Why did he say he was "Eduardo"? And where are all the messages he said they left? Why did the operator cut them off as soon as she said "Damir"?

"Isabella—" Damir stared at the receiver while he stood in the midst of shadows in the hall. "You fool," he thought. "She's been waiting for you to call! She hasn't been trying to avoid you, Damir, but someone is trying to keep you from talking to Isabella!" Damir quickly dialed the hotel again. This time the operator sounded like she had been crying—Damir heard the sniffling on the line.

"We were cut off," said Damir to the operator.

The operator put him on hold and then simply disconnected the call.

"I will call again and again until I speak to Isabella Gigli!" said Damir after calling a third time. He was furious and determined to stay up all night.

"I am sorry, sir. It won't do any good to keep calling," said Hortensia.

Hortensia thought that perhaps Beniamino Gigli was trying to keep his daughter from an unworthy suitor, because as soon as she had disconnected the boy, Isabella Gigli was ringing from her room demanding to know why the telephone conversation was interrupted. "I'm sorry, señorita," said Hortensia, "I have my orders." Then, the operator rang off.

If it had not been two-fifteen in the morning, Isabella would have stormed into her father's bedroom for consolation and an explanation of something she did not understand. Damir, on the other hand, was far less patient, and he crept quietly up to his sister's room.

The bronze Zeus was holding up the world (in the shape of a light bulb) with his hands. Instead of shaking Katarina out of her sleep, Didi turned on the light and pointed Zeus at Katarina. "Kati, wake up! Kati! Kati!"

It was another minute before Katarina sat up in bed, looked around, identified her brother and asked in a manner that showed she was still not fully awake, "Where am I?"

"Listen!" said Damir urgently. "I talked to Isabella!"

Katarina rubbed her eyes. "What time is it?"

"Past two."

"Why is it so dark outside?"

"In the morning! Will you wake up! I'm telling you—I talked to Isabella!" Damir shook his sister just a bit.

"Talked to Isabella! You did? When?" cried out Katarina just as Damir thought of going into the bathroom for water to splash on her face.

Damir refused to say anything else, for fear their mother in the next room might wake up. Once in the kitchen, brother and sister sat across from each other, leaning forward in their seats, their heads almost touching, with only their grey silhouettes visible in the nebulous, predawn light.

"Maybe the operator said that it was useless to call again because it was so late," observed Kati.

Damir did not think so. Someone was trying to keep Damir and Katarina from Isabella. Who? And why? The *why* was much easier to understand than the *who*.

Beniamino? The tenor had seemed to like Damir and Katarina. If not, he certainly could have stopped their friendship aboard the *Afortunato*, instead of waiting until they arrived in Buenos Aires.

Marija? Their mother liked the Giglis, and besides, Damir and Katarina knew that she would never lie to them. And suppose they put aside those very strong arguments; Marija would still need a way to prevent the calls at the hotel from getting through to Isabella. That alone meant she needed access to the telephone operators of the hotel and authority do have them do her bidding. It was, in fact, impossible. Then who?

"What's this!" Ante stood at the kitchen door, groping for the light switch with one hand and holding a gun in the other. It was the same Walther PP-K, the same small black gun Ante Pavelić used to murder Saša, the shepherd boy.

Damir was transfixed. The boy did not see the hand that held the gun or the man attached to the hand. Didi became unconscious of his sister and the room they were in; he only saw the diabolic little pistol. Suddenly, with the strength of years of suppressed outrage, the boy screamed, "No!" He threw himself at his father. "Kati, run, get away, he'll murder you, run get away! Murderer! You will not murder my sister! Murderer!" Damir knocked Ante to the floor—and was very lucky the safety catch on the gun was on, or it might have fired accidentally as it rolled off to the side. Ante had buzzed Rubén from his room before venturing downstairs to investigate the noises he heard in the hall. This was fortunate for Ante, because Damir was pounding him with all his might while yelling, "Murderer!" Marija heard the commotion and arrived on the scene about the same time as the bodyguard, and that too was a blessing, because the bodyguard would not have been able to pull Damir off el jefe unless he shot the boy, something that could possibly have cost Rubén his job. It took the combined efforts of the bodyguard, Marija and Katarina to stop Damir from beating up his father.

Then, it was up to Marija. "What have you done, you villain!" she screamed, slapping Ante across the face.

"Mama," screamed Kati, "Papa did not do anything! He did not do anything!" She helped the bodyguard hold back Damir.

"Are you mad!" Ante grabbed his wife's hands to keep her from hitting him. "You stupid fool! I heard a noise and—"

"Murderer!" screamed Damir, then, collapsed.

A few hours later, the songbirds skipped from treetop to treetop. Mornings in Buenos Aires are a spectacular affair, and Supi was admiring the beginning of another day from his office window. It was a small office with a telephone, a typewriter, a few pictures of dead relatives, one or two watercolors depicting the majesty of the pampas, and not much else, though it was quite enough for someone who spent all day running up and down the lobby supervising his staff. He was having his morning coffee and toast, enjoying a bit of peace before the morning rush, when Manolo Ortiz, the general manager of the Alvear Palace Hotel, called him on the phone. Ortiz did not waste time exchanging pleasantries. "Please, come at once to 8111."

8111 was, of course, Beniamino Gigli's suite. "What is wrong now?" thought Supi. He put down his coffee, looked at his watch and confirmed it was eight o'clock in the morning. He straightened his tie, made sure the flower on his lapel was as fragrant as when it was plucked, then made his way with a cheerful step to the elevator, quickly made it to the top floor and gingerly stumbled into a fiasco—which like any disaster, is never mindful of when it strikes.

Gigli stood by his daughter, who was sitting on the couch.

Sitting at a table on the same side of the room was Elvira. In the center of the room stood the general manager, sober for once, thought Supi, and looking more agitated than usual. Ortiz was an man of average everything—height, looks and age—all of which placed him around forty-eight years old. He wore an ordinary suit, though, like Supi, he also kept a flower in the buttonhole of his lapel. Ortiz did not have a mustache and preferred instead to keep all his brown hair on top of his head and on his thick eyebrows, which arched asymmetrically over his tortoiseshell glasses.

"Supencio," Ortiz addressed his front desk manager formally to indicate the seriousness of the issue, "Maestro Gigli has a complaint."

Complaints at the hotel ranged from getting a glass of tepid orange juice to having pigeon droppings on your window. The front desk manager knew that Ortiz would get around to the complaint sooner or later—and he was right. Ortiz explained what had occurred the night before between Hortensia, the operator and Isabella Gigli when a call came in at two in the morning.

"The operator said she was following orders when she disconnected my daughter from a friend. Whose orders? I want to know, who dared give the order to have my calls intercepted!" demanded the great Gigli, in a voice that would have been better suited on an operatic stage.

"I have informed the maestro," said Ortiz, "that it is not our policy to intercept or to listen in on the telephone calls of our guests. Anyone doing so will be dismissed on the spot. To my knowledge, in my fifteen years as manager of the Alvear Palace Hotel, this has never happened before."

Ignorance is bliss, thought Supi. He allowed the great Gigli to rage for five minutes, until the tenor ran out of breath and had gained considerable color.

"Don Manolo," said Supi at last, "may I have a word with you—in private?"

"In private!" bellowed Gigli. "I want you to know, sir, that the minister of culture is on his way here, as is the artistic director of Teatro Colón, who I believe is a personal friend of Madame Perón! Let's see if they want to talk in private when I tell them I am going back to Rome. I, Beniamino Gigli, will not sing in Argentina! This is a disgrace!"

"Maestro, I am sure it is nothing but a misunderstanding; please bear with me a moment." Ortiz then turned to the front desk manager. "Supencio, anything you have to say, you can say in front of the maestro, and I suggest you do it now!"

"Very well," said Supi, taking out his watch and looking at the time. He confirmed it was nearly eight-ten in the morning. "Yes, as much as I loathe and repudiate the practice," began the front desk manager, "some of your calls are being—as you say—intercepted."

"But—on whose orders?" inquired the general manager.

"This is—" Beniamino roared as loud as if he were singing *Pagliacci* at La Scala, "infamy!"

Someone else, some other spineless soul, would have dropped to his knees, embraced Gigli's ankles, kissed the tenor's feet and begged for mercy. Someone else maybe, but not Supi. He stood his ground, took out his watch, noticed it was eight-twelve, and told of the visit paid to him by two members of a security branch of the government, and their ensuing conversation and request.

"Why was I not informed of this?" the general manager demanded to know.

"I was preparing a memorandum when you rang just now," explained the front desk manager.

"It was *I* who should have been told at once!" screamed the great Gigli. "Did you, for a moment, consider the consequences of your shameful enterprise?"

"Shameful? Tsk, tsk, Maestro," Supi grimaced as if the stench of folly permeated the suite. "I think a better word might be *judicious.* I do not, never have, never will involve myself in other peoples' affairs. I do not, never have and never will care who *anyone,*" by his emphasis on the pronoun Supi apprised those in the room that the guidelines applied to all members of the human race, regardless of fame or notoriety, "who anyone consorts with, talks about, or is connected to. However, sir, when two properly identified detectives—I assume the two men were detectives in one way or another—request that I do my duty, my patriotic duty, and exercise my limited authority as front desk manager of the most prestigious hostelry in the world to intercept a few telephone calls—an action, that as I said before, I feel nothing but contempt for, sir, but that, as it might be related to national security was deemed absolutely necessary for reasons no one has shared with me—then, sir, I am afraid that Supencio Martinez del Arrollo has no choice but to nod, assent and comply." Supi's exposition, which lasted, by his own estimate, forty-five seconds, befuddled every one present, and taking advantage of their temporary inability to speak, the front desk manager added, "Perhaps, Maestro, if I told you the names of the people I was asked specifically not to put through it might help elucidate our differences, yes?"

"What were the names?" asked Isabella.

"They are foreign names, señorita," continued Supi with a frown. "One sounded like *kitty*, although I'm sure cats had nothing to do with anything. You must forgive my pronunciation but I've never heard names like these before. The other was Didi something or other, and the last was Marica or *Mariachi*—" Supi executed a flourish with his right hand, then put both hands behind his back and smiled.

"Oh, Papa!"

"For your information, sir," Beniamino addressed the front desk manager, "Damir and Kati are two children my daughter befriended on the way to Argentina. Are you telling me that in your country children cannot talk to other children!"

Beniamino was comforting his daughter when the doors to the suite flung open and Don Anastasio Gómez, minister of culture of Argentina and Don Fulgencio de Jesús, artistic director of Teatro Colón, the national opera house, entered with great dramatic flair.

"Finalmente!" cried Beniamino Gigli.

"Maestro! What is going on?" asked a very worried minister.

"Nothing! And not even opera will be going on!" With that Beniamino Gigli began fulminating against Argentina, the Alvear Palace Hotel and its staff of spies, especially the front desk manager, who did not look at his watch again until he left the room.

The minister and the artistic director took turns trying to convince the great Gigli not to cancel his engagement. "It would be a scandal," exclaimed the white-haired minister. "A national disgrace," added the thin, balding artistic director. "The president and the First Lady are expected opening night!" added the minister. "Maestro, we have a contract!"

"Oh, indeed, we have a contract." Beniamino moved to the piano. "As you know, in that contract is a clause which allows me to cancel any one or all performances if I get sick." And Beniamino Gigli developed a sudden cough and sneezing fit the likes of which had not been seen in Buenos Aires since the last outbreak of the flu.

The minister and the artistic director looked at each other panic-stricken, then the minister turned to the hotel managers. "I want you to know that if Maestro Gigli cancels I will personally see to it that both of you are fired, and you—" the minister turned to Supi, whose flower had wilted, "I will have you shot! Now, get out! And no more hanky-panky with the phones!"

"We are at your service," said the general manager.

"Sirs!" added the front desk manager as both retreated, bowed, turned and fled.

"Maestro, what is it you need from us?" asked the artistic director.

"I want to know who is trying to keep my daughter from talking to her friends, that is all, nothing much, is it? I want to know who has been so brazen as to dare meddle in my affairs. Otherwise, I am sure you can get del Monaco to sing for you. He's not Gigli, but then again, who is?"

The minister and the artistic director immediately held a mini-conference in a corner of the room, while Beniamino turned to Isabella and whispered, "This is all very strange!"

It took the minister and the artistic director less than a minute to get back to Gigli. "Maestro, we will find out what we can," said the artistic director.

"In time for opening night, I hope," said the great Gigli, between two wheezing coughs.

14

Damir moved about the room; it looked the same as before. The ceiling was just as low and Didi had to watch out for the crossbeam where he had bumped his head more than once. His bed was there, but Saša's crib was not. Damir guessed Ana had taken it back to the cellar since there was no longer a need for it. Damir thought how much he missed the baby. "I won't forget you, ever. I love you, Saša!" And where was the shepherd? Damir was sure Pero would be happy to see him. He wanted to tell the old man about Argentina and Isabella. The window was open and the moon was so beautiful, casting its unreal glow on the top of Mount Vlašić; there were many more stars than Damir remembered. He looked down on the empty space where Pero used to rest his bones after a long day in the field. "Pero!" No answer. The cot was gone, the dog was gone, the washbowl was gone. Where is the old man? "Pero, where are you, it's me, Damir!" The boy heard a wail from the house. Damir followed the moans and sobs. He left the barn and found himself in Ana Draganović's bedroom. There was a woman Damir had never seen before sitting by the door. She was in her late thirties and was crying. On the other side of the room was a little boy about six years old. The child had fallen asleep while kneeling beside the bed, his arms pillowing his head next to Ana Draganović's body. She was lying face-up, her arms crossed and her rosary, that string of beads she loved to play and pray with, held between the fingers of her left hand. "Ana—" Didi said in a voice that only he could hear. Then he noticed the clear veil covering the old woman's face and the lit candles around the room, most of them spent; the trails of white smoke accumulating on the dark ceiling. Damir had been fond of Ana. She had been kind and loving with him, she had been kind and loving with the baby. Where was the priest? Just as he thought of Father Draganović the door opened and remained ajar for a moment. Didi heard men's voices nearby. Then Ana's son joined the vigil. Father Draganović looked older and tired. He was dressed in work clothes. The woman sitting beside the bed took his hand and kissed the ring. It was a ring Damir did not remember. It was a bishop's ring. Draganović crossed himself, stood at the foot of the bed, said a prayer, walked to the little boy, and gently picked him up and carried him outside. Damir followed them to the attic. Once there the priest lay the boy on the bed Damir remembered as his own, took off the child's sandals, tucked him in and left the room. A moment later the little boy reached under his pillow and took the svirala, the little flute Damir had given him back long, long ago. How could he have grown up so fast? Was Damir having a dream? No, it was too real to be a dream. Damir caressed the boy's face, then kissed it. "Saša!" whispered Damir. "I love you." It was no more than a wisp of breath, yet somehow Saša must have felt it because his eyes filled with tears as he held the svirala to his cheek.

Damir was tired. His travels about the uncharted plains of the spirit upset him. It had been two weeks since he relapsed into the depression that almost killed him as a child, a depression that now reappeared due to the separation from Saša and the trauma of seeing his father holding a gun, as it seemed, on his sister. As before, Damir lacked the will to rise from bed and ate so sparingly he began to lose an alarming amount of weight. His eyes were bleary, tearful and expressionless, as if his life force had fled to where memories are stored to give comfort in trying times. Marija and Katarina took turns keeping him company, and music, the music Damir loved so much, played softly in the background all the time, in the hope that it would stimulate the boy's sensory awareness. Two doctors examined Damir, one an internist, the other a psychiatrist, and both insisted that he be placed in a psychiatric hospital for treatment with drugs and shock therapy against manic depression. It was that or face death. After eleven days, Damir's health deteriorated to a point where Marija agreed to have him committed.

In the middle of the turmoil caused by Damir's illness, in the midst of a series of charges and recriminations between Pavelić and his wife that threatened to expose their festering life together in more ways than one, there appeared on the scene one day, as if dropped by parachute, Juana Fritz, or the Fritz, as she came to be referred to.

It happened three days after Damir fell sick. Katarina heard the bell and looked out the door. She cast her glance across the lawn and saw a woman standing by the gate, waving from under a newspaper. Katarina did not know the woman, concluded she would not understand if spoken to in Italian, and so called Marija, who did what Katarina could just as easily have done—she called out, "Si?"

"Juana! Juana Fritz!"

"It's the maid," said Marija to Katarina. "Where are the dogs?"

"In the back."

"Open the gate please, darling." Marija motioned to Juana to wait a moment, while Kati ran to her father's desk and pushed a little green button on its side. Immediately, she heard the creaking of the heavy gate and by the time she returned to her mother's side, Juana Fritz was at the door.

Juana was in her mid-forties, tall, thin, with thighs like saddlebags and a neck and head resembling that of an ostrich. And yet, she was not so much ugly as curious to look at. It is true that her nose, black eyes, mouth and ears were too small to be in proportion with the rest of her features, and she kept her black, abundant, straight hair under a yellow handkerchief she tied in the back. It is also true the Fritz was often described as "undecorated," but she had a disarming wide-eyed smile, an honest face, and beneath the wrinkles and the hair and the distinctive clothing—which consisted of a black skirt and blouse and another piercing yellow handkerchief around her neck—there was an indomitable spirit, a spirit Marija felt would be necessary in dealing with the Pavelićs.

"Señora Bianchi?" The Fritz folded the wet newspaper that had protected her from the drizzle and placed it carefully in her large purse.

"Please, come in. My husband told me you would be calling." Marija liked the Fritz at once, and after a short interview decided to give Juana a tryout period of one month, a tryout period that began immediately.

Juana Fritz was the fastest, most thorough housekeeper Marija had ever seen. The Fritz cleaned downstairs, took care of the upstairs, cleaned the bathrooms and the kitchen, had a bite to eat around noon, and dedicated the rest of the day to whatever else needed done, which many times included laundry and always meant making supper. She was an excellent cook and an enthusiast of Mexican cuisine, so, every once in a while she introduced the Pavelićs to *huevos rancheros*, bean and meat *burritos* and many other delicacies from that nation to the north.

When Damir first caught a glimpse of Juana Fritz he thought he was looking at Marija through the clouded, distorted vision of an sick mind, like the effect of a warped mirror at a carnival. The second time he saw the Fritz he thought she was Katarina. It was not until his fourth run-in with Juana that Damir realized there was someone else besides his mother and sister coming into the room. Juana the Fritz approached Damir with great tenderness. She found out what foods Damir was fond of, then prepared them with special care—to entice the boy to eat. Unfortunately, she did not succeed.

The day before an ambulance was scheduled to take Damir to the hospital, Marija and Ante sat in the study—though not in each other's company—when Rubén opened the door and showed Beniamino Gigli and his daughter inside.

"Maestro." Marija greeted the great Gigli. "It's very kind of you to come. I know how busy you are. Isabella, my darling—"

Beniamino took her hand and raised it to his lips. "How is Damir? We have been very concerned because we did not hear from you."

Isabella did not say anything but rushed to Marija.

Ante stood by his desk as his wife stepped aside and introduced him, not by his real or assumed name, but simply as "My husband."

"Sir!" bowed the great Gigli. "This—is indeed an unexpected pleasure."

Isabella curtsied and again turned to Marija. "Oh, please, may I see him, please?"

"Come." Marija led Isabella by the hand, leaving the great Gigli and Ante Pavelić to get to know each other.

"Please, allow me." Pavelić helped Beniamino with his cape and hat. "I understand—you sing."

Halfway up the stairs, Marija stopped and looked at Isabella.

"I am not going to lie to you. Damir is willing himself to die, for reasons you may find out in time. Please, my darling, I know he likes you, and I'm hoping that when he sees you it will cheer him up. He is sad of spirit, and it's killing him. If his condition does not change for the better he will have to be hospitalized to save his life."

Katarina was holding her brother's hand and was very happy to see Isabella. She greeted her friend with hugs and kisses and immediately let Isabella take her place.

"Da-mir—" said the voice in his dream. "Damir," it said again. The music and the voice were almost one. "Damir, it's me. Isabella. Oh, please, please get well!" Isabella held the boy's hand to her face.

Didi moved his head to the right and remained in that position for a minute. It was enough of an event for Isabella, Katarina and Marija to take heart.

"He said something." Katarina tugged her mother's arm.

"Yes, he did," said Isabella, looking up at Marija. "But, I couldn't make it out!"

Marija immediately sat on the bed and caressed her son's face. "Didi, my sweet, Isabella has come to see you. Speak to me, my love, what is it?"

With a supreme effort, and almost without moving his lips, Damir whispered, "Saša."

"Who is Saša?" Isabella looked up at Marija.

"A little friend back home." Marija wiped Damir's forehead with a damp towel. "I'm sure Didi will tell you about him." And Marija addressed her son once more. "Won't you my darling? Isabella wants to know all about the baby."

Damir shook his head slowly and whispered, "He's—not a baby anymore."

Katarina walked over and stood behind Isabella. "Yes, he is! Of course he is a baby, what are you saying, Didi?" Katarina nudged Isabella on the shoulder.

Damir turned to Isabella and slowly opened his eyes. "How did you find me?"

Isabella answered that Marija had called the hotel and asked them to come to the house.

"Where is the great Gigli?"

"Downstairs, talking to your papa."

Beniamino Gigli did not know the kind of man he was talking to, thought Damir. "Mother—" he said, raising himself on the bed, "show Isabella what I found."

Marija went to the phonograph and picked up a record with Beniamino Gigli on the cover. It was a recording of *Tosca*. "He is wearing it out," said Marija.

"And—" began the boy with a little more energy, "Caniglia does not sing half as well as you." Damir meant Maria Caniglia, the Tosca in the recording, one of the most celebrated sopranos ever. What was a girl to do after such praise from the boy she loved? Isabella threw her arms around Damir and cried.

While Damir and Isabella were getting reacquainted, Beniamino was getting acquainted with Ante Pavelić. "Yes, that is what I do, I sing. And you, sir? I believe Madame Dávila—"

"Bianchi," corrected Ante. "You mean my wife? Yes, the name is Bianchi, not—that other name." Pavelić leaned back in his chair and looked intently at the great Gigli. It occurred to him that the man sitting on the other side of the room was perhaps not a singer at all, but an assassin from Belgrade who had made contact with Marija and the children aboard the *Afortunato*, preyed on their lack of caution, and by way of a complicated and melodramatic ruse had wormed himself into their confidence in order to kidnap Ante's family, assassinate Ante himself, or both.

"Oh, well," joined Beniamino. "What's in a name? That which we call a rose by any other name would smell as sweet," quoted the great Gigli.

Pavelić was not impressed. He did not think he looked or smelled like a rose.

"Do you know," added the tenor, "that I had a very dear friend by the name of Mascagni, Pietro Mascagni. Ever heard of him?"

"No, I can't say I have," replied Damir's father.

"He was a great composer." The great Gigli stopped, shook his head and waved his hand. "Forgive me, he was a *good* composer. He wrote *Cavalleria Rusticana*. Actually, it's the only decent piece he ever wrote," said Beniamino aside. "Anyway, Mascagni was friends with Mussolini and so was I. I'm sure you've heard of Il Duce."

"Of course." Pavelić put his hand in his jacket pocket and looked slightly bored.

"Yes, well," continued Beniamino, "we belonged to a group of artists dedicated to the fascist cause. It's disbanded now, of course." The great Gigli paused and sighed. "I miss the fashionable days of fascism."

Pavelić did not shift in his chair, did not look away, move his hands or indicate in any way whether he was for or against fascism.

"In '33," continued Gigli, "Mussolini held a banquet in Milan for his most fervent and influential admirers, over a hundred and fifty people." The great Gigli crossed his legs. "Halfway through the evening, I noticed a very moody, very serious man in the company of other moody, serious fellows who talked mostly amongst themselves. I was so taken by this man's no-nonsense demeanor that I turned to Pietro—Mascagni, that is—and asked, 'who is that over there?' 'That is the leader of the Croatian resistance, Dr. Ante Pavelić,' he said. Mind, you, this was well before you were known as the poglavnik. Of course, after that, it was only natural that every time I read your name in the paper, I would say to myself 'I know that man.' Small world, is it not?"

It is worth mentioning that Pavelić did not try to deny who he was or set in motion an elaborate fabrication. He simply let go of his pistol and took his hand out of his pocket. "So, you've come to Buenos Aires to sing?"

"Though I said I would not," replied Beniamino.

"But—will you?"

"Yes."

"What made you change your mind?"

"You did." And the tenor smiled but did not offer further explanation.

Pavelić walked around his desk, took out a bottle of inexpensive Argentinean red wine left there by the previous tenant but never uncorked, and offered the great Gigli a glass, an offer the tenor graciously declined. Pavelić put the bottle away, walked to the front of his desk, crossed his arms, leaned back, looked at Beniamino and said, "I want to thank you for the attentions you gave to Marija and the children. I am grateful."

Beniamino waved off the "thank you," as if to indicate that Damir and Katarina's company was its own reward.

"However," continued Ante, "there are a few things I must explain. You are here because my wife feels that having your daughter visit with Damir may relieve—whatever ails him. I am against the association between our families. This feeling has nothing to do with personal likes and dislikes."

Beniamino thought that if the poglavnik opposed Isabella's friendship with Damir and Katarina, his wife did not, and for the time it seemed she had the upper hand. Still, the tenor uncrossed his legs, leaned forward, rested his elbows on his knees, looked very serious and nodded at regular intervals to show that he was not only paying close attention but that he agreed with most of what Pavelić was saying.

"You are a charming man," added Pavelić. "But, as I have tried to explain to my wife, you lead a very public life, whereas we find it necessary to live in seclusion, something that I am sure you are aware of by now, and that cannot change. Please, I beseech you to keep to yourself whatever thoughts you have as to who is what and what is who. I personally find speculation distasteful, futile and at times," Ante paused longer than necessary and lowered his voice, "dangerous."

It was a moment before Beniamino got up, walked to one end of the room, turned around, stopped as if waiting for a conductor to snap his baton, walked to the other side and began to speak, nursing each thought and swaddling each phrase carefully. "What I do, sir, I do for the sake of my daughter. I will say to you that there is very little I would not do for my daughter, save make her unhappy."

Beniamino went on to describe the day Isabella was born, how his wife Edda, a woman he cherished, had given birth and then lived long enough to call out in her faint last breath "Isabella." Edda died, explained the tenor, for no apparent reason except that, perhaps, she had invested the baby with so much beauty, effervescence of spirit, and intelligence, and such a determined and yet thoughtful and generous disposition, that she had none to keep for herself. Isabella spent the first years of her life under the watchful and loving care of her grandparents, playing and prancing in the topiary garden in Gigli's Roman manor where golden butterflies twiddled "The Dance of the Hours," bees buzzed *William Tell*, bunnies whispered nursery rhymes, nightingales sang lullabies, two Persian cats—a white and a Russian blue—constantly hummed *Aida*, Pucho the Pekingese spent its mornings tooting *Turandot*, and a pair of crows—determined to add a little variety—harmonized to *The Magic Flute*. Even Isabella's pony, remembered the tenor, galloped about to the stirring measures of the *Light Cavalry Overture*. "I have tried to make her life one of fairy tales without goblins or stepmothers—evil or otherwise." Beniamino was about to sit down when he thought of something else. "I share with my daughter the adventure, the exhilaration, the satisfaction and the many, many, many privileges of my fame. But, it's not going to last forever. I have about five years left. Fifteen years from now, nobody will remember my name. But, I do not care." This time Beniamino sat down and leaned back on the sofa. "By then, Isabella will speak at least six languages, will have met some of the most important people of our time, will have gone down the Amazon and up the Nile, enjoyed breakfast in New York and supper in Canton!"

"Lucky girl," said Pavelić, amused with the tenor's intensity.

"In many ways she is, in many ways she's not, because she cannot enjoy being with other children, and children need other children. Surely, that is one of the reasons Isabella has become so fond of Damir and Kati." Beniamino stood, hitched up his pants and concluded, "I do not believe, sir, their friendship can be anything but a healthy experience for all three. Still, I am sensitive to your predicament and more than willing to oblige in any way you think is necessary. If you feel that it is too—how shall I say—compromising for Isabella to be with Damir and Kati for the short time we are going to be in Buenos Aires, say so, and so be it. If you do not, you will find me just as accommodating." Beniamino stopped and this time imitated Pavelić in his delivery. "God knows I am a very busy man who does not need to chase after ghosts or have his telephones intercepted."

Later, as the Giglis made their way back to the Alvear Palace Hotel, Isabella turned to her father with eyes full of smiles, smiles because she was helping Damir recover from something she still did not understand but knew was terrible enough. "Well," she began with a laugh, "is Damir's father Martin Bormann?"

The great Gigli looked at his daughter and shook his head. "Worse."

15

It was a slow process, but the effect of the Giglis' arrival at the house proved Marija correct. Isabella became a symbol of hope to the boy, demonstrated in its full power when Damir asked that the curtains be drawn to allow the sunshine to dissipate the gloom in the room. When she visited, the girl never left Damir's side, and she talked, laughed, shared pastelillos, laughed and talked some more. As was her nature, Isabella made plans, plans that included visiting Damir every day, going with Damir and Katarina to the park where they would enjoy long lazy walks in the sun, visiting the museums and the zoo with her friends, and attending Gigli's opening night performance of *Turandot*—all plans for which Damir would have to regain his strength and get out of bed. Every plan was approved by Ante Pavelić, provided that Rubén and two additional bodyguards watched over the children at all times.

It took Damir two days to be strong enough leave his bed, and two more days before Marija allowed him to go outside. That first outing was to the front lawn; Katarina went along with him, to be joined later by Isabella. The Fritz brought out a teapot and a tray of tiny sandwiches and placed them on the grass under the ombu tree. The food went unappreciated until Isabella arrived; then the little squares of bread, cheese and ham disappeared quickly, with Damir eating more than half. A few days later, Damir and Kati (looking smart in their new clothes) went with Isabella—as planned—to the park, where they fed the pigeons, helped a group of children untangle three kites, sat around enjoying each other's company and ate everything in the perfect picnic basket the Fritz had prepared for them. Next morning, they were supposed to visit Beniamino Gigli at the Teatro Colón. At the last moment, Katarina announced she did not feel well and would stay home. Concerned for the girl's health, Damir and Isabella said they would postpone the trip so Katarina would not be left alone. Marija would not hear of it. She refused to let Isabella and Damir cancel, and personally escorted them to the car and sent them on their way. Somehow, their departure had a medicinal effect on Katarina, who got out of bed as soon as her brother was gone and announced to her mother that she was feeling better than she had ever felt in her life.

On the way to the theater, Isabella detailed the process of putting together an opera. "It is the greatest spectacle in the world," she said. "It's greater than a circus and many times it becomes a circus! Can you imagine the sight of a flock of witches flying on brooms across a stage, or the spectacle of immense women—who are for the most part three times the size of the set—the spectacle of those mammoth females feigning death from starvation while they twitter like songbirds on a divan that is half their size!" It was enough to make the young, the very proper Isabella laugh aloud.

Rubén thought the conversation was foolish and showed great insensitivity on the part of the foreigners. It is true they were on their way to the greatest opera house in the world, but along the way so many splendid landmarks dotted every avenue, every side street, that it was stupid to talk about anything else. But what could he expect from two spoiled brats, one Hungarian and the other Italian?

Damir and Isabella arrived at the Teatro Colón where Beniamino was rehearsing *Turandot*; their car (and the small unassuming Fiat following it) pulling up at the backstage door. Damir had never been to a theater before, let alone to an opera house. Opening night was a week away and (as has happened in every theatrical production since the first cave man decided to get up in front of his tribe and scream) everything was behind schedule. The scenery was still being built, the singers were still learning their parts—all except for Beniamino—

the costumes were still being fitted and artistic sensitivities were being relentlessly trampled on.

Isabella led Damir past security; Rubén and one other of his associates followed them inside. Isabella took Damir's hand and showed him the Salón Dorado, with its impressive massive columns, chandeliers and ornate decorations in the grand style of the nineteenth century. A moment later they entered the theater itself, with over two thousand empty seats and elegant boxes where, on any given night, the privileged sat looking like an assembly of music loving penguins. Finally, they climbed up on the stage.

"It's huge!" exclaimed Damir, standing on the boards. The stage was lit by a single work light tied to a iron pipe. Didi had expected to see an ancient oriental city and a thousand orientals singing the music of Puccini. Instead, all the boy could see as he looked up was an infinitely high ceiling with thousands of ropes and counterweights.

From the stage, Isabella and Didi followed a set of tunnels busy with a hundred people going by, with their varied expressions of sadness, exuberance, doubt, exasperation, desperation, outrage, anger and finally horror. At the end of one of the tunnels there was a little room. In that little room, whence the dimmest, shyest light tried in vain to shed its feeble glow upon the universe, the loudest thunder reverberated and shook the legendary opera house. As Isabella and Damir approached, a very short, thin woman covered with measuring tapes, ribbons, needles and pins shot out of the shy little room. Because it happened so fast, it was impossible to notice whether she had left on her own or had been, in fact, expelled by force. Her two assistants—at least they looked like her assistants, because they too were covered with measuring tape, ribbons, needles and pins—flew out from the room with equal violence; one of them, a frail little wisp of a fellow, was in tears as he stood outside the door picking up trousers, coats, belts, buckles and shoes thrown in his face from inside. "You should not be designing costumes, sir, you should be growing figs! Get out of my sight and never, never, come near me again! Fool!" The poor man grabbed his armload of fabrics and leather and fled with a face that had "panic" tagged on its nose.

Damir and Isabella stood outside Beniamino Gigli's dressing room for a moment while the tenor vented another piece of bad news at the stage director. Gigli tore to shreds a libretto in the man's face. "I will stand where I will stand! Who do you think you are, telling me where to stand on that stage! I want you to know, sir, that Puccini wrote the part for me, for me. *He* never dared suggest where I should stand! I will stand where I damn please and you will not tell me where to stand! Now, get out of my sight!" The stage director—an extremely proud and very tall individual who towered over Gigli by at least one and a half meters; who carried himself with great panache, dressed in layers of gold rings, bracelets, silk handkerchiefs and wore large glasses—grew very red, very emotional and very offended. He flipped one of his handkerchiefs over his right shoulder, bowed to Gigli and left the room as "Moron!" rang in the air like a piercing midnight bell.

Damir was, to say the least, hesitant to follow Isabella into the dressing room. Even the bodyguards preferred to keep their distance. To Didi's surprise, the moment he was in the room Isabella cried out, "Papa, look who's here!"

Beniamino turned without a frown or ill humor, all of which vanished with the speed of a false musical note, as the broadest and the warmest smile emerged and Beniamino embraced a disconcerted and still anxious Damir. "Damir, my boy, how are you feeling? Isabella my sweet, how is *he* doing?"

"People in opera," thought Damir, "are bizarre."

At noon, Beniamino invited his daughter's guest to lunch at a quaint, excellent and very expensive restaurant not far from the Teatro Colón. "Maestro!" greeted Armand, the maitre d', with as many bows as his back allowed. "It is *such* pleasure, it is *such* honor to have you with us this day. Yesterday, we were all very sad because you did not come. Oh, the table was crying, she cried and made the floor very wet with the tears. She was so lonely, like a faithful cat when the master goes off to sea!"

Beniamino, his daughter and Damir were immediately escorted to Gigli's table—the same table the head waiter attributed such sentimental powers to, and that was reserved exclusively for the great Gigli.

In fact, the table was rolled out and set in the northwest corner of the room at exactly eleven forty-five in the morning, where it would wait until three o'clock in the afternoon for the Gigli to arrive. If Beniamino did not show up, the table was removed, its linen sent to the laundry, its silver utensils polished, and the entire ensemble returned to a back closet to await the morrow.

The restaurant was nothing more than two discreetly lit and impeccably white rooms with ten tables between them. The walls were decorated with many soft watercolor renditions (originals, as Armand liked to point out) of the French countryside.

"How do you do, Armand?" Two waiters helped Beniamino remove his coat and took his fedora. "Yes, yesterday I went to La Cabaña for a press conference."

"Ah, that insidious little hole in the wall where the bread is always stale and the food—" Armand pinched the ends of his pointy little nose with his fingers. "*Mais, j'ai comprend*! I do! I will go home tonight and flail myself on your behalf in penance!" Armand, a terribly affected man whose French was worse than his hairpiece, was, of course, not French at all but as Argentinean as a bowl of chimichurri. He had a thin head, eyes like a fish, small ears, a mustache of Hitlerian fashion, and was dressed, at the moment, in tails. "Your wine will be right out!" Armand declared, and whipped around, snapped his fingers and called out, "Pepe!"

Joining Beniamino Gigli at any restaurant other than Armand's meant having people constantly stop by the table to ask for an autograph, have their picture taken alongside the great voice, and other impositions to which the tenor was more than willing to submit himself. "Those people," he would say, "pay the outrageous ticket prices to hear me sing. That means they pay my generous salaries and support my extravagant lifestyle." At Armand's, however, no one except the staff was allowed to go near his corner, and anyone trying to do so would be asked in the most polite manner to leave the restaurant.

Rubén sat across the room, keeping an eye on the door with the other security men. Shortly after Beniamino ordered appetizers, Elvira rushed in looking for the tenor. The bodyguard immediately stood in her way.

"Excuse me?" said Elvira in her deep voice, casting a menacing stare upon the little man.

"It's all right," called out Beniamino from his place. "She's with me."

Elvira shoved Rubén to the side and approached the great Gigli. "Maestro, you forgot your lunch with the minister, the president and the First Lady."

Beniamino stared at his secretary for a moment. "Are we too late?" he said, getting up suddenly and with unusual agitation.

"Not unreasonably so," returned Elvira. "The car is outside."

"My darling," said Beniamino to Isabella, "I have to go. I am sorry. Damir, you will forgive me, won't you?"

Damir rose from his chair and Beniamino patted him on the cheek.

"Armand!"

The head waiter suddenly appeared behind Elvira. "*Oui,* Maestro?"

"Only the best for my daughter and her friend!" Armand assured the great Gigli it would be so.

"And those fellows over there," and the tenor pointed to the bodyguards, "tell them to enjoy themselves. My treat." Beniamino kissed his daughter. "I'll see you at the theater," he said, and dashed out the door followed by his tall, brown secretary.

And there it was. Whether by accident or by design Damir and Isabella had their first candlelight lunch. The conversation revolved around opera and the Giglis, which in Damir's mind were one and the same. Damir ordered the veal Florentine not because he knew what he was ordering but because he once lived in Florence, and Isabella savored the grilled trout fillet. Both accompanied their meal with a bottle of wine chosen for them by Armand, and both appreciated several samples from the dessert tray, each item topped with whipped cream.

It was almost two o'clock when Damir and Isabella left the restaurant. Isabella took Damir's arm and suggested they take a walk to browse the displays of the small shops in the neighborhood. Rubén and his colleagues were forced to follow on foot, something they would have preferred not to do after spending the last few hours eating too much meat and drinking too much wine and brandy. Their immoderate midday meal inspired conflicting feelings of gratitude toward Beniamino Gigli and Isabella and hostility toward everyone else.

Isabella and Damir crossed the street to a small park lined with narrow, winding paths flanked by slender palms trees, bushes, iron lamps, two fountains, three statues, and wide benches where old men sat to read the newspapers, young mothers nursed their babies, and lovers cuddled under the midafternoon winter sun.

Talk of opera led to talk of music in general, Argentina, music in Argentina and the tango.

"The what?" Damir never heard of the tango.

"The tango. It comes from here, from Argentina, but it is famous all over the world. It's great fun to dance."

"Do you dance the tango?" inquired Damir.

Isabella thought for a moment. "A little. It is very involved."

"Why?"

"Because you need two people," observed Isabella with a smile. "You should only do the tango with someone you adore."

It would be another minute or so before Damir finally decided to ask Isabella something that he had wanted to know for a long time. "Why do you like me?"

It was a fair question. What had attracted Isabella to Damir in the first place? What was it that made her profess her love for him seconds after she met the boy looking ragged and lost, scared and bewildered that night aboard the *Afortunato*?

"I do not like you, Damir. What gave you that idea?" Isabella looked at Didi with a look of surprise that was returned with greater astonishment.

"You don't?"

"I love you. As to why I love you—I don't know why, I just know I do."

Love, as romantics, philosophers and cynics agree, is nothing short of a confounding miracle that can be both creator and destroyer at the same time. It is a divine spark that sends every particle in the body into a condition of extraordinary happiness or inexplicable despair. It blurs the vision with tears of joy or melancholy; at times endows a person with superhuman strength, while at others it leaves him in a state of total weakness, suffering from headaches and mood swings of depression and elation aggravated by eating and sleeping disorders. There is no formula for falling in love. It appears when one least expects it and withers and dies just as capriciously. It is as impossible to fall in love wittingly as it is impossible not to fall in love when you do. And Isabella had fallen victim to that impish whim of human indiscretion.

"I think we have to talk." Damir took Isabella by the hand and to an empty bench. "You don't know who I am, you don't know where I come from, nothing!"

"Your name is Damir Pavelić. You are the son of the exiled president of Croatia, Ante Pavelić. My father met your father at a reception for Mussolini in 1933. What else?"

"What was Beniamino doing there?"

"Papa, like many others at the time, was a follower of Mussolini," replied Isabella.

"Beniamino Gigli is a fascist?"

"Beniamino Gigli was a fascist."

"Do you have any idea what it is to be a fascist?"

"No," answered the girl. "I know what Papa tells me and what he tells me is that, in those days, Mussolini was a great leader that most people in Italy liked very much. Then, one day, he was not liked anymore and those that were fascist in Italy became something else. I don't understand anything about it, and I still love you."

Damir looked away for a moment, took a deep breath and said, "I know very little of Mussolini, I know too much about my father and when I tell you the things he has done, you will not want to see me anymore."

"That is not possible," said Isabella firmly.

Damir's voice suddenly acquired an urgency, like a signal calling those nearby to flee from danger. "Isabella, my father is a monster, a mass murderer responsible for the deaths of hundreds of thousands of people."

"I love you," was all she said.

Damir told her about Jasenovac.

"I love you!"
Damir told her about Glina.
"I love you!"
Damir told her about Saša.
"I love you!
"You don't care about any of what I've said?" Damir was alarmed.
"Of course I do!" Isabella was truly appalled that Ante Pavelić could live the comfortable life of a don in Argentina while the remains of his victims were scattered throughout Yugoslavia. She felt sick when she learned that as a little boy Damir saw his father murder another child. "Oh, Didi, I wish I could get rid of all the demons that reach out to you in the middle of a happy thought and turn it into a nightmare. I wish they would take over my dreams so you are spared. What can I do to ease your suffering? I will do anything so you can think of love—not death."

"I have his blood! That evil is in every cell of my body!"

"And it will be cleansed and made good by your gentle virtue." Isabella took Damir's hand and kissed it.

Damir was unable to say anything else.

That night Didi did not sleep very well. The day had been perfect, and opening night, the most exciting night (in terms of *good* excitement) of his life, his first time at the opera, was less than two days away. Didi would be there with his mother, his sister and with Isabella. Isabella. Isabella. Isabella—he thought of the name, he thought of the face that went along with the name, the eyes, the smile, the voice—Isabella. Saša would have loved Isabella, he thought. "Oh, God, oh dear, dear God—" Damir buried his face in the pillow and began to cry.

☩

At five-thirty on the afternoon of the performance, Marija and the children were driven to the Teatro Colón by Rubén and one other bodyguard. Marija looked like she used to when she was known as the wife of the poglavnik, the President of the Independent Nation of Croatia. She was dressed in an exquisite black silk evening gown beautifully embroidered with silver and gold, a pearl necklace and a mink stole. Katarina looked just as lovely in her pretty blue dress and silver slippers, but Damir—in his brand new tuxedo—looked positively dashing. The Fritz whistled and stated candidly that the boy was prettier than his sister. Instead of taking offense, Katarina remarked that Isabella would be hard-pressed to look as beautiful as her brother did that night.

"Stop it, you two!" ordered an embarrassed Damir.

The Pavelićs arrived at the theater fifteen minutes before curtain. Isabella was splendid enough—thank you—in a charming green silk gown with grey trim that made her blue eyes sparkle more than usual, and a fabulous emerald tiara that kept her golden hair perfectly in place. She greeted the Pavelićs at the backstage door with her usual hugs and kisses. "Kati! Where did you get that dress? It is positively dazzling. Madame," Isabella turned to Marija, "we must keep an eye on Kati tonight. There are dozens of handsome boys here, especially the son of the Venezuelan ambassador. I'll be sure to introduce him to you." Isabella winked at Katarina. "Of course," continued Isabella, "he's nothing like Damir." And Isabella gave Didi a kiss that made Damir turn very red. "You must forgive me if I'm a little nervous, but I am."

"Is everything all right?" Didi thought that perhaps the great Gigli was not in good voice.

"Oh, yes, it's just—opening night. Papa is as cold as ice. He worries only about his voice, which is what he should do. But me—I worry about everything!"

"Will you sit with us?" inquired Marija.

"Some of the time. You will forgive me, won't you? Papa likes to have me in the wings when he sings."

"Of course, darling, don't worry about us."

"Look at this place!" exclaimed Katarina as she walked through the magnificent opera house. "Isabella, is Evita—"

"No, not yet, but I'm sure the president and Madame Perón will be here any moment now."

The box from where the Pavelićs would watch the performance was but six boxes away from the presidential box. Every box on the mezzanine level of the opera house, including the Pavelićs', was guarded by security men because each box was occupied by someone important, by this or that minister or this or that general or admiral, every one of them waiting for Beniamino Gigli to sing Calaf in *Turandot*. This meant that Rubén, who had to borrow a tuxedo to stand in the hall, was going to have company. As agreed, the Pavelićs would remain in their box until the end of the performance, when Isabella would take them backstage to congratulate the great Gigli and to thank him for an unforgettable evening.

As soon as Marija, Damir and Katarina were seated, Isabella excused herself and rushed to be with her father. An usher arrived with the programs, thin little booklets that described that evening's opera, its cast and some of the future events planned at the opera house.

"He looks thin," remarked Katarina when she saw Beniamino's picture on the cover of the program.

"And tall," added Marija.

"So, Didi, what is this thing about?" Katarina made herself comfortable—as if she expected to sleep through the performance.

"This *thing* is a fantastic opera called *Turandot*," replied Damir with as much condescension as he could possibly pack into an uplifted brow and a sigh.

"Well?" His sister was not going to make it easy for him. "Is it fun?"

"Fun?" Damir rolled his eyes, looked at his mother as if to say, "She is such a child," and described the plot—

Turandot was the last opera composed by Giacomo Puccini, the greatest of operatic composers (according to Damir). It was the story of a Chinese princess called Turandot who has a vendetta against all males, especially those that would like to marry her.

"Why?" interrupted Katarina.

"Never mind why, she does, that's all," said Damir in his most patronizing tone.

So Turandot gives every man of royal blood who wants to marry her—

"Why of royal blood?" interposed Kati again.

"Because she's a princess! She's not going to marry just anyone, you know!"

—Turandot gives every suitor three riddles. If the suitor does not answer all three, he is executed.

"Good for her!"

"Now comes Calaf—that is the role that the Gigli will sing. He is a prince but no one knows it. After an exchange with his father, who was lost and was suddenly found, Calaf sees Turandot and falls in love with her."

"Why was his father lost?" Katarina was curious.

"It's not important!" shot back an impatient Damir.

—Calaf begs to be given the chance to answer the riddles so he can marry the princess.

"That's stupid," observed Damir's sister.

"Do you mind!"

"Kati," Marija was forced to intervene, "let him finish."

"Anyway, Calaf answers all three questions. But now, Turandot does not want to marry him. She tries to have the whole thing thrown out, but her father the emperor does not allow it. Calaf replies that he does not want to marry the princess Turandot if she does not want him, so, if she can guess his name, he is willing to give up his life. Immediately Turandot orders everyone in Peking to find out the name of the stranger so she can have him executed. When nobody can come up with the name, Calaf takes Turandot in his arms and gives her a kiss. Then, he tells her his name, putting his life in her hands. Turandot is so taken by the kiss, she falls in love with Calaf and tells her subjects that his name is *Amor*, Love."

"That's it?"

Damir did not reply but sighed, and was about to open his program when there was a great commotion in the audience.

"*Perón! Perón! Perón! Perón!*"

At the same time, Isabella entered the box. "Kati, look!" Isabella pointed to Juan Perón, dressed in a very becoming Italian suit, and his wife Evita, who matched her husband's elegance with a lovely Chanel gown and a diamond necklace that must have cost many shirts from the backs of the couple's supporters. The crowd cheered: "*Perón! Perón! Perón!*"

Isabella noticed Damir remained in his seat.

"Didi, are you all right?"

A look from Damir and Isabella understood. No, he was not all right. As a little boy, Didi had witnessed similar manifestations, except that instead of *"Perón!"* the crowds cried out *"Pavelić!"* Fascism was very much alive in Argentina.

"I'm sorry," whispered Isabella. She gave Damir a kiss, and left the box.

While Perón and Evita waved to the crowd, Damir returned to the program. He was read about the future productions at the Teatro Colón, when *Maria Stuarda* caught his eye. It was an opera by Donizetti and one of the characters was Elizabetta, that is, Queen Elizabeth of England—

Suddenly, the house went dark and the conductor walked out to the accompaniment of "Bravo!" The man bowed once to the presidential box, once to each side of the house, turned, and the Teatro Colón exploded in a fantasy of music. Damir almost fell from his chair. Real music! Certainly not the kind he was used to cranking out of a phonograph.

When Beniamino Gigli walked onstage, the house went wild. They were not calling out "Perón" anymore, they were screaming *"Gigli! Gigli! Gigli!"* Damir was not crying, but if anyone had seen him then, they would have sworn he was. Tears were streaming down his face as he joined the crowd yelling: *"Gigli! Gigli! Gigli!"*

The first act was over and the curtain call was pandemonium when the great Gigli stepped in front of the curtain for the traditional curtain call: *"Gigli! Gigli! Gigli! Gigli!"*

A few minutes after the lights for the first intermission came up, Isabella joined the Pavelićs again. This time she brought along a little girl with a tray of refreshments. Rubén was tempted to frisk the youngster for a concealed weapon but decided not to, given that she might get scared and spill the drinks.

"You like it so far?"

"It's great!" said Kati.

Marija laughed and Damir could do nothing but shake his head. Isabella remained with them for a few minutes until the first bell announced that the second act was about to begin. Then she dashed off to be with her father.

It is the great talent of the human mind to take one thought and connect it to another by logical—or sometimes illogical—association. When Damir returned to the program he stared at the name *Elizabetta*. The boy had studied enough European history to know that Elizabeth of England had been a great queen. But why did that fact hold his interest? Elizabetta. Isabella. No. The two names were different, no doubt about it. Elizabeth, or Elizabetta, as was written in the program, was Queen of England; it was also the name of the empress of Austria and the czarina of Russia.

The lights went out, Damir put aside the program and was caught in the heavenly music vibrating in the air. The second act ended like the first, with *"Gigli! Gigli! Gigli! Gigli!"* except that, as Beniamino walked in front of the curtain, the audience tossed flowers at his feet. "Just wait," Damir warned his mother and sister. "You haven't seen anything yet."

"What do you mean?" asked Kati.

"Wait," was the only thing Damir said.

"Isabella has not come up this time," observed Katarina.

"She must be busy helping her father," suggested Marija.

Damir read the program. Yes, he thought, Elizabetta and Isabella were two different names. Isabella, of course, was the name of Isabella d'Este, an Italian noblewoman of the Renaissance, famous as a patron of the arts. And then, there was Queen Isabella the Catholic, who made it possible for Columbus to travel to the New World.

The third act of *Turandot* began. Damir laid the program on the floor as the house became quiet, so quiet you could hear people shuffling in their seats. The silence was solemn and absolute as Beniamino Gigli began *"Nessun dorma—"*

Damir edged so far forward he might have fallen off. He closed his eyes, and suddenly every moment, every sight, every smell of that night aboard the *Afortunato* hit him like a tidal wave. He remembered how he almost killed himself had it not been for that voice.

After *"Vincero! Vincero!"* the house sat stunned. For an instant, not a sound was heard after the great aria, when suddenly, there was an eruption of noise so incredible it was heard outside the Teatro Colón. It was not only *"Gigli! Gigli! Gigli!"* but *"Bravo! Bravo! Gigli! Bravo! Gigli! Bravo! Gigli!"*

Screaming so loud that he could be heard above everyone else, calling out "Bravo!" and making such a scandal Evita turned and looked at him from her box, was Damir—on his feet, clapping so hard that his hands hurt for days, and wiping tears from his face. The ovation lasted ten minutes and the great Gigli was forced to do an encore of the most inspiring aria in opera. The second ovation lasted fifteen minutes and only when Beniamino walked off the stage after much bowing and throwing kisses, was the performance allowed to continue.

All of a sudden Damir became very quiet; he stopped paying attention to the music and stared into space. He searched on the floor for the program, and, with the help of a little beam of light that had escaped from the hall, read the name *Carmen*. The opera by Bizet was going to be presented at the Teatro Colón as part of the next season. It was all about a Gypsy—

Damir stood up suddenly, as if his seat been electrified.

"Didi!" Marija whispered loudly and grabbed his arm to make her son sit back down. He would not.

"What's the matter with you!?" asked Katarina.

Damir looked at his mother and sister before rushing out of the box as the opera was reaching its climax. Marija and Katarina dared not make any more noise; they had become the targets of several nasty stares from their neighbors. Rubén ran after the boy and left his partner to look after Marija and Katarina. The little bodyguard waved off the other security men, who were tempted to stop Damir from running down the hall. Didi flew down the stairs, into the main house and out a side door he knew led backstage.

PETER'S CHOICE

"Find the sovereign that will give you comfort and cheer your days."

Damir went to Beniamino's dressing room but did not find Isabella. She was onstage, in the wings, watching her father. "Isabella!" Didi called out. Fortunately, the music was so loud the audience did not hear "Isabella!" Didi rushed past several members of the chorus trying to get onstage, past the stagehands and the stage manager. He looked everywhere for Isabella.

"Damir, what are you doing here? Get out!" Elvira was trying to keep Didi from distracting the singers on stage.

But Damir did not see Elvira, did not see the singers, did not even see the great Gigli raising his arms and his voice; Damir saw Isabella. She was standing stage right, which was a problem because Damir was stage left. "Isabella!"

The girl did not see him waving at her from the other side. There were too many people in the way. The Rumanian brat was going to get hell for what he was doing, thought Rubén.

Damir went out and around to the other side, all the time screaming for "Isabella!" Damir reached stage right.

Isabella could not help hearing him then, even though the trumpets, the bassoons, the French horns, the trombones, the tubas, the drums and the cymbals were sounding and crashing, and a million strings lifted the scene to glory. Damir tripped on two steps that led to the stage, picked himself up and ran to Isabella.

"Isabella!"

"Damir!"

They were finally face to face. Didi was out of breath, and Isabella looked up at him with concern. Then, with the tenderness of true worship she wiped the tears from his face.

"*So il tuo nome!*" sang Turandot. "*I know your name!*"

"Amor!"

The full chorus raised its voice like a sea of angels. "*Gloria a te! Gloria!*"

And Damir said the words he had wanted to say for too long. "I love you, Isabella!"

THE BISHOP

16

"Papa!" screamed the little boy. His father tried to hold onto him, but one of the soldiers whacked the man in the face with the barrel of his rifle, leaving a gash across his cheek. The same Ustaše kicked the shepherd's son in the rear, making the boy trip and fall, lacerating his knees and elbows. And yet, the child did not drop the svirala. Three other Ustaše regulars decided to entertain themselves; one of the soldiers scooped the boy's legs from behind and the boy fell back, landing with a heavy thud. He got up—oh, sure he did—a little dazed, but there was no keeping him down. Unfortunately, the moment he was back on his feet, a second Ustaše kicked him in the ribs and the young shepherd fell on his right shoulder. Tears were now evident on his dirty little face, but he did not make a sound; he was resigned to bearing the humiliation and abuse. The purpose of the game, of course, was to make the little boy cry out in pain. A third Ustaše pushed him back so hard, the boy hit his head on a rock and cracked his head. Still, the boy never let go of his svirala; he never made a sound.

"Do what they say, do what they tell you! Don't make them angry!" yelled his father, almost hysterical. A trace of foam dribbled from his mouth and his words were muffled by terror. The shepherd and his son had been in the field looking after the family's two sheep while the shepherd's wife and baby stayed at home. Then the soldiers arrived.

"What's your name, asshole?" asked a soldier, ramming the rifle butt into the man's side.

The shepherd could not answer right away because he could not breathe. It took an additional slap in the face before he screamed, "I-van!"

"Is this your brat?" asked the same jovial fellow, raining another series of blows on the shepherd's head.

"Yes, yes, he is—please, please! We weren't doing anything!" screamed Ivan. "We're poor people, we don't hurt anyone! I beg you!" Ivan threw himself on his knees and pleaded. "Don't hurt my boy!" Ivan Seve sobbed, afraid for his son, afraid for himself.

"Shut your face up, you sniveling Serb sheep fucker, or I'll do both of you right now!" The soldier seized Ivan by the throat, pulled him to his feet, and beat him some more. This time the shepherd almost passed out.

"Papa!" The boy tried to hold onto his father, but one of the Ustaše grabbed him by the neck and yanked so hard it almost tore off his windpipe. The boy coughed and spit blood, unable to breathe until the soldier that had been beating up his father jabbed him in the ribs with the barrel of his carbine.

"Move it, sheep fucker!"

Ronnoco screamed and sat up in bed. He was sopping wet. He did not want to be awake, of course, but he knew he could not go back to sleep. Death waited, death was impatient. Outside his bedroom window the day was well on its way. The alarm clock flashed its red, bold "six." He felt a headache coming on and staggered to the bathroom. He slid open the clear acrylic door to the shower and let the hot water rush out a few minutes until the steam filled up the bathroom and bedroom as well. Ronnoco removed his undershorts and stood in front of the mirror; he hated shaving. The hot steam from the shower fogged the mirror and created a cascade of crystalline drops that raced down the white tiles. If nothing else, the steam would soothe his muscles and soften his beard.

He had been sitting in the shower half an hour when he heard the phone in his room ring, and ring, and ring again.

"Excellency!"

"Yes?" Ronnoco yelled over the sound of the strong pouring of water.

PETER'S CHOICE

"Serafio is on the phone!"

"Serafio? What time is it?" yelled Ronnoco, surprised at the early call from the pope's secretary.

"Six thirty-five!"

"Tell him I'll be there by nine."

There was a slight pause, then the voice of the old nun continued. "I am going to open the windows. The apartment is full of steam."

"As you wish, Sister," said Ronnoco, not to the nun who was in the other room but to himself.

Sister Angelina opened the bedroom window, and quickly went to the closet to pick out Ronnoco's clothes for that day: a black cassock with purple buttons, a purple zucchetto and purple sash, along with the peripherals that included a silver chain and cross, underwear, socks, and black shoes. Once the clothes were neatly laid out on the bed, Sister Angelina left the room for the kitchen, where she already had breakfast waiting for the bishop. She was almost sixty-two years old and Ronnoco believed—no, not believed—he was sure that in her youth the nun from Calabria must have been quite beautiful. That was in her youth. Sister Angelina was now typical of nuns caring for the comfort of high-ranking church officials, plain, full of piety, and in Sister Angelina's case, possessing a quick mind and a wit ready to lash out at anything she felt was improper. "You look awful," she said, looking up from the newspaper when Ronnoco walked into the kitchen.

Ronnoco set his small briefcase by the door, took the demitasse, sipped his espresso, took a bite of toast, and shrugged.

"Will you be home for supper, Excellency?"

"I don't know what the Holy Father has in mind. I'll let you know by twelve." Ronnoco drank the grapefruit juice, grabbed his case, and was off.

Bishop Ronnoco arrived in his office at the Government Palace in Vatican City at seven forty-five. It was an interesting space at the end of a long, dark corridor at the back of the Palace, from where Ronnoco, when he felt like it, could sit and watch helicopters take off and land from the heliport. The doors to his office were of cast iron, thick and heavy. They were equipped with a Zeffir combination lock, guaranteed not to allow any unauthorized person inside, regardless of how hard they tried to pick or drill the lock. The office had plain white walls, two large windows with pale yellow curtains, and a portrait of Saint Jerome that concealed a large safe. Across the floor was an antique desk and the only chair in the room (behind the desk). On the desk were two telephones, a silver letter opener, and a couple of pens. There was a utility table in one corner of the room, with a fax machine, a laser printer and a "burn basket" (a disposal mechanism, looking much like a regular wastepaper basket, that allows its contents to be incinerated at the close of the business day).

Ronnoco opened his briefcase, pulled out a small notebook computer and placed it on his desk. He plugged the computer to a telephone jack on the wall, logged on to the Internet via the Vatican server, reviewed his e-mail, logged out, and began to get ready for his meeting with the pope.

He opened the safe behind the portrait of Saint Jerome, pulled out a large manila envelope labeled "Secret," placed it on his desk, and studied its contents carefully. Then he wrote a summation of his conclusions in a memorandum that he would deliver personally to His Holiness. The header of the memorandum also read "Secret."

His secretary arrived fifteen minutes later. Father Giorgio d'Stesi was from the diminutive Republic of San Marino. He was in his mid-thirties, small and thin; his hair was wavy, dark brown, and abundant. It was swept up in a crest that put his wide forehead on full display. His nose seemed to have suffered a contusion in his youth (though it could smell a rat from the next room). Father d'Stesi's eyes were the color of his hair, reflected careful thought, and were topped by a brow that was always creased and attentive to any of the seven languages he had mastered. Like his predecessor, d'Stesi answered only to the Guardian of Saint Jerome; unlike his predecessor, d'Stesi boasted a fastidious mind that complemented Ronnoco's often distracted nature.

"Good morning, Excellency."

"Good morning. You're rather early, today."

D'Stesi answered that he wanted to make sure His Excellency had everything needed for the meeting with the pope.

"I do. Thank you."

"You are also supposed to meet the Four Horsemen—at two o'clock. You would like me to call and confirm?" asked the secretary.

Ronnoco looked up from his papers, and after a brief pause shook his head. "No, not yet. Let's wait until I'm finished with Leo. I don't know what His Holiness has in mind." The Four Horsemen, as Bishop Ronnoco called the men, were the four most influential members of the Curia and Pope Leo's closest advisors—after Bishop Ronnoco. They included Giuseppe Cardinal Pino, secretary of state; John Cardinal Bailey, in charge of Vatican public relations and communications (and the only American in the group); Lorenzo Cardinal Numa, secretary of the Vatican's Congregation for the Causes of Saints, and Paolo Cardinal Tomaso, prefect of the pontifical household.

D'Stesi nodded and turned to leave. "Coffee?"

"No, thanks. I already had my quota of caffeine for today." Ronnoco smiled and the secretary left the room.

About the same time, Ronnoco was putting the finishing touches on his memo to the pope, across the Vatican, at his papal apartments, His Holiness Leo XIV paced back and forth in his private study on the third floor of the Apostolic Palace. He was forcing himself to concentrate on the correspondence laid on his desk by his secretary. Of the thousands upon thousands of letters received by the Vatican each day addressed to the pope, only a trickle were actually read by the pontiff, and they had to be very special, very unusual, or of incredible urgency. Most of the letters addressed to the pope were handled by ten clerical workers, who would open them, read them, and distribute them to those experts within the bureaucracy of the Vatican that could best reply, if indeed a reply was necessary. For instance, if a letter requested an audience with the pope, it was automatically routed to Cardinal Tomaso, who, depending on the individual making the request, would then forward his recommendation to the pontiff. Otherwise, the cardinal's assistant would answer with a polite and usually brief turndown. The most common petition was for a papal blessing. For that, the letters were automatically forwarded to Father Luciano Tenebroso, who would answer back in a form letter indicating the letter was being studied, and upon a decision, would then be passed along to His

Holiness—which meant that the sender could make up his own mind about whether he had been blessed by the pope or not.

That morning one letter did make it to the pope's attention. It was from America and talked about an—*apparition*.

Apparition. Leo sat staring at the word. He suffered the chief ailment of the Vatican—grand antiquity—with every other bone and joint corroded by arthritis. Ten years into his tenure as Vicar of Rome, Leo had developed clogged arteries and had undergone heart surgery. As a consequence, he wore a pacemaker. Glaucoma had also been of concern in the past, but although he suffered a slight blindness in his right eye, his vision of a greater, more powerful Church forced him to wake up every day and battle the impossible. Every one of his sixteen years on the papal throne had been excruciatingly difficult. Then again, he had expected nothing else. Leo XIV was the first non-Italian pontiff in the Roman Church in almost 500 years.

His rooms were spacious but modest, if the term modest can be applied to anything in the Holy See. The walls were of an off-white color, the ceilings were high, and the delicate cream-colored curtains fluttered back and forth in the gentle summer breeze. A thick white and yellow rug covered the parquet floors, and huge, tall vases full of plants and flowers complemented the Renaissance images of the Madonna and Child that hung on the wall in elegant but plain gold frames. The papal desk was hand carved, with deep grooves in the dark wood. On the desk, there was a bronze lamp with a tall rectangular shade that matched the exact color of the curtains. Beside the lamp there were two telephones, one white, one red—giving the impression that Leo had a direct connection to heaven and to hell. Behind the desk, the pope's chair symbolized the regal status of the one and only man allowed to sit on it. It too was handcrafted, with short, thick legs and white satin upholstery. Across from the desk stood three bookcases, tall and elegant. They were made of light oak and were relatively modern; therefore, the bookcases did not reflect anything but graceful lines and functionality.

His secretary was a Franciscan friar from Argentina, Brother Agustino Serafio. Leo XIV felt that having anyone of higher rank so close to the papal throne—someone likely to have an agenda of their own—was not in the best interests of his papacy.

Brother Agustino had first served His Holiness when His Holiness was a bishop. Serafio was sixty years old, with sharp features and a complexion as smooth as a marble tabletop; there was not a trace of hair anywhere, not even where his eyebrows should have been. Brother Agustino was also endowed with a most uncommon voice, a voice that, while it was somewhat lyrical, was also high pitched and not very steady; indeed, when meeting the brother for the first time, one felt in the presence of an old, bald songbird that was losing its voice.

"His Eminence Carelli is waiting outside, Holiness," said Brother Agustino, entering the room.

"Carelli? What is he doing here? What does he want?" asked the pontiff impatiently.

"He obviously would like to talk to you. He was here yesterday, and the day before that." The fact that Serafio had worked for the pope for such a long time allowed for a degree of familiarity, although the good brother was very careful never to step over the line where an offhand reply sprinkled with sarcasm could be interpreted as insolence.

"Well, I don't want to talk to him. Tell him to go away. He's an insufferable bore. I don't want to see anyone now but Felix."

"As you wish, Holiness." Serafio turned and left.

Antonio Cardinal Carelli occupied two chairs in the narrow antechamber outside the pope's door because a single chair would have collapsed under the eminent load. The "Humpback of the See" (as his detractors called him) was reading the Italian edition of *TIME* when the lyrical Serafio announced, "His Holiness is not receiving at this time."

The cardinal did not look up from the article, which described the upcoming environmental disaster in the Brazilian jungle. In total, stealthy silence, His Eminence folded the magazine and started to glide away, looking more like a hovercraft than a prince of the church. Brother Agustino, who by then was sitting behind his PC, reminded His Grace of "The magazine, please." As personal secretary to the pope, Serafio was only polite to His Holiness and those well-placed others who carried influence with the pontiff. Cardinal Carelli was not among them.

The cardinal did not break stride but slowly banked to the left, retraced his steps, and gently reinstalled the publication in its berth. He was stung by the papal indifference. Leo XIV did not like him. Why? Was it his appearance, perhaps? Cardinal Carelli was the widest representative of the Curia. He had a slight hump on the back of his right shoulder, but it was kept well hidden under a special cope that was padded on the left side. As chief of daily operations for the papal state, Cardinal Carelli was burdened with more responsibilities and influence than he had folds in his neck. Still, Pope Leo never consulted him on anything. Why?

"Good morning, Brother Carelli," greeted Ronnoco, walking quickly past the cardinal. Carelli acknowledged the bishop with a slight and aloof nod before turning the corner.

"Good morning, Excellency," sang Brother Agustino.

"Good morning, good morning," answered Ronnoco without stopping.

"Shall I—" Brother Agustino was about to ask if he should announce Ronnoco, but by then, the bishop was inside with Pope Leo and Serafio had no choice but to raise his bald eyebrows, pucker his lips, and get busy.

"I see Serafio has a new toy." Ronnoco meant the computer on the friar's desk. He shut the door behind him and walked to the pope.

"It's about time you got here." Leo got up, embraced and kissed the bishop. "Yes, we've made it to the twentieth century."

Ronnoco walked about with relaxed authority. His relationship with the Holy Father went beyond protocol. There was no formality in their exchanges; no titles, no condescending attitudes, nothing but love, trust, and respect. Only when others were in their presence did Ronnoco attend to the Holy Father with the veneration and homage reserved not for his mentor, but for the head of the Roman Church. As could be expected, gossip, sneers, jealousy, and resentment were rife among the nobility of Holy See, who craved in vain the same pontifical favors.

Bishop Ronnoco and Pope Leo XIV met almost every day, usually early in the mornings. In those meetings the bishop briefed the pontiff on any number of issues having to do with the Holy See and its archdioceses around the world; from the progress being made by a secret federation of Catholic states in Europe established by pontifical mandate to block the spread of Islamic fundamentalism in the continent and the Eastern Church's supremacy in the Balkans and in Russia, to the handling of a brother, be it a lowly priest or a cardinal, whose indiscretions had mired the Holy See in scandal.

The topic for discussion on this particular day, however, was the challenge the Catholic Church itself faced from governments around the world because of their open disagreement with Rome on several questions of morality and ethics (issues such as abortion, contraception, and divorce). This challenge was promoting dissent and divisiveness among the eight hundred million Catholics worldwide. In order to best confront and deal with the problem, the pope, at the urging of Bishop Ronnoco, had ordered a secret research study that would—hopefully—give him a better understanding of the attitudes and the reasoning of his increasingly rebellious flock. There was nothing the study did not cover, no question it did not ask, and no answer that was not carefully noted; nothing like it had ever been done before and the study, with an impressive two hundred thousand respondents out of a sample base of five hundred thousand, took two years to complete.

Ronnoco placed a chair in front of the pope's desk, opened his briefcase, and pulled out the secret memorandum he had prepared in his office.

"I have one question," said the pope before Ronnoco was even able to sit down. "Are we in trouble?" he asked, returning to his desk.

"I have summarized the findings." The bishop placed the memorandum on the desk, in front of the pope. "The numbers speak for themselves."

"I don't want to read anything; you tell me what's going on." Leo pushed away the memo.

Ronnoco shrugged, retrieved the paper, and returned to his chair. "The bottom line is that in the last fifteen years there has been a twenty-five percent drop in attendance at church services. That translates into a twenty-five percent loss in revenues from collections. However, that does not reflect the total loss in contributions; that number is approximately thirty-five percent, since those who have remained in the Church are giving ten percent less than they were before. The situation is not improving; in fact, it's getting worse and threatens many churches, especially those in remote and underdeveloped areas.

"We did not reach this critical stage overnight. This trend is part of a phenomenon that goes back almost thirty years, to the advent of mass communication—especially television—and the fostering of democratic principles around the globe. It is interesting to note that it is precisely this odd mix of democracy and mass media that has affected the way Catholics think of their Church.

"For centuries the Catholic Church was a huge part of people's everyday life. Children went to schools operated by the local church, and their parents belonged to men's and women's societies connected to the church. If people had problems, they discussed them with their priest. Catholics felt secure that they could depend on the Church. Today, you will agree, things are quite different.

"Many Catholics today refuse to follow Church teachings. Some are against Church actions and have protested, demanding changes in Church policy. This has not happened, and many believe the Church remains an inflexible monolith unable to face up to the varied problems of modern society. Sixty-four percent of Catholics around the world disagree with the Church on abortion; they do not believe that ending a pregnancy is morally reprehensible in every case. Seventy-six percent disagree about divorce; they do not believe that ending a marriage is morally wrong in every case. And forty-eight percent disagree about homosexuality; they do not believe that having sex with a person of the same sex is morally wrong."

"This is worse than I ever imagined," remarked Leo.

"One of the problems—and I don't think this will surprise you—is that we don't have enough priests. Fewer men enter religious schools that train priests. Since 1985, the number of priests has dropped by thirteen percent, and many Catholics say that since only priests are permitted to lead the holiest ceremonies, that lack of leadership threatens to deny many church members the main experience of being a

Catholic. As it stands now, ten percent of Catholic churches around the world do not have their own priest. Priests visit these churches, but, most of the time, the churches are run by ordinary church members; most are women. These nonclergy leaders do much of the work traditionally carried out by priests. They advise church members, they operate religious schools, and they speak during religious services."

"Enough! I've heard enough!"

"Don't you want to hear the good news?"

"Good news!" said the pope in a loud, angry voice.

"Eighty-five percent of respondents like you."

"But they question every decision I make. Not long ago, the idea of Catholics doubting the wisdom of the pope would have seemed shocking!"

"We are not dealing with illiterate peasants anymore. People today have a degree of sophistication that is bound to make them question everything. If it makes you feel any better, I don't believe the problems I just described are exclusive to the Catholic Church. I am sure the Protestants, the Muslims, and the Jews are also experiencing a change in attitude among their followers.

"In conclusion, we have to become relevant again, we have to be able to make a difference—a real difference in the lives of our members. For that we need leaders that can take the message to the people, and that comes down to urgently training and recruiting more priests. Only after we have enough competent, caring priests can we address the other problems faced by the Church. I have a list of recommendations for you to consider."

"How many people know about the study?" asked the pope, looking worried.

"You and me."

"What about the people who did the research?"

"This project was designed in four parts to make it impossible for anyone to know what was going on at any given time, and it was further disguised with sections of the questionnaire having nothing to do with what we were trying to find out. The results were tabulated by computer, and once I was given a hard copy of the findings, I ordered the data and all the material related to the project destroyed." Ronnoco smiled. "Satisfied?"

The pope leaned forward in his chair. "You cannot tell anyone about this," he said.

"What about the Four Horsemen?"

"Especially them. Before you know it, they'll tell the others and soon they will be having meetings and issuing proclamations without ever getting a thing done. I mean, what is the Curia? Just a bunch of old farts afraid of their shadows." Leo pushed back his chair and walked around his desk. "Dear God, how did we ever get into this mess?"

"Look, there is no doubt we have made mistakes, but I also think this crisis was, in some ways, inevitable," said Ronnoco.

"Why?"

"We have lost the magic, the mysticism that made us unique among the world religions. We have embraced communications, technology, and progress openly, thinking that we would benefit from them, when in fact, all they have done is promote incredulity and dissent. Somewhere along the way we forgot that the Catholic Church is founded on faith and the supernatural. Sure, the taking of the Eucharist is intended to make a holy union between man and the Lord Christ, but—did you know that ninety-five percent of Catholics believe that transubstantiation is symbolic?"

Leo looked dumbfounded. "Ninety-five percent?" Transubstantiation is the Catholic rite performed by a priest in which the bread and wine used in the Eucharist are in fact changed into the body and blood of Christ.

"And the other five percent have no idea what the word means," concluded Ronnoco.

Leo stared into space for what seemed a very long time. "Come back this afternoon," he said at last, "about four. I have to think about what we have to do."

"Yes, Holiness—four o'clock," said Ronnoco putting the papers back in his briefcase.

He had barely walked in his office when his private telephone rang. "Come now," said the voice at the other end.

"Yes, *Holiness!*" said Ronnoco with a laugh. He hung up, turned around and left.

"One of those days, Excellency?" said d'Stesi when Ronnoco walked by his desk.

Ronnoco smiled. "It's my new exercise regiment; better than jogging or playing tennis and it's blessed by the pope."

D'Stesi laughed and Ronnoco returned to the papal apartments.

As soon as he opened the door to the pope's study, Leo rushed out to meet him. "You are right! You are one hundred percent right!"

"About what?" Ronnoco sat down.

Leo showed him the letter from America that described how two young children in a small town in the United States claimed to have been visited by the Holy Virgin. The apparition had caused such a sensation that thousands upon thousands of pilgrims had invaded the small community.

"This is what they want, what they are waiting for!"

"A miracle?" asked Ronnoco, returning the letter to the pope.

Leo nodded. "It is amazing," the pope said with a chuckle. "We forgot the one element that made all this possible!" The pope opened his arms to embrace the Holy See. "Can't you see? Miracles justify their faith!"

"And I thought I was cynical," said Ronnoco, also smiling.

"Cynical? I am not being cynical. I am being truthful. Think back, Felix. We are the holy guardians of a trunk-full of miracles, that is our heritage!"

Ronnoco conceded as much.

"We have been too busy looking at the future, when we should have been keeping our finger in the past. Oh, we need a miracle, Felix, one that will fire the imagination, one that will fix the attention of the world on the Roman Catholic Church, a miracle that will convince the skeptics that we hold the key to everlasting glory!"

Ronnoco pointed out the canonical procedures set up to establish the validity of reports of apparitions, revelations, and the myriad of other such phenomena, most of which were due to feeble minds, charlatans, and fraud.

"Unless I say the miracle happened," said Leo. "My word is the law of the Catholic Church. If I say those children saw the Mother of our Blessed Savior, they saw the Mother of our Blessed Savior!"

"And what could Mary have possibly said to those kids?" asked Ronnoco, playing along.

Leo returned the smile. "Your guess is as good as mine."

"But we don't have to guess, do we?" said Ronnoco. "The Blessed Mother of Christ was—is upset. She feels abandoned. She wept and made a pronouncement—a pronouncement that will make every Christian tremble, and hail Mary with unmistakable joy."

"And what is that?" asked the pope, like a little boy waiting for his surprise.

Ronnoco smiled. "I don't know. I have to think about it." He got up and headed for the door.

"Where are you going?" asked the pope.

"Back to my office. I have a lot of work to do. Are you sure you don't want me to brief the Four Horsemen?" asked Ronnoco.

"I said no!"

"But we need to start thinking about how the Church is going to respond to these findings."

"With a miracle!"

Ronnoco let go of the door handle and walked up to the pope. "Are you serious?"

"When have you known me not to be serious?" Leo took Ronnoco by the arm and led him to the door.

"Tata, I was kidding just now." *Tata* was what the little children back home called their papas.

"I was not," said Leo.

"This is positively silly. It's absurd!"

"It's not absurd. It's outrageous, that's why it's perfect!"

"You'll never make it work," said Ronnoco, concerned.

"I have no intention of making anything work. That, I leave to you."

"Me?"

"You." Leo stopped and stood face-to-face with Ronnoco. "I'll take care of the bureaucrats; they are a nuisance that can be easily circumvented or—ignored. But you—you, my boy, will be the ringmaster, the miracle-worker. I want magic! Go, find out what happened to those children. Get rid of the loose ends and make the apparition—the Blessed Mother's, not yours—true. Leave as soon as possible; we have no time to lose."

For a second, Ronnoco pondered the problem—*his* problem, actually. In all the years he had been in the service of the Church, or in the service of the pope (which to Felix were one and the same), during all that time Ronnoco had been a zealous defender of the faith. He viewed his mentor as the embodiment of justice—Catholic justice, of course, with its all-encompassing love for mankind. Felix had never questioned the motives of the pope, because the logic, the reasoning behind his policies was always clear and correct. But to fake a miracle, an apparition—this was a blatant attempt to manipulate world opinion to achieve a goal that could have been best achieved by righting what was wrong with the Church. But Felix's love for Leo was unquestionable, his loyalty unshakable, even if, as Felix knew only too well, His Holiness was pursuing a course that he, as a man of conscience, was loathe to follow.

Leo kissed Ronnoco on both cheeks. "We have work to do. Go!"

Ronnoco walked to the door. He looked back at the pontiff. The old man looked frail. Ronnoco smiled and left.

Outside, Serafio was busy typing a letter when Bishop Ronnoco left the pope's chamber. The friar's concentration was intense and conspicuous. Ronnoco walked up to the friar's desk, stopped as if he was going to say something, changed his mind, smiled to Serafio, and walked away, heading back to his office behind the Zeffir lock—a brief stopover on his way to America.

17

Yes, it was an inconvenience to rip a hole in the roof to install a glass-bubble sunroof exactly where the Blessed Mother appeared in her glory to little Teddy and Alice Miltedew. But Ray felt, with good reason, that since they were asking for a two-fifty donation for two minutes in the shrine, the pilgrims would better appreciate the full impact of the apparition if the sun blinded them when they raised their eyes to the ceiling. A small font was erected under the sunroof, from which water flowed and where, for an additional dollar, those interested were able to cool their foreheads—unless, of course, they would rather take a sample home. For two dollars anyone could acquire a light-blue vial with an ounce of water that might or might not be holy but was certainly wet.

Ray and Harriet installed a fence around two empty lots they rented next to their humble shack to provide extra parking, so that the thousands who had traveled from around the country to catch a glimpse of the blessed children would not have to walk far. The faithful donated three dollars an hour per car for the parking privileges and another dollar to sit for fifteen minutes on one of thirty benches Ray himself had built in front of their brand-new porch. There, every once in a while, Teddy and Alice made an appearance, though how often this happened was anyone's guess. Harriet believed that for the children to exhibit themselves on schedule would be anticlimactic.

Pictures of Teddy and Alice in one of three different settings were available in vibrant color: Teddy and Alice in sparkling white satin, kneeling, facing each other, their little hands clasped in prayer as they looked up to the heavens; Teddy and Alice side by side, their adoring heads together as they looked at camera, holding a figurine of the Blessed Mother between them; and Teddy and Alice sleeping (this was the favorite of most devotees) while the blessed Mary and a crowd of angels gathered lovingly about their bedside. Fame proved to be a terrible but also a profitable imposition for the Miltedews, and they were not complaining. America is a land of opportunity and when opportunity descends from heaven—well, it would be downright un-American not to seize it, tie it up in colored ribbons and share it with others.

Harriet never imagined that things would go as far as they did the night she returned home from work and found her children and husband huddled in a corner, praying feverishly, expressing their love for Mary, who had chosen them from amongst all others. It was, as Ray told the newspapers the following day, "An honest to goodness humdinger." And they thought about it for at least one day before telling Father O'Malley of the apparition. It was, after all, a religious experience, and if anyone knew what to do with a religious experience it was that very pious and saintly of men, the local priest. Unfortunately, like many priests stuck out in small parishes, Father O'Malley had very little else to do except gossip with his parishioners—a select group, mind you, that included Mrs. Lindgren. Mrs. Lindgren thought the apparition was the most wonderful news for the parish and took the trouble to phone everyone she knew to tell them that the Mother of Christ had dropped by the Miltedews.

Five minutes on the local news gave way to wire stories from the AP and UPI; CNN, better at news of wars on the other side of the globe, was the last to pick up the story. Ray and Harriet signed an exclusive contract with Channel 21 in New Orleans because everyone wanted to know more about the children, everyone, that is, except the Protestants, the Jews and the Muslims (no one had ever seen a Muslim in town but Mrs. Lindgren swore they existed nonetheless). All marveled at the story: the children were young, innocent, beautiful, and there were two of them! It could not be fabrication or fantasy, or the dream of a child with an overdeveloped Catholic imagination. Here we had a little boy and girl who had seen the Blessed Mother at the same time. Unless they suffered from hallucinations induced by drugs, or a stomach virus, or were pathological liars, Teddy and Alice were, then, telling the truth. Besides, as any person who met them could attest, they had blessedness written all over their sweet little faces.

Father O'Malley referred all questions pertaining to the apparition to Bishop Cuyas in New Orleans, who in turn stated, "The matter is under investigation." In truth, although a seal of approval from the Church would have helped the sale of the book and its accompanying single (entitled "Angels in the Bayou"), it was a great time for the parish—especially for the 7-11, the town's one motel and the diner, not to mention Harry's gas station and several local entrepreneurs selling oysters and crayfish side by side with figurines of the blessed children and Mary in roadside stands not far from where the miracle took place.

After years of being unemployed, Ray was now the manager of a shrine, while Harriet was in charge of bookkeeping and dealing with the press. No one asked Teddy and Alice if they liked being the center of so much attention, but they seemed not to mind. They were always polite, never without a smile and forever—mum. The lack of communication between the children and their many admirers was a shrewd precaution on the part of their parents, because, if it was true that their little boy and girl had been visited by the Blessed Mother, it was also true that neither Teddy nor Alice remembered what had happened after they passed out. Therefore, to avoid the children being made uncomfortable with the needless but almost certain questions that would arise when meeting the faithful, Harriet and Ray decided not to allow them to talk about the apparition, with the apology that it was a sacred and very personal matter between Mary, Teddy and Alice.

One of the few drawbacks, for Teddy anyway, was that he missed going out hunting with Ray. As his mother explained, killing defenseless—though wild—beasts was not in line with the image of one who had been visited by the Virgin Mother. Another drawback was that because he attended public school, which in La

Place included children from a variety of religious and nonreligious backgrounds, some of his classmates took it upon themselves to taunt Teddy with sacrilegious pranks, even having a fat Protestant boy sit on him during recess, an action that could have been a metaphor for the diminishing influence of the Catholic Church in the parish. The kids in school nicknamed young Miltedew "Blessy Teddy."

One day Teddy came home from school with a bloody lip, and Harriet decided that enough was enough. She made up her mind to place her son in the only private and also very Catholic school in the parish, Saint Luke's Academy.

"I won't stand by and watch my Teddy be sacrificed by the Protestants and the Jews, Father!" said Harriet to Father O'Malley. She was younger than her husband by five years; not a beautiful woman, but not ugly either. Harriet was—simple. She was as tall as Ray, with long strong limbs, blue eyes, a small nose and a mouth that was not altogether symmetrical; when she smiled, however, which was as often as circumstances allowed, Harriet displayed an excellent set of teeth.

She found Father O'Malley helping the altar boy move the pews against one side of the church so the priest could practice his backhand indoors. "I sympathize with you, Mrs. Miltedew. Let me see what I can do," said O'Malley. He was a short, thin man around five and a half feet tall, in his mid-fifties. His hair was grey and his eyes were blue and sharp—set in a face whose middle-aged flaccidity was already giving way to the gaunt and leather-like complexion of more advanced years. "Remember I'm just the parish priest, I have nothing to do with the school."

"My Teddy is not just another boy, Father," said Harriet. She was wearing a pretty pink dress, full of red and blue flowers and her concern for her son transcended tennis. "My Teddy has been chosen by the Mother of our Christ. I am sure that you can convince whoever you have to and get Teddy enrolled at Saint Luke's."

"Perhaps you should talk to Father Zaragai; he's the headmaster." Father O'Malley looked at Harriet, at the same time taking the cover off his racquet. "That would do two things. It would eliminate a go-between—in this case, me—and it would expedite matters considerably by making Father Zaragai aware of your urgent needs."

Harriet looked away for a second. Though not wanting to sound arrogant or inconsiderate, she said, "You understand, Father, that I can't take a chance of Teddy getting hurt. I mean, think of it—the Blessed Mother comes all the way to La Place, picks out my Teddy among a hundred million children—and for what? So he gets beat up in school? I don't think so, Father, I really don't."

"I'm just an ordinary priest, I have no opinion."

"I feel strongly about this."

"I'm sure you do. I would too—probably—if I were in your place." Father O'Malley took a tennis ball from his pocket.

"I am thinking of writing to the pope."

"Why, Mrs. Miltedew, that is an excellent idea! Why didn't I think of that! It's brilliant! That's exactly what you have to do." Father O'Malley dropped the ball on the floor to see if it still had its bounce. "You see, once the Holy Father receives your note, he'll give it to one of his many aides who do nothing all day but look after such—unusual requests. Before you can say one Hail Mary, little Teddy will be at Saint Luke's. You must have been inspired, Mrs. Miltedew, honestly!"

Harriet had not really thought of writing to the pope, but after Father O'Malley's enthusiastic response, why not? Four months had gone by when, one Tuesday morning, as the clock in the hall chimed eight, Father O'Malley received a telephone call from the Vatican. Things were never the same again.

☩

"Excellency!" called out Father O'Malley as Ronnoco left the customs building. "Let me take that, please." The priest tried to take Ronnoco's suitcase from him, but the bishop would not let him. "Welcome to the US of A!" The priest opened the trunk of his green Buick (the car was two years short of becoming a classic), which stood parked outside the arrival terminal.

"Thank you, Father," said Ronnoco, getting into the car.

"Ever been in New Orleans, Excellency?" asked Father O'Malley after he had slammed the trunk.

"No," replied Ronnoco.

"In my humble opinion," continued the priest, "they can give it back to the French." Father O'Malley was not a native.

Bishop Ronnoco took in as much of the landscape as was possible, given the time of the day. They drove north, along Route 10, a four-lane highway flanked by swamps, full of bumps, possums, possums that had become bumps on the road, and other exotic wildlife with their entrails spread across the lanes. "Do you mind if I smoke?" asked the priest.

"Yes," returned the bishop.

Father O'Malley stepped on the gas and less than a half hour later they reached their destination. The small church was in the town of La Place, in Saint John the Baptist's Parish. It was unassuming, irrelevant and ignored by the folks in the parish—at least until it became part of the cause célèbre of the apparition, since the church was where Teddy and Alice had been baptized and where they went to mass three times a week. The little church was the standard local house of worship, white on the outside and brown on the inside. It rested on a foundation of thick wooden posts that kept it from sinking into the bog, while several species of moss ate their way up from the ground with rotting efficacy. Two magnolias and one large cypress stood around the structure, leaning against its walls as if overcome by the warm mist that rose from the swamp and danced with the morning fog before the sun showed its face. Behind the church was an old churchyard that had long since stopped taking guests, and that was divided by a dirt path that led from the back door of the church straight to the front steps of the rectory. The two-story edifice had none of the grace and old southern charm of its neighbor, and was built in the best tradition of utilitarian modesty. It too rested on a bed of posts, and its chief features were the four uniform and unattractive windows that indicated the four points of the compass.

The Buick crunched hundreds of locusts that covered the road like a black winged blanket, and stopped along the side of the building. Father O'Malley jumped out and opened the door for his guest. "You better go inside. Mosquitos here love to suck priestly blood." He opened the trunk, took out the bishop's suitcase, left it on the front steps, unlocked the door and said, "I'll be back in a sec."

"Where are you going?" asked Ronnoco.

"To have a smoke—unless, of course, you have any objections to my seeking death in private." A Marlboro was already dangling from Father O'Malley's lips.

Ronnoco shrugged and went inside. He found an office just to the right of the hall. It was decorated with fake wood paneling and enjoyed the amenities of a fireplace (which makes no sense in Louisiana), a wooden desk with an easy chair, a couple of floor lamps, beige curtains, a small closet, two additional wooden chairs, a medium-sized couch, a pink marble coffee table with an embedded ashtray, an air conditioner and a small Kenmore refrigerator next to the desk.

"I'm back!" said Father O'Malley, reeking of nicotine. "Do you want to see your room?"

"Not right now. I want to talk to you." Ronnoco opened his briefcase, pulled out the letter from the Holy Father and gave it to O'Malley. "I am assuming responsibility for the parish," he added.

Father O'Malley read carefully the papal order and whistled.

"Where is the file regarding the Miltedews?"

"The what?" inquired Father O'Malley, still looking at the papal seal.

"The children visited by the Blessed Mother." This was the reason Ronnoco was in Louisiana in the first place.

"Oh, that—yes, well—I'll get it for you. You don't need it now, do you? You know it's a crock of shit."

Ronnoco moved away from O'Malley. "I need it now, and please, Father, keep your opinions on the matter to yourself."

"Yes, Excellency. I'm sorry."

Ten minutes later Father O'Malley placed a sign on the door of the church: *"Closed until further notice. Any questions, please contact the archdiocese."* Then, he was ordered to gather the records of the church—reports to the archdiocese, bank statements, account logs, letters (personal and parochial), memoranda, a list of anyone employed by the parish past and present, and anything else that had been put on paper since Father O'Malley had taken over as priest. In one word, everything. Bishop Ronnoco instructed that the papers and documents be separated into two sets, those that made reference to the Miltedews—whether concerned with the apparition or not—and the rest.

"Do not, I repeat, do not omit anything. Have it ready by ten. Then, we'll pay the Miltedews a visit."

"Yes, Excellency."

"Now, please show me to my room."

It took His Excellency most of the afternoon to read every document in Father O'Malley's file cabinet. Two items caught his attention: Father O'Malley's dismissal of the janitor Louie Peps for stealing, and the complaint filed with the police, listing the items that Louie Peps had taken but which were never recovered. Father O'Malley, having better things to do, did not pursue the matter. Ronnoco lit the fireplace, delivered all records of the incident to the flames and stared at the fire, enthralled by the flickering flames, their orange glow reflecting off the walls. The flames whipped and crackled against the red bricks as Father O'Malley said, "Anything else you'd like to set on fire, Excellency?"

"Yes," answered Ronnoco, not specifying what.

At three o'clock Father O'Malley drove the bishop into the bayou to meet the Miltedews. They crossed the railroad tracks, turned right onto a two-lane street, cut across two large open fields and ran into the bumper-to-bumper traffic making its resolute way to—

"Mary's Haven. All are Welcome."

There were many cars parked alongside the fence and more than a few inside the gate. A crowd of three hundred milled around like Catholic ants, going here only to turn and go there, their Bibles and rosaries always at hand. Most of the women covered their heads with a shawl or a handkerchief, and sooner or later approached the house. It took almost ten minutes before Father O'Malley was allowed to cut in front of a line of cars that extended a good half mile toward La Place. Ray's cousin, Billy, opened the gate and welcomed the priests.

The crowds notwithstanding, attendance was slacking off. Ray attributed the diminishing interest in the miracle to the searingly hot and humid weather, which did not allow anyone to sit outside on the benches too long. Harriet was not too happy about this and thought that the least the Blessed Mother could have done was provide a favorable climate—at least around their residence—for those who traveled to pay homage.

Harriet was surprised, though, when she saw Father O'Malley, in the company of another priest, climb the steps and walk toward her. Many of the people Father O'Malley passed along the way said hello and smiled. Nobody, of course, knew Bishop Ronnoco.

"Hello, Harriet," greeted Father O'Malley, stepping up to the porch.

"Hello, Father! And what brings you 'round these parts, anyway?" Many of the faithful gathered around the green Buick and tried to listen in on anything the priests might communicate to the mother of Teddy and Alice.

"This is Bishop Ronnoco. He's come all the way from Rome to talk to you and Ray," said Father O'Malley, moving aside and allowing Ronnoco to come forward.

"Mrs. Miltedew, is there a place where we can talk—in private?"

"Bishop?" It was difficult to tell whether Harriet was happy to be visited by such a high-ranking Church official, whether she was worried for the same reason, or whether she did not care. "Well, dear me, this is a surprise. Is it very important? As you can see, we're rather busy at the moment."

"I think, Harriet," interjected Father O'Malley, "I think you should listen to His Excellency."

Ronnoco walked up to Harriet, leaned his head to the right, and whispered in her ear, "Tell everyone to leave. If you don't, I will. I view this mercenary display as a shameful reminder of the time when our Lord so indignantly whipped the merchants out of the temple."

Harriet beckoned to her husband, consulted with him for a moment, and then husband and wife pointed to Ronnoco and revealed to the faithful that due to an unforseen visit by a bishop from Rome the shrine would close for the day and would they all please come back another time. The people exclaimed "Oh!" and "Ah!" Most were impressed, leaving the premises without further ado, but one man asked for his parking money back and was graciously obliged. In less than half an hour there was not a soul in search of salvation, or of anything else, in sight.

Ray invited Bishop Ronnoco and Father O'Malley inside the air-conditioned shrine, then brought out a pitcher of ice-cold lemonade.

"You say you're from Rome, Italy?" Ray sat in his favorite chair, leaning forward and resting his forearms on his knees. "Well!" Ray slapped his knee and leaned back.

"I wish to inform you," began His Excellency, "that the Holy Father has taken an interest in the apparition. I have come to find out what happened the night when the children saw the Blessed Mother. If, as you say, the children were indeed visited by Mary, the Church will legitimize the event at once, not wait a few hundred years as is usually the case. Nonetheless, there are a few things I am afraid you will have to do. You must stop this grotesque commercial exploitation of the apparition. You will not receive anymore people, and you will stop selling pictures and souvenirs."

"But, Excellency—" Ray protested. Ronnoco put out his hand and did not let him continue.

"You will not talk to anyone any more about the apparition—"

"B-b-but why?" Harriet finally joined the debate.

"That is not for you to question." Ronnoco turned and looked straight at Harriet. "If you don't do as I say, I will hold a press conference and say you're charlatans and that the apparition never happened."

Harriet was slightly out of sorts. "Excuse me, Excellency, but my children saw the Virgin!"

"That, Mrs. Miltedew, is beside the point." Ronnoco walked to the door. "Be at the rectory at, let's say, tomorrow morning at nine. I will first talk to the children alone, one at a time, and then I will meet with you and Mr. Miltedew. Father O'Malley—"

"He's not a bishop, that's what I think," said Mrs. Miltedew as Father O'Malley drove away.

"Well, if he ain't, he's got me fooled," returned Mr. Miltedew.

Next morning, as instructed, Harriet arrived with Teddy and Alice in tow. Father O'Malley led Teddy into the office while Harriet and Alice sat in the kitchen.

"Teddy Miltedew, Excellency," announced the priest in a formal voice, then closed the door and left the bishop to begin the interrogation.

All things considered, Teddy was as easygoing and friendly a little boy as he was supposed to be in the presence of the bishop. He was relaxed and talkative, and looked, in his shiny white suit (the shine came from the polyester) as if he were celebrating his first communion. Teddy and Ronnoco faced each other under the air conditioner—Ronnoco on the sofa and Teddy in a chair. Ronnoco explained to the boy that the Holy Father, the pope, wanted to know what had happened when Teddy and his sister saw the Mother of Christ. Ronnoco had to repeat his questions as many as three times because it was often difficult for Teddy to understand the bishop's foreign accent.

Teddy described his encounter with the Virgin in words that were as sincere as they were innocent.
"Were you scared?"
"Oh, yeah, lots!"
"And what did the Blessed Mother say to you?"
Teddy sat very straight, his hands resting on his knees.
"Nothing."
"Nothing?"
"Nope. I passed out."
Ronnoco took the boy's hands in his and said, "Teddy, you did not pass out. The Blessed Mother wanted you to fall asleep so the little angels could hold you in their arms and bring you to her. Then, she whispered in your ear."
"Really?"
"Yes, Teddy—really," said Ronnoco softly.
The look of wonder gave way to a curious wrinkle of the brow. "What did She say?"

Next it was Alice's turn, and she talked endlessly about everything, particularly about her older brother. It was Teddy this and Teddy that and Teddy likes this and Teddy likes that and Mommy says that Teddy is this and Daddy says that Teddy is that—
When she finally got around to talking about the apparition, Alice recited word by word the story the bishop had heard from Teddy.
"Were you scared?"

"Oh, yeah, lots!"
"What did the Blessed Mother say to you?"
Alice shrugged. "Nothing."
"Nothing?"
"Nope. I fainted!" said little Alice candidly.
"Oh," said Ronnoco, and laughed.

Harriet was far more anxious than her children, but Ronnoco was particularly friendly that morning and did his best to put her at ease. "Mrs. Miltedew, I am not here to judge. I am interested in what happened, that is all."

"What happened is this," began Harriet. She had come home late one night and found her children and husband praying and crying because, they said, they had seen the Virgin. Harriet believed her husband, but more than that, she believed the babies. It was simply not possible for the little ones to have made the story up and—"Excellency, we never ask for money. It is very important that you know that! We accept donations that help us keep the shrine, that's it. We don't sell pictures, we give them away. We're lucky the folks who visit the shrine are willing to pay for the costs of making the pictures, otherwise we could not give them away. We're poor people, Excellency, and don't have money to—"

"I understand, Mrs. Miltedew, believe me, I do." In another time and place perhaps, Bishop Ronnoco would have taken the time to explain to Mrs. Miltedew the ethical nuances of her enterprise. But as Ronnoco wanted to finish quickly with Harriet, he allowed her to talk about the generous people of the community, about the letters and calls from all over the world asking for Teddy and Alice to hold special prayers for those in need, about the gifts and letters people—total strangers—sent with money for the kids. At first, she thought she should return all of it—

"Why didn't you?" interjected Ronnoco.

Because being very poor and in need Ray had decided that it would be in the best interest of the children to make their lives more comfortable so they could carry out the mission for which they were chosen by the Virgin.

"And what mission is that?" asked the bishop.

"I don't know," answered Harriet. "Don't you? I hope someone can tell me. What does it mean? Why pick on my children? Why us?"

At three o'clock Mr. Miltedew came in.

"Please, sit." Ronnoco pointed to a very uncomfortable-looking wooden stool he had brought in from the kitchen for the interview. "Now, Ray—may I call you Ray?"

"Yes, of course, of course—"

"Tell me what happened—in your own words." Ronnoco walked back and forth, tossing questions at Ray like crumbs at a flock of pigeons.

Mr. Miltedew related that on the night of the apparition he had not been feeling well and was depressed because he had been out of work for so long. He was waiting for his children to come home but fell asleep on the couch. When he woke up, Teddy and Alice were unconscious on the floor.

As was his style, Bishop Ronnoco did not waste time with irrelevant chitchat. He stood in front of Ray and asked, "Do you know a man called Louie Peps?"

"I—I don't remember."

"I think I should explain the rules of the game."

Ray looked up and caught the bishop's uncompromising glare. "I ask questions and you do not lie to me. If you do, you'll wish you'd died and gone to hell. Now—" and Ronnoco waited to see the reaction of his threat on Mr. Miltedew. "Harriet told me you do know Mr. Peps. That he used to come to your house often. As a matter of fact, your wife said this Mr. Peps was at your house the night of the miracle. Is that true? Did Louie Peps drop by your house before the apparition? Well?"

Ray nodded.

"That's better, that's better." Ronnoco paused long enough to walk behind Ray. "Of course, that brings us to another matter. You know that Mr. Peps used to work here, at the church?"

Ray nodded again.

"And you know he was dismissed for stealing?"

"Yes."

"Do you have any idea what he stole from Father O'Malley?"

Ray shook his head.

"Come, come, Ray, you were doing so well! You know what I'm getting at, don't you?" continued the bishop. "You may not remember everything but you do remember the movie projector—the one Father O'Malley used to show movies? Most were of a religious nature, yes?"

Ray was so still that Ronnoco wondered if he was breathing.

"Let's try and make some sense of what happened, shall we? And please, feel free to correct me at any time. What I think happened, Ray, is this. I think Louie, as your wife calls Mr. Peps, stole the movie projector from the church, took it to your house, sold it or gave it to you—it really does not matter which—and you used the machine in a desperate attempt to get out of the awful situation you were in. How long were you without work?"

"Two—two years," replied Ray, his lips quivering.

"Two years! You just had to do something to get out of the hole, out of the rut, as you Americans call it. And what did you do? You waited for your children to get home, and the moment they walked through the door, you played one of Father O'Malley's short films on the Virgin. In their innocence, little Teddy and Alice thought they were in the presence of the Holy Mother of Jesus Christ! But they were not—right Ray? It was just a silly movie, one that you used in a stupid plan to fleece the simple and trusting men and women who want to believe, who have to believe in a miracle in order for their faith to have meaning. You have made fools of everybody. You made fools of your children, made fools of all the people you have been taking money from, and you have made a fool of your wife. I wonder what Harriet will say when I tell her what really happened. It'll break her heart, Ray, that's what it will do, she'll never forgive you." Ronnoco brought his face right next to Ray's ear and added, "Isn't that right?"

Ray shook violently and began to weep. He protested and said he never planned the "apparition," that it had been an accident.

"Liar!" said Ronnoco loudly.

Ray confessed that Louie forgot the projector at the house after they argued and when Louie left, Ray was so despondent he wrecked the house and tried to kill himself.

"Obviously, you failed."

"I knocked myself cold. A beam fell on my head," said Ray between sobs.

"Liar!"

Ray said that because there had been no lights in the house when Teddy and Alice got home that night, because it was all so dark, the children tripped over the projector. The machine went off by itself—

"You're lying, Ray!"

"No, I swear I'm not!"

"Did you tell your wife you tried to kill yourself?"

"No!"

"And you never told her about the projector?"

"No!"

Ray thought of the disgrace he would bring upon his children. They would be ridiculed and the family would have to leave town. Harriet would take the children and leave him. He might as well be dead.

"I'll tell you what I'm going to do," said Ronnoco. "What you have done is insulting, pathetic but—it's done. Listen carefully, because I have decided to help you. What you have told me just now never happened. As of this moment, the miracle, the apparition—I don't care what you call it, it is now out of your hands. Where is the machine, the projector and the movie of the Blessed Mother, Ray? What did you do with them?"

Ray could not get the words out.

"Again, where is the projector? Where is the film?"

"I—I—it's b-buried," Ray stuttered. He turned around quickly and looked up at the bishop; Ray had the strange feeling that he was about to be murdered. He was wrong. Instead, Ronnoco grabbed him by the shirt and pulled him up off the stool. "Listen to me, you imbecile, and listen well—you're going to dig those things up and bring them to me, understand? Or, shall I call the police and the newspapers? You don't want that, now, do you?"

Ray shook his head with such force that Ronnoco had to let go.

"Now, where is this—Louie? Have you seen him lately? Do you know where he lives?"

"He's—he lives by the tracks, 'bout three miles south—in a shack he built himself. I'll fetch him if you—"

"No, Ray, you will not. You will let me handle everything from now on. If you're good, Ray, if you're very good, you'll come out of this—a better person. Your children will be taken care of for the rest of their lives, and you and Mrs. Miltedew can reap the benefits of being the parents of the children who saw the Mother of Christ. Of course, you never wanted much, did you? Just enough to get by." Ronnoco took Ray's face in his hand and just as he had done with the man's son, made Ray look him in the eyes. "Now bring me the projector and the film!"

Ray Miltedew left and returned an hour later, lugging a green plastic garbage bag with everything that Louie had delivered to his house that fateful night when Teddy and Alice saw Mary. Ronnoco received the man in his bathrobe. "Is this everything?" he asked.

"Yeah."

Ronnoco relieved the man of his burden and closed the door, leaving Ray standing outside. Two hours later, having examined the contents of the green bag, Ronnoco threw the film in the fire and put away the projector. There was no need to worry any further about Louie, he thought. There was nothing that Mr. Peps could say that anyone would believe. Everyone in town knew that Louie Peps was a liar and a thief.

18

Pope Leo XIV met with his advisors. They sat in the pope's study, two on each side of the papal throne. On the pope's right there was Cardinal Pino, and Cardinal Bailey. On the other side was Cardinal Numa and Cardinal Tomaso.

"The evidence speaks for itself." Pope Leo pointed to a stack of papers and pictures on top of a small table at his side. "We have lie detector tests that prove the children are telling the truth. Their mother and the father were also examined. The results are conclusive." If anyone had taken the time to see the results of the lie detector tests, or risk offending the Holy Father with a few simple questions, they would have found out that it was the pope who was not telling the truth; the tests had never been administered.

"But, Holiness, that doesn't mean the Blessed Mother was there. At best it means that these people believe she was." Cardinal Bailey was almost as tall as the pope, with a handsome, aristocratic face, a good head of hair streaked with grey, and a resonant, baritone voice.

"That makes sense, Holiness." Cardinal Pino was a little too small, a little too fat, a little too amiable, with a smile that was a little too quick, eyes that were a little too black, hair that was a little too unkempt and a mind that was a little too sharp.

The pope got up and the four red hats sprang to their feet. "I will tell you what makes sense. It makes sense that I travel to America and meet with these two children. It makes sense for the Church to recognize the apparition as a miracle because that's what it is!" The red hats looked at each other but never questioned—even raised the possibility—that maybe the pope was being a bit too impulsive. "Must I remind you that one of the tenets on which our Church is founded is the miracle of the resurrection? Christ died on the cross and a few days later walked out of his tomb and rose to heaven! An apparition by the Blessed Mother is nothing compared to that. And why did Christ rise to heaven? Why?" Leo waited and looked at each of the men standing at his side. "He had to! Man was condemning himself to hell and His Father, God Almighty, in His magnificent wisdom, sent His only Son to intercede for us. I put it to you, are we going to allow the technocrats, the skeptics and the atheists to shake our faith? Because if we do, we might as well become lawyers and forget that the existence of our glorious institution is based on that which is not tangible, that which cannot be measured with instruments and computers, but that which is as real as the blood Christ shed for us; as real as the love in our hearts and the faith in our souls!" The pope paused to gather breath, but though his strength may have been lagging his determination was firm. "After two thousand years," he continued, "man is again slaughtering children by the tens of thousands, hunger and famine are rampant, crime, perversion, drugs—where will it end?" Leo pointed his finger at the cardinals. "I tell you this apparition is not a hoax. It is a warning for Man to reflect before it is too late!"

"I beg your pardon, Holiness." Cardinal Tomaso measured his words carefully. At seventy-four, he was the senior member of the group, as well as a staunch conservative and ally of the pope. He had never been a handsome man, and he had never cared. He kept his weight down, his hair white, his nose flat and politics as far away as possible. "Do we know what the Blessed Mother said to the children?"

Leo looked him squarely in the eyes. "That is a sacred secret between the children and Mary. The children were told to reveal the message exactly thirty-three days from now."

"Holiness, I take it the children are American?" asked Tomaso.

"They are," confirmed the pope.

"Mary spoke to them in English?"

Leo walked up to his friend, looked him squarely in the eyes and answer that, "Mary spoke to the children in the language of universal love."

"Holiness, as you know, in the last several hundred years there have been many apparitions; apparitions that have surfaced all over the world. From Japan to Rome, from Ireland to Greece; from Mexico to your own homeland of Croatia. The latest apparition was to a seer called Yolandita, and before that, there were reports in early December, 1996, of an image appearing on the windows of the Seminole Finance Company of Clearwater, Florida, in the United States. It resembled the Blessed Virgin Mary as Our Lady of Guadalupe. It is extraordinary that a building owned by a finance company should become a shrine, but so it has. Nevertheless, the Holy See has kept its distance from all these apparitions because as you know none of them—including that of Yolandita—stands up to scrutiny."

"What is your point, brother," asked the impatient pope.

"Who has met with the children, Holiness? Who is making sure that the information we get is correct?" asked Numa.

The pope returned to his throne. "His Excellency Bishop Ronnoco."

"Ahhh!" The eminent exclamation was accompanied by nods and smiles.

"Tomaso, do me the kindness of arranging my travel to America. Bailey, this must be the religious event of the century! For once we are going to legitimize a contemporary miracle. Pino, make sure that the American president is in on this. He is Catholic and should be proud of what will take place in his country." The pope beckoned Cardinal Numa aside. "Numa, I do not want, nor will I tolerate meddling, you understand?"

"Yes, Holiness."

"Holiness, I want to be clear about everything." Tomaso walked up to the pontiff. "You want the miracle to be authenticated by the Church and the children beatified in life?"

"I do. Any objections?" He pope looked around the room. Since there were no objections, he asked everyone to leave the room. "Let's get to work!"

Across an ocean, Bishop Ronnoco invited Father O'Malley to dinner at one of the finer restaurants in New Orleans. La Colombina had sparkling white tile floors, white stucco walls, big, indolent fans, round potted plants and watercolors of the French Quarter rendered with dazzling originality by a host of local artists.

Bishop Ronnoco and Father O'Malley dressed in civilian clothes, Ronnoco in blue jeans and a peppermint-green striped shirt, Father O'Malley in a pair of black trousers and a white shirt. Both ordered the same dish, grilled rack of lamb with wild rice, accompanied by an excellent bottle of California Barbera (a new experience for the bishop), coffee, fresh raspberries with cream, flan, and brandy. At one point, Father O'Malley remarked that Bishop Ronnoco was unlike any other high-ranking Church official he had ever met. "Where are you from?"

"Croatia."

"Like His Holiness!" observed the priest.

"Like His Holiness," agreed the bishop.

"What do you do, Excellency, in the Holy See?"

"What do I do?" Ronnoco sipped his wine.

"Yes, if I may ask—what do you do for the Holy Father—besides making sure that miracles happen?"

"You know, Father, I like men who speak their minds."

"Oh, I do that."

"I know, I read your file. You're tagged as a troublemaker. Did you ever wonder why you're stuck in this godforsaken place?"

"Punishment for being a big mouth, I guess." Father O'Malley shrugged.

"I don't think it is meant as punishment, though it is certainly a way to keep you from getting in trouble. They thought of sending you to an even more insignificant outpost in New Mexico—to teach native Americans about Jesus and Mary. The only reason you are here, and not there, is because the bishop who had your life in his hands, thought—rightly, I might add—that you would have less opportunity to do mischief in this climate. The heat and humidity in Louisiana has a tendency to smother initiative." Ronnoco smiled.

"Ha! And you just arrived!" Father O'Malley stuck his spoon in the flan.

Bishop Ronnoco sipped his brandy. "You've been a troublemaker forever."

Both men had shifted their attention to the coffee before Father O'Malley asked the bishop where he had gone to school.

"The Gregorian Institute."

"I went to Saint Joseph's myself," said the priest.

"You have been priest at La Place for twenty years. In that time the congregation has fallen to a fourth of what it was when you took over. Do you think there is a connection, or is it a coincidence?"

"People are disillusioned and disappointed with the Church," explained O'Malley. "They feel the Church doesn't have a clue, that it has lost its sense of purpose and become just another bureaucracy selling a little mysticism to perpetuate its existence."

"That is a strong condemnation, Father."

"It's not! It's—criticism, and from the heart. I love the Church, otherwise I would have left years ago. It needs to open its eyes, that's all, to look at what is happening in the world. If it doesn't, it might as well go into real estate."

Ronnoco laughed and offered the priest another brandy. "So, tell me, Father, what I should do with you?"

"Do? With me? I didn't know you were supposed to do anything with me." Father O'Malley laughed.

"Things are going to get pretty busy around here in a few days."

"You're not afraid I'll spoil the miracle for you?"

"You wouldn't do that." Ronnoco smiled.

"No, I wouldn't." O'Malley returned the smile. "What do you want from me, Excellency? Tell me what to do and I'll do it. Despite what people say, and despite my big mouth, I've never disobeyed my superiors."

"You're a good man. It may be that I have a weakness for idealists. Why don't you take a vacation—if you like, after that, I'll talk to His Holiness and perhaps rescue you from the swamp. You can work at the Vatican."

"Me? Work in the Holy See?" It was the first time since Bishop Ronnoco met Father O'Malley that the priest seemed interested in something. "Doing what?"

"It really doesn't matter, does it?"

A week and a half later, on orders from Pope Leo XIV, a contingent of Franciscan friars arrived in La Place to be secretaries, messengers and watchmen. They slept in cots inside the little church, and Brother George, a tall, muscular man with small eyes, a long nose and not much hair, became Bishop Ronnoco's lieutenant. Ronnoco assigned three of the brothers to be with the Miltedews day and night. The men helped Harriet with the groceries, took out the garbage, kept out the tourists, the curious, most friends and most relatives, and screened all calls.

The fence was reinforced and electronic sensors and surveillance cameras were added. A dozen devices that discharged "white noise" (an acoustical or electrical interference used to mask conversations and make them unintelligible to someone trying to listen in from a distance) were aimed at the gate from the roof of the house. Also, Bishop Ronnoco warned the family not to talk about the apparition with anyone outside the house.

It was during one of those frantic afternoons that Ray stood outside his door—a beer in one hand—and watched mesmerized as a hundred men built the white and yellow canopied stage from which Pope Leo would address Catholics around the world (with Teddy and Alice at his side, of course). Ray felt a shortness of breath and staggered into a rocking chair. He pressed the cold can to his forehead as his stomach tightened and his body quivered. Mr. Miltedew had finally realized that his family was being held hostage by the Catholic Church.

✝

The local paper carried a headline that was repeated around the world: *"Leo XIV Travels to Meet with Blessed Children."*

Cardinal Bailey's press kits complimented the propaganda machine of Vatican Radio and its web of confederates throughout Europe, the United States and South America. Some in the commercial media (controlled by Jews and Protestants, according to insiders at the Vatican) wondered why the Holy See had decided to place its considerable prestige behind such an unbelievable story. In the end, the press resolved not to express its opinion, fearful they might be labeled intolerant by disgruntled Catholics. Instead, the media sent dozens of trucks and vans equipped with long-lens cameras and high-power microphones, parked them outside the gate and waited. Bishop Ronnoco smiled; he was ready for them.

While New Orleans hummed with news of the papal visit, a brown Ford stopped at a gas station on its way to Destrehan. It was one o'clock in the morning. The driver bought a two-gallon plastic container and quickly filled it with high octane gasoline. He was the sort of fellow who, even in the light of day, and regardless where he stood, looked like his own shadow, grey and flat; a silhouette without features or color, that allowed him to move in and out of crowds with no one taking notice. He wore black pants, a black windbreaker and matching leather gloves. It took this specter less than half an hour to reach the overpass, though the torrential rains made it difficult to see the road and rivers of mud overflowed both sides. He parked next to the railroad crossing, opened the trunk and took out the container of gasoline. He was amazed and annoyed by the insistence of the numberless flying pests that buzzed about his head—in the dead of night and in a rainstorm. It showed remarkable determination on the part of the mosquitos, several of whom could have been drowned by a single raindrop. "Shit!" His heart stuck in his throat when the biggest rat he had ever seen (it was in fact a possum) dashed from a bush less than a meter away and disappeared into the swamp. Joining the parade of flying insects were thousands upon thousands of colorful lovebugs copulating in the air. The grey man in the black jacket spat out a few of the darlings he inadvertently inhaled. He shook his head and waved his arm in a fruitless attempt to keep the insects off his face. He walked toward the underpass and there, about five meters from where he stood, he found the shack (if the few pieces of plywood on top of each other could be called a shack) and inside it the worthy Louie Peps, lying underneath a green garbage bag as added protection against the downpour. Of course, Louie was used to vermin; mosquitos were not unlike distant relatives, locust were cousins once removed, and water rats and possum were his next of kin.

"Good evening. Hello!" The stealthy shadow took out a tiny flashlight and approached the makeshift dwelling.

"Eh! What, what?" Louie blinked at the weak but persistent beam shining in his face.

"Excuse me, is your name Louie?"

"Who the fuck are ya?" Louie was not in a good mood, but who would be? It was very late and it was pouring buckets, not to mention the inconsiderateness of *whoever the fuck this asshole was,* waking him up.

"Are you Louie Peps?"

"Who wants to know?"

"I'm from the Red Cross and have some money for you—if you are a—" and the fellow read from a piece of paper, "Mr. Louie Peps."

"Ya fuckin' out of your pissing mother-fuckin' brain!"

"Sorry I disturbed you, then. Goodnight."

"Wait! Ya said you got somethin' for me?"

"If you're Louie Peps."

"How much?"

"Twenty dollars."

Well, twenty bucks was twenty bucks in any weather. And although twenty bucks did not amount to much in modern times, it was enough to let Louie eat for a few days, enough even to pay for a pint of moonshine from the Dooley brothers. "Yeah, I'm Louie," he admitted at last.

But the representative from the Red Cross was no fool. He asked Louie for identification.

"What kind of 'dent'fication?" The Fox showed his toothless grin. "Driver's license?"

Louie did not have a driver's license. He had never learned to drive because he had never owned a car. So he produced his welfare card, which was good enough.

"I can see you are Louie Peps. Here you are." The man from the Red Cross held out a wilted twenty dollar bill. Louie did not jump up and down (he was still half asleep) but it hardly mattered. The moment his wet paw grabbed the money he was stabbed in the heart with a switchblade and then doused with gasoline. Louie the Fox went up in flames.

About the same time Louie Peps lit the dismal night-skies of Louisiana, Father O'Malley arrived in Rome, left the airport terminal and was immediately whisked into a waiting black Mercedes-Benz with tinted windows and Vatican plates. There were two priests inside; the one who sat in the back with Father O'Malley was thirty-something, big and fat, with short hair, a long nose, thin lips and buck teeth. The other, who was driving, had hard features, a rough beard, a complexion that had seen its share of inclement weather, a broken nose, long oily hair that reached his shoulders and eyes that said nothing.

"Welcome to Rome, Father," said the first priest in fair English as they left the airport. "I am Father Humberto," he added. "I am personally to see to your comfort."

Father O'Malley engaged in some light conversation as he looked out the window and recognized the sights of the Eternal City. He remembered the time that, as a young man ambitious to be a shepherd for Christ, he toured the Holy See. Yes, thought Father O'Malley, Bishop Ronnoco, had kept his word.

The car never stopped at a traffic light, and almost never stopped for people either, speeding into the center of capital. After thirty-five minutes on the road, it entered an alleyway, turned sharply several times and pulled up to the back of a building.

"Follow me, if you please, Father," said Father Humberto to Father O'Malley. The driver opened the door for O'Malley at the same time another young man appeared from the building. "Please," he said. It was the only word he knew in English and he said it with such grace that Father O'Malley thought it should have been accompanied with a smile. Father O'Malley, flanked by the two men, walked quickly into the Institute of Saint Jerome, which had changed very little since Ante Pavelić had been a guest there. Since Father O'Malley was not a VIP, he was lodged in one of the smaller rooms. Then he was told to wait. The room had four cement walls, a desk with a lamp and a Bible on top; at one end of the room was a toilet and sink, and at the other a stained mattress on the floor. As the door closed and the lock was secured, Father O'Malley realized he had traveled all the way to Italy to be thrown in a dungeon.

Three hours later, Father Humberto returned. "If you please—" he said, moving aside and inviting the American priest out of the room.

"Excuse me, but I think there has been a mistake. This is not what I had in mind," protested O'Malley. "I was told by Bishop Ronnoco to—where are you taking me?" It was no use. Father O'Malley was surrounded by four men, who led him in utter, eerie silence through the hall, out the back door and into another car, this one a black Citroën. The car, with Father Humberto and O'Malley in the back seat, sped away and O'Malley, who by this time was a bit uneasy, thought of jumping from the car the first time it stopped at a traffic light, then running to the American Embassy. Unfortunately, the car never stopped at a light and was going so fast that jumping out would have been suicide. Of course, O'Malley was unaware that the doors to the automobile were secured so they could not be opened from inside. He did notice that it was a half moon, and the sky was full of stars.

The car zoomed out of the city limits like a rushing ghost and into the countryside. After an hour, it stopped. The driver opened the door and courteously directed Father O'Malley to get out and follow. The three men walked up a small hill that was barren except for a shrub here and some grass there. When they reached the top, Father O'Malley saw Rome and its millions of lights spread out in the distance. It was beautiful. Unfortunately, O'Malley was unable to enjoy the sight for too long because the men accompanying him were in a hurry. They walked down the other side of the hill until they reached a fruit tree that stood in the middle of a field. The man in front motioned Father O'Malley to walk to the other side of the tree. O'Malley had enough time to look down and see a large, deep hole in the ground near the base of the tree before he fell quietly into it, as dead as anyone could be after being shot twice in the head.

Humberto and his partner worked quickly and with thoroughness. First, they removed every piece of clothing from the body; then they cut off the head and hands, covered the body completely with fresh earth, placed several plants and shrubs on the grave, put the severed head and hands in a plastic bag, returned to the car and drove back to Rome. Once inside the Institute of Saint Jerome, they entered a well-guarded room and placed the plastic bag on a table. There, they removed Father O'Malley's head and hands and painstakingly crushed them with mallets until the bones were pulverized. Once this was done, the remaining bone fragments and skin were put through an industrial grinder and the results placed in the garbage bin. So much for Father O'Malley's Roman holiday.

☩

Less than a week later, Ronnoco sat in the office at the rectory. It had become the command center for the pope's visit to the United States and had been equipped with three fax machines, a burn basket, a paper shredder, special electronic gear to prevent bugging, and telephone scramblers.

The bishop had just gotten off the phone with the pope. He had called Leo to advise him to take emergency precautions and prepare the Holy See for a possible sudden and monumental increase in the number of people attending church worldwide the moment Mary's message was revealed. He reminded the pope of the severe shortage of priests and of the weakened infrastructure of the Church. Ronnoco wondered if the pope had ever sat down to consider the consequences—positive and negative—of what they were trying to do.

"Excellency?" said Brother George walking in the room. "Thomas, Brother Thomas says Mr. Miltedew is acting strange."

"Strange?" It was too close to the pope's arrival in New Orleans. Ronnoco could not afford second thoughts, guilty consciences or instability on the part of the players. "Let's find out what ails Mr. Miltedew today."

A short and stumpy friar opened the gate the moment he recognized Ronnoco. "Good afternoon, Excellency!" The bishop waved at the brother and drove the car slowly through the mass of reporters, paparazzi and others until he reached the front porch. Another friar, a much larger man than the one manning the gate, opened the door to let Ronnoco out of the car. As soon as His Excellency stepped up to the door of the house, Harriet greeted him with a kiss on his ring.

"Excellency!"

"Hello, Harriet. Where is your husband?" asked Ronnoco.

"Playing catch with Teddy. Ray!"

Ray had not shaved in several days and his overall appearance left a lot to be desired. Besides a shave and a change of clothes, Ray looked like he needed sleep.

"What is the matter?" Ronnoco and Mr. Miltedew stood in the backyard beside the clothesline that stretched from one side of the white fence to the other, and which, at that moment, had nothing hanging out to dry. The matter was, according to Ray, that he was a prisoner in his own house. "These friars are not friars, they are thugs!"

"That is no way to talk about men who are here to help you, Ray. Listen to me," said His Excellency softly. "You brought this upon yourself. You wanted comfort, you have it. You wanted your family looked after, you have that too." The bishop pulled Mr. Miltedew away from the fence in case the high-powered microphones on the other side (from the press) should pick up their conversation. "Unfortunately, this type of enterprise—and that's all it is, Ray, a business deal, you know—in this type of enterprise the parties have to be extremely careful and make sure nothing is said or done to invalidate the agreement. I don't think that is too much to ask. The brothers are here to protect our interests. Take a little time, if you will, and think what would happen to us—to the Church, to the reputation of the Holy Father—if something went wrong. That just cannot be allowed to happen and I am here to make sure it does not. Now, what else? Speak up; I've had a busy day and if you don't mind—"

Ray pulled out a newspaper clipping from his shirt pocket and handed it to Ronnoco. It was a short notice from the police blotter. It said that a Louie Peps, a resident of La Place, had been found murdered underneath an overpass. It added that the deceased was stabbed before he was set on fire. The inquiry was continuing, although the police didn't have any leads in the case. Ronnoco carefully refolded the clipping and gave it back. "Poor man, God have mercy on his soul." Ronnoco noticed that Ray was lighting a cigarette. He had not been aware that Ray Miltedew smoked. "Is that why you are upset, Ray? Look, as sad and tragic as it is, men like Mr. Peps meet with misfortune—often."

"What happens after the pope leaves?"

"What do you want to happen, Ray? Do you and Mrs. Miltedew—with the children, of course—do you want to go on vacation?"

"Vacation?"

"Yes."

"Where?"

"Europe. You can fly back with us, in the pope's plane. First Italy—you'll stay in a palace."

Ray's eyes widened. "A palace!"

"Would you like that, Ray? Do you think Harriet would enjoy living like a queen, if only for a few weeks?"

"Yeah! Sure!"

"You see, Ray, all I want is to make you happy. You keep your side of the bargain and I'll keep mine. Relax, everything will be fine."

19

Leo XIV's arrival in America promised to be a spectacle of such magnitude that the television networks preempted their programming to show live the pageantry of the papal visit. A pope was arriving in the United States. That in itself was not unusual, of course. What made pope Leo's visit such an extraordinary wonder was the legitimization of a miracle.

The empty, state-owned lots in the vicinity of the Miltedews' were sprayed by crop dusters two days prior to the event so those standing in the swampy fields could attend the pope's mass without being eaten alive by the mosquitos. Almost half a million of the faithful were expected to be there, standing a hundred feet behind the press line, roped off by local and state police. From there, they would witness the astounding and history-making service.

The whimsical local climate that has managed to disrupt every outdoor activity in Louisiana since time began—from jazz funerals to political rallies to barbecues sponsored by the KKK—was on this occasion on its best behavior. It allowed for an unusual spell of dry and cool weather that promised the loveliest of days for Leo's visit. This was no accident, of course; after all, the pope knew those who ruled the elements firsthand.

Ray and Harriet Miltedew followed the event, like everyone else, on television. The day before the pope was scheduled to land they were up at five, running last-minute errands and hoping that in the commotion nothing would be left out. The only ones unfazed by the whirl of activity going on around them were little Teddy and sweet Alice.

For her meeting with the pope, Alice would wear a simple white chiffon dress with tiny yellow sunflowers and pink ruffles. Teddy would put on a celestial blue suit that Jenny Tarr, Harriet's friend who ran a boutique from the kitchen of her mobile home in Destrehan, had made for him. Bobbie Black, a hair stylist from Baton Rouge who was rumored to have done Jimmy Swaggart, drove from the capital to do Alice's hair and give Teddy a haircut.

Sweet Alice was not required to do much except meet the pope, wait for the Holy Father to bless her and then move aside. Teddy, however, was expected to wait until the pope had celebrated his first mass in America in front of a record-breaking crowd, then stand by while Leo introduced him to the world. The boy, with help from Bishop Ronnoco, had rehearsed for over four hours the moment and the words to say then. He had shown a remarkable talent for sounding sincere and truthful, all the while looking like a little angel. What nobody was aware of—including Harriet—was that since the apparition Teddy had acquired a taste for the morning evangelists who crowded the airwaves of local television. Sometimes the little boy stood in front of a mirror and imitated his idol, a man who, though not Catholic, could storm and rage on stage and even make his nose turn bright red (if not long) at the drop of an almighty dollar. Teddy could not sing very well yet, and he had never learned to play the piano. Still, he knew he could beseech the faithful with offers of salvation, or scold them and threaten them with damnation. He could also beckon them with grateful eyes overflowing with tears of sadness, remorse or simple joy, depending on the sentiment required at the moment.

Around noon, Ray and Brother Thomas went to the local supermarket. On the way back to the house, Ray stopped to buy fresh oysters from a buddy who went out each morning to the gulf and returned to sell his catch by the roadside, from the back of his van. Ray and Teddy loved raw oysters, especially when swimming in Tabasco, horseradish and lemon.

"Georgy!" called out Ray.

"Yo!"

The transaction did not take long. Five dollars for a five-pound bag of oysters. Ray took home three bags, enough for everyone, including the friars. Harriet and Alice loved steamed and fried oysters.

"You think His Holiness likes oysters?" asked Ray, as they drove home. "I'll put a bag aside for him."

"Teddy!"

"Yes, Daddy?" The little boy was sitting barefoot on the floor, watching a movie on television.

"Oysters! Want some?"

"Yeah!"

Ray dropped a bag of the mollusks in a bucket of ice and placed the others (including the one for Leo XIV) in the refrigerator. He took out the Tabasco, the horseradish, five lemons, a beer for himself, a Coke for his boy, and joined Teddy in front of the TV.

"Where's your ma?"

"I'm here, hon—" Harriet entered from the bedroom. "I heard on the radio that there are so many people in town—come to see His Holiness!"

"Tell me about it. I spent fifteen minutes waiting for a light to change. It's crazy, plain crazy!" Ray and Teddy settled down to an oyster feast while Harriet went to prepare something dead for lunch.

"What are you watching, son?" Ray asked his son.

"An old movie," said Teddy dipping his first oyster in hot sauce. The movie Teddy was watching, and that Ray now sat down to watch with him, was on a religious channel owned by the archdiocese. It was the turn-of-the-century tale of a precious little boy named Marcel, who—

"Daddy—" said Teddy softly.

"Yes, Teddy?" Ray saw that his son had turned a sickly green and was wincing in pain. "What's the matter?"

"I—" That was all Teddy Miltedew was able to get out, in the way of words anyway. He threw up violently and then fainted. Tainted oysters do not take long to do their nasty bit of work.

☦

The white jumbo jet landed as delicately as if it had been set down by a legion of angels carrying the airship on their silken wings. The TV cameras zoomed in on the ramp that was immediately attached to the front of the plane, and half the world saw the receiving line of national

VIPs, including the American secretary of state and his wife, the governor of Louisiana and his First Lady, and the mayor of New Orleans with his son and three daughters. There were also half a dozen children from as many parish schools bearing flowers for the pope. The bishop of New Orleans was also there, in the company of a dozen priests and nuns. First in line, however, was His Excellency Bishop Felix Ronnoco. Half the world witnessed that same bishop, with his purple cope fluttering in the wind, make his slow and dignified ascent up the ladder and vanish inside the plane.

In the forward section of the 747, Leo XIV sat on a large and supple white velvet seat built by the airline especially for His Holiness. It could have been described as a papal throne with a seatbelt.

Cardinal Tomaso and his secretary—an Ethiopian priest, tall and black as an American basketball player, who answered to the name of Father Ricci—stood next to His Holiness. Cardinal Bailey was there as well with his own aide, a languid and pale young priest by the name of Rostentini, as well as Cardinals Pino and Numa (traveling without secretaries). In addition to the clergy, there were the pope's personal bodyguards (who numbered about twenty and answered to Bishop Ronnoco), the pope's chef, his physician and his secretary, the ever-musical Brother Agustino Serafio. All in all, there were not so very many people traveling with the pope—just enough for an impressive show.

"Excellency!" called Leo from his seat when Ronnoco entered the plane. Cardinal Tomaso had been whispering something in the pontiff's ear, to which Leo simply nodded before going to embrace his friend. "How is the little boy?" asked Leo XIV, quite concerned.

"Not well, Holiness," replied Ronnoco. "He is very, very sick." Ronnoco looked as if he had not slept much during the night, and in fact he hadn't, spending the time in the hospital with little Teddy instead. "He is in critical condition and this morning fell into a coma."

"What!" Leo took Ronnoco aside. "How can this happen! Who did this? I want him found! Are you telling me no one tasted his food?" For some reason His Holiness thought it was a premeditated attempt on the child's life.

"Tata," replied Ronnoco in the same tone of voice, though not as alarmed, "we're not in the Middle Ages. The oysters were bad. His father was also taken ill."

The pontiff grabbed the bishop by the elbow. "I can't afford to go home until this child recovers!" Leo XIV looked rather cross.

"I'm afraid there is very little we can do." Ronnoco spread his hands in a gesture of resignation.

Leo summoned Tomaso, Pino, Numa and Bailey at once. What began as a private conversation between the pope and his bishop now turned into a mini-conference.

"I beg your pardon, Holiness." Cardinal Bailey was standing at the partition that on routine flights would separate coach from first class. "I believe we should consider the alternatives."

"Explain what you mean, Eminence!"

"It is not complicated," said the American prelate. "An apparition is a wonderful miracle, no doubt about it." The cardinal addressed everyone in turn. "But, if the child succumbs without delivering Mary's message, we will have wasted a tremendous amount of time and money, not to mention that our enemies will have a field day. The Holy See will become the butt of every joke for the next five hundred years." Cardinal Bailey clasped his hands and fixed his eyes on the pope. "On the other hand, if we use this unfortunate accident to our advantage, and present to the world, not an apparition, but an ascension, now that would be a formidable event!"

Cardinals Tomaso, Pino and Numa stood like a wall of red behind the pope and listened—carefully. "Think about it," Bailey went on. "What is more impressive—an apparition without a message and possibly without a witness, or an ascension where the party in question is raised to heaven in body and soul?"

"Begging your pardon, Eminence." Ronnoco stepped forward. "The boy is plugged into a respirator. He has tubes in his mouth and nose and has needles feeding him antibiotics. An ascension might be very dramatic but I doubt very much if this little boy will float!"

"Felix!" Leo was peeved. He could not afford dissent or, worse, discord among his advisers. There were a great many people waiting outside. He had to act quickly. And so, he decided: he would visit Teddy in the hospital. He would be in the room alone with the child when, or if, the boy expired; what would then follow would be possible to describe as an ascension—its interpretation a matter of faith, of course.

Bishop Ronnoco protested. The pope immediately overruled him. Ronnoco bowed, nodded and was about to leave the airplane when the pope called him back. "I want the boy to get well, Felix, believe me!" Leo made sure nobody else was listening. "Now, please, don't be angry. We have a lot to do. The world is watching, Felix, keep that in mind!"

Leo XIV stood at the top of the ramp, his perfectly white cassock and matching zucchetto beautifully set off by the azure of the Louisiana sky, a sky so bright and pure it was as if the Almighty had cleared away the clouds. The pope extended his arms toward the citizens of the world and, a moment later, stepped onto the red carpet that had been rolled out to receive him. Leo acknowledged the flowers from the children, blessed each and every one, shook hands with some of the men and women on the receiving line, kissed others, then climbed into his white, custom-made Mercedes-Benz and led the way to New Orleans.

At the head of the convoy was a police motorcycle escort, followed by three vans full of television crews from around the world. Next was the van with the pope's security contingent. Then came the pope himself, in his hybrid off-road vehicle, its rooftop and rear seat replaced by a tight but air-conditioned cubicle made of bulletproof Plexiglas, from where Leo stood and waved at the faithful. A detachment of US Secret Service men (which included the driver) and another group of Vatican bodyguards—all dressed in dark suits and ties, sporting two-way radios, and armed (surreptitiously) to the teeth—maintained a protective cordon around the pontiff, riding on footboards and on an open platform at the rear of the vehicle.

Bishop Ronnoco, Cardinals Tomaso, Pino, Numa and Bailey rode in a van behind the pope. They were trailed by two ambulances and five additional vans packed with more Secret Service men, more local police and the rest of the Vatican staff.

Both sides of the interstate were closed to traffic. Hundreds of thousands of spectators—Catholics and non-Catholics—lined the streets. They mingled with thousands more who were hawking everything from the oysters that sent little boys to the hospital to ceramic figurines of the Blessed Mother, little Teddy and sweet Alice. Police and media helicopters buzzed overhead, crisscrossing the skies like dutiful bees and supplying an exciting, airborne accent to a spectacle that was bigger and more outrageous than Mardi Gras.

As the pope made his way to Saint Paul's Hospital, the throng in front of the Miltedews' dwelling transferred itself to the parking lot in front of the hospital, creating a traffic snarl the likes of which had never been seen below the Mason-Dixon line. Confusion, anger and frustration replaced the goodwill that lingered in the hearts of those who had waited for days for a glimpse of Leo, Teddy and Alice.

The hospital wing where Teddy was being kept was vacated. Teddy's doctor, who happened to be from Bombay, was told to step out of the ward. Twenty-six other patients in the ICU were moved to a different part of the hospital, and Harriet and sweet Alice were permitted to visit only with Ray (in a room across the courtyard), not with their son and brother.

Leo XIV was welcomed at the entrance to the hospital by Monsignor Stevens, the chubby and agreeable hospital administrator. He led the pontiff and his train into the executive elevator and up to Teddy's floor. Two friars then escorted Stevens back to his office, while the pope, Bishop Ronnoco, Cardinals Tomaso, Pino, Bailey, Numa and Dr. Gotovać (the pope's personal physician) called on little Teddy Miltedew.

Dr. Franko Gotovać was an extremely tall and thin man with small, round wire-rimmed glasses and a long hooked nose. He was always dressed in black, and in proper lighting was easy to mistake for the angel of death.

Of course, a contingency plan had, in fact, been worked out in case of Teddy's unfortunate passing. The body of the little boy was to be put in a body bag, placed in a laundry basket and taken to the graveyard behind the little church in La Place, where it would be buried in the churchyard—in a previously occupied plot whose owner had passed away in 1875 and who was not expected to protest. Once that was accomplished, and all evidence of the existence of little Teddy Miltedew made to disappear, the pope would announce the miracle—an ascension. Still, for the plan to be put into effect it was of course necessary that Teddy expire; Dr. Gotovać was on hand to confirm the sad end. But, just as he was listening to the little boy's heartbeat, and as the machine that tracked Teddy's vital signs seemed to slow to a crawl and its "beep, beep, beep" take on a frightening, elongated rhythm, Teddy opened his eyes, took one look at Dr. Gotovać—with his long skeletal fingers—and screamed. Dr. Gotovać blamed the incident to hallucinations caused by the lingering effects of oysters on the half shell, but whatever the cause, a flurry of activity followed the little boy's awakening.

"Teddy, the Holy Father is here to see you," Bishop Ronnoco whispered in the boy's ear.

It was little short of what was supposed to have happened anyway. Half an hour later, Teddy was fully awake, surprising everyone with his remarkable recovery. He recognized Bishop Ronnoco and said, "Hello." Then, he recognized the Holy Father and saluted the pope as well. With the energy and resilience of his young age little Teddy Miltedew now tried to sit up in bed. After a brief examination, Dr. Gotovać proclaimed that Teddy was on his way back to health.

The pope, the cardinals and the bishop fell on their knees and thanked the Son of God for His intervention, and because He had kept Teddy from ascending to His side just then.

It was an hour before Leo XIV allowed the boy's personal doctor—that Indian fellow—to return and resume caring for the little boy. It was also a stroke of luck—or Providence was just playing out its hand—that the window in Teddy's room faced the front of the hospital where at least a million people, including the media, were now stationed.

Half the world was thus watching when the blue curtains were pulled back; half the world observed a microphone suddenly appear at the window; half the world witnessed Leo XIV approach the window in his sacred vestments; half the world saw and heard the pope say mass and bless the half of the world that was watching him spreading a little smoke, sprinkling a little water and raising the large silver cross above the mass of humanity assembled below (many of whom fainted when sunlight, reflecting from the cross, struck their eyes like a bolt from the heavens). Whatever half the world thought was going on, Leo hoped it would be over soon because his miter was getting too hot for comfort. Finally, the moment that half the world had been waiting for arrived. Leo stood to one side and little Teddy's bed was rolled to the window. Leo XIV blessed the child, then turned back to the microphone and in heavily accented but clear English announced, "My children! There has been a miracle!"

"Amen!"

"The Blessed Mother of our Lord Jesus Christ, in Her loving heart, has deemed it necessary to appear to these children!" And half the world noticed that sweet Alice was now sitting beside her brother on the bed, as Leo XIV feebly pointed at them.

"Amen!"

"It is an extraordinary and sacred moment. This child, Teddy Miltedew, who from among all others in the world was chosen, will now convey what Mary, in Her glorious sanctity, demands!"

"Amen!"

Leo XIV turned his head and fixed his eyes on Teddy. The Catholic world held its breath.

There was a moment of silence—only a few seconds, but it was enough for suspense and anxiety to build to such a point that, when little, beautiful Teddy, faint and sickly, uttered his first words, Catholics and everyone else watching, regardless of religious affiliation, became convinced he was special indeed. In that brief pause, Teddy himself thought of crying out "Hallelujah!" He considered taking the microphone off the stand, so as to have the freedom to jump and prance about on the bed. He even thought of going into "Good Golly Miss Molly," which had nothing to do with the purpose at hand but had a hell-raising chorus. But since Teddy still did not feel perfectly well, and since he did not know if it was proper to raise hell in front of the pope, the little boy stuck to his lines, and in his soft, sweet child's voice (weakened by medication), he said at long last:

"Hail Mary, Mother of God! She did weep. She was sad. Begs Her children to come back. With Her Son She returns in the year twenty-ten. To bring love, reign in peace. Everlasting glory be!

20

The message from Mary had exactly the effect Leo XIV hoped for. He did not really have to say anything else, but he did anyway.

"In the name of God Almighty, in the name of the Blessed Mother, open your hearts and join your Church. Let us welcome Jesus Christ, the Son of God, and His Blessed Mother back into our lives as Jesus fulfills his sacred promise in this, His Second Coming!"

The Crusade of 2010 would be something to behold.

From every corner of the world, even from those far-off lands where only a few lived in hiding or in isolation, Catholics rejoiced. Others, critics and detractors of the Church—especially the Protestants—claimed that the Holy See had overplayed its hand. Muslims scoffed and ridiculed the announcement, Jews scratched their heads, and almost the whole world, including many Catholics, wondered what would happen if Jesus and Mary did not show up as planned in the year 2010. The press, who up until then had remained skeptical and uncharacteristically quiet, jotted the year 2010 in their calendars (just in case) and moved on.

Criticism aside, the crusade exceeded Pope Leo's wildest expectations. In a little over three months the Crusade of 2010 was responsible for a Catholic revival that registered a fifty-percent boom in church attendance and a seventy-five percent rise in donations and contributions, especially to local parishes. But, as Bishop Ronnoco had warned, the event stretched those same parishes to the breaking point. As a growing number of urgent calls for help reached the Vatican, its lumbering bureaucracy was caught off-guard and did not offer much except countless apologies. To complicate matters, as soon as Leo returned to the Vatican from the United States, he took to his bed with the sniffles. Since no one dared to make a decision without his consent, the Crusade of 2010 began to spin out of control.

There was little anyone could do, including Bishop Ronnoco, who had returned to Rome as well, glad the episode of the apparition was over, and glad he was not looking after the Miltedews anymore.

Of the Miltedews, Teddy recovered fully from his encounter with the oysters, but even before the pope had left Louisiana—indeed, even before the pope had left the hospital after Teddy delivered Mary's message—Ray suffered a setback, first developing a fever, then falling into a coma and finally dying. He was buried in the same churchyard and in the same plot that had been reserved for his son. Given the turn of events, and with a little financial help from Bishop Ronnoco, Harriet decided not to go on vacation. Instead, she sold the house (at an unreasonably high price, since it had been blessed by the pope and consecrated as a shrine), moved with the children to California, enrolled little Teddy in a professional children's school, and dedicated her time to his promising acting career in a land where apparitions, annunciations, and even resurrections happen every day.

In the meantime, as it never fails to happen when someone becomes entangled in controversy (in this case Pope Leo), loyalties were split, factions formed, and conspiracies hatched.

Early one Thursday morning, Cardinal Tomaso was in his office when Father Ricci announced that Bishop Ronnoco was outside and wanted to have a word with His Eminence.

"Ronnoco?" Tomaso looked up from the letter he was writing. "What does he want? No, never mind. Tell him to come in, of course." Father Ricci went outside to fetch the bishop while Tomaso put away his pen, placed the unfinished correspondence in a drawer, got up, and walked around his desk to receive His Excellency. Cardinal

Tomaso's office was, by far, the largest and most lavish in the Holy See, conforming precisely to the needs of the most influential member of the Curia. Not even the papal apartments dared display the conspicuous affluence that adorned the walls of Tomaso's office—with masterpieces from the Renaissance (paintings as well as tapestries), Napoleon's traveling desk, and furniture that Louis XV himself had had made for the marquise de Pompadour. Since the cardinal liked a well-lit space, one wall was nothing but tall windows—now open to the morning air—framed with delicate off-white curtains that waved ever so gently in the breeze. On top of the Napoleonic desk were the usual inkpads, inkwells, lamps, and telephones—all unusually extravagant—and two photographs in silver frames: one of Cardinal Tomaso as a priest in the company of Pope John XXIII, and the other of Cardinal Tomaso as a bishop in the company of Pope Paul VI. A third photograph of Tomaso as a full prince of the Church in the company of Leo XIV was framed in gold.

"Excellency, this is a surprise. Would you like something to drink? Coffee? Tea?" Ronnoco shook his head and smiled in such a way that Tomaso instructed his secretary that they not be disturbed; Tomaso then closed the door, showed Ronnoco to a wide sofa underneath a Titian, and gave his visitor his full attention.

"Thank you," said Ronnoco, sitting down. Cardinal Tomaso sat on the other side of the sofa. Neither man leaned back on the soft cushions; rather, they sat bolt upright, each attentive to what the other had to say.

"Eminence," began Ronnoco, looking quite concerned. "We have a problem, and I come to you because, first, I know that His Holiness does not have a more loyal servant than yourself, and, second, because the Holy Father treasures your counsel, as well—in my humble opinion —he should."

What followed was not so much a conversation as a monologue, with Cardinal Tomaso doing the listening. The Crusade of 2010 was unraveling, said Bishop Ronnoco, and had to be stopped. The Holy See was under fire; it was being attacked by its own leaders, bishops and cardinals who did not believe Leo had been in full control of his faculties when he traveled to New Orleans. Several bishops were speaking openly against the pope, and some had even gone so far as to write to Leo and demand he abdicate. "Eminence," added Ronnoco, *"Hannibal ad portas!"*

Whether Hannibal, that legendary nemesis of the Roman Empire, was at the gates or somewhere else was of little importance to Cardinal Tomaso. What concerned His Eminence was that he did not understand why Bishop Ronnoco was seeking his advice, since His Excellency had never done so before—in fact had never needed to, because, as was common knowledge, the bishop was the pope's closest confidant.

"That is true, Eminence," replied Ronnoco. "But we both know that when the Holy Father sets himself on a course it is very difficult to make him switch lanes. You understand what I'm saying?"

"Yes, of course, but you are far more able to describe the dangers to the Holy Father than anyone else. You are in the vanguard of this movement, are you not?" It had begun to rain and Cardinal Tomaso got up and shut the windows halfway.

"Yes, but I have not been able to convince His Holiness to yield to reason. That being the case, it is my duty to inform the Curia. We have to do something before the damage becomes irreversible. Eminence, we risk alienating our members to a point that not even a miracle will bring them back. In Mexico, fifteen churches had to close because there were no priests to say mass and the peasants rioted. In Canada, six; in Spain three, in Argentina four—and the list goes on."

Cardinal Tomaso stood by the window for the longest time before he turned, extended his hand to Bishop Ronnoco, and led him to the door. "I understand the problem. Let me give it some thought. I promise to get back to you no later than tomorrow morning."

Bishop Ronnoco nodded and left. The moment he arrived in his office he received an urgent call from the pope. Ronnoco rushed to the papal apartments and found Leo in bed, covered to the neck in white silk sheets and a comforter. Dr. Gotovać was there, and the doctor noticed that when Ronnoco walked into the room his patient's pulse accelerated.

"Franko, I have to talk to His Excellency now." Leo XIV took back his hand, sat up in bed with the doctor's help and coughed up an unsightly mass of phlegm into a spittoon.

"Holiness, you cannot exert yourself; you are very ill," warned the doctor, before turning to Ronnoco. "He cannot exert himself!" The doctor left his instruments behind and stepped outside; he knew he would be returning soon.

"What's going on? It's bloody depressing in here. Can't you open the windows a bit?"

"Stop swearing, Felix," said Leo, with a cough that shook every inch of his ailing frame. "I should never have gone to America. God, what a mess! I can't get sick now, I can't!" The Holy Father smiled ruefully, but pain soon wiped the smile off his face.

"Here." Leo took a white envelope from under his pillow and gave it to Ronnoco. "Read it." Leo coughed again and had to close his eyes and breathe deeply to regain his strength.

"I know about the letter," said Ronnoco, giving it back to the pope. It was the letter Ronnoco had described to Cardinal Tomaso a few minutes earlier in which several bishops asked Leo to step down. "They're feeling the pressure," observed Ronnoco.

"They're like a bunch of—"

"They are what they are, Tata," Ronnoco interrupted. "You can't expect anything else from them. They are complacent, happy bureaucrats, always were, always will be; they are enamored of their positions and with the elevated opinions they have of themselves. Why should they roll up their sleeves and risk everything for an ideal; or do you think they believe that Christ will descend from heaven in a cloud of stars accompanied by Mary to the music of Handel? This is your doing, Holiness, and we know why it's your doing, but they—they didn't want to rock the boat."

"'Rock the boat'? The boat is sinking! They should be terrified of becoming a nonentity!" said the pope. "Ah, I'll deal with them soon enough! Call Serafio."

Ronnoco popped his head out the door and was about to call for the secretary when he noticed Cardinals Tomaso, Pino, Numa, and Bailey waiting in the vestibule. Ronnoco acknowledged the cardinals with a nod, summoned Brother Agustino, and closed the door.

"The Four Horsemen are outside," said Ronnoco, turning back into the room.

"Have them come in."

And the cardinals filed in, each one expressing his concern about the pope's health. "The red hat," the pope ordered his secretary.

Serafio opened a drawer in the pope's desk and brought out a white velvet cushion on top of which sat a red zucchetto. With wonderful agility for a man his age, Serafio turned around and showed the pope the cushion and the hat. Then, he spun on his toes and placed the cushion on the desk. He followed with a half twist of his body, faced the door, took half a step, and left the room.

Ronnoco looked stunned. There was no one in the room aside from himself who could be created a cardinal. Instinctively, Bishop Ronnoco turned to Leo. "I beg your pardon, Holiness, what are you doing?"

"What does it look like I'm doing?" The pope smiled.

"You can't!" protested Ronnoco.

"I can't?" The pope's smile disappeared and he seemed annoyed.

"I—don't do this to me!"

"This is not your decision, Felix, it is mine."

Ronnoco looked as if he had been sentenced to death. "Please, Holiness—I can't accept it, I am not worthy!"

Tomaso, Numa, Bailey, and Pino each took turns trying to persuade His Excellency that to become a prince of the Church was not so much an honor as an obligation—once the Holy Father had decided to confer the title. Ronnoco listened, walked up and down—his arms alternately at his sides and waving in the air—all the time looking at the red hat as if it were a dead animal in the middle of the road. Finally Ronnoco paused, looked at the pontiff, and shook his head.

"My brothers," began Leo. "Many years ago, our late dear Pope Paul blessed me with his favor. The only witnesses on that occasion were two other brothers much like yourselves, close friends of His Holiness, and a boy, young Felix Ronnoco." Leo described the afternoon he was made cardinal and young Ronnoco's reaction to that event, so important in the life of the former priest Draganović. "Felix Ronnoco has been at my side through the best, and he has been at my side through the worst. He has risked his life to serve our Church as legate to Vietnam and Cambodia, as well as in Jerusalem, Iraq, behind the Iron Curtain, and most recently in Bosnia. His love for Christ and his dedication to the Holy See are unquestionable!"

Tomaso, Pino, Numa, and Bailey clasped their hands and nodded at everything the pontiff said—and he said more. "No one else could have undertaken the delicate assignment in America. No one else could have cleared the way for that most glorious event. I do not know of anyone who is more worthy—" and with nod, Leo XIV beckoned Ronnoco to kneel.

It was a short ceremony. Ronnoco had arrived as a bishop and would leave as a cardinal, the purple on top of his head replaced by red. He was now a member of the Curia, the governing body of the Catholic Church.

After the congratulatory formalities and a brief conversation relating to the state of the world, all the red hats were asked to leave, and Dr. Gotovać returned to take charge of his patient.

Next morning, even before he had a chance to stop by for his morning meeting with the pope, Ronnoco received a call from Tomaso asking the new Eminence to drop by. When Ronnoco arrived at Tomaso's office, he found Pino, Bailey, and Numa milling about and drinking coffee. "Good morning," said Tomaso.

"Good morning, good morning, good—"

"I have explained your concerns, Eminence," began Tomaso, nodding at Pino, Numa, and Bailey, while at the same time laying added emphasis on *Eminence*. "They concur one hundred percent. Something must be done."

The agenda for that meeting was to find out what this "something" should be. They could draft a letter and have every member of the Curia sign it; they could request an urgent meeting with the pope and try to convince him to scale back the Crusade of 2010, or to change his mind; but they could not tell the pope what to do. The Church of Rome was not a democracy, and the pope was in every way an autocrat.

"He's not going to like it, I can tell you that much," said Pino.

"Nevertheless, it is our duty to tell him what we think, not what he wants to hear," added Numa.

"I'll call Serafio to tell him we need to meet with His Holiness this afternoon," followed Tomaso.

"Regardless of the outcome, we have to do everything possible to make him understand!" pressed Bailey.

"It must be done," concluded Ronnoco.

Simple as one, two, three—and four and five—except that the pope did not want to see anyone that afternoon. He was weak and his doctor recommended against getting out of bed. Therefore, the Eminences had to wait until next day.

That evening, Ronnoco went home at eight. Sister Angelina prepared a simple but delicious chicken and *prosciutto tortellini al pesto*. It was a heavy dish, but since eating was one of the few luxuries that Ronnoco allowed himself, and since he did not have a weight problem, he enjoyed the dish with half a bottle of Chianti. After dinner, he stepped into his study, turned on his PC, logged on to his office in the Vatican, and worked until his vision blurred. It was one in the morning when Felix logged out and went to bed.

☦

"Papa!" the little boy cried out again. He heard the dark man ask him his name.

"A-lek-s-sandar," he answered in a soft voice.

"Aleksandar, your name is Aleksandar?"

The boy nodded.

"And—" the dark man looked at the priest, "tell me, Aleksandar, they call you Saša, eh? Is that what your papa calls you? Saša?"

More silence. Saša tried to look up, but the sun positioned itself behind the dark man, and he could only nod and blink a few times at the towering silhouette asking questions.

"Of course they do, of course they do," said the dark man. He looked at the little boy next to him, again looked at the priest, and finally at the soldiers, before turning his attention once again to Saša. "Do you know how to cross yourself, boy?"

The little shepherd looked at his father, who was wringing his hands, unable to hold back the tears, reflecting nothing but dread and impotence.

"Come, boy, cross yourself."

Saša lowered his eyes, gave a deep sigh and began the ritual learned as a toddler from his grandmother. His thin, bony right hand moved slowly across the chest. First, he touched his forehead, then brought the hand down to his breast, and was about to touch his right shoulder when the sun exploded. He let go of the little flute he had been holding in his other hand and his body fell to the ground. A soldier crushed his head with his boot. The priest gave him the last rites. Nobody heard him scream. Another soldier stabbed his papa in the eye. Saša realized there was nothing to do. Death was impatient. The needs and wants of his pitiful life ceased—the hunger, the cold—exterminated in the blackness that ensued and in the river of blood. Saša was dead.

☦

The meeting was scheduled for ten o'clock. Ronnoco was last to arrive, the dark circles under his tired eyes proof of the horrible nightmare that haunted his sleep. He found Leo sitting on his throne, wearing a long and heavy white robe and red velvet slippers. The pope looked better than he had the day before, although he was still suffering from influenza. Brother Agustino was kind enough to bring an extra chair for Cardinal Ronnoco, who sat down next to Tomaso.

The meeting began with a short and brusque comment from the pope. "This had better be important. I should not be out of bed!"

At that point Cardinal Pino approached the Holy Father. "Holiness, your brothers in Christ have respectfully written up a list of concerns—" and he put out his hand to Bailey, who handed the letter to Numa, who passed it to Pino, who presented it to the pope. Then, after the expected obeisance, Cardinal Pino returned to his seat. The list was written on an official, and long, piece of stationery—long because it required the signatures of every member of the Curia. The silence in the room was absolute. While the pope studied the document, the other five men did nothing, not even play with their rosaries. They entertained themselves by exchanging looks. Thirty seconds later, Leo turned to Tomaso, handed him the letter, and said, "Request denied. What else?"

Tomaso took the letter back and began to protest, but Leo turned sharply and said, "That is nothing but a childish attempt at a palace coup! I won't have it!"

"But, Holiness!" Pino did not get very far.

"I said no!" thundered the pope, pointing from one cardinal to another, including Ronnoco. "What kind of men are you? You are supposed to be the leaders of the Church! So what if hundreds mobbed a church because there was no room for them inside! Mary's call was a call to arms! There is no turning back, and we must get ready for 2010!" Leo coughed so hard he could not remain on his feet and was forced to sit down. "I am ashamed! I am ashamed of you! I won't stand for it!"

With the exception of Ronnoco, none of the cardinals present—they were, after all, men whose careers depended on the goodwill of the pope—thought of challenging the pontiff. Doing so would immediately place all they had worked for at risk. Ronnoco, however, left his chair, clasped his hands in front of him, and in a voice that was firm, direct, and determined spoke for the rest. "Holiness, we have to slow down. People are getting hurt, and worse, they are being disappointed. What for? For an ideal that, although magnificent, is flawed and untrue!"

"Silence!" ordered the pope.

"I beseech Your Holiness, I can't be silent while so much confusion is going on. We are to blame! It is not right, it is not just, and it is not Christian!"

Tomaso, Pino, Numa, and Bailey looked like four sticks of wax dressed in red; their blood drained from their faces and plunged to their heels. Tomaso darted an urgent look at Cardinal Ronnoco, but Ronnoco was not looking at anyone except the pope.

"How dare you speak to me in that tone!" bellowed Leo. "How dare you!"

"As God is my witness, I dare because it is my duty! I love and revere Your Holiness, but your actions are pernicious and the Holy See is suffering! Not since the Middle Ages have we been more vulnerable, not to attacks from our enemies but from our own brothers in Christ, and from our flock as well! It is a situation that cannot—must not—continue!"

Leo XIV got up and walked to Ronnoco. The sick old man trembled as he took his friend by the arm and shook him with all his might. "You think because you're wearing red for the second day in your life you have a right to question me!" roared the pope.

"As a true servant of the Church, as a true servant of Christ, and your true servant as well—yes, I do!"

Tomaso put out his hand and tried to interject an "Eminence!" It was inaudible and his arm remained outstretched; no one was paying attention to him.

"Anywhere else," said the pope, standing now in the middle of the room, "anywhere else what you are trying to do would constitute treason!"

Pino and Numa were not able to contain themselves and spoke in unison. "No, no, Holiness, how can you even think we're—" while Cardinal Bailey shook his head so forcefully it seemed in danger of dropping off.

"My word is that of the Church. To stand against me is to stand against the Church! To stand against the Church is sedition, heresy! I thank God He has given me the chance to unmask your treachery!"

"Holiness, I beg you—this is not fair!" said Ronnoco, helping the pontiff return to his throne. "You are a man known for justice and charity, how can you—"

"Stop! I forbid it!" screamed the pope. "Serafio!"

The friar entered the room so quickly that one could almost have thought he had his ear to the door, although this was unlikely, given the presence of two Swiss Guards outside.

"Paper and pen, now!"

Whether Brother Agustino knew what was going on or not is unimportant. What is important is that to hear Leo rage was enough to make the good brother wish that he had not come into the room after all. As soon as he had given the pope a pen and notebook, Brother Agustino moved across the floor, hoping that he would be told to leave. But Leo XIV had other things in mind. The pope wrote quickly, his pen sweeping across the piece of paper like a painter's brush. "You think you know better?" Leo stopped writing for an instant and stretched out his arm. With a dramatic wave of his hand, the pontiff called down the wrath of God on each of the red hats in the room in turn, addressing them in a voice that was hollow but firm. Tomaso was first. "You want to be the new Bishop of Rome? The Vicar of Rome?"

"No, no, Holiness! How can you think that!" Tomaso had no choice but to throw himself on his knees and beg forgiveness.

The pope then turned to his right and with the same accusing finger aimed the next volley at Pino. "What about you? Does the title of Vicar of Christ and Successor to the Prince of the Apostles fill your perfidious heart with pride?"

Pino was just as eloquent as his colleague, crying out, "No, no, no! Oh, Holy Father, show a little mercy!" He too ended up on his knees, then raised his hands and requested divine assistance.

But the pope did show mercy. He got to his feet and walked straight to Numa. "You look like you could be Supreme Pontiff of the Universal Church, Patriarch of the West and Primate of Italy! You would like that, yes? Tell me! Coward! I can make it possible for you!"

The pontiff's uncompromising stare forced Numa to his knees beside his brothers. He did not say anything, but prayed to Mary.

"Ah, my American friend!" Leo turned to Bailey. "Your country has enslaved half of humanity with its flagrant exploitation of the world. Now you want to conquer the Holy See. It's so like you Americans to want to buy into power—and to let yourselves be bought by it! Imagine, a cowboy as Archbishop and Metropolitan of the Roman province!"

Bailey fell to his knees and cried, "Oh, Holy Father, have pity!"

"Let it be, then!" Leo sat down and with one last stroke signed the piece of paper. "Wax!" Brother Agustino immediately fetched a stick of red wax and a candle. The pope stamped the hot wax with his ring and handed the document to Serafio. "Read it!"

"M-me?" stuttered Serafio, trembling so much his habit swayed back and forth.

"Oh, give it here, you fool!" yelled the pontiff, taking the paper back from Serafio. Then he turned to Ronnoco. "Of all the base, deceitful recreants in this room, you, Felix Ronnoco, are the worst! To think—" Leo straightened his infirm body, so used to the debilitating burden of arthritis, and for the first time in years stood to his full height, towering above the others in the room like an ancient grey specter, "—to think that you would attach your name—a name I gave you—to betray me! Judas!"

"Holiness, please calm down! We only—" said Ronnoco in a broken voice as tears rolled down his face.

The other cardinals crossed themselves and raised their clasped hands to heaven with tears of repentance and cries of protest. It was too late.

"You!" screamed Leo, shaking his finger at Ronnoco. "You shall rue the day! You will suffer worse than any!" Leo stood before the papal throne and proceeded to read the document he had signed in a voice that seemed accompanied by thunder and lighting. "It is my wish and command that I, Leo XIV, Bishop of Rome, Vicar of Rome, Vicar of Christ, Successor to the Prince of the Apostles, Supreme Pontiff of the Universal Church, Patriarch of the West, Primate of Italy, Archbishop and Metropolitan of the Roman province, Sovereign of the state of Vatican City, Servant of the servants of God, choose as my successor Felix Cardinal Ronnoco! To make the succession immediate and irrevocable, I, Leo XIV, hereby renounce my titles and my obligations! That is my last command as Supreme Pontiff of the Universal Church!"

THE CONFESSION

21

It remained an unusual happening, but one that was well within the bounds of reason and acceptability where the Catholic Church was concerned, especially when you consider all the Church has gone through in its two-thousand-year history. For example, the succession of Felix Ronnoco to the papacy was nothing compared to what happened in the year 1032 when Benedict IX was made pope at the saintly age of twelve. Benedict grew up so depraved and led such an unrestrained life that the people of Rome chased him from the city. He eventually recaptured the papacy, but soon got tired of the position and sold it to Gregory VI for one thousand pounds of gold. Now, Ronnoco did not buy the papacy, nor did he bribe anyone or exert undo influence in the way of extortion or blackmail, as happened during the spirited tenures of the Borgias and the Medicis. Ronnoco was appointed by Leo XIV, much as John XXIII had chosen Pope Paul VI as his successor. While the uncommon investiture did raise more than one set of brows, the Curia faced a fait accompli. In the end, what really stunned the noble princes of the Church, including the Four Horsemen, was not so much that a relatively young man of forty-nine was chosen as the supreme pontiff immediately upon the abdication of his predecessor, but that upon being asked what name he would take as pope, Felix Cardinal Ronnoco paused, pondered and answered "Felix," followed by the Roman numeral "V."

Pope Felix V decided to postpone his coronation for three weeks to give cardinals from all over the world time to assemble in the Vatican. In the meantime, the former Leo XIV exchanged apartments with Felix V. The musical Brother Agustino followed his master to Trastevere, and Sister Angelina transferred her activities to the apostolic kitchen, which was bigger and better equipped than the one in the cardinal's former living quarters.

Leo XIV, now retired, recovered from the ill effects of influenza and lived in seclusion under the protection of the Holy See. Pope Felix provided a live-in bodyguard and two nuns to care for his friend, while local *carabinieri* were stationed permanently outside the door to the apartments.

Three days after becoming pope, Felix V dropped by to see his old friend in Trastevere. He arrived in a Vatican limousine and was wearing a black cassock. "Popes come and go, but the curtains remain the same," said Felix, entering the study that up until a week before had been his own.

Draganović was resting in a large new chair that allowed him to watch television comfortably or take a nap if he felt like it.

"Holiness!" Draganović did not get up. He was too old to do so, even for the new pope. "I am riddled with arthritis. My knees are swollen and I'm having more trouble than ever walking."

"Do you want a wheelchair? I'll have—"

"A wheelchair? Heavens, no! The day I can't move on my own I'll take hemlock, thank you, that's it. I don't have to stick around longer than my Maker wants me to. I have left the Church in capable hands—my worries are over. They are yours now, my boy," said Draganović with a wry smile.

"Thank you," said Felix sourly. "I still get confused when they call me 'Holiness.'"

"You'll get used to it, trust me."

Felix pulled up a chair next to Draganović and sat down; they talked for three hours. Their conversation covered many topics, but most of all Draganović offered counsel to the new pope, and tried to smooth out the bumps Felix V was likely to encounter along the way as head of the Roman Church. If Tomaso, Pino, Numa or Bailey had been present they would have been astonished at the civility with which the new and the old pope treated each other, and the seeming amiability and love between them; at the way they laughed and joked without a trace of the antagonism that had led to the abdication. The cardinals also would have been quite shocked to learn that the fiery and explosive theatrics displayed by Leo the day he resigned had been just that, theatrics; a ruse premeditated and agreed upon between the pope and then Bishop Ronnoco. Leo XIV could not afford to die and risk that someone else, for whatever reason, became pope. "We live to die," Leo XIV was fond of saying. He was not about to leave unfinished business behind. He had long determined to resign before becoming too old, too sick or disabled to carry out his obligations; he wanted to secure a successor he could trust, one who shared his ideals and dreams; one who would make sure the Crusade of 2010 continued till the Catholic Church regained its prestige and influence in the world; in short, a man whom Leo XIV had trained himself, one whose name was Felix Ronnoco. That the time was due became apparent following Leo's trip to America, where events had gone so wrong, and where all his actions and decisions had been so lacking in clarity and purpose. Upon reflection, Leo XIV understood that haphazard escapade as a warning: it was time for him to step aside. However, Leo XIV did not want to risk opposition from the Curia upon naming his successor. That was unacceptable; hence the need for the theatrics. By the time Leo abdicated and named his man, the most influential members of the Curia were on their knees, in tears, and praying. They were too stunned to realize they had been duped.

Two days after his meeting with Draganović, Felix received an urgent call. "Come at once," said Brother Agustino, his light operatic voice taking on a pessimistic Wagnerian tone.

The pope rushed to Trastevere and found Draganović in bed, attended by Dr. Gotovać, Serafio and the nuns. The bedroom was outfitted with the latest emergency medical equipment. "He was going to the kitchen when he stubbed his toe against the table. The pain triggered a heart attack," said Dr. Gotovać outside in the hall.

Suddenly, a red-eyed Serafio opened the door. "He's calling for you!"

"He cannot exert himself, Holiness!" warned the doctor as Felix went to see his friend.

Draganović lay in bed attached to several machines, including one that fed him oxygen through two thin plastic tubes in his nose. "Tell them to get out!" said the old man in a barely audible voice. Felix waved the nuns and Brother Agustino out of the room.

"My time—my time is come, I wish—need to confess!"

Felix V took the old and bony hand of his dear friend in his, leaned forward in his chair, placed his forehead against the edge of Draganović's bed, and felt the tears rolling down his face. How could it be otherwise? Felix Ronnoco had never known a sadder day in his life; he was losing his mentor, his guardian—his Tata. "Confess and be absolved," he began in a tremulous voice, before he continued with the ritual that both men knew so well. *"In nomine Patris, et Filii, et Spiritus Sancti. Amen."*

"I confess," said Draganović with great difficulty, "to Almighty God, to Blessed Mary ever Virgin, to Blessed Michael the Archangel, to Blessed John the Baptist, to the Holy Apostles Peter and Paul, to all the angels and saints, and to you, Father, that I have sinned exceedingly in thought, word, deed through my fault, through my fault, through my most grievous fault, and I ask Blessed Mary ever Virgin, Blessed Michael the Archangel, Blessed John the Baptist, the Holy Apostles Peter and Paul, all the angels and you, my brother, to pray for me to the Lord our God, I confess—I confess—"

☦

Rostas returned the baby to the farm a week later and the toddler spent his days sitting by the road looking out for Damir. "Where Damir? Nana, Damir here soon?" The old woman looked into the sad little eyes and said nothing. When nighttime arrived, Ana went outside, picked the boy up and carried him into the house. When winter covered the mountain in a blanket of white, the child was confined to a little side window in the parlor where he sat by a roaring fire—his small chin cupped in his hands, his eyes ever vigilant for anything or anyone outside the house as he waited for Damir—until he was put to bed. He often turned to Ana, who was never far away, knitting or mending—clothes or the baby's hopes—and asked, "Nana, where Damir?" or "Nana, Damir soon?" The old woman put the yarn away, sat the baby on her lap, kissed and caressed him, and said the only words she knew would soothe him, "Soon, Damir will be back soon." Damir's face, his smile, playfulness, tenderness, his hugs and loving nature were sealed forever in the child's fondest recollections. And there they would remain, never to be lost in the unpredictable maze of his unfolding life. Ana, of course, was not aware of this, nor did she wonder about the importance of one little boy's fate set against that of so many others—the hundreds of thousands who died in the war, the latest victims of a bizarre melodrama in which, for centuries, outside interests incited a nation's children to fratricide.

Because Pero died suddenly, Ana was left with the baby alone on the farm and Father Draganović was required to seek outside help for his mother in the form of Rostas and his wife, Olga. The couple did not need much persuasion to abandon their small apartment in town and move to the comfortable house on the mountain. Yes, they would have to put up with the old woman, but neither Rostas nor his wife expected it to last for long. Yes, Rostas had to assume the chores of a shepherd, but that too would not go on forever. Most babies grew up; some even learned to tend sheep. All in all, it was a worthwhile compromise, one that in the end the couple hoped would prove to their advantage.

They were right. The boy grew up, took over caring for the animals, and Ana Draganović died in her sleep on a sparkling summer night, while the stars and the moon attended her rising spirit. She was laid to eternal rest a day later at the top of the incline behind the house, among the flowers and the fruit trees she loved so dearly. After a brief service around the insignificant mound of dirt, Draganović commended the spirit of his mother to Christ, walked down the windswept hill, went in the house, put away his ceremonial garb, changed to a black suit and tie and walked outside where Olga was waiting for him with a twig basket. It was lined in white cloth and was full of dried meats, fruit, cheese, wine and a thermos of Puerto Rican coffee for the long journey back to Rome.

"Where's the boy?" asked Draganović.

"Saying good-bye to the cat," sighed Olga. She was thirty-three, rather plain, but with a healthy, youthful look—although her hair was beginning to show traces of grey. She had small black eyes that became slits when she was angered. Her temper, as her husband had discovered more than once during their eight-year marriage, was as severe as the knot of hair she kept tied at the back of her head.

"Felix!" Draganović walked to the car.

"The suitcases are in the trunk," said Rostas. He looked as fit as ever.

Felix ran out of the barn in a dark grey wool suit at least one size too big for him, a suit that thirty-six years earlier had belonged to young Krunoslav Draganović. The suit did not come with a tie, so the little boy buttoned his white shirt at the top. In his arms, Felix carried a kitten of infamous lineage, one he called Tito.

"Don't run, you'll get all sweaty. Come here." Olga did not wait for the little boy to go to her, but cut him off as he approached the automobile. She waited for Felix to kiss and hug the kitten half a dozen times, then took the little cat from the boy, dropped it on the ground, took out a handkerchief and wiped his face.

"You have black circles under your eyes—like an old man. Give me a kiss." Olga pushed back the light brown curls from the boy's face. Felix gave Olga not one but several kisses and embraced her longer than she thought was necessary.

"It's almost three o'clock. We have to go!" called Draganović, holding the door for the boy.

"Promise you'll take good care of Tito," said little Felix to Olga.

"I promise, I promise—" She let go of the boy, turned him around and pushed him gently toward the car. Once Felix was inside, Olga shut the door.

Rostas shifted gears and released the brakes. Slowly, the car began its long journey down the mountain. Felix waved at Olga from the back seat and Olga waved at the boy until the Citroën vanished behind a turn. Then, she went back into the house—her house now, in a way, since Ana was dead and Draganović was taking the boy to Rome. Rostas would have to start taking care of the animals again. Oh, well—

✠

"Tell me, Felix, are you excited you are going to Rome?" asked Draganović. It was Felix's first trip outside Travnik.

"I don't know."

Rostas kept an eye on both through the rearview mirror.

"You are going to make many friends," added Draganović, smiling. Up until then, Felix had counted Tito the cat, the sheep and the other animals at the farm as his only friends.

"But I don't speak Italian."

"Ah, you—you'll learn soon enough," said Rostas from the front.

They reached the town of Split seven hours later. The waterfront, which had been destroyed in the war, was still being rebuilt. The cranes, the trucks laden with lumber, cement, sand and rock—all were hidden in the shadows, resting like giants for the time being, waiting for daybreak so they could begin anew the work of reconstruction. Rostas stopped the car next to the ferry that would take Draganović and Felix across the sea.

"Thank you, Rostas." Draganović got out of the car. He was followed by Felix, who was just waking up from a nap. "Felix, look! Do you see the water?" The boy did not answer but looked up at Draganović. "That's the Adriatic Sea; on the other side is Italy."

"Why is the water black?" The only bodies of water Felix had ever seen were the small rivers running down the mountainside in Travnik.

"The water is black," explained Draganović, "because it is night. During the day the water is as blue as the sky."

"Well, look who's here. Hello, Draganović," said a man who sat at the end of the pier, stamping the papers of those boarding the ferry. The man wore the grey uniform of a customs officer. His desk was set up on a platform made up of four planks from the same lumber that was being used to rebuild the port. He was a burly fellow with a short beard, no neck, a few oily ringlets, big popping black eyes, a thick voice, a large flat red nose, and beads of perspiration on his forehead.

"Good evening." Draganović stepped up to the platform and handed over his Vatican passport and Felix's traveling papers.

The officer stamped the passport without looking at it, then turned his gaze on Felix. "Who is that?"

"My cousin. He will be traveling with me. Those are his papers." Draganović pointed to the official-looking document beside his passport.

This time the man was forced to pay a little more attention. "Ronnoco? Italian, eh?" The man stamped Felix's papers, gave everything back to Draganović, and looked down again, hoping the priest would go away.

"Thank you." Draganović retrieved the documents, stepped off the platform and walked back to the car.

Rostas opened the trunk and took out two small suitcases and the basket of food (some of it already consumed). Draganović took the provisions and one suitcase. Felix took the other little valise, which held everything he claimed as his own.

Two loud toots from the boat alerted everyone within two kilometers that the ferry was shoving off.

"I guess I will not see you for a long time, now, will I?" said Rostas to little Felix. "And when I do, you probably won't remember me."

"I won't forget you," said the boy. There was a time when Felix thought Rostas was his father and Draganović his uncle. Then, he got confused and thought Draganović was his father and Rostas his uncle. It was the reason why Felix began to call Draganović "Tata." But Felix learned the truth from Ana three weeks before she died. Felix did not have a father, and he did not have an uncle.

"You take care, you understand?" Rostas patted Felix on the side of the face with as much affection as he comfortably could demonstrate in Draganović's presence. As the man in the suit and the little boy boarded the ferry, the boat's lights framed their silhouettes—one tall, black and wide, the other short, black and thin. Rostas looked after them until the plank was removed from the dock and the ship glided silently into the solid darkness of the sea. It was not without a sense of loss that he went back to the car and drove away.

✠

The old red and white boat was operated by a shipping concern on the Italian side of the waters. It was wide, heavy, slow and uncomfortable. There were four small rowboats hanging from its sides, not nearly enough to save the several hundred passengers the ship could accommodate. That meant, of course, that in the case of an accident the proprietor of the shipping line had decided to write off at least three-quarters of the passengers, three-quarters who would either have to swim ashore or drown.

"It's moving!" said Felix, feeling the swaying of the craft. "Ooohhh!" He took hold of Draganović's hand.

"You'll get used to it." Draganović pulled Felix closer to him.

"What if it sinks?"

"Then we get on one of those little boats you see over there." Draganović pointed to the rowboats hanging from the sides of the ferry.

"They can sink too," observed Felix.

"They certainly can," agreed Draganović.

"And what if they do?"

"We swim."

"I don't know how to swim," Felix reminded Draganović.

"Then I hope you have been a good boy."

The trip to Italy was as tedious and uneventful as anyone crossing a large body of water in an old boat might be thankful for. Ten hours later, Draganović and Felix were met ashore by Marco, His Excellency's chauffeur. *"Buon giorno, Eccellenza,"* greeted Marco, first taking Draganović's suitcase and then relieving Felix of his. Marco immediately led Draganović and the boy to a long and sleek Cadillac limousine with Vatican plates. Marco was in his fifties, had a long nose, dark complexion, cropped grey hair, a stout body and the quiet, impeccable manners of a professional servant.

"Marco, this is Felix," said Draganović.

"Buon giorno, Felix." Marco merely glanced at the boy.

Felix looked up at Draganović.

"He said 'good morning,'" translated the bishop.

The last leg of the trip to Rome meant more hours in a car; unlike the Citroën, however, the Cadillac limousine was long, wide and comfortable. Moreover, driving though the Italian countryside was far different from driving in Yugoslavia. The road to Rome was dotted with factories, public buildings, ancient ruins, churches, houses and other cars and people. All the same, Felix was so very tired that nothing caught his attention—nothing, that is, until they hit the outskirts of Rome. He was startled at the unexpected mass of automobiles zipping past at any speed, by the pedestrians, by the tall office buildings left and right, and by not one but a thousand monuments in all sizes and shapes, such as the monument to King Emmanuel II (known affectionately as "the cake"). Then there was the *colosseo*, a perfect example of Roman antiquity that, along with its brother the *circo massimo*, elicited from Felix the one comment that told Draganović the boy was taking notice. "This is incredible! There are so—many—and they're huge!"

At a quarter to ten in the morning, twenty hours after they had left Travnik, Felix and Draganović crossed the Ponte Palatino and entered the district of Trastevere, where the limousine maneuvered through a series of back streets until it reached a quiet alley, and the uncommonly plain and inconspicuous little door to the bishop's residence.

The building was two stories high. It had not been painted since the war and therefore looked older than it actually was, though it was at least four hundred years old. There was a balcony on the second story that was rarely used by anyone except Sister Ornella, who filled it with flowerpots and plants.

Marco held the door for Draganović and Felix, then took the suitcases out of the trunk and set them on the sidewalk. *"Grazie, Marco,"* said Draganović. *"A domani."* Marco, nodded, bowed, walked around the back of the car, got in and drove away without saying another word. Draganović took out a set of keys and unlocked the door. "Are you hungry?"

Felix nodded. He had not eaten since the night before when the food in the basket ran out.

"Are you tired?" Draganović opened the door and clicked on a light switch on the wall behind the door, turning on a bare light bulb on the high ceiling.

Felix nodded again.

"Are you more tired than hungry, or more hungry than tired?" Draganović bolted the door from inside.

"More hungry than tired," replied Felix with a grin. He found himself in a cramped hall with a door to the left leading to the cellar and a staircase to the right going to the apartments.

"Well, if I know Sister Ornella, she'll have a plate of pasta with meatballs and sausage waiting for us." And Draganović took to the stairs.

No sooner was Sister Ornella mentioned when the nun opened the sliding doors to the receiving room. *"Buon giorno, Eccellenza. Ma, che bel ragazzo! Benvenuto a Roma, Felix."*

"Felix, this is Sister Ornella."

Felix smiled, but because he could not reply in Italian, he decided not to say anything.

"Did you have a comfortable trip?" inquired the nun in passing Serbo-Croatian. Sister Ornella was not beautiful, thought Felix. She was a broad-shouldered woman with high cheekbones, a wide forehead creased with wrinkles, big hands, a long nose, short dark-brown hair she kept tucked under her coif, a very tight smile that never revealed itself unless her head was leaning forward, a set of yellow teeth (one of them chipped), a firm tone of voice, and a tendency to be kind that ran contrary to her nature and had taken years of penance to mold. "I am sure Felix is hungry, yes?" The nun lowered slightly her head and led the way into the apartments.

"Before we eat," Draganović nodded to Sister Ornella, who was busy setting the food on the kitchen table, "I want to show Felix his room." Draganović beckoned Felix to follow him out of the kitchen. They crossed into the living room, where Felix stopped when he saw three photographs on top of a slender mahogany end table by the sofa. One of the pictures was in a white ceramic frame and showed Ivo and Ana Draganović sitting by the front door at the farm.

"Nana!" said Felix pointing at the picture.

"Yes, that's Nana," said Draganović.

Then Felix turned to the other photographs. They were in plain silver frames. Felix first looked at the one on the left. It was a picture of Draganović and another priest taken a couple of years earlier on the steps of Saint Peter's. The priest in the photograph with Draganović was a tall young man with a thoughtful, unsmiling face which could not have been more than twenty-five years old. "Who's that man?" asked Felix looking up at Draganović.

"That is your namesake," answered the priest smiling. Felix did not understand what 'namesake' meant and he did not get a chance to ask for an explanation because the moment he turned to look at the picture on the right, the little boy recoiled, turned away, threw his arms around Draganović, shut his eyes and held on tightly.

"What's the matter, Felix?"

Felix did not answer. He shook his head and refused to look at the photograph of Draganović and Aloysius Stepinac standing side by side on a street in Banja Luka.

"It's just a silly old picture. Come now," And Draganović led Felix out of the living room, and across the hall. "This is my bedroom," said the priest pointing to a door on his left. "And that is your room," he said pointing to the door at the end of the hall. "Go ahead," he said moving aside so Felix could walk in front of him.

Felix opened the door slowly, as if not sure what he was going to find inside. What he found was a bedroom five times the size of the little attic at the farm with big windows and clean white walls that reflected the sunlight, keeping the room bright and fresh. There was a portrait of Baby Jesus and his Mother, but what caught the Felix's eye was the collection of toys such as he had never seen in his life, all lying neatly on the floor and on his wide, comfortable-looking bed. There were balls, balloons, several armadas of toy soldiers, toy airplanes and trains, building blocks and coloring books; as many toys as any little boy Felix's age might dream of playing with. Felix put down his suitcase, looked up at Draganović with eyes that said, "For me!?" The boy walked around slowly picking up a ball and putting that down to pick up a train and putting that down to pick up a soldier and putting that down to pick up a coloring book—

"Things will be different here, Felix. This is your home now. This is your bedroom. These are your toys. Tomorrow, you'll see your school; then, we'll get you some clothes, the kind of clothes boys in Rome—not shepherds—play and go to school in. You're going to be here a long time and you will grow up and learn everything you can and become a wise, wise old man." Whereas the children who, on occasion, roamed the halls of the residences of high-ranking Church officials were typically those of the staff, Draganović had adopted Felix as his own. And while he was strict and sometimes inflexible with most people, to this little boy Draganović showed understanding and love.

After his meal, Felix took a short nap and spent the rest of the day playing in his room. At sundown the boy stood at the window and saw clotheslines (all but one were full) crisscrossing an inner yard. Across the yard, in the building next door, Felix saw an old man sitting in a large chair reading the newspaper, in a room that was otherwise bare except for the one light bulb shining down on him. He saw a family of five—three children, all of them older than Felix, sitting with their mama and papa having dinner in the kitchen. In another apartment Felix saw a grey cat looking out a window, maybe like Felix waiting for the rising moon. And—there she was, bright, big and yellow, just like at home.

"Felix, Felix, Felix, come and stay,
Not in there but out to play!
Felix, Felix, Felix, come and stay—"

"She remembers me! The moon did not forget!" The boy smiled, jumped in his new bed and in a few minutes was fast asleep.

At six o'clock the next morning, Draganović entered Felix's room and found the boy holding a yellow locomotive in one hand and the little flute he liked to keep under his pillow in the other. "Felix," said Draganović softly. "Felix—" Draganović took the yellow locomotive, put it on the floor and sat on the edge of the bed. "Wake up." He put his hand on the boy's wet cheeks and Felix slowly opened his eyes and smiled. "Another bad dream?"

Felix nodded, yawned and stretched his limbs.

Draganović sat quietly for a moment, stroking gently the boy's face, then kissed the child on the forehead and said, "Brush your teeth and take a bath. Sister Ornella is making breakfast—though you ate enough yesterday for a week." Draganović got up and left the room.

Forty-five minutes later, as the city was beginning another Roman day, Draganović, dressed in a dark grey suit and tie, took Felix by the hand in and out of a noisy, talkative crowd, through the tight alleys and narrow streets of Trastevere. (Felix had no choice but to put on the same oversized suit he had worn the day before, though his shirt had been washed and ironed by Sister Ornella.) Felix was fascinated and bewildered by the multitudes of fine-looking people rushing by—not farmers or peasants, but secretaries, lawyers, doctors, businessmen and hordes of salesmen. The little boy had several head-on collisions because he kept looking left and right at all the things he had never seen before, which was everything around him. For instance, the life-sized dummies in Antonia's dress shop (Felix had never seen a mannequin), and the haberdasher's store across the street; the counting house where a dozen young, beautiful girls punched the keys of strange-looking machines; a tailor shop where the bald little tailor with a chalk in one hand, a measuring tape around his neck and needles in his mouth knelt beside a client who was standing on a metal box; the flower shop that specialized in wedding and funeral arrangements, several examples of which were displayed on the pavement side by side as if to advise passersby that the inevitable outcome of marriage is death. And the barbershop with a waiting line of six men, none less than eighty-five years old.

"Stop running into people, it's embarrassing," said Draganović after the boy almost knocked over an old woman on her way to mass.

The little boy shaded his eyes with his right hand, looked up at Draganović, and said, "But, Tata, there are so many of them!"

Madame Berini's Scuola Inglesa was only six blocks from the house. It was a green building with a crenelated door, surrounded by a tall green concrete fence. The strains of Jerome Kern's "They Didn't

Believe Me" could be heard from a faltering trombone, mingling with the voices of children on the school grounds. Draganović rapped on the door several times, and it was opened by an extremely large woman who seemed as wide as she was tall, with red hair, brown eyes and a little too much rouge. She stood sideways in the doorway, half her body inside and the other half outside the building, in case any of the children were thinking of escape. *"Eccellenza, che piacere!"* said Madame Berini, for it was the educator herself who was greeting them. "And who is this?" she continued in fluent Serbo-Croatian—something hardly surprising, because Madame Berini had been born in Zagreb and lived all her young life there before escaping to Rome during the war. After the war, Madame Berini married a trombonist named Berini. "Is this little Felix whom we've heard so much about?" She was not surprised to see Draganović dressed in a suit; she had never seen him wearing anything else. Draganović and Madame Berini had met on several occasions at the Institute of Saint Jerome—the same Croatian nationalist organization that would extend its hospitality to Father O'Malley—where she had gone for assistance and advice. It was perhaps for this reason that Draganović chose the Scuola Inglesa for Felix to attend.

"Please, come in, come!" Madame Berini opened the door a little more and stepped aside. The school was located in a large, two-story truck and construction machinery depot abandoned after the war. In the center of this unusual structure was an open, unpaved area that had been used in the building's heyday as a dumping ground, and which Madame Berini, after ingratiating herself to local officials, converted into what she described as "a playground." Five small compartments on the first floor were classified as classrooms, each equipped with a clutter of tiny desks, a map of the world and a blackboard. The second story had been appropriated by the Berinis as living quarters, from which her husband was often heard practicing his trombone. The institution had been established to teach the young children of wealthy Roman families to speak what Madame Berini, a language instructor by profession, thought was the lingua franca of the future, English. Of course, if the Germans had won the war, Madame Berini would have been teaching German instead. Though she might have been an opportunist, Madame Berini was also an excellent teacher, and the school was an instant success, both because of its academic excellence and because many of the children at the school were, in fact, the children of the United States and English embassy staff—who wanted their offspring to learn not English but Italian. "I am sure Felix is going to like it here," the educator declared, offering Draganović a chair in front of her metal desk. Felix sat in a smaller chair specifically designed for a child.

Madame Berini's office was painted a light blue. Piles of papers and stacks of books were everywhere, including on a small table by her desk. The wall behind her desk was hung with photographs, photographs not of kings, or popes, or presidents but of many of the children who had excelled in her school. Each picture had the name of the child on it and beside the name a gold star.

"Felix knows how to read and write," said Draganović.

"He does? Well, that's wonderful!" said Madame Berini leaning forward. It hardly mattered, she thought, whether the little peasant knew how to read and write because even if he did—and Madame Berini had no reason to doubt the bishop—the boy could only read and write Serbo-Croatian. He could not speak Italian, and certainly knew no English, which was the reason he had been enrolled in school to begin with.

"Nana taught me," said Felix, speaking for the first time.

"Nana?"

"My mother," clarified Draganović.

Madame Berini leaned back in her chair, clasped her hands and said, "Of course!"

At that moment the bell sounded and the hundred or so little boys and girls playing in the courtyard suddenly became very quiet. The children scrambled like little soldiers and formed three lines in the center of the yard. They waited patiently and quietly until four young women of very serious academic mein marched them inside.

"Yes, I know Felix will flourish here," said the educator.

After Draganović and Felix were finished with their tour of the school—accompanied by a trombone rendition of "Ain't Misbehavin'"—Felix found himself once again colliding with strangers, as Draganović took him to Bambini, a clothing store for children not far from the school.

Because Draganović had never bought clothes for a child, he allowed the pretty young woman behind the counter to recommend, measure, collect payment for and deliver to the house ten shirts, five pairs of shorts and five pairs of slacks, ten pairs of socks, two suits, two pairs of sandals and three pairs of shoes, ten pairs of underwear, three belts and two pairs of suspenders. All in all Draganović bought Felix enough clothes to last the boy—well, at least until he outgrew them, or until Sister Ornella could not alter them any more.

When Draganović and Felix returned home, Sister Ornella had ready and waiting a plate of polenta and sausages for Felix to enjoy. The boy did not like cornmeal so the polenta remained untouched. He did however eat two portions of sausages with onions accompanied by a glass of diluted red wine. Draganović did not join Felix at the table. Instead, he retreated to his rooms. A short time later, after Felix finished his meal, Draganović called to him from the living room.

Felix ran quickly to Draganović, and was surprised to find the priest wearing a long black skirt (a cassock), a purple sash, a cape (the cope) and a little cap (a biretta). Felix remembered, of course, that Olga and Rostas always addressed Draganović with deference, and Ana used to tell Felix how her son became a man of God. She also showed the boy pictures of Draganović in Rome in his priest's collar and skirt. That was the only time Felix saw Draganović wearing anything other than what he wore at the farm. Even when Draganović held mass at the farm, or the time when he buried his mother, Draganović dressed in regular slacks and a shirt.

"Come, sit here, Felix, please." His Excellency pointed to a footstool in front of his chair. Draganović leaned forward and took the boy's hands. "Do you know what I'm wearing?"

"No."

"These are the clothes I wear most of the time outside the house. Here, of course, I always change into something more comfortable because these robes are hot and heavy." Draganović brushed Felix's hair from his face, thinking the boy needed a haircut, and continued. "You know I am a bishop?"

"Y-yes," answered Felix.

"Do you know what a bishop is, Felix?"

"N-no."

"Well, a bishop is a priest, but an important priest, one that other priests look up to and one who is always treated with great respect. If I had worn this outfit when I took you to the school or to buy your clothes, people would have been bowing to me and greeting me all the time and that is the reason I did not put on my bishop's clothes. In most cities of the world, but especially in Rome, a bishop is a very, very important person. Do you understand what I'm saying?"

"I think so," answered the boy.

"I am going to ask you to do something that will be very difficult for you at first, but, as with most things, I'm sure you will get used to it."

"What?"

"Whenever we are with other people, including Marco and Sister Ornella, it is important that you call me 'Excellency' and not 'Tata.'"

"Why?" Felix's first thought was that Draganović did not love him anymore.

"Because that is the way to address someone in my position, that is the correct way to address a bishop." Draganović noticed that Felix had acquired a worried look. "That's not to say I don't care for you, or that I don't love you. It's not that at all. Of course, when we are alone, I want you to call me what you've always called me—"

"Tata!"

"Yes, but only when we are alone."

"I understand," said Felix smiling.

"Above everything else, you must know that my feelings for you do not change with a change of clothes. But, there are traditions and rules that must be observed." Draganović looked at Felix for a moment, then added, "Another thing. It is important that you do not tell anyone at school or anywhere else that I am your father, because I am not, and could never be. Remember I am a priest, and priests do not have children—in the traditional sense. If someone asks who I am, tell them I am your cousin. Believe me, Felix, some day, when you are older, you will know why we've had this conversation." Draganović kissed the boy on both cheeks. "Now, look out the window and tell me if the car is here."

Felix rushed to the window, put out his head, walked back to Draganović, looked to his left, looked to his right and said with a big grin. "Yes, Tata, the car is downstairs."

Half an hour later, Draganović arrived in his office at the Government Palace. He was the Holy See's link to Intermarion, an obscure organization first established in the 1920s by the French and English Secret Services. His field of operation included Poland, Hungary, Austria, Romania, Germany, Czechoslovakia and Croatia. The mission of Intermarion was to inflame Catholic sympathies in those countries and spark a holy war against international communism. Unfortunately for the federation, by the end of the Second World War all but Austria and half of Germany had fallen under the totalitarian boot of the Soviet Union. In 1946 Intermarion was reorganized, revitalized and newly funded by Britain's MI6 and the CIA to recruit, train and run anticommunist insurgents in a campaign of sabotage, disinformation and assassination against the Soviet Union and its satellites, as well as against left-wing labor unions and regional communist parties.

Because of Draganović's leadership, the Commissione d'Assistenza Pontifica was a smashing success helping Croatian and Nazi war criminals vanish in the murky and rusty ballast tanks of the Ratlines. Pius XII was so impressed he lavished unrestrained praise and a bishop's title upon the priest. Archbishop Montini, by then pro-secretary of state at the Vatican and Pius XII's confidant, saw the bishop as the only man in the Apostolic See with the expertise required to deal with Intermarion.

"Anything happen since I've been away?" Draganović asked his secretary.

"These arrived yesterday, Excellency." Brother Agustino stood just inside the heavy doors with a pile of telegrams and a writing pad. He approached the desk and placed all the telegrams on the desk except for one. "This came in today—from Buenos Aires."

Draganović read the Argentinean telegram, opened the right-hand drawer of the desk, placed the telegram inside, then closed and locked the drawer. "What else?"

"His Eminence Roncalli called to offer condolences on the loss of your mother, and would like for you to call him at your convenience. His Excellency Montini has also been coming around asking when you were coming back."

"You did give him a copy of my itinerary, yes?"

"Yes, Excellency," sang Serafio looking at his notes.

"Thank you."

Serafio was straining to open the doors when Draganović called him back. "Call Roncalli. Ask him if I can come over at four."

"Yes, Excellency." With a huff and a puff Serafio returned to his modest cubicle, from where he received anyone expecting to meet with Draganović, prepared His Excellency's schedule, answered his telephone and brewed his Puerto Rican coffee.

As soon as Serafio was out of the room, Draganović took Saint Jerome off the wall, opened the safe, removed enough bundles of Argentinean currency tied up with rubber bands to finance a small army, took out a brown diplomatic pouch with the Vatican seal, placed the money and the pouch on his desk, locked the safe, put Saint Jerome back in place, returned to the desk, placed the money inside the diplomatic pouch, called Serafio through the intercom, sat back and waited for the brother to return.

"Yes, Excellency?"

"Here." Draganović tossed the pouch to Serafio. "For Brother Martín." Brother Martín was Draganović's go-between with Ante Pavelić. The pouch was sent from the Holy See by special courier to the Alitalia office at the Rome airport. It would then be put aboard the next flight to Argentina, where Brother Martín would pick it up and deliver it to the poglavnik.

"Yes, Excellency. Oh—His Eminence will be waiting for you at four."

"Thank you."

Serafio left the room. For a moment the bishop stared into space and thought of Felix. Then, he opened the drawer, took out the telegram from Buenos Aires, read it again and stopped at the word *wedding*. Draganović walked to the other side of the office, tore up the telegram and tossed it in the burn basket. "Good."

22

Next morning, Sister Ornella insisted that seven-year-old Felix not be left to wander the streets of Trastevere by himself, and volunteered to walk the boy to and from school every day if necessary. His Excellency Draganović reminded the good sister that the Scuola Inglesa was but a few blocks away, and that Felix was used to taking care of himself plus a flock of sheep and goats besides, in a wooded valley infested with predators. But the nun prevailed and escorted little Felix to his first day of school.

He looked positively Roman in a new pair of brown shorts held up by suspenders, a cream-colored checkered shirt, matching socks and sandals. His hair was combed back with brilliantine.

Still distracted by the novelty of everything, Felix managed to crash into a little girl, an old man and a priest before Madame Berini greeted him at the school door, while "Anything Goes" tried to play in the background. It would be several days before the new, strange town and its amazing sights no longer demanded the boy's undivided attention and he was able to get to school without mishap.

His dress and bearing aside, Felix's first day in school showed him that it would take time to adapt to the academic life. He could not remember a day in his young life when he had been asked to sit down for hours at a time and pay attention to an unattractive matron speaking a foreign tongue. He could not remember a time when he had to ask permission to go to the bathroom—something that required the intervention of Madame Berini because no one in the school understood what he was saying. And although some classmates made an effort to befriend Felix, they too were frustrated by the language barrier, leaving Felix on the sidelines watching the other children enjoying themselves at play.

Le petit Croat—as the French teacher called Felix—soon became alienated and lonely, though he was never one for giving up. He pondered a whole morning the question of "communication," and remembered that while the sheep and the goats back home didn't speak Serbo-Croatian either, they did seem to understand Felix and Felix always understood them. It made perfect sense, then, to treat his classmates like his herd: whistling and waving, running after the boys, chasing after the girls, knocking them on the head and shaking them by the arm, poking their sides or pushing them from the back to make them move along. Felix certainly made his point. It was lucky for the boys and girls of the Scuola Inglesa that Felix had left his shepherd's stick in Yugoslavia.

It was not long before the indignant parents of Felix's classmates descended on the headmistress to complain about the mad little Croat. One mother, the wife of the secretary to the military attaché of the English embassy, went so far as to demand that Felix be expelled because he "lacked the refined upbringing" essential to associating with her dearest Jimmy and darling Ruthie. Madame Berini had no choice. She summoned Felix to her office and delivered an awful scolding along with a terrible workout of her index finger which would have gone on forever had Felix not looked up at the headmistress as she paused for breath and said, "You are beautiful."

Madame Berini had just refilled her lungs, opened her mouth, and was about to renew the assault on the boy when her mind suffered a short circuit. Her finger halted in midair, her jaw dropped, her brows wrinkled and her eyes blinked a few times. She walked around her desk, sat down, leaned back, threw her gaze across the room at Felix and said, "What was that?" She was sure Felix had been coached to flatter his way out of trouble.

"I think you are beautiful," insisted the little boy sincerely.

After all, next to Ana Draganović, who was dead, Olga, who was young and spent, and Sister Ornella, of whom it did not matter whether she was old, young, spent or dead, Madame Berini was as beautiful as a rose. The headmistress got up from her chair with the feathery grace of a ballerina, skipped to one side of the room, turned quickly to look back at the little boy, and asked, "Would you like some milk and cookies?"

In six months Felix learned enough Italian from Madame Berini to communicate with his classmates without herding. He made many friends among the little girls of his class and was admired by the boys for his physical agility and endurance. The teachers were enchanted with Felix's wide-eyed innocence and endearing country charm. They never suspected that, as he had demonstrated with Madame Berini, little Ronnoco disguised shrewd diplomatic skills behind this simple façade. It was a talent Felix had acquired early on, living with four adults who did not allow him to cultivate the art of being just a little boy.

When Felix was home he spent a lot of time running errands for Sister Ornella. She made things easy for the boy by telling him exactly what to ask for from the butcher, the baker, the fishmonger and the wine seller. The "bishop's boy," as he was known, would go into the baker's shop and call out *"Ciao, Carlino! Bisogno pane!"* Then, he would cross the alley and burst into the wine shop with *"Ciao, Roberto! Bisogno vino!"* All of them, the baker, the wine seller, the butcher and others, tried to find out about his relationship to the bishop. "Oh, he's my uncle," Felix told the butcher. "He's my cousin," he told the baker. "He's my neighbor," he told the fishmonger. "He's my friend," he told the florist. "He's my brother," he told the wine seller—it was enough to keep inquiring minds perplexed, off balance and thirsting for more.

The nights when Draganović was home, Felix sat on the floor beside His Excellency and chatted for hours about what had happened in school that day, a new friend or about something interesting he had witnessed in town. The experience was enlightening for both the bishop and the boy. One time Draganović arrived home later than usual. Felix had already eaten and was in his room playing with his toy soldiers when the bishop walked in. "Tata!" cried the boy, leaping out of bed to give His Excellency a hug.

"What on earth happened to you?" Draganović held the boy at arm's length.

Felix grinned, a large gap evident in the middle of his mouth because he had lost his first tooth.

Draganović suddenly realized that there was a world of difference between spending a few hours with Felix at the farm, where Ana and Olga cared for the boy, and now, where every day-to-day event in Felix's life was intertwined with his own.

Days later, Felix asked Draganović if he could visit a friend after school.

"What is your friend's name?"

"Robert."

"Robert? Where is he from?"

"England."

"That's good," said Draganović for no particular reason. "Just make sure you're home by six, and don't forget to tell Sister Ornella where you'll be, just in case."

A week went by and Felix approached Draganović to ask if Robert, his English friend, could come to the house after school. Draganović thought about this for a long time. "What for?"

"To play."

"Ah—" Draganović pondered some more. It seemed that raising a little boy was full of unpredictability. "Make sure Sister Ornella knows when your friend will be visiting."

"Yes, Tata."

Two days later, as Felix was leaving for school in the morning, he announced to Sister Ornella he was bringing home his friend from *Inglatera*. The nun had been warned of that possibility by Draganović and did not think anymore about it. She tried very hard to keep an open mind and not criticize His Excellency for allowing Felix far too many liberties.

At four-fifteen, just as Sister Ornella removed her coif, she heard the door to the house slam, followed by a noisy dash up the stairs. "Why can't that boy walk like normal people?" thought the nun, as Felix and his friend appeared in the room carrying their heavy backpacks.

"This is my best friend Robert—" Felix could not think of the boy's surname.

"Goldsmith," offered the boy. He and Felix were flushed and sweating. They had run all the way from school. Robert was a little taller and a little fatter than Felix. He had an oval face, curly sandy hair, two little brown holes for eyes beneath two copper-colored brows, an elf's nose, an extremely pale complexion and a set of very small teeth. He was dressed the way any boy his age might have been dressed in London, with a pair of brown slacks, socks and sandals, a white T-shirt with a dark blue knitted sweater on top.

Sister Ornella did not reply but dropped her head slightly, which meant Felix had permission to leave the room.

"La tua mama?" Robert chased Felix down the hall.

"Sorella!" Felix hollered as he threw open the door to his bedroom. Though little Ronnoco meant to say that Sister Ornella was a *sister*, in other words, a nun, neither he nor Robert knew enough Italian to discern the ambiguity of the word, and the distinction between "sister," meaning "nun," and "sister," meaning "daughter to your father and mother" was lost in translation. The idea of Felix having such an odd-looking woman for his sister mystified the English boy.

That evening, Draganović arrived at the house about eight o'clock. As soon as His Excellency walked in the door, Sister Ornella described the events of the afternoon, then returned to the kitchen to fix the bishop's supper.

Felix was lying on the floor of his room looking over a coloring book and winding down from a very fun and exciting day when Draganović came in the room.

"Tata!" Felix rushed to Draganović.

Draganović gave Felix a kiss and sat on the bed while the boy related everything he had done with his friend. "He likes movies, Tata, and asked if I could go to the movies with him next Saturday! Can I, please? I've never seen a movie!" Felix stopped and frowned, then looked at Draganović. "What's a cowboy?"

"My boy," said Draganović with a sigh and in a way that required little Ronnoco to pay attention. "I would prefer if you did not bring that boy here again."

"Not bring him here? Why? You don't like Robert?" asked Felix. The happiness that had been so evident in his face vanished. "Why don't you like Robert? He's not a Serb." Felix knew of Draganović's special dislike for Serbs.

"No, he's a Jew." To think that Madame Berini allowed Jews in her school! But the bishop understood that the Americans and the English had the money to pay her high fees and everybody knew the Americans and the English were a strange mix.

"A Jew?" Felix remembered on many occasions Draganović and others saying the Jews betrayed Jesus, that they turned against Christ and had him crucified. "I'll beat him up!"

"No, you will not."

"But, the Jews—they killed Jesus!" cried Felix getting angrier and angrier.

His Excellency held Felix by the shoulders. "Stop it, Felix. I mean it. I just don't want you to bring him here, that's all. Remember I am a high-ranking member of the Catholic clergy! I can't have little Jews, big Jews or Jews of any size running up and down my halls. It's just not—right."

Felix was not sure what all of this meant or what it had to do with Robert, but he wanted to cry. To think that he had brought home a Jew. "I hate Jews!"

"You mustn't hate the Jews, Felix, we must pray for their salvation, pray for their repentance. We musn't hate them, for it's not Christian to hate."

Felix cast his eyes to the floor. "I'm sorry."

Draganović kissed the boy goodnight, and just as he stepped out in the hall, he heard the boy call out, "I didn't know he was a Jew!"

The melody the following morning was Gershwin—disguised, since the lazy undulations of the trombone that tried to interpret "I Got Rhythm" had everything else but. Felix, tired after a troubled night's sleep, filed into the schoolyard with the rest of the children. Robert was waiting for him inside but Felix ignored the boy and walked past.

"Hey, Felix!" called Robert, thinking that perhaps his friend had not seen him. But Felix did not answer or look at Robert. He ran across the yard to where a group of boys had assembled to talk about what boys talk about in schoolyards. "Felix!" Robert insisted again, this time loud enough for everyone else to hear him—everyone, that is, but Felix. Thinking that maybe Felix had gone deaf overnight, Robert ran to his friend and slapped him playfully on the shoulder. Felix turned sharply and looked at the English boy in a way that instinctively made Robert recoil. "What's wrong? What did I—" Robert was left standing alone and confused in the middle of the yard.

After this unpleasant affair, Felix became wary of associating with anyone unless he knew beforehand the person was not a Jew. Of course, he would not be caught dead talking to a Serb, or a balija (as Rostas called the Muslims), but he had left those back in Travnik. Felix tried very, very hard not to hate them too.

Once, he was crossing the schoolyard when he looked up and saw a white dove making its way downward through the sky in wide, lazy circles. The resplendent ball of the sun outlined the bird with its blinding rays. The dove touched the ground and dissolved into a puddle of blood. Felix closed his eyes, crossed himself and said a short prayer. When he opened his eyes the apparition was gone.

"Felix!" It was an American boy calling him. The kid had recently joined the school and wanted little Ronnoco to look at a collection of baseball cards he had brought from America. Felix did not know what baseball was but was curious to find out. But, before taking a look at one of the colorful rectangular pictures of men in funny uniforms holding thick wooden clubs, Felix looked at the boy with a serious face. "Are you a Jew?"

"No. Why?"

"Let me see that!" Felix smiled and snatched a couple of the cards from his friend.

Felix and Freddy—that was the boy's name—became pals, chums and plain best friends. Freddy was shorter than Felix but built like a little tank. He had brown eyes and hair, and the friendliest smile of all the children at Scuola Inglesa. He did not care for soccer, which did not win him any friends in school, but loved the one sport that no one in Rome (not even the other American boys) seemed to know anything about—baseball. Freddy had a passion for the sport that was certainly contagious. At least Felix felt the lure of the all-American pastime. Freddy spent long hours (mostly during recess) talking about the game, telling Felix about its heroes, the incredible money they made, and one day, even tried to give a demonstration how baseball was played. Unfortunately, the closest thing Freddy found to a baseball was a tennis ball, and the closest thing to a bat was a long, frail twig.

Meanwhile, although baseball season was just starting in America, the most important holiday in the Christian world was about to arrive—Easter. Several days after Freddy tried to teach Felix how to use a bat, school let out for the holidays. Christian love and goodwill prevailed and forgiveness was in vogue during the religious observance that culminates on Easter Sunday, the most sacred of Christian holidays, commemorating the resurrection of Jesus Christ after his crucifixion. The Holy See was buzzing with thousands upon thousands of worshipers who had traveled from all over the world to witness Pius XII give the traditional Easter greeting from the central loggia at Saint Peter's. The pope was frail and rumored to be sick; still, it was Felix's first time in Vatican City and he was as eager as anyone to catch a glimpse of *il papa*. Draganović had secured passes for the boy and Sister Ornella so they could stand in front of the crowd just behind the VIPs. Draganović was sitting not too far away, with other important members of the government of the Vatican and the Curia, and though Felix could not see him, he could see the Felix whipping his head left and right, now pointing, now tugging at the nun, now pulling the nun forward to try and get a better view. Draganović's smile disappeared, however, when he saw Felix talking to a Swiss Guard.

"What is he doing?" His Excellency thought.

Simple. Felix was trying to get the Swiss Guard to allow him and Sister Ornella to sit with the VIPs. The bishop sighed in relief when he saw the guard shake his head and courteously but firmly point to the boy to get back. A minute later the crowd roared with cries of *"il papa!"* and there he was, his tall white and gold miter reflecting the Roman sun like an angel of light against the sparkling blue of the Easter sky. Felix noticed that almost everyone was crying, crying from joy as they set their eyes on the perfect mirror of love up on the balcony. The only people not crying were the Swiss

Guards and a few men and women dressed in funny clothes—some with straw hats—and carrying little cameras around their necks, cameras that were, of course, aimed at the loggia from where the pope delivered his message of peace to the rest of the world.

As quickly as it began, it was over. The pope was helped off the balcony, the crowd dispersed and Felix and Sister Ornella joined the mob and went home.

During the summer holidays Felix was allowed to sleep later than usual. When Sister Ornella protested (she felt that allowing Felix to sleep late was ill-advised because it only reinforced the child's natural lack of discipline), His Excellency explained that although he and the nun were compelled by vows and rules to maintain a simple and rigorous discipline, Felix was not. Felix, said the bishop, was but a little boy, and, as such, had to be given a greater margin of freedom.

A week before he went back to school, Felix was awakened at seven by Draganović and instructed to bathe; meanwhile the bishop brought out a brand-new grey suit, white shirt and a bright yellow bow tie he had bought Felix earlier in the week.

"Where are we going?" asked the boy, getting ready to get in the tub. "It is a surprise. Hurry, the car will be here shortly."

At eight-thirty, as planned, the limousine pulled up and His Excellency, Bishop Krunoslav Draganović, dressed in his clerical best, and little Felix, looking quite handsome and smart in his new suit, got into the car and headed to Vatican City. The limousine zigzagged through the streets of Rome until it reached the walled domain by way of the Viale Vaticano, giving Felix a good idea of the size of the papal city-state. The car drove past Saint John's Tower, turned left and entered the Vatican through a gate where Swiss Guards checked ID's. The car continued slowly and stopped in front of the Government Palace.

"This is where I work, Felix," said Draganović as he and Felix got out of the car. The bishop pointed at the building behind Saint Peter's basilica as the car drove away.

The Government Palace was the nerve center of the Holy See. It was from here that the bureaucracy of the Vatican ran its day-to-day operations. It was made up of one five-story building, with a small, columned bell tower capped with a statue of Jesus. That building was ensconced between two identical, protruding three-story extensions that faced a manicured garden with a topiary rendering of the Vatican's coat-of-arms.

"You mean this is all yours?" The boy's eyes widened.

"No!" Draganović laughed. "I work here, I have an office."

"Are we going to your office? Please!"

"No, we are not. Very serious things go on in that building and it is not a place for children. But, I'm going to take you to see the most wonderful treasures in the world. Would you like that?"

"Oh, yes, very much!"

Draganović patted the boy on the head, took his hand and had started walking away, when he heard a familiar voice.

"Excellency! Draganović!"

The bishop and the boy turned to see Archbishop Montini walking quickly toward them.

"Excellency!" greeted Draganović as he went to meet the archbishop.

"And who is this?" Montini looked carefully at Felix. "Is this your little cousin, Excellency?"

"Yes, he is." Draganović moved to the side. "Felix, say hello to His Excellency, Archbishop Montini." Felix, on cue, bowed, took Montini's hand and kissed it.

"How old are you?" asked Montini.

"About—eight years old, Excellency," replied Felix with a firm voice and an ingratiating smile.

Montini laughed at the *about* part of the answer. "You're a charming young man."

"Thank you, Excellency." Felix bowed again to Montini, then smiled at Draganović.

"Where are you heading?" Montini started to walk again and Draganović and Felix followed.

"I was going to show Felix the Academy of Science, you know, give him a little tour. This is his first time at the Holy See."

"It is inspiring," said Felix in a calm, meditative voice. Both Draganović and Montini looked at each other, then at Felix, who smiled innocently. Both—Draganović even more than Montini—were surprised at Felix's choice of words.

Montini took Felix's chin in his hand and looked the boy in the eyes, but addressed Draganović. "There's more to this boy than meets the eye, Excellency."

Draganović did not reply. He waited until Montini turned to him and smiled, then Draganović returned the favor and followed Montini, who had begun to walk ahead.

"Why don't you come with me, Excellency, you and Felix."

Draganović followed without inquiring where they were going. Instead he asked about the pope.

"He's as well as can be expected. The doctors told him to cut back; that's the reason you have not seen him much lately. But, come, you can ask him yourself."

As Draganović suspected, Archbishop Montini was on his way to meet Pius XII. "But—Excellency, I can't very well—" Draganović meant he could not very well take a little boy along to see the pope as if they were visiting an old uncle.

"Nonsense. His Holiness is always asking about you—and our friends *you know where*." Montini did not want to mention Intermarion in front of the boy, but the point was conveyed to Draganović well enough. "And don't worry about Felix, I'm sure Felix will love meeting the Blessed Father."

Felix glanced at Draganović with disbelief and felt his knees start to shake. But the look his tata gave him was enough to instill courage and joy at the possibility of meeting Pius XII face to face. Minutes later, the archbishop, the bishop and the boy entered the papal apartments from a side door, went past a couple of Swiss Guards, climbed the wide stairs to the third floor and reached the antechamber to the pope's study. Two cardinals and three bishops were lounging about, waiting for any word or command from the pontiff. They did not know Draganović by sight, but Draganović knew each one of them. As a matter of fact, the Vatican's man to Intermarion had been collecting information on the two Eminences for a while, information he kept in a red folder behind Saint Jerome.

Of course, the sight of the little boy raised the prelatic brows, especially after Montini ushered His Excellency Draganović and his cousin in to see the pope.

"Excellency!" called out a feeble Pius XII. "Come, come!" the Blessed Father beckoned Draganović to approach. Montini was already standing beside the white satin throne. Draganović walked quickly to Pius XII, took his skeletal hand and kissed the sacred ring. Felix remained at the far end of the room after a sudden squeeze of his hand by Draganović made it clear that he should not move, not talk and if possible not breathe until he was called—and, if he was not called, to imagine he was a potted plant, period. The room was not as grand as the Sistine Chapel but it was grand enough. The Blessed Mother watched over the proceedings and eight scarlet chairs, four on each side of the white throne, remained empty atop a thick rug with the papal seal.

"Kruno, how nice it is to see you again," said the pope in the faintest of voices.

"Thank you, Holiness."

His Excellency Bishop Draganović and Pius XII talked for a moment in whispers that were difficult even for Montini to understand. On the other side of the room, Felix focused on the white, shimmering vision on the illuminated throne. It seemed, at least to Felix, that light was emanating from behind the throne and from its sides, an aura of all-goodness and love that radiated from the small figure talking to Tata, while a chorus—it must have been angels—sang a sacred hymn. The light was so bright he could hardly look at it. But Felix did not blink for fear that in the opening and closing of an eye, Pius XII might vanish in a puff of magic smoke and ascend to the heavens to take his place next to Christ. The pope was, after all, that one human link with the Son of God.

All of a sudden, Pius XII moved his head ever so slightly, touched his glasses with his right hand and cast his eyes on Felix. He said nothing, but the child knew the pope wanted Felix to go to him, as if the pope had in fact uttered the words "Felix, come to me, my son." It was a moment before Felix realized he was walking toward the Holy Father. The boy wanted to stop his feet from going forward but he could not. Neither Draganović nor Montini made an attempt to stop Felix from approaching His Holiness, but actually stood aside to give the boy some room. As soon as Felix was within reach, Pius XII put out his hand and touched the boy's face. For a moment Felix was confused. He had intended to kiss the papal ring but was never given the chance. The pope held the boy's face in his long and translucent grasping fingers. Looking Felix in the eye, he remained silent for a moment, then said, "You are a boy, yet you seem old. Tell me, Felix, what do you want to be when you grow up?" It was a simple question from a very complex man.

"A baseball player."

"Really?" The pope looked at Draganović.

"I think, Holiness," said Draganović leaning forward to speak softly in the pontiff's ear, "I think it has something to do with sports." Draganović darted a look at Montini as if to say, "This was your idea," and stood by in case more translations were required.

Pius XII got up, stood in front of Felix and laughed. "I know what baseball is, Excellency, I do!" The pope took Felix by the hand and led him to the far end of the room to a tall mahogany cabinet with cut-glass doors. The pope opened one of the doors and took out a small, dark blue lead crystal globe with the initials "NY" etched in silver; the bottom half of the globe was flattened to prevent it from rolling over. "Take it."

Felix looked at the pontiff, then at the blue crystal ball the pope placed in his hands. The ball was heavy, much heavier than it looked. "Open it, go ahead," said the pope, smiling. Felix noticed that the ball was divided in two. He lifted the top part with one hand and saw that inside the glass ball there was another ball; this one covered in white leather, with red stitches, and signature on it.

"Do you know what that is, Felix?" asked the pope, taking the leather ball in his hand.

"No, Holiness," answered the little boy, fearful that, in his ignorance, the floor would swallow him whole and send his soul to hell.

"That, Felix, is a baseball."

Felix was amazed (and a little angry with himself) for not having recognized the baseball. Then again, Freddy had never shown him one.

"You know, Excellencies," Pius XII turned around to Draganović and Montini. "I don't remember a time when I've asked a little boy what he wanted to be when he grew up and was not told by that same little boy that he wanted to be a priest!" The pope laughed some more, seemed to acquire new strength and even flipped the baseball once or twice.

"Felix, can you read the name on the baseball?" asked the pope.

Felix looked at it carefully but he was barely able to read, let alone read a scribble on a ball.

"That was signed by a great baseball star, an Italian-American by the name of DiMaggio who came to see me a couple of years ago. Here, keep it. I certainly—" and the pope began to laugh again, "I certainly have no use for a baseball. A bat, maybe—I could use it on some of the red hats around here, but a baseball—take it my boy, with my blessings!" It was the last time Pius XII had any fun.

Felix could not wait. He paced his room anxiously, unable to sit still for a moment. He wanted to yell to the world, but particularly to Freddy, about his gift—and what a gift, straight from the hands of the Holy Father himself!

Unfortunately for Felix, Draganović sensed that the boy wanted to show off and would not allow it.

"But why? Why can't I take it and show Freddy?" pouted little Ronnoco.

With great patience, Draganović explained that the present from His Holiness was not to leave the house. "It is too valuable and I would hate for you to get hit over the head and robbed. This is Rome, Felix, not the mountains, and we have to be extra careful. If you want to show it to your friend, you'll just have to bring your friend here." Felix protested, cried, protested some more and sulked. It did not change Draganović's mind.

A week after the Easter holidays something happened that forced His Excellency Draganović to pay an official, but covert visit to the Scuola Inglesa.

"*Eccellenza*, thank you for coming," Berini greeted him, surprised to see the bishop dressed in his religious clothes. She escorted Draganović into her office, closed the door, offered His Excellency coffee (which he declined) and begged him to make himself comfortable.

After a quick exchange of "How nice to see you again!" and "I hope everything goes well?" Madame Berini got down to the point. "*Eccellenza,*" she began, "I apologize, for I know how busy you are, but—we have a problem."

"Felix?"

Obviously, thought the educator.

"What has he done?"

"He has been asking other children if they are Jews."

"I was in your school today." Draganović and Felix had just sat down to dinner. Felix did not ask why Draganović had been to his school. He guessed there had to be a reason for His Excellency to have gone there and that reason was, in all likelihood, himself. "Felix, will you please tell me why on earth you are going around asking other children if they are Jews?" It was the kind of question that makes children despair of grownups. Draganović knew why Felix was going around asking his classmates if they were Jews—and Felix knew that Draganović knew he knew—and yet, there it was, an inquiry into the most obvious, presented at the dinner table next to the salt and pepper shakers.

"Well?" Draganović waited for an answer while Sister Ornella placed a plate of cannelloni in front of him.

Felix darted looks from His Excellency to the nun, hoping that she would intervene so Felix did not to have to give Draganović an answer that would make him feel silly.

"Felix, I'm talking to you. Why were you asking the children at school if they are Jews?"

Another pause. Felix tilted his head to one side and opened his eyes wide. "Because!" He left it at that.

"Because? Because what?"

"You don't want me to play with Jews!"

"I told you not to bring them here. I did not tell you not to play with them and I certainly did not tell you to find out which child is a Jew and which is not!"

"But if you don't want me to bring them here it is because you don't like Jews and I shouldn't either! So I won't play with them.

But how am I to know who is a Jew and who isn't if I don't ask them first?" The whole point made so much sense to Felix his voice took on a slightly irritated tone.

"Finish your supper," said Draganović calmly. "And please—" he lifted several pieces of cannelloni with his fork, chewed for a moment, swallowed, took a sip of wine and added, "—don't ask anyone else if they are a Jew."

A few days later, Felix invited his American-baseball-loving-friend Freddy to the house to see the amazing blessed baseball. At four-thirty, fifteen minutes later than usual, Felix stormed into the building with his new friend. They ran up the stairs and into the kitchen where Sister Ornella was waiting for them.

"This is my friend Freddy Benton!"

"Hi!" said Freddy with his engaging smile.

Sister Ornella inclined her head quietly as Felix pulled his friend into the toy warehouse he called his room.

A minute later a *"Holy Yogi!"* rang in the hall. Freddy had paid homage to the sacred baseball.

It had not been a good day at the Vatican. Draganović learned that the British Secret Service's man at Intermarion had been a British traitor, a KGB mole named Kim Philby. That meant that all the agents recruited by Intermarion since the end of the war had been compromised to the Soviets. Dozens of agent-provocateurs working for Intermarion had been sent to their deaths. Draganović was not happy. He went home seeking peace and quiet but was met by Sister Ornella, who, as always, gave Draganović an accounting of that day's events.

"Are you serious?" The bishop knew perfectly well that seriousness was as much a part of Sister Ornella as salt was of seawater. "Felix!" Draganović met the boy in the hall.

"Yes—" Felix caught sight of Sister Ornella behind Draganović "—Excellency?"

"What's this? First you bring home a Jew, now you bring home a colored boy? What's the matter with you?"

"B-but he's Catholic!" stuttered Felix.

The bishop threw his arms up. *"Madonna mia!"*

23

It was just a matter of a year or so. In the end, little Felix applied himself (with substantial encouragement from Draganović), settled down and did surprisingly well in school. By the time he left Madame Berini's, the boy was not only fluent in Italian, but had a good grasp of Latin, English and French as well. Felix was by then about eleven years old, old enough to be delivered to Saint Pius.

Saint Pius X was the Vatican's preseminary for altar boys. Naturally, many of the lads at Saint Pius looked forward to the priesthood. Felix, however, had never displayed evidence of religious devotion, nor did he possess the serious and meditative turn of some of his colegionnaires. The only sign of Felix's personal aims remained his comment to the pope—where an interest in baseball was expressed—and an offhand remark to Draganović and Sister Ornella one night after supper (Felix was about nine), when the boy announced his intention of becoming a Roman emperor in the tradition of Marcus Aurelius.

Saint Pius was, at least on the surface, strict and upright. The school was in a building that never meant to be a home to thirty-odd rambunctious youngsters in the prime of adolescence. It was as sterile as a hospital, lacking in warmth and devoid of grace. Its mustard-colored walls, as old as any in the Vatican, were hot and stifling in the summer and cold as a penguin's breath in winter. The boys were lodged in semi-private rooms as barren as four walls could be, with just enough space for a desk, a lamp, a chair, two trunks and two cots placed side by side.

The arrangement lent itself to pranks, mischief and sexual experimentation—especially during the long winter nights when the boys shared their beds in order to mitigate the cold.

The daily routine for the boys of Saint Pius began at dawn. After a breakfast of bread and chocolate, accompanied by coffee, milk or cocoa, the boys filed out like Catholic cadets to assist the priests of Saint Peter's in celebrating mass. They returned to Saint Pius at noon and spent the rest of the day in class.

Responsibility for teaching the altar boys of Saint Pius fell upon seven priests under the guidance of Father Uncelli, rector of the school. The housekeeping and clerical chores were carried out by some of the most dutiful sisters in all of Christendom.

While at Saint Pius, Felix grew into a lean, healthy and graceful boy, he retained his charming smile and disposition, and won many friends. The younger boys in school looked up to him, and Felix did his best to steer them away from the trouble schoolboys get into—such as smoking, fighting and, on rare occasions, stealing.

Although everyone knew that Felix had a powerful mentor, one who was an influential member of the Vatican elite, Felix—instead of taking advantage of this—undertook more than his share of duties and study. If, for instance, another boy was sick or unavailable, Felix replaced him during mass. He was also always on hand to help those priests the rest of his schoolmates shunned like the plague—like Father Catalini, whose cassock reeked like a boiled onion (Felix doused his surplice with cologne and spiked the holy water with perfume). In time, the priests, the sisters—even Father Uncelli—learned to depend on and to trust young Ronnoco as much as they did one of the staff.

When time allowed, Felix took it upon himself to explore the libraries, treasure rooms, warehouses, catacombs, secret archives and the tunnels in and around the holy city. His red cassock became as familiar to the grounds keepers, the clerks and the men in charge of security (who, unbeknownst to Felix, reported to Draganović) as the robes of any bishop or cardinal. In less than three years, few people in the Vatican knew the grounds of the Holy See as well as young Felix Ronnoco.

One Friday afternoon—when Felix was about sixteen years old—as the boy strolled the grounds behind Saint Peter's, he noticed a flurry of activity at the Government Palace. Priests were running in and out, and more than a few bishops, archbishops and cardinals (along with their acolytes) were milling around the papal apartments. *"He was such a good man!"* Felix heard them say. He guessed that Pope John XXIII was dead. History was, once again, being made. The Catholic Church was without a pope.

Later that day, Felix went home for the weekend. He found Draganović in the bathroom, shaving. His Excellency had just enough time to take a bath and change his clothes before having to return to the Holy See. His hair was turning grey on the sides, but other than that, Draganović looked pretty much the same as he had when Felix moved to Trastevere. Of course, every one of the bishop's views concerning raising a young boy, now a teenager, had been revised or discarded long, long ago. Nothing teaches like experience and Draganović had had more than his share.

Felix leaned against the door—half his body in the bathroom, the other half out in the hall—and with the brazen curiosity of his age inquired, "Do you know who will be pope?"

His Excellency did not halt the careful glide of his blade, did not turn and did not lose a second before he replied, "It is my business to know," and proceeded to work the other cheek. Intermarion might be a thing of the past, but the systems and procedures learned by Bishop Draganović then had been copied and improved. The bishop had organized an internal security section at the Holy See— one that, like others of its kind, did not officially exist, and that answered to only one man, "Your friend, Montini."

Felix did not reply. Only his gaping mouth and raised eyebrows acknowledged his surprise. His Eminence toweled off and left the bathroom without so much as a word of caution or a warning to Felix to be discreet. He knew he could trust the boy with the greatest secret in the Catholic world, the name of the man who would be chosen Vicar of Rome.

A few weeks later, after the new pope had been properly elected and life in the Holy See returned once again to normal, Draganović called the boy into the living room. "Tell me, Felix, have you given any thought to what you want to do when you leave Saint Pius?" Draganović closed the door to keep Sister Ornella out of the conversation. He sat back in his favorite chair, crossed his legs and looked up at the boy standing in the center of the living room dressed in blue jeans and a black sweater.

"Yes."

"Good. And what is that?"

"I want to be like you."

If Draganović's chest did not swell with paternal pride, it was because he was not sure if Felix understood what he was saying. "But Felix, I am a priest."

"I know." Felix indeed knew His Excellency was a priest, and a rather important one at that.

Draganović spent the next hour explaining to Felix the sacrifices a man assumed when he gave his life to the service of Christ. But Felix had heard all of it before, many, many times—from the priests at Saint Pius, from friends of Draganović, and from Draganović himself. Yet, Felix was firm; he wanted to join the Church and spread the Catholic faith.

Draganović kissed the boy on both cheeks. "You make me very proud. However," His Excellency took the boy's face in his hands, "know that you can change your mind. You don't have to do or be anything except what you think is right for you. The world is full of possibilities. I've made my choice; you are entitled to make yours."

Months later Father Uncelli sent for young Ronnoco. The priest was a wiry little man with enough charm to entertain Felix for hours. He was bald, with large brown eyes, a wide mouth, a long face and a very long nose that, Felix felt, made Father Uncelli look like a pelican in black. The priest ordered Felix to put on a clean cassock and surplice and go immediately to the papal apartments. Five minutes later, Felix flew out of Saint Pius thinking that the pope was holding mass and had requested Felix to be his altar boy. This would be a great privilege, because to serve the pope on the altar was a duty (and honor) normally granted only to young seminarians.

When Felix reached the papal apartments, he was met by Brother Agustino. "Follow me!" sang the friar. "Quick, quick!"

"What's going on?"

"You think they tell me anything?"

Felix was quickly led into the room he remembered from his boyhood, the same room where Pius XII had given him the baseball in the blue glass globe. And it was in that room that His Excellency, Bishop Krunoslav Draganović, now stood with Pope Paul VI, two bishops and a cardinal. On the pope's desk there was a white velvet cushion with gold stitching and a red biretta on top. "Surely," thought Felix in a panic, "I'm too young to be a cardinal!"

"My goodness, how you've grown!" Pope Paul greeted the boy.

Felix remembered that there had been several boys who were created cardinals during the Middle Ages and the Renaissance—except that he was not living in the Middle Ages, nor was he a member of the powerful Medici clan.

"Come here, Felix." The pope put out his hand and Felix kissed it. "You still want to be a baseball player?" The pope turned to his guests and smiled.

What a silly question, thought the boy; he would prefer to be a prince of the Church anytime.

"When Felix was a small boy—in this very room—" The pontiff told of the meeting between Pius XII and little Felix Ronnoco. Everyone laughed and thought it was splendid story, including Draganović. His Excellency grinned, as any proud father would. "Well?" Pope Paul patted the boy on the cheek.

"It's not practical, Holiness," answered Felix with a sheepish smile.

The answer caused the pope to laugh aloud. "See what I mean?" The Blessed Father laughed again. Then, he asked Felix to pick up the cushion on his desk.

For an infinitesimal half of a millisecond, Felix thought of turning down the nomination, regardless of what anyone might say. He did not have any idea what a cardinal was supposed to do!

"Felix, I asked you here this afternoon because it is fitting that as the only living relative of—"

Felix was standing next to the pope holding the cushion and felt his knees shake, much like they had done years ago when Pius XII beckoned him to approach.

"—our dear brother in the faith, Krunoslav Draganović, you will be proud to know that from now on he will be Krunoslav Cardinal Draganović."

Tata!

Pope Paul VI placed the red biretta on Draganović's head.

After a brief and very personal ceremony, in which His Eminence Draganović embraced the pope and the other prelates, Felix hugged his tata and was so happy that he even cried a little. It was not until many, many years later that Felix thought back on the naive idiocy of his youth, and laughed.

☦

Life resumed its dull, daily round of school and church, church and school, with the monotony broken only by weekends in Trastevere. It was a consistent and predictable life—but God has a sense of humor, and the moment a person becomes too complacent, or looks the other way, He throws a pie in your face.

Felix's roommate of almost a year went home and another boy moved in. His name was Nino Lubri. Nino was from Florence and he was younger and smaller than Felix, though not by much. Nino had straight sandy blond hair cut in page boy style, large oval grey eyes and a mouth that was as sensuous as it was inviting. He had a fine, narrow nose and an attractively delicate, if somewhat androgynous, face. His hands were those of an artist, with long slender fingers—although Nino did not do anything particularly artistic except, perhaps, read a little more than most boys his age. Nino was from a wealthy family, had traveled extensively in Europe and America and was more precocious than any other of his classmates. This fine-featured angel, who could have modeled for Leonardo or Raphael, was a natural seducer. His voice had not undergone the imminent transformation from childhood to adolescence, and it fluctuated between that of a boy soprano and that of a young man. At Saint Pius, Nino Lubri was adored by the nuns (and one priest), loathed by some of the boys and enjoyed by others.

There was something about Nino that captivated Felix, something about the boy that made Felix want to be in his company.

Young Ronnoco, of course, did not remember that there had been another boy, with the same kind of sweet face and thoughtful stare (though far more chaste), who had loved and nurtured Felix during the first years of his life; another boy who had left his indelible loving stamp on a baby known by another name.

Now, because of the strict moral standards kept at home (and, supposedly, at his school as well), and despite his innate curiosity, Felix had managed to remain indifferent to that singular preoccupation of youth that turns sweet, innocent little boys and girls into fiendish, insatiable ghouls; that adolescent obsession that transforms the introverted and quiet child into an aggressive tormentor, Daddy's girl into a vixen and a childhood buddy into a rival; that one fixation that dominates the senses of almost every teenager since Adam looked at Eve and realized there was something behind the fig leaf—sex. Part of Felix's charm was his innocence, innocence due in great part to his absolute ignorance on the subject of sex.

For the first couple of weeks after Nino moved in with Felix, they spent many hours at night talking, getting to know each other. Nino told Felix that his father was a tyrant and that his mother was a pitiful submissive woman totally dependent on her priest. Nino's mother wanted him to join the priesthood (his reason for being at Saint Pius), but Nino himself found the idea laughable and grotesque. He was determined to leave school as soon as he was able to, so he could do whatever he wanted to do in life, though at the moment Nino had no idea what that was. In turn, Felix related the story of the svirala that was always under his pillow—a short enough story, because he did not remember a day when the flute was not under his pillow. One day he confessed to Nino that he wanted to be a priest because it was his destiny. Felix was surprised to hear the word "destiny" come out of his mouth and laden with so much purpose.

Late one November evening, around two in the morning, Felix woke up in terror, sobbing and sweating. He had had another nightmare. He heard the rustling sound of sheets and blankets coming from Nino's side of the room. In a voice groggy with sleep he asked Nino what he was doing. Nino, in a raspy, distracted voice, answered that he was thinking of Felix. The rustling of the sheets continued. Felix asked again what Nino was doing; Nino offered to show him.

In the cold darkness of the room, Nino left his cot, and the next thing Felix knew Nino was in bed with him.

"Go back to your bed!"

"No, I want to be with you."

Since Nino was a boy who bathed regularly and did not smell like Felix's former roommate, Felix sighed, warned Nino against kicking in his sleep or snoring, moved over to give Nino some room, then turned and faced the wall.

But the rustling under the blankets began once more, and Felix, a little annoyed by now, asked Nino to stop. Nino laughed. He could not believe, he said, that Felix did not know what he was doing. Felix replied that he did not care to find out and that he wanted to sleep. Nino offered to show Felix, but Felix would under no circumstance turn on the lights and risk a reprimand from Father Uncelli. Since Nino was still moving around more than Felix thought was necessary, he ordered the boy to stop and go back to his own bed. It was then that Felix heard the question that would stay with him for years—

"How about if I eat you?"

Felix could not see his friend in the dark, but felt the warm breath of the other boy close to his face. His pulse quickened. "W-what?"

"I want to eat you." Nino indeed sounded a bit hungry.

Felix did not answer right away. Things were happening that he did not understand; he felt like he was entering a cave without knowing where it led. In a nervous, halting voice Felix asked Nino if "eating" was like kissing, since Felix had kissed some of the younger boys in school before, much like a big brother does, as a sign of affection.

Nino chuckled. "In—in a way. Well?" Without waiting for an answer Nino pressed his body against Felix. He also slipped his hand under Felix's shirt and slowly, ever so gently, stroked first one nipple, then the other.

Felix's voice faltered and the answer was hardly audible, but it was what Nino wanted to hear. Nino immediately ducked under the covers, and Felix was seized by rapture. He became a puppet willing to be manipulated and toyed with. He felt a mounting excitement that had begun the moment Nino had touched him, and that was gathering momentum, numbing every nerve in his body. "Are you eating me?" Felix moaned.

But Nino was taught as a little boy never to talk with his mouth full, so he let out a muffled, "Uhhuh!"

Felix could not think. Heavy sighs were his only means of conveying his pleasure, though for an instant, he wondered if he should have protested. He did not. Zeus placed Felix on a cloud, and thunder and lighting struck down his misgivings; Felix wanted to be sacrificed. A moment later he opened his arms and took Nino in his embrace; his breathing turned to gasps and his body went into spasms of such delight it frightened him. It was the most extraordinary sensation he had ever felt. "Ohhhhh!" Felix suddenly stood up in bed and realized that he and Nino were naked, and that for the first time in his life the lower part of his bed was as wet as his pillow.

Next morning everything was different—the room, the sun, the sky and, especially, Nino. "How do you feel?"

"Great!" said Felix a little too fast and with a smile that was a little too wide.

"You're lying." Nino laughed. "You're feeling all that Catholic guilt. Don't worry, it'll go away!"

For Felix, the day went by so slowly it seemed the sun and the clouds refused to move in the sky. During mass, he almost dropped the chalice. In class, he could not sit still and was scolded several times. Felix couldn't concentrate or think of anything except Nino. He had not seen his friend since breakfast but wanted to very much. There were a million questions he needed to ask, a million questions he needed answers to. He had heard that for a priest carnal love was forbidden, spilling the seed was a sin, and physical affection between boys was a particular aberration. Well, he thought, first of all he was not a priest, not yet, anyway. As far as the other doubts, he would ask Nino.

Felix looked for his friend at supper and saw Nino enter the dining room in the company of two other boys before he came over and joined Felix at the table. "How do you feel?"

"Why—why do you keep asking me how I feel?"

"Because—"

The boys retired at eight o'clock. They did their homework and read some, but did not speak. In fact, Felix avoided looking at Nino, and, every time Nino looked at Felix, Felix turned away. At nine o'clock Father Leoni dropped by and found Nino beside his bed, praying. Felix was already in bed. "Lights out, Nino, come on." The priest waited until Nino climbed into his cot, then turned off the lights and left. It was at least an hour and a half, after the last sounds of the evening had died out that Felix turned from the wall. "Have you done it before?"

"Yes—a couple of times." (Including, he did not mention, with an older altar boy at Saint Pius who had since left.)

"Who—who taught you?"

"Nobody. Didn't you ever see a sheep on top of another?" Nino tried not laugh.

"I thought they were playing."

"They were making baby sheep!"

"Are we going to make babies?" The question triggered such a laughing fit that both boys had to bury their faces in the pillows not to wake up the school. "Nino, is it right? I mean what—we did?"

Nino answered bluntly and without regret that according to the Bible it was quite possible they would both end up in hell.

"Oh, God!"

Seeing how much his friend was suffering, Nino got out of his bed and climbed in next to Felix. In an instant, guilt made way for desire. The boys explored each other's bodies with utter fascination, soft kisses and gentle caresses without regard for the afterlife.

"I love you," said Felix.

"And I love you." Nino returned the kiss. "Are you hungry?"

"Yes."

"Let's eat!"

Two weeks later found Father Uncelli walking quickly down the hall. If anyone had come upon the priest just then, they would have heard him uttering Felix's name over and over again. Uncelli had been at Saint Pius for almost twenty-five years and he knew the signs, had seen them often enough. Two boys would start by ignoring the other boys and everyone else; they would become inseparable. They would eat together, play together, study together, work together, do *everything* together. They would sit next to each other in class, even go so far as ask to be placed on the same work schedule for mass. The situation was not unusual; it was but a matter of numbers and probabilities. In every barrel there are likely to be one or two rotten apples. Still, he was disappointed. Felix Ronnoco of all people, a boy who was admired by his fellow students, a hardworking, honest boy with a good heart. It was not, however, up to Father Uncelli to judge, but to protect the other children from immorality and, above all, from a scandal. As confessor to Felix and Nino, Father Uncelli had drawn a blank. "Bless me, Father, for I have sinned—" followed by trivia and lies. The priest inspected their room. He went through both trunks and all four drawers in the small desk. Nothing. He would have to see the boys in his office.

"Why are you running?" The priest was about to make a telephone call when Felix burst into his office. Father Uncelli put down the receiver and placed his hands on the desk. His office was sedate and comfortable with furniture that had been acquired from several Vatican warehouses. The room had two tall bookcases accessible by a ladder on rollers, several potted plants, a large figurine of the pope and saint after whom the school was named, a picture of Jesus Christ that according to myth was six hundred years old, and four windows with a view of Piazza Santa Marta.

"Felix, there is a new boy joining Saint Pius. He is to move in with you. Nino will go to another room."

"Father—" said Felix after a pause, "that is not a good idea."

"Why not?"

Felix paced the room, "We study together, Father. I-I help Nino with his Latin, he—he helps me with algebra. If Nino moves—if he moves out our grades will suffer."

Father Uncelli reminded Felix that if he was really interested in studying with Nino they could do so in the peace and quiet of the library, and asked him to please carry out the orders for Nino to move in with Marcello.

"But Father, Nino hates Marcello!" Marcello was a bully, and Father Uncelli had obviously not considered the facts well enough.

Father Uncelli walked over to Felix. He saw the boy was confused. "Fine. If you think Nino will not get along with Marcello, then you move in with Marcello and Nino can room with the new boy."

"But I hate Marcello, too!"

"You're trying my patience, Felix. I told you what I want. Now, do it!"

Felix did not understand why Father Uncelli was giving him such a hard time. He thought they were friends; after all, they spent hours playing chess and talking about airplanes (Father Uncelli had a passion for flying things). There had to be a reason why Father Uncelli was being inflexible when he never had been before. Felix also knew that the more he argued the less chance he had of the priest changing his mind. "Please," he pleaded, "Nino is my best friend. He's used to my nightmares in the middle of the night—he's used to all that!" Felix looked away so the priest would not see he was beginning to cry. He wanted to die, to throw himself out the window.

It was too late. The priest had seen enough. Father Uncelli picked up the phone and called for Nino. Then, he turned to Felix. "Sit down."

"I don't want to, Father."

"Is there something you're not telling me?" asked the priest softly.

A knock on the door broke the momentary lull that found Father Uncelli returning to his desk. Felix knew Nino was in the room, but he did not dare turn to look at him. If he had, Felix would have seen that Nino was not the least frightened.

"Lubri, our friend Ronnoco is very upset because I told him that you are moving out. Perhaps you can tell me why Felix is acting so—unlike Felix?"

Nino looked from the priest to his friend and back to the priest. "I think Felix has become a glutton, Father." Felix felt the hairs on his neck bristle. "Yes," continued Nino, "Felix loves to snack in the middle of the night. You didn't know that, Father? Well, it's true!"

Even though Felix felt wretched and sad, and indeed a little angry at his friend, he had to bite his tongue to keep from laughing.

"I keep a little this and that in the room. When Felix gets hungry he just—takes it. What can I do?" asked Nino, innocently, "He's my friend. I give him what I have."

There was a very long pause while Father Uncelli glared at Nino. He leaned back in his chair, turned to Felix, then back to Nino and repeated his order for Nino to move in with Marcello.

"W-when, Father?" Nino's voice took the higher end of the scale.

"Now!" screamed the priest. Nino bowed and left the room. "As for you, young Ronnoco—"

Felix wiped off the tears and walked into a trap. "I will call my cousin, Father; I'm sorry, but I have no choice."

"No, Felix, you are wrong!" Father Uncelli jumped from his seat. "*I* will call His Eminence. You are dismissed!" Felix had played his hand, and, as the saying goes, Father Uncelli had called his bluff and raised the stakes.

Felix found Nino packing. "You bastard! You were trying to make me laugh in front of the priest!"

"Well, I thought you needed cheering up! Wasn't it cute?"

"You're mad!" Felix shut the door so they could talk in private. He was going to call His Eminence Draganović, he said. He would not allow Nino to leave.

"Don't. It'll only make things worse. I don't want you to get in trouble. Besides, I'm not going anywhere. I'm moving across the hall, that's all."

"No!"

"We'll see each other every day—"

Felix began to curse in Serbo-Croatian and smacked a pillow against the wall. Nino grabbed the pillow and threw it at Felix. "Don't worry, everything's going to work out fine!"

"It better, or—we'll run away!"

Just then, Marcello, the same Marcello whom Felix and Nino despised, threw the door open and said in that whiny voice of his, "Well, girls, I understand one of you bitches is moving in with me. La-di-da! Won't *we* have fun!" Marcello was not ugly, he was plain. Nor was he unkempt, though he was not particularly concerned about whether or not his very small, tight black curls received their proper ablutions once a week. Marcello was, on the other hand, tall—much taller than Felix or Nino—and dull. He never smiled, no, not unless someone else was in pain. No one liked Marcello; not even Marcello liked Marcello.

"Listen to me, fuck-face," began Felix in a voice too soft for anyone except Marcello to hear, "you touch my friend and I'll rip out your heart and stick it up your mother-fucking ass, got it?"

"Why, you Slav piece of shit!" Marcello's upper lip curled into the beginning of a sneer, and his right hand closed into a fist. But he was not fast enough for the shepherd boy. Felix kicked him in the groin so hard that the only thing Marcello could do was grab his crotch and double over in pain. That, of course, was the worst thing he could have done. Felix was about to punch him on the back of the head when he found his hand grabbed—by Draganović, who was standing there in his scarlet cope and zucchetto. Father Uncelli stood next to His Eminence.

"Father," said His Eminence, "why don't you take the boy and see that he's all right?"

Father Uncelli led Marcello between the students, priests and nuns who had gathered outside the room. The priest reproached the onlookers for not having anything better to do and finding delight in the misery of others.

The towering presence of Cardinal Draganović was enough to chill the eternal memory of Saint Pius, wherever he was.

"Let's go, Felix." His Eminence stepped aside and waited for Felix to start walking. Felix and Nino looked at each other, but never said good-bye.

24

Felix was still crossing the Adriatic when Draganović received a telephone call from Father Uncelli, telling His Eminence that Felix had been expelled from school. Less than an hour later, His Eminence, an imposing symbol of authority with his red cope sweeping the floor, dropped by the school to have a little chat with the rector.

"Your Grace, please!" Father Uncelli pointed to a comfortable chair across his desk.

Cardinal Draganović, however, preferred to stand because, he said, "I won't be long."

Father Uncelli inquired half-heartedly after Felix. Why, Felix was fine, just fine, replied Draganović, just as carefree, walking around and looking at the books on the walls. His Eminence could tell a lot about a man from the books he read. In Father Uncelli's case, Draganović felt that the priest should have been an aviator.

"The reason I'm here, Father, is because I need something explained," said Draganović.

"And what is that?" Uncelli leaned forward in his chair.

"Did you decide to expel Felix because he was insolent, or because of something else?"

The priest pondered the question, staring at the red hat as he did so, and replied that the decision was a result of Felix's threat and the boy's challenge to the rector's authority. He added that in the years Felix had been a student at Saint Pius he never once mentioned His

Eminence as a way of gaining special favors. Father Uncelli was disappointed and shocked.

Draganović indicated that it was out of character for Felix to be impertinent.

Uncelli raised his hands. "Felix was upset because his roommate was told to move to another room."

"Why?" asked the inquisitor in the scarlet hat.

Father Uncelli did not like to have anyone second-guess his decisions, but because Draganović was who he was, the priest took great care to explain himself. "Something was wrong."

"Wrong?"

Father Uncelli tried to tiptoe around the unpleasant subject, explaining that Saint Pius had to be uncompromising about discipline and the moral excellence of its boys, most of whom go on to be clergy.

"Yes, yes, I know—but were the boys fighting? Were they lacking in discipline, not cleaning up after themselves, maybe? Were they quarreling with other boys, or being disrespectful to teachers or members of your staff? Did they spend so much time playing, talking or doing—doing whatever it is that boys do these days—that they did not study, attend mass or do what was expected of them?"

For a moment the priest had a vision that the cardinal had been transformed into a woodpecker, hammering him with question after question. But the priest was a stolid man and only the slight twitch of his right eyelid signaled his irritation. "They behaved much like everyone else," Father Uncelli said, adding quickly, "I must be vigilant, Eminence; it is my responsibility to the other children."

"Vigilant? Mmmm—" Draganović paused long enough to leaf through a small volume on the Stuka that lay on the rector's desk. "Could it be that you wanted to separate Felix and his friend because you had a hunch there was something more to their friendship than simple camaraderie?"

A trace of moisture became evident on Father Uncelli's upper lip. He thought *hunch* too careless a word, under the circumstances. "Not a hunch. The word I would use is *intuitio*."

"Intuition?" Draganović stopped smiling. "Father, who was Felix's confessor?"

"I was, Your Grace."

"And what about the other boy, were you also his confessor?"

"Yes, Eminence."

"So, you hear the confessions of the older boys?"

"I do, Eminence."

To accommodate a powerful prelate is a delicate balancing act, thought Draganović, and Father Uncelli was about to trip. "I know that the intimacies entrusted to us during the rite are sacred, but did Felix or his friend ever intimate anything that made you wary of their friendship?"

"No, they did not, Your Grace."

"Then, I must be frank. Felix should have been reprimanded, but to expel him from school I think is unjustified. It casts an unfavorable light upon him."

"But, Eminence, he also struck a boy."

"Yes, he did that, did he not?" returned Draganović, almost as an aside.

Father Uncelli was about to say something but the cardinal cut him short.

"You are rector of the school, not I." Draganović declared, examining Saint Pius, who was standing as always on a nearby table. Without moving his head, Draganović fixed his eyes on Uncelli. "I hope you will reconsider and allow Felix back in school."

A half grin slowly appeared on the rector's face. He liked having bishops and cardinals asking favors. "I'm afraid I cannot do that, Your Grace. If I did, I would have to allow the other boy to come back as well. And that is impossible."

Draganović grabbed his cope, whirled around and approached Uncelli. He stood so close to the priest that when he leaned forward Uncelli was forced to push back his chair, feeling he was trapped between the cardinal and the wall.

"I don't think it is impossible at all," said Draganović taking out a large manila envelope from inside his cope, tossing it on the desk, and walking to the other side of the room, where he remained with clasped hands in his most practiced, devotional stance while the priest finished looking at the pictures.

There were seven photographs—seven large black and white photographs. Two or three of the pictures had been taken from a distance and showed Father Uncelli from different angles sporting a raincoat, a large hat and sunglasses. Another picture revealed the priest from the waist up knocking at the door of a building in a neighborhood that, while being so close to the gates of heaven due to its proximity to the Holy See, had its foot caught in hell. It was a neighborhood of dark alleys and streets teeming with garbage and of pimps. But the most interesting of all the photographs, had been taken inside a bedroom. They were of high quality and of excellent resolution. Beyond that, the pictures offered fascinating images of Father Uncelli naked, in bed and in several rather compromising positions. The most engrossing and entertaining of the pictures showed the rector sticking his face between the legs of a naked, obese female with too much makeup on her face and a wearing a blonde wig.

Father Uncelli had trouble breathing and thought he would faint. "This—this is blackmail!" He gasped, unable to look at anything but the photographs that had fallen from his hands and were now strewn on the floor.

"No, it's more than that," corrected His Eminence in a loud whisper. "You are a sinful, wicked, lecherous hypocrite. You are a disgrace to your brothers, a disgrace to this institution and an embarrassment to the Holy Father. Your life is blasphemy and it would give me great pleasure to smite you with the sword of righteousness!" Draganović went to the door, threw it open and turned one last time to face the priest. "But, I am a most forgiving and understanding man."

✠

Felix arrived in Split in a perfectly sunny day that unfortunately did not do much to brighten his mood. "Come here!" yelled Rostas, taking Felix in his arms. "I almost didn't make it! His Eminence should give me a little more time!"

Felix did not reply. He hugged his friend and began to cry.

"What's this? Oh, shit. Don't tell me you've been exiled! And I thought you were coming to see your old friends. Come, Felix, you can tell me about it in the car."

And Felix did—well, almost. He relayed only the prejudice against him and his friend by a stupid priest (Father Uncelli) and a Neanderthal altar boy (Marcello). Rostas listened and shook his head. "Terrible, awful. I tell you, Felix, priests can be so arrogant. That's what I admire about His Eminence, he's never been like that. He's so—down to earth."

Felix opened the window and filled his lungs once again with the clean, fresh air of his country.

"Don't worry. I know Draganović. He's a fair man, Felix, you'd better know that, because he is."

It was past midnight when they reached the farm. Olga was waiting in the kitchen with a pot of peasant soup hearty enough to raise the lowest spirit. He kissed and embraced her affectionately, but noticed that the strain of the farm was finally taking its toll on Rostas' wife. She looked much older than her husband; her face had become drawn, wrinkled and pale, and her hair was completely grey; her once compact body was flaccid and her bones brittle. They talked for an hour, then Felix excused himself, kissed Rostas and Olga goodnight and went up to his old room.

Walking in, he banged his head on the low beam. Felix rubbed his head. This had never happened to him before, but then he had never stood so tall in the attic. Everything was the same, so much so that Felix wondered if the sheets on the bed had been washed since his last visit two years ago. He opened the window and saw the beaming moon welcoming him with a smile. "I'm not happy and you know why." The moon's smile turned into a sad frown. Felix lay down on his bed, threw off his shoes and cried himself to asleep.

Next morning, Felix remained in bed later than usual. He went down to the kitchen around nine o'clock, led there by the sweet smell of fresh-baked bread and coffee left for him by Olga. He breakfasted by himself because Olga and Rostas had gone to town for provisions. After eating an entire loaf of the delicious bread with homemade butter and downing three cups of coffee, the boy took a bath and changed into a clean set of clothes—black slacks and a black shirt, black like his mood. Winter had yet to unleash its severity on the mountain, and the weather was warm for mid-October. After his bath, Felix wandered about the house for a few minutes and he found himself in the living room. There, resting on a dark, blue cushion on top of a chair, Felix found a copy of the Bible, with a note from Olga that read simply, *"Felix."*

The boy picked up the book, but put it down when he saw through the window someone taking the sheep and goats to graze. Felix could only see the person from behind; Rostas and Olga had obviously gotten themselves a farmhand. Felix sat by the window and watched the flock go down the hill. He knew the routine so well, remembered the happy, carefree days of his childhood, chasing after sheep and goats and playing with his dog. That, in turn, reminded him of the day he went to Rome, which brought back memories of Madame Berini's, Saint Pius—and Nino. Misery cast itself once more upon the boy, and he wept. He picked up Olga's Bible and opened the book blindly, without looking for anything specific, and found himself reading *The Song of Solomon: "His banner over me was love. Stay me with flagons, comfort me with apples: for I am sick with love."*

Young Ronnoco needed air. He went to his room, banged his head on the beam, picked up his jacket, went downstairs and ran outside, just as he used to do years before—before he was sick with love.

He went looking for the flock, vaguely curious to meet the shepherd. Felix knew the way to the pastures, and after walking for fifteen minutes he saw the white shapes of sheep and scraggy goats grazing on the side of the mountain. He walked slowly toward them and saw the sheepdog—one he did not know—already with its ears pricked, staring at him, trying to decide if he was friend or foe. Felix had come within thirty meters when he was tackled from behind and thrown to the ground. "What the—!" yelled Felix looking up at another boy, a bit older than himself, with green eyes, a mass of red hair, freckles and thick eyebrows so blond they were almost white. The boy wore a wool and leather jacket with colorful embroidering; dark, coarse baggy pants; and boots. It was the typical clothing that shepherds wore to protect them from the cold days and nights on the mountain—except, in this case, for the colorful touches typical of Muslims. "There must be a reason why this fool is laughing and punching me in the shoulders while I'm pinned underneath him!" thought Felix, screaming obscenities at the shepherd.

The shepherd's expression suddenly changed from one of raucous, playful humor to one of terror. He jumped off Felix and began to apologize, trying to brush off Felix's clothes with his dirty hands. "I'm sorry! Oh, God, I'm sorry, I—I thought you were my—oh, I beg your forgiveness!" yelled the boy in a shrill voice.

"Take your hands off me! Fucking *balija*! Attacking people from the back!" Felix considered beating up the boy. "I live here, you know!" Felix turned and walked back to the house, cursing in his native and very earthy tongue as he made his way up the hill.

That night Rostas talked to the shepherd and demanded an explanation. "He's sorry and so embarrassed," said Rostas, walking into the kitchen where Felix and Olga were sitting at the table. "He's afraid I will let him go."

"He's a witless fool," observed his wife.

"Well—he thought Felix was his cousin," added Rostas.

"His cousin! What, he goes about pouncing on his kin, does he? And what would his cousin be doing here, I ask? I tell you, it's a joke!" Olga had opposed hiring a Muslim to work at the farm.

"Is it?" If it was a joke, Felix was not laughing. He was not even cracking a smile.

"Is it—what?" asked Olga.

"A joke?" It was all too clear that Felix could have been related in any of a dozen ways to any one of, say, roughly five million souls living in the country.

Olga tried to gingerly steer the conversation from this uncomfortable course to a more palatable topic. "Are you going to listen to what that fool says? Don't you know people with red hair are like snakes—I don't trust them, not one bit!"

"Come with me," said Rostas to Felix. He lifted the boy from his chair and told him to get his jacket and go outside. They were going for a ride. But Felix did not want to go anywhere. Rostas insisted. He took his large hand, laid it on the boy's face and begged him to come along, if only to humor his old friend.

"Where are we going?" asked Felix.

"To Paradise."

"Paradise" was a house on the outskirts of Travnik. It was bigger than any house around, but there was a reason for that; it was also more comfortable than any house around, and there was a reason for that too. Outside, it was all white stucco with a ribbon of red tiles, an attractive, well-kept garden and a gravel driveway. Inside, it was red satin and frills from end to end. In addition to lace window curtains, a large parlor with an enormous and extremely cozy fireplace, and garish replicas of Victorian chairs, sofas and divans, there were imitation Tiffany lamps, a baby grand piano and hardwood floors so well waxed that many visitors had been known to slip and end up on crutches. The house had been owned before the war by a Jew who ran the town's printing plant. When the war was over the Jew vanished—no one knew what happened to the man or to his family—but the property remained. It had fallen into disrepair when a Croat entrepreneur from up north saw it, knew that it could be gotten for almost nothing, bought it from the authorities, fixed it up and sold it to an acquaintance (also from the north) who quickly became personally known to almost every man in town, as well as (by reputation alone) to their wives and girlfriends.

Her name was Esmeralda, and she was suspected to be a Swabian, a Yugoslavian of German descent, who had chosen her professional name (Esmeralda) because it sounded more interesting and exotic than, say, Helga. When Esmeralda arrived in Travnik she did not arrive alone. She was accompanied by her husband—a tall and very thin man with a face that resembled a rusty cleaver, who was killed in an accident shortly after arriving in town (he fell from the roof where he had gone to patch a leak)—and four girls between fourteen and twenty-two. The girls, needless to say, were not Esmeralditas but Magdalena, Esperanza, Caridad and Voluntaria, each girl named after one of many legendary eighteenth century Spanish madams. Why Spanish and not Danish? No one ever tried to find out.

Esmeralda's clients ranged from peasants in town for a night, to his honor the mayor, his staff and his oldest son. Other frequent callers included the chief of police and his men and members of the militia.

"What is this place?" Felix looked around while they were led inside by an attractive girl who was too old to be dressed like a child.

"Rostas!" From the end of the hall, a voluptuous white-haired matron yelled, ran the whole six meters, flung herself into Rostas' arms and showered him with kisses. She was tall and strong-looking, had perfect teeth, too much rouge on her face, and seemed the very embodiment of sensuality and delight. This was a woman who liked giving pleasure, whether for money or not, a philanthropist *de rigueur* who spent most of her life in men's and women's arms listening to their woes, their dreams and even their despair.

"Esmeralda, you look ravishing—as always!"

Ravishing! Felix could not believe his ears. He had never heard Rostas speak that way before; more to the point, Felix had never heard Rostas expressing any such sentiments, not even to Olga.

"How's your dear, lovely girl?" Esmeralda was still in Rostas arms.

"She's not lovely anymore, but she's still very dear," answered Rostas.

"Tell her I miss her. Oh—" and here Esmeralda finally unlatched herself from Rostas and did a little dance, holding the side of her red satin chemise. "She should come down and have a drink with me, like in the old days."

"She might do it, too. I think she's getting bored; the farm is a lot of work." Rostas sounded genuinely concerned. "But I did not come all the way here to talk about the old days, my love; I came because we have to look after the future, and here he is in the flesh!"

Felix was trying to hide behind Rostas, so Rostas grabbed Felix by the end of his jacket and swung him around, setting the boy right in the middle of the conversation.

Esmeralda put her hands to her face. "Oh, he's beautiful, Rostas. Is he your own?"

"Almost."

"And he looks so—sad!" There was not one fake note in Esmeralda; every phrase, every gesture and every expression was as true and sincere as a heartfelt love song.

"He is. I need you to make him happy." Rostas put both hands on Felix to make sure he would not run out of the house.

"Oh, I wish I were fifteen," complained Esmeralda.

And Felix wished to be struck by lighting. But he was not. He was struck instead by a gorgeous girl his own age, who was now shown into the room by the madam. She was small, had long, light brown hair down to her waist, and eyes like amethysts—eyes so strange in color they seemed suspended in space beneath a pair of copper-colored eyebrows. She was barefoot, and dressed in a pair of loose men's pants (which may have belonged to an older brother) and a delicate white silk blouse. She wore no makeup. Her skin was soft as the petal of the most exquisite flower and her voice like a nightingale's. Her name was Sofisticada, and she was, Esmeralda declared, a virgin: untouched, untainted—and only just arrived.

"What! I—don't want to! I—can't! I—" protested Felix and pulled back his hand.

It did not matter; Felix was in the hands of a professional. As Rostas and Esmeralda retired to the next room to sip brandy by the fire, Sofisticada took over. First, in a voice that was like warm honey, she asked him his name and entreated him to follow her. But Felix would not move, would not even look at the girl, but kept eyeing the door. It was at that moment, when she saw that Felix was about to bolt, that Sofisticada put her finger to her lips and looked sideways in the direction of Rostas and Esmeralda. "Shhhh—I don't want them to hear me!"

"What?"

She cornered Felix and whispered, "Look, I don't want to do this any more than you do, but I have to make a living. I have my mother, my old grandpapa, two little brothers and my uncle depending on the money I make. Let's go to my room; I'll close the door, we'll talk for a while, you'll come out buttoning your fly, say everything was just great, smack your lips a few times; I get paid, you go home and everybody's happy. Please, Felix, be nice!" Sofisticada had the scent of a flower bud in the freshness of spring. "Please!" Her eyes were moist, and Felix thought the girl was going to cry.

Felix was—Felix felt sorry for the girl. "Fine!" Still, he was determined, he was not going to do anything!

Before he had a chance to realize he was being suckered, Felix was led to a room in the back of the house. It was neat and clean, with a good-sized and comfortable bed with perfectly white and fresh linen, one chair, a small table with a bottle of brandy and a glass, and a mirror on the ceiling that Felix did not notice when he first entered the room. He sat down in a chair as narrow and straight-backed as any in Saint Pius, and just as hard and uncomfortable—as it was meant to be. Sofisticada lay down on the bed.

"Where are you from?" she asked.

"Here." Then, Felix looked up for the first time and was mortified. Reflected on the mirror above him, he saw Sofisticada sliding her hand inside her pants and between her legs, spreading them out a bit, still within the bounds of decency. She went on to express her admiration for the boy's eyes, his nose, his inviting mouth, and begged to see the rest of him. She asked if Felix had a girl, although she was sure he did not. But Felix was not listening, not really; he was looking at the ceiling, watching how Sofisticada loosened her blouse and caressed her left breast, how she removed her pants and parted her legs, now totally shameless. She pouted, and in a forlorn voice begged him to tell her why he did not want to make love to her.

"Because," Felix cleared his throat, "I don't know you." Felix swallowed hard and shifted his weight. The chair was becoming impossible.

"I want you more than anything—" cooed Sofisticada.

Felix replied—in a voice that chilled the room—that Sofisticada said the same things to every man in exchange for money. Felix's eyes, still pointing upwards, widened and his breathing quickened. He had never seen a naked girl before and could not avoid thinking that Sofisticada was indeed very beautiful, that her body seemed soft and as delicious as Nino's. Nino! Felix grew suddenly angry, furious that he had been led like a sheep to slaughter to the whore's den, while Nino was alone in a cold room hundreds of kilometers away. Felix buried his face in his hands and began to cry.

Now, if there is one thing a whore can't stand, it is a man (or boy) crying when they are supposed to be doing something else. But it so happened that Sofisticada really liked Felix and felt sorry for him. She knew he was scared and that he was not in Paradise by choice. She quickly got up and went over to his side, though she did not touch him, knowing that this would probably have made things worse. She sat down on the edge of the bed. What was wrong? she asked, and was there anything she could do for him? Felix began to shake, and for a moment Sofisticada thought she would have to call the whole thing off. She went to her little table, poured a glass of brandy and handed it to Felix. "Take it; it's not going to make you feel better, but it will keep you from shaking." Felix accepted the liquor, but since he had never had liquor before—other than wine every now and then—the brandy set his windpipe on fire. "Why are you so sad, Felix? Why? You're not the only person who's never done it before, there's nothing to be ashamed of."

"I love someone," confessed Felix.

"But Felix, this has nothing to do with love."

Well, to say Sofisticada performed beyond the call of duty is to say choirboys sing. She was whispering so close to his face that he felt her lips kissing his hair and then his ear until, slowly, Felix leaned back on the chair, too sad to protest. He embraced Sofisticada, his tears streaming down her naked breasts. Sofisticada raised Felix's head gently and kissed him on the wet cheeks and then on the lips. She kissed him as only one other person in his life had done before. Then, she took off his shirt, removed his boots, his socks—his pants—and led Felix to bed. It is true that at the beginning Felix was not a willing participant. It is true that Sofisticada had to employ every trick and weapon in her repertoire of seduction. But, although she was young, she was a virtuoso, with a good idea what was the matter with Felix. She stroked his body with her hand and kissed his nipples and his belly button and—oh, well—slowly and with the greatest gentleness pried open his legs, which were as smooth as her own, and slid her fingers firmly between his buttocks, running them up and down—prodding here and there until she elicited cries of pleasure.

"You have loved before, Felix," murmured Sofisticada, "and someone has loved you."

When Felix got in the car, his feet hurt. He did not want to go home, either. He wanted to stay with Sofisticada for at least—at least until he was sent back to Rome. But, as Rostas reminded the boy on the way back to the house, to get to Paradise you had to pay a price.

Olga allowed Felix to sleep late. He awoke at noon and looked out the window from his bed. It was another beautiful day, not as warm as the day before but warm enough to go back to Paradise. He could hear the chickens outside and the shepherd yelling at the dog. A bee had made its way inside and was buzzing from one end of the room to the other. Felix put on his pants and went downstairs, his hair messed up, his eyes half-shut, his thoughts divided between Saint Pius and Paradise—where he would have to pay to get in.

"Hello, Felix."

Felix turned and saw Draganović in his work clothes, sitting in the living room, reading a magazine and sipping coffee. They looked at each other, then Felix walked to His Eminence, knelt and placed his head on the eminent lap. "You have an interesting smell. Musk, I think." Draganović noticed the boy looked exhausted, dark circles evident under his eyes. "Go wash. Better yet, take a bath and come down. We have to talk."

In one hour Felix was revived to a semblance of his former self and Draganović and Felix went out for a walk. Like all important moments in a person's life, the sequence of events began haltingly, as Felix tried to arrange his thoughts into a set of ideas that could be communicated clearly and without his sounding like a cretin.

"Are you going to tell me about Paradise?" inquired His Eminence.

Oh, God! How was he going to explain the whorehouse? "It was not my idea!"

"No, it was mine."

They had come upon a small brook surrounded by poplars, and Draganović sat down on a boulder by the rushing stream. The sound of the water was soothing to Felix, and he needed to be soothed. "Why?" he asked, sitting down against a tree and pulling his knees up to his chest.

Draganović picked up a fallen twig at his feet and looked at it. There was something he was curious to find out. "Do you know what a homosexual is, Felix? Have you heard that word before?"

"Y-yes."

"I tell you—when a man has a child, it is usually not by choice. As often as some men love their children, others do not. I could have sent you away, put you up for adoption, or left you to live your life on the farm. I did not. I baptized you—I made you my own." His Eminence got up and walked back and forth.

"So, why did you call me Ronnoco, not Draganović—like you?"

"I would have been proud and honored to have you take my name, Felix, but you can't." Draganović lowered his voice. "I have made many enemies. It's not fair or practical to place you in such disadvantage. So, I made up a name for you. Ronnoco—O'Connor spelled backwards."

"O'Connor?" asked a surprised Felix.

"It's an Irish name."

"Irish!?"

"Yes. I had a friend from Ireland whose name was O'Connor. A real Catholic, a patriot. He was murdered in Belfast in '46. He's the one in the picture—on the steps of Saint Peter's, remember? Anyway, it doesn't matter; what matters is that you speak several languages, that you're getting—or were getting—the best education I can think of for you; what matters is that you will continue to excel, to grow, to become a man so that you can bear my legacy."

A minute or so went by, and the talk gave way to something Felix thought more important than anything else. "Were you ever in love?" This time Felix's voice carried a little more strength.

"I grew up on this mountain, much like you, but it was another time. Until I was fourteen I had three people in my life—my mother, my father and the old shepherd, no one else. I almost never went to town. I spent my time working on the farm and reading. And I didn't have a great selection of books, either, just the Bible and my father's books—all about the heroes of Croatia, the empire, things like that. At fifteen I was sent to the Franciscans. There's nothing much I can add." Draganović smiled, but his smile was shadowed by regret. "God and country, Felix. I have been in love with God and country since I was ten."

"You never made love to another person?"

"No. I was young, too young maybe, when I took my vows. I was only eighteen."

"What if you'd fallen in love—before you took your vows?"

The conversation had taken an interesting turn; here was the boy interrogating the priest, rather than the priest interrogating the boy.

"Like—you think happened to you?"

"Yes, Tata, like happened to me," answered Felix.

Draganović sat next to Felix. "Maybe I would have done what you did."

Felix sighed.

"But I didn't," Draganović was quick to add. He opened his arms, and his gesture encompassed everything in sight, the entire mountain. That was his passion, that was the air that sustained him; that gave him life, nothing else. His goal was to see his land and his Christ united again. Croatia—Catholic Croatia, as in those few, terrible years before Felix was born; when many people suffered, many people died, only to see their vision of a great nation turn to dust. Draganović would help bring it about, he told Felix, no doubt about it. "Croatia will once again be independent and Catholic." Draganović tossed the twig into the brook. "Maybe I should have been a politician and not a priest."

Felix realized that he had never seen Draganović so relaxed, that he was seeing a side of the priest that no one else had seen before. There was a moment of silence; Draganović wanted the boy to reflect on what was being said. He moved around so he could face Felix, then brought his knees to his chest, like the boy. "Which brings us to why we are sitting here in a beautiful valley beneath a tree, instead of you being in school and me tending to the pope."

Felix closed his eyes, afraid of what Draganović might say next.

"You can't afford to lie to me, Felix, just as I can't afford to lie to you. Nothing you say or do will ever make me love you less, not now, not ever—unless I find out that you've lied."

Felix was trying hard not to cry, but the tears were already running down his face.

"Look at me!"

It was difficult but Felix raised his eyes.

"I had the most awful time convincing Father Uncelli not to kick you out of Saint Pius." In fact, he had had no trouble at all. But then, Felix did not know that Draganović had every brothel within five square kilometers of the Holy See on his payroll; had paid informants at police headquarters and within the American, British and French Secret Services (relics of Intermarion); that Draganović ran agents in every country where the Holy See kept a diplomatic mission; and that he directed the clandestine activities of thousands of loyal Catholics serving the Church quietly behind the Iron Curtain. "So what is it with you? Do you like boys or do you like girls?"

Felix did not hesitate; he relished Sofisticada, but he loved Nino.

"Do you know the Church holds your type of affection for Nino a great sin?" Draganović shook his head and smiled. "Look, you are a boy. In twenty years—no, in ten you will think back on today, on your so-called love for your friend, and look upon it as one of those mistakes we all make in our youth. You may laugh, then, or you may shudder when you remember the things you've done and said." Draganović walked to the edge of the water. He kneeled, leaned forward, cupped his hands and drank from the mountain stream. Felix watched His Eminence spring back to his feet like a man half his age. "You will go back to Rome. If, as you once said, you want to be like me, God will absolve you of your sins through the loving grace of the Son. But you must renounce your infatuation with Nino. Boys, men, girls, women—you will serve them, you will not take pleasure from them." Draganović knelt down and took the boy's face in his hands, bringing it so close to his own that their noses touched. "Through Christ the Redeemer you will find the comfort. Without Christ, Felix, you do not have a chance. It is up to you." His Eminence was digging deep for the soul of the boy and came up with hope. The battle would continue. "I guess you can be of great service to me as a lawyer."

From far away Enes, the shepherd, saw the priest and his boy climb the hill and head back to the house, the tall man walking a few steps in front of the boy.

25

It was after five when Draganović and Felix returned to the house. Felix did not feel like being sociable so he went up to his room, lay down, stared at the ceiling and sulked. Draganović joined Rostas in the living room and they talked about plans to acquire a shortwave radio in lieu of telephone service. Olga was in the kitchen cutting, slicing and chopping when Enes the shepherd returned with the animals. He penned the little creatures, bid them goodnight, and, unbeknownst to anyone who might have been interested in his whereabouts, got on the horse and went home.

He was not supposed to, but he did anyway. It took him almost four hours to ride down the mountain and reach the collective farm where his people lived, three kilometers south of Komar. Tall mounds of wheat and barley abounded around the six small cottages built of dirt-brown bricks and red tiles. Each little house had two windows and a door in the front, and two windows and a door in the back. They were practical but not in any way representative of Muslim architecture, because one of the objectives of the central government in Belgrade was to take the different ethnic groups—Croats, Serbs and Muslims—throw them into a socialist melting pot and transform them into responsible proletarians. What better way to promote that socialist and egalitarian ideal than by supplying the new breed of Yugoslav with drab housing free from ethnic differentiation?

Enes jumped off the horse, tied it to the fence and rapped on the door as hard as he could. It was already past eleven o'clock and no light was seen from inside. He knew that everyone was sleeping or in the back room sitting around the sheet-metal stove, complaining about life and doing nothing about it. At last, a light went on in the front room and a boy about fourteen years old answered the urgent call of the shepherd. Though a bit short for his age, he was a good-looking boy, with wavy sandy-colored hair, big, brown eyes and a lovable, innocent smile. Adnan, or Ady as he was called, was Enes' cousin. He wore a pair of coarse, dark grey trousers, a thick hand-knitted sweater and no shoes. Ady was surprised to see Enes standing outside and even more surprised when the shepherd pointed his finger at the boy and screamed, "I knew it! Just like you! Just like you!"

Enes quickly stepped inside and Ady closed the door. The front room was small and plain and lit by a single, bare bulb that dangled on a wire from the ceiling. In some parts of the room the stucco on the walls had flaked away, exposing the bricks underneath. Two brown curtains, fashioned out of a rough fabric and decorated with green leafy patterns, hung from two warped wooden slide bars, which never allowed the curtains to be fully closed or fully opened. On one wall was a old photograph—it must have been taken in the 1920s—which seemed to show the family's more recent ancestors. On the opposite wall was an old calendar, kept there not for scheduling (since it was ten years old) but for its monthly depictions of native flowers. The floor was bare cement and two narrow beds along opposite sides of the room provided sleeping accommodations for the house's occupants.

Hamdai heard the noise and came out from the back room. He was a thin man about forty years old, as tall as his son, which is to say not tall at all. He had a distinguished nose, though his face was rough and weather-beaten. He possessed intelligent eyes, full lips, curly brown hair and a wide mustache that curled up at the ends. His dress was as nondescript as his son's except a shade darker and he wore a fez. "Enes! What are you doing here? And why such a ruckus?"

Enes did not answer. He pointed to his uncle and laughed, stopped, turned serious for a moment, then started laughing again.

Each fit of laughter was accompanied by a jerk of his head and a slap on the thigh.

"Papa, I think Enes is drunk," said Ady.

"I found Nermin! I found Nermin! I found Nermin!" yelled Enes pointing at his cousin Adnan. "He is just like you, I tell you!"

"What's that?" Elma, Hamdai's wife, had joined the group and was standing at the door. "What do you mean, boy! Nermin?" Elma had once been beautiful and proud, but her blue eyes were now tired and sad. She had long brown hair that she kept tied back and a mouth that was adorned with a gold tooth. She was a stout woman, and each year of her difficult life was recorded in a thousand ways on her forehead and hollowed cheeks. Her complexion was pale and her lips were chapped after a long illness. She was out of bed for the first time in days, wearing a long white cotton nightshirt and slippers. The family was wretched and they were poor; no doubt many times they were hungry, too. But there was a difference between Ady and his parents. Hamdai and Elma were resigned to their life and had no hope for a better one. Ady, on the other hand, had expectations and dreams that his would be a better, perhaps easier life.

It was a few minutes before Enes—barely able to contain the joy of his incredible discovery—explained that Nermin, Ady's older brother, the one who had disappeared after the war when his grandmother took him into town, was living in Rome with his employer, the priest Draganović.

"Rome?" said Elma, almost a whisper.

"I thought he was you!" screamed Enes and pointed again at Ady, then quickly raised both arms. "Oh, he looks so much like you, that when I saw him, I hid behind a tree and jumped him—only, it's not you, but this kid Rostas calls Felix!"

"Felix?" echoed Hamdai.

"Yeah! Felix is the priest's cousin from Banja Luka, but I don't believe it. He has no mother, no father—but forget all that, forget all that! What is incredible is how much he looks like Ady! Or how much Ady looks like him—well, he looks older, as old as Nermin would be now if he had not disappeared! It is Nermin, I know it is!"

If a meteor had crashed through the roof it would not have caused as much commotion. The tragedy of Ady's grandmother found dead on the road to Komar and the loss of the baby were part of a dark family legend told and retold around the sheet-metal stove year after year. Hamdai had tried to get help from the authorities to look for his baby, but he had vanished right after the war, and in those days the police was the militia, and the militia was undisciplined, uncaring and unwilling to search for a child, especially when it belonged to an impoverished Muslim clan.

"Nermin is dead! My baby is dead!" screamed Elma, falling into a swoon.

Hamdai reached out to keep her from hitting the floor. "Why do you do this?" Hamdai yelled at Enes. "You know she goes crazy when you talk of the baby!"

"But Uncle, I tell you, he is Nermin, he has to be!"

"How did you get here?" asked Hamdai.

"By horse, I took the—"

"Get back before they say you stole it and have you arrested, you stupid boy!" ordered his uncle.

"But—I came to—"

"Yes, I know, I know! Go!"

"So, what about Nermin?" Enes yelled from the door.

"Nermin is dead! Dead! Dead!" Elma screamed with such fury that Enes thought she was going to attack him.

"Don't believe it!" he screamed back. "He's alive and doing better than you and me!" As he rode away Enes heard his aunt scream after him. "Dead! Nermin is dead! My baby is dead!"

The following day, Inspector Durković arrived at the police station at ten o'clock in the morning. He was tired, with red, bleary eyes and a stuffy red nose. Time had redrawn the inspector's face, giving him deep grooves on his forehead. His cheeks were puffed up and so was his belly. As a member of the party, he enjoyed certain privileges that made it possible for him to drink, eat and smoke more than he ever did as a simple, unobtrusive comrade. Crime in the country did not pay (or make sense). In Travnik no one had anything that anyone else wanted to steal—except a wife, a lover or a sheep. Therefore, most violations of the law in that small town were due to passion, revenge or misadventure. Inspector Durković often spent his days just filling out forms sent from Belgrade, and rarely left his office in pursuit of his vocation.

"Comrade!" called the man sitting on a bench under Tito's picture. Since he did not call the inspector by name and Inspector Durković was a busy man, the policeman did not feel he had to reply. He ignored the Muhammadan who, along with his wife and child, had arrived in a horse cart. Durković was walking slowly and tiredly toward the green door when he heard his name called. "Damn!" he thought, he would have to turn around and acknowledge the fez after all. "What is it?" Inspector Durković did not move.

"You don't remember me—" began Hamdai.

"You're right, I don't. Why should I?"

"I didn't say you should remember me, I said you don't," corrected Hamdai.

Durković sighed, looked at Hamdai for a moment, then closed his eyes and said softly, "What do you want?" Durković kept his eyes half shut and heard not the reply to his question but something else.

"My name is Hamdai Hadzimulić."

"What do you want?"

"I need help and the man at the front desk said I should talk to you."

"What do you want?" repeated Durković for the third time. Because he would not open his eyes Hamdai could not tell if the policeman was thinking, taking a standing nap or suffering from abdominal pain. "I have things to do. What is your problem? You lose a goat? Someone steal your sheep?"

"No," answered Hamdai. "Someone stole my son."

The morning began with a thin layer of fog that made the shepherd, the sheep and goats seem to be walking on clouds. Olga was making breakfast, Rostas was in the back of the house fixing a leak in the roof, and Draganović was still in his room when Felix decided to go for a walk. No one saw him leave in his heavy jacket, or step into the haze like a ghost wandering between the real and the netherworld. He walked for a few minutes and heard the sheepdog bark, the sheep baa, and the shepherd's whistle and call. They were about fifty meters in front of him, and Felix knew that he could not get any closer without the dog getting wind of his scent. And yet he wanted to do just that. Or did he? He was both curious and fearful. Why was he following the shepherd? Many people remind others of someone else; that is a commonplace experience. To Felix, however, that everyday happenstance meant, perhaps, a clue to the unanswered questions of his life. Felix often wondered what kind of family he came from, the family he never knew. It was possible that they were dead, but it was just as possible they were not. Did he really want to find out? Was Felix willing to take that risk? Was he willing to give up his privileged life in the greatest city in the world to live in a shack with heaven knows how many brothers, sisters, uncles and aunts, grandads and grandmas—just so he could share that which others call "family"? If so, everything he had worked for in life would be wasted. There was no need to have ambition or aspire to great things. There was no need to speak Italian or French; to meet popes, cardinals and bishops when you were nothing but a lowly sheepherder or a farmer's son! And what about Tata? How would Draganović feel if Felix left? Abandoned and betrayed. Could Felix do that—trade so much for so little?

Felix kept out of sight, moving from tree to tree just inside the edge of the forest, almost like a wolf watching the prey. The fog was lifting and Felix saw Enes in the distance lie down on his blanket, cover himself with a quilt and fall asleep. Why not? What else could a shepherd do on a cold day? The dog did most of the work anyway. Felix thought of waking up the shepherd. "Hey, balija, who do I remind you of?" He did not. He sat against the tree and looked up at the top of the trees that surrounded him. A narrow crack high up between the branches allowed Felix a glimpse of the sky. He wondered what it was like to see the world from up high. Would he be able to see the whole valley? Would he be able to see clear to Travnik? Rome? A hundred images flashed in front of him—Saint Pius, Nino, Paradise, Sofisticada, Enes the balija. Felix wondered if Sofisticada was a Muslim, Croat or Serb. She was delicious, whatever she was. He loved Nino, he wanted him, and he wanted Sofisticada. But—what if Sofisticada—what if she—what if she—

Felix had trouble putting his thoughts in order because what he was contemplating was outrageous, but not impossible, not at all. It was a small world and an even smaller town. What if Sofisticada was related to him? How could he know for sure? A cousin, maybe? A sister! Felix had screwed his own sister! He chuckled and decided to think of something else lest the tightening pressure in his groin got worse. He decided it was better to go back to the house. He would be returning to Rome in a few hours and the confounding questions of his life would have to wait to be taken up later, to be considered at length when the need to know overrode the need to be happy.

A pointed knob from the tree was digging into his side, and Felix had turned sideways to avoid it, when his eyes fixed on two words that had been entrusted years ago to the tree's brown bark: *Damir*, and beside it *Saša*. Felix's heart pounded, his blood rushed to his head and tears were not far behind. Why? He did not understand. He was spellbound. He gently outlined each letter with his fingers. *Damir*? "Didi!" He whispered the name that was so familiar to him, and yet Felix could not put a face to the name, no matter how hard he tried. He did the same with *Saša*, whispering the name over and over again, until he could no longer hold back, and placed his wet cheek against the rough of the tree, closed his eyes and kissed one, then the other. *Damir* and *Saša*. There were so many things Felix did not know, so many things he did not understand.

"His Eminence is asking for you," said Rostas. He was working on the engine of the Citroën when Felix walked up the hill.

"Where have you been? We're leaving soon. Get ready and—you better eat something before we go." Draganović had finished eating his breakfast of ham and eggs, and the empty plate lay in front of him, waiting for Olga to place it in the sink. Draganović saw the boy's face was wan and his eyes red. He had to get Felix back to Rome, as soon as possible.

"Who is Damir?"

There was a moment of silence before Draganović looked at Felix with a tired frown. "I don't know where you heard that name, Felix, but I will ask you not to repeat it, please."

"Who is he?" Felix asked again, making sure not to say the name aloud.

Draganović knew Felix well enough. The boy would not stop trying to get an answer. "He was the boy who found you and brought you here."

"Why don't you ever talk about him?"

"There are things," began Draganović slowly, "that are better left alone, even after so long. It's just not safe to talk about those people."

"What people? Why?"

"Felix!"

"Did he kidnap me? Did he kill my parents and—"

"Stop it!" Draganović raised his voice. Olga was just coming into the room when she heard the exchange. She turned right around and left Draganović and Felix alone. "That person you mentioned is dead," added Draganović.

"D-dead—" whispered Felix, his disappointment evident in his downcast eyes.

"Felix, I don't have time for this!" Draganović did not know if he should get angry, or tell the boy the truth.

"What—what happened to Damir?"

"I told you not to say that name!" screamed Draganović. In all the years Felix had been with Draganović, it was the first time the priest had yelled at the boy. The anger behind the voice confused Felix, made his cheeks flush and made his imagination take flight. What was His Eminence afraid of? Draganović pushed back his chair, stood up, put both hands on the table and leaned forward. "He—" began His Eminence in an angry whisper, "was the son of the poglavnik!" Felix did not say anything but stared at Draganović in shock. "After the war—*he* came here with his mother and sister. It is something I can't talk about! You were a baby and used to spend a lot of time with—that person. He even had a name for you—" and when His Eminence said the name Felix closed his eyes. "He was a brooding and morose young man, Felix. They left here, and not a moment too soon. While in South America there was an attempt on his father's life; he—the son—was shot and killed."

"*Saša,*" he whispered. "That's a Serbian name! Why did he call me that? Am I a Serb? You would hate me then!"

"Hate you!" There was indignation in the cardinal's voice. "How can I hate you? What's the matter with you?"

"Rostas would hate me—he was Ustaše! He hates the Serbs!"

"For crying out loud, boy, who cares if you're a long lost Obrenović," said Draganović, meaning the Serbian royal line. "Who cares if you were born to Jews. I wouldn't even care if you were born to a—Chinaman!" Draganović noticed the boy was biting his nails. "Enough!" Draganović was about to leave the kitchen when—

"Eminence!"

"Get ready, we're leaving!" said Draganović, and went outside.

Rostas wiped his greasy hands on a rag, then pointed to a police car that was making its way up the road. The small automobile coughed and backfired before it went into a mechanical convulsion and stopped. Five people got out of the car: one uniformed policeman, one man Draganović thought he recognized, and three people he did not.

"Do you know them?" asked Draganović.

"That's Hamdai, Enes' uncle," said Rostas.

"Well!" Draganović went out to meet the new arrivals. "Is it Comrade Durković? Could it possibly be? Is it you, Inspector?"

"Cardinal Draganović." Inspector Durković was aware of the implications of Draganović's rank and his diplomatic immunity. "I didn't know you were here." Durković scolded the uniformed policeman by his side. "Why didn't you tell me His Eminence was home? I am sorry to disturb you, Eminence, but I need to ask you a few questions. Do you mind? Are you very busy? Would you like for us to come back some other time, perhaps?"

His Eminence remembered those words exactly from the last time Durković dropped by the house. There was something to be said for consistency in the constabulary.

"Still hunting for treasures, Inspector? You are a full inspector now, are you not? I'm glad to see life treating you well after so many years of devoted service to your community. It's nice to see a dedicated civil servant get his just rewards."

Durković did not want to prolong the encounter with the priest longer than necessary, so he got right to the point of his visit. "These people have a complaint." Durković pointed to Elma, who was dressed all in black, from her shawl to her long, wide skirt.

"And pray, who are these good people and what are they complaining about?"

"This woman's name is Elma Hadzimulić. She says you have her son living here," said the inspector, as if he were describing the noonday weather.

"Her son?" Draganović turned to Rostas. "I thought he's their nephew, and he's not living here, Inspector, the boy works here. He is the shepherd."

"No, not Enes," interjected Hamdai. "Nermin."

"Nermin? I'm sorry, but I do not know anyone by that name." Again, the cardinal turned to Rostas. "Do you?"

Rostas shook his head.

If Draganović had half a smile on his face, it vanished when the Muslim woman said, "You call him Felix!"

"Are you mad?" Rostas screamed at Hamdai.

No, he was not mad, interrupted Elma. She grabbed the boy next to her and brought him to the forefront. "Look at this boy!" she said aloud. "Look at him! Does he look like your Felix? Like my Nermin!"

"Inspector, may I have a word with you?" His Eminence and Inspector Durković stepped to one side. "You know, Inspector, you have an uncanny ability for coming up with the most tortuous but, I must add, original ideas and plots I've ever heard of. First, the—*episcopal treasure* as I like to call it. Comrade Tito was quite amused by the story."

"Tito?"

"Yes, we met by chance at La Scala—that's an opera house in Milan. Josip Broz was there on a state visit—I think he was going out with a soprano singing that night. He loves opera, did you know that? Anyway—" and Draganović smiled—"I was on official business, you know, and we were introduced by the Egyptian ambassador. Well, we talked during intermission, and when I told him about your treasure hunt, he actually held his sides and laughed! I put in a good word for you, mind you. But Inspector, if I were paranoid, I would think you have a personal vendetta against me. You realize this woman is crazed?"

"Is she?"

"Felix is my cousin. He was born in Banja Luka. You must remember him from the last time you were here. He was the baby my mother was holding in her arms."

"Ah, I do remember, yes."

"How you dare come to my house and accuse me of—"

"Cardinal Draganović, no one is accusing you of anything," interrupted Inspector Durković.

"But you are, you certainly are!" Draganović let it be known by the flourish of his hand and the softness in his voice that he was slightly aghast, somewhat mortified and quite unable to make sense of any of it. "I have all the papers you would ever need to establish Felix's identity—his birth certificate, his identity card, records and photographs of the baby with his real parents just before they perished in an automobile accident. I will get them for you immediately. Mind you, Inspector Durković, Belgrade has made it a point to promote religious tolerance in Yugoslavia, but your behavior seems to contradict official policy. I will protest to the central government, you know that, don't you?"

"Cardinal Draganović, you are at liberty to do as you see fit."

As Hamdai consoled his wife, he looked over and saw Draganović standing in front of the inspector, with his hands raised and clasped in front of him as he made one point after another. Hamdai thought he had never seen anyone so vertical as the priest.

"Really, Inspector," Hamdai heard Draganović say, "you have other means, other procedures available to, in effect, investigate this sort of thing, rather than bringing these people here." Without looking at them, Draganović pointed at Hamdai, Elma and their son. "By doing so, you validate their claim! It is outrageous! How many other families are you going to disrupt with the same charges? Is this woman going to run to the police every time she sees a boy that looks like her son? How many other parents will have to prove their children are who they are? The whole thing is absurd!"

"You did say you have the papers that show the boy is your nephew?" Inspector Durković was unruffled.

"Nermin!" Elma rushed at Felix, who had come out of the house with Olga. Felix cringed and slammed against the side of the house.

He found everything about Elma disgusting, from her gold tooth to the distinct stench of poverty. The tall policeman grabbed her by the elbow and handed her back to her husband.

"Nermin!" Elma screamed again and she was going to do so again when—

"Silence, please!" commanded Draganović in a loud, forceful voice of such authority that it restored order immediately. Not even Inspector Durković dared interrupt. "Felix, this woman says she is your mother." The expression of horror in Felix's face was enough to make Elma fall to her knees, throw her arms up in supplication and wail. Felix and Ady looked at each other. Everyone but Draganović thought they were almost identical, except that Felix was the taller.

It took Draganović less than a minute to produce the documents necessary to establish Felix's identity. The evidence was overwhelming and irrefutable. There was no mistaking the baby in the dozens of pictures with his father and mother, with his great aunt and with the priest Draganović. "I admit there is a resemblance to this boy," Draganović pointed at Ady, "but we are all children of God."

"That is Nermin! He is my baby! I am your mama! Your grandmother—" and Elma gasped, "she died for you! They found her—" Elma was sobbing so that Hamdai had to take his wife in his arms.

Inspector Durković informed Elma and her husband that Draganović had established beyond any doubt Felix's identity, and that it would be best to leave. Draganović approached Elma, and in a voice full of Christian compassion and understanding said, "You have suffered a great loss and I pray for you, but please believe Felix is not your son."

Inspector Durković cleared his throat and interrupted. "I think we should be moving on. We have bothered these people enough already." Case closed.

Elma began to cry again—no, not cry, she wailed. Ady helped his father take her back to the car as Hamdai apologized over and over to Draganović. Felix ran into the house, into the bathroom and threw up. Rostas looked at his wife, and both realized Draganović was going to demand they get another shepherd. Enes was going to pay for his aunt's impudence.

Draganović found Felix sitting on his bed. "Are you all right?" Felix did not answer. He was crying. "I hate them!"

Draganović put his arm over the boy's shoulder. "You should not hate them, Felix. They have suffered greatly, they have lost many loved ones."

"Yes? Well, I'm not one of them!" Felix looked up at Draganović and His Eminence saw the doubt and fear in the boy's eyes.

"Listen," said Draganović softly, "the worst thing you can do is deny the obvious. Nobody knows where you are from. You could have been born anywhere and to anyone. That said, it is important you understand that you are Catholic. I baptized you in the name of Jesus Christ, and no one can take that from you. You have gone through confirmation. Even if you had been born to a Muslim tribe it would have been an accident. It does not make you one of them." Draganović paused long enough to give Felix time to ponder. "Felix, there were millions of refugees after the war wandering up and down the country looking for food, shelter, hoping not to die of exposure or famine. It was an awful time—awful. Your parents could have been among them, I don't know."

"Where did you get the pictures, the ones you showed those people?"

"I had them made years ago, just in case," said Draganović.

"In case what?"

"In case anyone dared lay claim to you. This happens all the time, Felix. Again, many, many people lost their children in the war."

So true. But even if Inspector Durković had been a good policeman, which he was not; even if Inspector Durković had had a sharp investigative nose, which he did not; and even if Inspector Durković had taken the time to write down names, numbers and any other information on the documents Draganović showed him, and had followed up with a few perfunctory telegrams and telephone calls—even then he would only have confirmed that, in fact, there had been a young couple by the name of Ronnoco killed in an accident in Banja Luka just after the war; that in fact they had been the parents of a little boy named Felix; and that in fact all this information was chiseled on a humble, forsaken gravestone covered with dirt and grime, and abandoned by time, in a cemetery outside Banja Luka.

"I love you!" Felix threw his arms around Draganović.

"And I love you, Felix," returned Draganović.

"I've been an ass," said Felix softly. "I was a selfish brat. I'm ashamed of myself. I'm sorry for all the trouble, for getting thrown out of school. I swear, it will never, never happen again! I want to take confession and ask to be forgiven."

"You are not an ass, you are a boy. I pray this is the worst thing that happens to you. Life has a way of handing out suffering the likes of which you cannot imagine," said Draganović, stroking the boy's hair.

"I want to be like you," said Felix with tears in his eyes.

"You will, you will," His Eminence assured the boy. Felix would follow in Draganović's footsteps after all.

THE SAINT

26

"You are my legacy! You cannot allow distractions, can't allow anything, not even people to get in the way!" said the old man in a croaking voice that was hardly audible. "Bless me Father, bless me!"

"Confess and be absolved," Felix repeated, and buried his face in his hands.

"I—" Draganović gasped. The tubes supplying him with oxygen were making it very difficult for him to talk. In a last, desperate attempt to be heard, Draganović let go of Felix's hand and pulled off the plastic tubes taped to his nose.

"What are you doing!?" Alarmed, Felix reached over and tried to stop him.

"Listen!" cried out Draganović. "Oh, listen to me!"

"Tata, you can't take that off, you will—"

"What's the use! Let me finish! I—I violated the most sacred commandment! Men have died on my orders, most of them I never met. Holy Father, I confess—"

"What did you say?"

"The thief," blurted Draganović.

"The thief?"

"The one that stole from the church—in, in America!"

Felix stared the old man and wondered if he meant Louie Peps.

"He—he had to be sacrificed, like the priest, O'Malley; I also had him killed—and the little boy's father. Even Pero—the old shepherd, who was my only friend when I was a child, he found the treasure! I—I couldn't take a chance! I murdered Pero with my own hands!" The struggle for the final breath had begun and Draganović was barely holding his own.

"A treasure? What are you talking about?"

"Pavelić!"

"What!"

"No loose ends, Felix, Your Holiness, no loose ends!" He stopped talking for a minute and Felix heard the heavy, hollow sound as the old man's chest heaved, fighting the conclusion of his extraordinary life. "Nothing, nothing can get in the way of the Church!" The words lingered in midair long enough to be understood, then dropped to the ground and seeped quickly through the cracks of the hardwood floor. "I have sinned for my Church, for my Christ—for my country!" Draganović seized Felix's hand as tight as he could and closed his eyes. He was not dead, no, he was just waiting to hear the words that would excuse him for his earthly transgressions.

"You are a priest! How can you justify murder!" cried Felix. "Life is sacred!"

"The Church is sacred!" Draganović opened his mouth, stretched out a long, skeletal arm and clutched Felix's sleeve.

Felix was horrified. There was no way to measure his disillusion and heartache. All his life he had thought "his tata" the most honest, just, loving, human being on the face of the earth; a man who unselfishly dedicated himself to an orphan who was not even a member of his family. Felix stared at the man he once thought was his father and wept; wept for the sins of a confused old man, wept for the Christ in whose name the innocents died. He pulled back his hand and made the sign of the cross on the wrinkled forehead of Draganović. *"Misereatur tui omnipotens Deus, et dimissis peccatis tuis, perducat te ad vitam aeternam. Amen."* May almighty God have mercy on you, forgive you all your sins, and bring you to everlasting life. Amen.

At that moment, Draganović closed his eyes and expired. Felix knelt beside the bed, prayed and cried, cried as he had not done since he was a boy. "You lied to me!"

Felix left the room ten minutes later and informed those outside that Leo was dead. He did not wait for anyone to give him condolences, nor did he want any.

That night, outside the papal apartments, the Swiss Guards exchanged looks and wondered. Someone was playing a flute.

☨

"Holiness," began Cardinal Bailey, "we're being bombarded with requests from the media for your photograph. Father d'Stesi was able to find one but it is at least ten years old. I'm afraid it just won't do."

"It will have to do for now. I don't have pictures of myself, never cared for photographs. Everything in good time, Brother," replied the pope.

"Yes, Holiness."

"Bailey—"

"Yes, Holiness?"

"Prepare a news release to be sent out at once. Pino, you are to coordinate with His Eminence and inform anyone interested. Let's stop this nonsense now. Say that after a detail investigation, the Holy See found out that the predictions of a Second Coming of Christ in 2010 are wrong. You can also say that the Holy See apologizes for any suffering caused by the announcement from America and that it will work very hard to prevent anything like this from ever happening again. Enough is enough."

"Yes, Holiness," said Pino.

"Yes, Holiness," echoed Bailey.

"And Pino, the Institute of Saint Jerome—" Felix turned and fixed his eyes on the secretary of state. "Shut it down."

Father d'Stesi entered the room, walked up to the pope and whispered, "Holiness, the president—Zagreb is on the line."

Felix begged to be left alone, waited for the cardinals to march out of the study, and picked up line one. "Milo—my friend, well?" President Milo Babić had been an old acquaintance of Draganović; they had known each other since the end of World War II. When in 1991 Croatia seceded from the Federal Republic of Yugoslavia, Babić emerged as an important political force thanks to his coalition of ex-fascists, most of whom had been closely connected with the Ustaše. "Yes, that's good, yes." The pope wrote down the information he had called for. "Thank you, Milo. God bless you." He put down the pen and hung up.

Next morning, Pope Felix met with Tomaso and Bailey and informed them he was going on a trip.

"But, Holiness," said Tomaso, quite alarmed, "the coronation is two weeks away."

"I'll be back in four days, five at most. Relax, Eminence."

"What should I tell the Curia? They'll want to know where you are," said Pino.

"Tell them I am settling family business. That's not too difficult to understand, is it? It is up to me to oversee the proper care of our late brother Draganović's estate."

An hour later, Pope Felix V was in a helicopter on his way to the airport. The pope was alone and dressed in dark grey slacks, a matching turtleneck, a thick, dark brown leather jacket and black loafers. The man behind the shades could have been a movie star instead of the Vicar of Rome.

Felix carried on him his diplomatic passport—although this named him as Bishop Felix Ronnoco and not Felix V—a thin cellular phone that allowed him to call or be reached anywhere in the world and the svirala.

☩

The small, white Vatican jet zoomed across the Mediterranean. It landed in Madrid an hour and fifteen minutes later. Felix went through customs and into a waiting limousine sent by Bishop Ernesto Vidal, bishop of Madrid. Bishop Vidal was informed that an important guest was arriving and to please provide transportation, although how important a guest the bishop was never told.

Bishop Vidal's chauffeur was a young man by the name of Fernando. He was quite an unseemly creature, large, with a very long and twisted nose, three layers of flesh under his jaw and small eyes that squinted all the time. He did not smile much, but when he did the bishop's chauffeur displayed a full set of shiny braces. Still, Fernando was an agreeable chap who used a light but pleasing cologne.

"Is it far?" Felix gave the young man the address on a piece of paper.

"No. It's in the center of town, Excellency." Fernando looked at Felix through the rearview mirror.

The limousine pulled up to a luxury high-rise. "I will wait for you, Excellency."

"Yes, thank you." Felix turned to the doorman who was holding open the door to the building. "Contessa Folinari, please," said Felix as he walked in the elegant lobby, with its extravagant chandeliers, dark wood paneling, marble floors and columns, and large mirrors in ornate golden frames.

"Your name?"

"Bishop Felix Ronnoco."

When Felix got out on the fifteenth floor he found himself in the foyer of a large apartment where he was met by a tall butler dressed in a white bolero and black trousers. "This way, please." The butler led him down two marble steps, across a wide hall, up a flight of stairs and through another long corridor. They reached a double door that the butler opened at the same time he announced, "His Excellency, Bishop Ronnoco—Contessa Folinari." The butler stood aside to allow Felix into the room. The butler closed the doors and left Felix looking at a slim, beautiful and elegantly dressed woman in her early sixties, standing at the far end of the room next to the fireplace. Her grey hair was combed back, and she wore a black dress and a pearl necklace. Behind the contessa, on top of the fireplace, was a large portrait of Ante Pavelić, the poglavnik, in military uniform.

"Excellency." The contessa walked up to greet Felix. Felix put out his hand. She took it and kissed the ring, though, in the moment of introduction, Contessa Folinari did not notice that the man she thought was a bishop was wearing a ring that indicated a somewhat higher ranking in the Church. "Please—" And the contessa led Felix to a chair, then sat down. "Have you had lunch? May I offer you something to eat?"

Felix replied with a smile and a shake of his head.

"Something to drink, then?"

"No, I don't want anything, thank you. I don't have much time," said Felix.

"Our friend in Zagreb said you have something important to ask me."

"My name is Felix Ronnoco. Of course I don't expect you to remember me because the last time you saw me I was a baby. It was right after the war. You were staying at a farm in Travnik, at the home of Ana Draganović—" Felix stopped because he saw Katarina's eyes open and a slow but extremely wide smile light up her face.

"Oh, my God," she whispered, putting her hand to her mouth; her widening eyes took on that glistening quality that shows tears are about to surface. She searched his face for a hint of the baby she knew as, "Saša?"

"You remember me, then?"

Katarina was only able to repeat, "Oh, my God!" She leaned forward and gently touched his face. "It is you! You were taken away by the militia! Oh, my God!"

"Contessa—"

But the contessa could not contain herself, and she began to cry. "It broke our hearts!"

"Contessa," Felix tried again. "I need to ask you something."

"My poor, poor brother! He loved you so much! He was devastated when you were taken!"

"Why—why do you call me Saša? I have to know this, it's very important!" Felix placed added emphasis on *important*, trying to make Katarina focus on his reason for traveling to Madrid to meet with her.

"Why Saša?" Not taking her eyes away from his, Katerina was clearly trying to remember back to when she was a young girl. It was impossible. The problem was not that so many years had gone by, but that she had never known the reason why. "I don't think he ever told me."

"Who? Who are you talking about?"

"Didi. He never told me why he called you Saša. I don't think he told anyone."

"Please, try to remember, anything, even if you think it's not important." Felix saw his hopes dashed, realized that the search for his identity would end in a luxury apartment in Madrid.

"Damir was quite peculiar, you know, and very moody. Heaven knows why he called you Saša. I just remember we were on our way to the farm; it was very late at night and we were terrified of getting caught by the communists. We had an accident and had to stop. Damir found you by the side of the road. He said your name was Saša. That's all I remember." The contessa paused and shook her head sadly. "If you want," she added, "if you want I can write and ask him. I'm sure he'd love to—"

"Who? Ask who?"

"Didi. I can—"

"Didi! Ask Didi? You mean Damir is alive?" Felix was out of his chair.

"Why, yes. Well, at least I hope he is."

"Where, where is he?" Felix's voice cracked and his hands shook so hard he had to stick them in his pockets.

"He's in Bosnia. I haven't heard from him lately. The situation there is not good, even with the cease-fire. Sometimes it takes a long time for the letters to get through."

It was Felix's turn. "Oh, my God!"

☩

"Brightbird, this is mother—over!"

"Mother, this is Brightbird! Come in, over!" answered the pilot.

"Caution is advised. Area is known for sniper fire, over!"

"Roger!" The UN Bell Iroquois helicopter buzzed the trees when it hit an air pocket and the pilot was forced to pay a little more attention to his flying. "Look," he yelled at Felix, but without turning his head, "I'll drop you off but I can't hang around. This bird's a great target, and there are reports of snipers in the hills! Give us a ring. I'm sure Colonel Giraud will send another chopper to pick you up!"

"Fine!" yelled Felix over the roar of the engines. Things were moving too fast, and not just the helicopter ride either. Twenty-four hours earlier he had been in Madrid; now he was flying into Serb held territory, in Bosnia.

"There it is!" The copilot pointed to a white and green rectangle in the distance. He was the opposite of his burly colleague at the command of the ship—a very small and frail man, whose bright black eyes darted anxious looks left and right, and who seemed not a minute older than his twenty-two years.

The site was outside Srebrenica, isolated by hills and accessible only by a country road. Its parking area, about ten meters in front of the main building, was adequate for a landing. "What is this place?" yelled the pilot.

Felix cupped his hands and answered as loudly as he was able, "Orphanage!" It had not been built for this purpose, of course. The thick-walled, two-story structure, made of concrete and stucco, and with red tiles on the roof was built in 1983 to house athletes participating in the Sarajevo winter Olympics of 1984. The distance from Sarajevo made this, to say the least, impractical, and the building was abandoned to the fairies of the woods one day before it was to be inaugurated.

The helicopter did a fly-by and hundreds of children ran out to see it land. The attendants did everything possible to keep them from getting in the way of the helicopter, the copilot waving them back with an urgent thrust of the arm from his side of the cockpit. As soon as the helicopter touched down (the pilot never cut the engines) the children ran to it from all sides. There were little kids, big kids and in-between kids. There were boys and girls, blonds and brunettes, redheads and those with black hair; there were blue eyes so blue they shamed the sky and black eyes blacker than coal; there were Serbs, Croats, Muslims and Gypsies. All children, all orphans.

The copilot unbuckled his seatbelt, went into the rear of the helicopter and pushed out from the left side of the craft several large bags of clothing, medicine and food they had brought for the orphanage, while Felix climbed out the other side and ran to the entrance of the building. No sooner had Felix cleared the helicopter, that it took off, made a sharp about-face and disappeared behind the hill.

Felix noticed that the walls of the orphanage were pockmarked and part of the roof was scorched. A little boy about six years old, with big brown eyes, was tugging at his sleeve when Felix noticed the sign on the building. It read *"Saša."*

A young woman in dungarees, with long sandy-colored hair and a face whose only attractive feature was its many freckles, ran to meet Felix.

"I'm Bishop Felix Ronnoco. I am looking for Miguel Bianchi," Felix yelled over the voices of the excited children running everywhere.

The woman scolded some of the kids before she answered that Don Miguel had been taken away. "This morning—a group of men dragged him into a car at gunpoint!" She called out to an assistant to help get the children back in the building. "It is very dangerous to stand like this in the open," she said, darting nervous looks at the hills surrounding the compound.

"Who took him? Where did they take him?" asked Felix anxiously.

"The police." The woman was very frightened, not only for herself but also for what might have happened to Don Miguel.

"I need a car," said Felix quickly.

"A c-car? But it's very dangerous to—"

"Do not argue with me!"

The woman quickly ran inside the building and returned thirty seconds later with the keys to Miguel Bianchi's beat-up red Fiat. "Thank you," Felix said to the woman, as he shifted gears and stepped on the gas.

The road out of the compound was full of holes. It led into the hills that were—Felix guessed—teeming with lookouts and snipers from the Serb factions that controlled the area. He wondered why they had kidnapped Damir. He would soon find out, hopefully before Damir was used for target practice.

Twenty minutes after leaving the orphanage, Felix downshifted and swerved to avoid a giant pothole in the middle of the road, then saw the road up ahead blocked by two grey Russian made jeeps with the word "Police" written in bold black letters on the doors. Six men stood beside the jeeps, smoking and talking, all wearing the blue-grey uniforms of the Serbian police. Felix stopped, got out and was immediately surrounded by the men.

"Papers," growled a short, stocky fellow of about twenty-five.

Felix pulled out his UN safe conduct and his passport.

"Are you carrying weapons?" asked the officer.

"No," said Felix.

Another policeman, this one a tall, muscular fellow with the swagger and tone of voice of someone in command, ordered Felix to raise his arms. "Let's see what we have here." He stuck his hand inside Felix's jacket and pulled out the cellular phone, the passport and— "What the fuck is this?"

"It's a svirala," explained Felix.

"What is a *svirala*?" The officer, who had been born and raised in a tenement in the center of Belgrade, was ignorant of what shepherds called—

"A flute," answered Felix.

"A flute?" And because things are frequently not what they seem—especially in a war torn country—the officer blew on the little musical instrument to see if, in fact, it was a flute, and not some special device fitted with a miniature transmitter that could be used to track its owner with the help of satellites, or an innovative and diabolical piece of hardware that could expel poisoned darts.

Having never played a flute before, he grinned when he heard its high-pitched toot. He was even more baffled when he glanced at the passport. "Well, it seems you made a wrong turn, priest," the officer said to Felix. "Rome is that way." He pointed to his right.

"I am looking for Miguel Bianchi," said Felix matter-of-factly.

"Who?"

"Miguel Bianchi, the director of the orphanage," Felix continued. "I understand you had him picked up."

"We did?" The policeman looked at his partners.

"I would like you to let him go. He has done nothing to you."

"I don't know what you're talking about."

"Then, please, take me to someone who does." Felix smiled. He was gambling with his life. Even with the IFOR soldiers patrolling the area, Srebrenica was still considered no man's land unless you were a Serb. He knew he could be made to disappear and no one would ever find his body.

Two policemen climbed into the back seat of the Fiat and ordered Felix to follow the same winding, steep and very bumpy trail up the hill as far as it would take them. Less than fifteen minutes later they arrived at police headquarters in the center of town. Felix was ordered out of the car and made to stand with his hands on top of the hood and his legs spread wide while he was searched—more carefully—for a second time. The Fiat also underwent a thorough inspection. A distance away, Felix saw an IFOR armored vehicle and a group of soldiers milling about, their heavy weapons at the ready. They did not see Felix being searched, or if they did, they did not care.

"Come!" ordered one of the policemen, and Felix was shown inside the windowless, brown, square cement building. They passed an empty front desk and went in a room with green walls, two chairs, a dark grey desk, a file cabinet of the same color and a light bulb hanging from the ceiling. "Wait here," said the fellow, stepping aside.

Ten minutes later, Felix heard voices outside, and soon a small, thin man of about sixty-three entered the room carrying Felix's cellular telephone, the svirala and the passport taken from him earlier. He was the captain of the police force, a fellow who, the year before, had been a general in the Serbian army that overran Srebrenica.

The captain placed the objects on the table in front of Felix and offered a cordial, "Good afternoon." His manner was businesslike, and his voice had that deep and gravelly quality that bespoke many years of enjoying the pernicious effect of cigarettes. The captain sat down across from Felix and never offered to shake hands. He had a small nose, very little hair and lots of wrinkles—most etched on his face not by age, but by suffering.

The moment the captain walked in the room Felix was seized by a strange feeling that he had seen the man before. He stared at the brown eyes that seemed a little too big for the rest of the face, and which now stared right back at him.

"Well?" began the captain.

It was almost thirty seconds before Felix replied. "You—you are holding Miguel Bianchi."

"No, we are not. I don't know anyone called Miguel Bianchi."

"The director of the orphanage," said Felix.

"Oh, that fellow!" The captain paused, leaned back on his chair and laced his hands around the back of his head. "You know, Father, you speak our language very well."

"I was born here."

"Where?"

"Travnik."

"But you're Catholic, not Muslim."

"Yes, I am."

"And a bishop with a diplomatic passport bearing a name that is on every Catholic's lips these days," said the captain with a smirk.

"How much?" asked Felix.

"How much? How much what?" asked the captain.

"How much do you want for the old man?"

"I'll pretend you did not say that."

"No," Felix shot back. "Don't pretend anything. You've kidnapped a civilian who had nothing to do with your crazy war, an old man who has spent years taking care of children left orphaned by insanity!"

"Insanity that has been fueled by your Church. Don't lecture me, priest. And don't talk to me about orphans. You're lucky I don't have you taken out and shot." The captain delivered every word calmly, never moving a muscle or raising his voice. "This fellow you call Miguel Bianchi is the son of Ante Pavelić, the mass murderer. Ever heard of the poglavnik, Father? I understand he's still greatly admired in Croatia; your politicians are even trying to rehabilitate his reputation."

Felix closed his eyes and sighed. Damir was as good as dead.

It had taken Serbian intelligence a year to find out the real identity of the director of the orphanage, explained the captain. At first they had thought Miguel Bianchi was a spy, but they were appalled when they traced him to Argentina and learned the truth. "I'm afraid this is not *business as usual*, Father, this is personal." The captain looked away. Without meaning to, he fixed his sight on the svirala in front of him. He knew all about shepherd's flutes. "Ever heard of Glina?" he continued softly, looking again at Felix. "In 1941, Ante Pavelić visited our little town. He had everyone in town killed. My mother and I were two of fifteen people who survived the massacre. We wandered the countryside for months eating grass and dung to stay alive. Later we learned that the poglavnik himself shot my nine-year-old brother in the head, and his henchmen stabbed my father to death. Where were you then, priest? You've probably never heard of Glina, have you?"

Felix grabbed the side of his chair. He thought his head was going to explode. His eyes glistened as he stared at the old man across from him. He must have looked awful because the captain called for a glass of water.

"*Saša,*" whispered Felix under his breath.

The captain tilted his head and frowned. "What was that?"

Felix shook his head and waved both hands, trying to fend off the demonic nightmare that had haunted him since childhood. He wondered if the captain had ever seen the name on the orphanage.

The amiable face of the old soldier became hard and unforgiving. "It was very arrogant of you, driving up here like you did, priest, so confident that nothing would happen to you. Then you have the nerve to offer me a bribe. Is your show of emotion supposed to soften me up, make me take pity on Pavelić? You're wasting your time. That son-of-a-bitch is going to die."

"Why?" asked Felix. "He had nothing to do with what happened over fifty years ago! He was a just a child!"

"So was my brother."

"Yes! I know, I—I understand, believe me, I do! But where is it going to end? How many generations have to die before your thirst for vengeance is satisfied? This cycle of senseless retribution is madness! The murder of innocent people has to stop!" Felix got up and stood looking down at the captain. "One second of satisfaction, that is all you're going to get if you kill Damir Pavelić. It is not going to bring back your family!" Felix put both hands on the desk, leaned forward and lowered his voice. "Show me you are not just another Ante Pavelić."

The policeman remained silent for five minutes. Then, he sat up straight, clenched his teeth and said, "Fine, let's see how much that old man is really worth to you, Holiness."

27

"Eminence, your three o'clock has arrived," said Father Subraggi, popping his head in the door.

"Let him wait. Come here, Marcello. I want to show you something!" ordered Cardinal Carelli.

Marcello walked quickly to the prelate's side. He was the same Marcello who had condemned himself to shame and irrelevancy because, as a boy, he had committed the unforgivable sin of calling the future pope a *Slav piece of shit*.

"Where is it?" Carelli stuck his head in the safe. Every so often, he would resurface, take a breath and address Marcello. "This will make your hair stand on end!" assured His Eminence.

Making Marcello's little tight curls stand on end would have required a miracle, something that, given Cardinal Carelli's diminished authority in the Church, was unlikely to happen. Still, the little piece of paper that Carelli showed Marcello elicited a prolonged whistle from the priest. "That is a check made out to the Croatian National Council. Do you know what the Croatian National Council is—or was? Pope Leo's secret fund set up to buy weapons for the Croatian army during the civil war in the Balkans. That is what this cost me!" Carelli knocked on his zucchetto. "Look at that number, 1,522,500,000 lire! Do you think it is fair that after I've given these foreigners so much money I should be treated like a pariah? No, you don't! Of course you don't! It's unjust, I tell you, it's un-Christian, and it's pure and simple evil!" His Eminence returned the papers to their secret hideout, slammed the door to the safe and sought the comfort of his chair. "Alien maggots have taken over the Holy See! Parasites, infecting our glorious Church with their despicable habits. Ah, yes, Marcello, the throne of Peter is being held for ransom—by scum!"

His Eminence's remarks tapped Marcello in the forehead, because in all the time he had worked for Cardinal Carelli, the secretary had never expressed sentiments even remotely close to those pronounced by his superior. Marcello had, on one or two occasions, voiced his displeasure over an incident that had happened in a distant past when he was humiliated in front of his classmates. But Marcello never inferred that his lack of advancement within the Church was due to Felix Ronnoco or his mentor. Was it a coincidence that, during the years he was employed as secretary to Cardinal Carelli, Marcello never ran into Father, Bishop, or Cardinal Ronnoco, much less Felix Ronnoco the pope? Was fate doing its best to keep the two from ever coming face to face again, notwithstanding the fact they both worked within the walled city, and for almost a decade, had offices (on different floors, to be sure) at the Government Palace? Was the lack of contact between Marcello and Felix Ronnoco a continuation of their last two years at Saint Pius, where they never shared a table at mealtime, never worked the same detail, never even bumped into each other in the hall?

Once, Marcello had been determined to receive satisfaction (in the form of an apology) for the drubbing he had received at the hands of the younger, smaller Ronnoco. He felt Felix should never have been allowed back into school, and could not help but look upon Father Uncelli's transfer except as a reminder of his disgrace. In his quest for justice, Marcello sulked, whined, grew bitter and angry, and planned to whack Felix on the head with a tennis racquet. But administering injury with a Dunlop is incompatible with Christianity, which advocates a turning of the cheek. So before Marcello could carry out his assault, guilt took over, helped avert a tragedy, and led the penitent boy directly to his confessor, one Monsignor Antonio Carelli.

Upon leaving Saint Pius preseminary, Marcello confronted the difficulties any young man, whether religious or not, faces in life when furnished neither with charm nor family fortune. He enrolled in a second-rate seminary in Lombardy, embraced the all-encompassing humility of poverty, grew less arrogant, more tolerant, and took his vows at twenty-two.

During that time, Monsignor Carelli used the power of his purse to rise above lesser mortals in the hierarchy of the Church. When Monsignor Carelli became Bishop Carelli, he invited Father Subraggi to be his aide. Misery loves company, especially when it lacks self-esteem, is easily manipulated, and yet manages to carry out duties competently and with the resoluteness of a zealot.

"Shall I show the gentleman in?" asked Marcello.

Carelli nodded and waved. He was still mulling over the indignities he had suffered at the hands of the Balkan popes, when Roberto Ponti entered the room. Ponti was not a young man, being in his mid-sixties. He had a full head of grey hair (thanks to a successful transplant), was thin, nervous and always in the latest Armani suit; he was also greedy and completely unethical, but possessed a remarkable talent for persuasion, which was underscored by the animated exercise of his limbs—Hamlet's advice on the subject notwithstanding.

"Good morning, Eminence," said Ponti.

Cardinal Carelli put out his hand languidly and waited for Ponti to kiss the ring. But the lawyer was an atheist with a vehement dislike for the Catholic Church, so the meeting got underway with only a shaking of hands. "You said you have information that is extremely important to the Holy See," began Carelli. "You said it was urgent. What can I do for you?"

Ponti took out a thin, black leather card holder, took out his card and presented it to His Eminence. Then, he crossed his legs and assumed an air of familiarity that His Eminence thought highly inappropriate. "Eminence, I have a client who is in a terrible fix."

Cardinal Carelli was as imperturbable as the Mona Lisa.

"I cannot say he is a good man, for he is not," continued the lawyer. "Indeed, I can state that he is a terrible, horrible human being who should never have been permitted to leave the womb alive." Lawyers are used to assaulting the sensitivities and values of others if it suits their purposes, but even Ponti should have been a bit more reserved when talking about the extrication of life from the womb before a representative of the Universal Church. "My client is a drug pusher, a pimp, and a murderer. In the course of his life, he has had many customers, customers who have paid him to carry out some of the most heinous crimes imaginable."

"I pray he is repentant," said Carelli, stifling a yawn.

"Humberto Venavić is not the type of man who looks back, except to get even," said the attorney, giving his arms a rest and leaning his head forward.

"Ahhh, well, we know where he will end up, I'm sure," added Cardinal Carelli, dryly.

"He has as good a chance as any," quipped the counselor.

Cardinal Carelli cast his impassive eyes on the Madonna behind the lawyer.

"Now, the reason I've come to see you is that my client once had a business relationship with the Holy See. My client and I concur that in view of the close ties that have bound him to this august institution—"

"Please, stop fidgeting. What are you talking about? Get to the point."

"Yes, well, then—Eminence, to be perfectly blunt, my client's whores have left him and moved across town. The police put his drug smuggling out of business. Two other gangs took over his protection racket. His bodyguard was murdered (fortunately for Humberto, since the bodyguard was not the intended victim), and his green Mercedes has been firebombed. On top of everything else, it is my professional opinion that the prosecutor has enough evidence to put my client away for the rest of his life. Now, that's the good news. The bad news is that the court has seized his assets. We are talking about a serious and complicated case, Eminence. My client can't afford to be left without representation—" Ponti placed his hands on his bosom to demonstrate his sincerity, "—and I can't afford to provide it without getting paid."

"I don't understand what this sordid affair has to do with us?"

"Ah, yes, of course, I was getting to that," added the counselor.

"Please do," interjected the cardinal.

"My client murdered a priest—"

Cardinal Carelli's eyes widened and acquired a subtle glint.

"—on orders from the pope."

Another cardinal would have denounced the cheap attempt at blackmail and called a guard or the police or, at the very least, would have kicked the lawyer out of the Vatican. Not Carelli. In fact, Ponti— a fellow experienced in human unpredictability—was surprised when the prelate suddenly became quite friendly. "Which pope?"

☦

Cardinal Carelli lived in a fifteen-room villa forty-five minutes north of the city. The property, along with a substantial cache of gold, had been given to Maximilian Carelli (the founder of the line) in 1808 by Napoleon, in exchange for Maximilian's help in putting down an insurrection against invading French troops.

The two-story building stood in the midst of spacious gardens surrounded by wooded hills. The interior was quite rustic, except for the walls, which were adorned not only with a sculpted frieze of garlands and an elaborate cornice, but were hung with a splendid collection of Baroque art (acquired by Maximilian's heirs) that included works by Van Dyck, Caravaggio, Rubens, Vermeer and de La Tour. Two cartoons by Leonardo da Vinci were also on exhibit. The ceiling was *a casselle*—that is, with bowl-shaped bosses—and the floors were set with black marble tiles that bore the Carelli coat of arms chiseled in silver.

For Cardinal Carelli, maintaining a proper standard of comfort was not always easy, and most of times it was expensive. He employed a tall, dark, Spanish butler who answered to the name Rodrigo, a Filipino valet, a French chef and his assistant, three gardeners and four maids. The upkeep of the estate was paid for by the fortune Carelli inherited from his father, who inherited from his father, and so on— the same wealth that had bought the red hat from Pope Leo XIV.

At exactly seven fifty-eight Cardinal Carelli went outside, dressed in a black cassock, and waited for the Vatican limousines to arrive. The first delivered Cardinal Pino. "Welcome, Eminence!" exclaimed Carelli with arms outstretched.

"I always marvel when I visit you, my friend," said Pino getting out of the car, "how pure and sweet the air is out here."

Pino and Cardinal Carelli were about the same age, though Carelli looked younger than sixty-eight.

"Yes. If ever I considered moving to the city, the fresh air and the fragrance from my gardens would change my mind."

Pino was followed by Cardinal Tomaso ("My dearest brother. It has been too long!"), who was followed by Cardinal Bailey ("My friend, how are you? It's been ages!"), who arrived just before Cardinal Numa ("You've lost weight, Eminence.")

The poached salmon fillet was wonderful, the wine superb; the dessert was obscenely chocolaty and smooth, and the coffee was not to be believed. "You are a man who lives well, Eminence," said Numa, looking sideways at Carelli. "This brandy is wonderful!" said Bailey.

At ten-thirty, the Eminences retired to the comfort of soft leather chairs—matching the rich paneling of the library—where they sat absorbing the heartwarming glow from the fireplace, every detail under the gracious supervision of an immense portrait of His Eminence (minus the hump) atop the mantelpiece.

"It is Duque de Alba," said Cardinal Carelli of the brandy.

Pino shrieked and giggled like a silly schoolgirl. "He was a horrible man!"

"But very Catholic," Tomaso pointed out. "Besides, they've named the best brandy in the world after him."

Carelli smacked his lips. "Rodrigo, that will be all, thank you." The butler left the room. "My dear brothers, has any of you ever met my secretary?"

The prelates exchanged looks, shook their heads, kept their noses in the snifters, and said almost in unison (voices muffled by the glass) that they had talked to him on the phone often enough.

"He was a student at Saint Pius, you know, the school for altar boys," said Carelli.

"Oh?"

"And he was a classmate of our brother Ronnoco."

Pino tilted his head, indicating, if not outright interest in the subject, at least some curiosity.

"I am told that young Felix Ronnoco was kicked out of school by the rector, a Father Uncelli. A week later Father Uncelli was transferred, and Ronnoco was back in school."

"Transferred?" asked Tomaso.

"Relocated."

"Fired," guessed Bailey.

Cardinal Carelli offered each of his guests a Cuban cigar.

"No, thank you," said Numa.

"I'll take one." Bailey reached over.

"What year was this?" asked Pino.

"Oh, in the early sixties."

"And?" Tomaso was looking around for the brandy.

Carelli shrugged. "I'd love to know what happened, wouldn't you?" He lit the long and pungent Havana that, along with the brandy, was as close to heaven as Cardinal Carelli would ever get on earth.

"The rector stepped on the wrong toes, that's all. Our late brother Draganović was Ronnoco's—mentor." Pino placed a mischievous emphasis on "mentor." He paused long enough to take his nose out of the snifter.

"And Draganović was a man to be reckoned with," added Bailey.

"Even then?" Carelli's tone bore an inflection meant to sound naive.

Numa was not fooled. "Draganović was Pope Paul's man."

"And he was arrogant, secretive, devious and had no regard for anyone except Ronnoco," said Bailey.

"And we know what that was all about," added Pino.

"Hmm."

"Leo XIV was a tyrant and so is his successor," continued Pino.

"I am sure Brother Carelli has not brought us together to gossip about things we can no longer do anything about," said Tomaso, arching one eyebrow.

"No, I certainly did not." Carelli puffed a few times on his cigar, took a sip of brandy and described his meeting with Humberto Venavić's lawyer.

The Four Horsemen heard the story in disbelief. The secretary of state was so stunned he was unable to stop staring at Cardinal Carelli through the glass.

"And pray, brother," said Bailey, "what is it they want?"

"A settlement," said Carelli at last.

"A settlement?"

"An arrangement, if you will. Can you imagine the repercussions if the press gets wind of this? A priest, murdered on orders from Pope Leo!"

"It's a nightmare! How much time do we have?" asked Numa, in a tone that showed he was very upset.

"A week," replied his host.

"What's to keep that man from coming back a year from now and demanding more money?" asked Tomaso, leaving his seat and standing by the fireplace.

"Indeed!" asserted Pino. "How do we prevent the blackmailer from keeping the Holy See on a very tight leash?"

"I think the question we should be asking ourselves is, is it true?" said Numa, blinking several times.

Carelli did not speak for a moment, admiring the ethereal emanations from his mouth with distracted fascination. "Do you remember," he said finally, "that the children who professed to have seen the Blessed Mother—the little darlings that triggered the Crusade of 2010—do you remember they lived in America? In New Orleans, yes?"

One by one the cardinals said they had been there, part of the spectacle. Pino and Numa could still feel the suffocating climate of Louisiana.

"I took the liberty of calling New Orleans. The diocese confirmed that a Father O'Malley—that was the name given by the lawyer—was parish priest in La Place, and that he disappeared around the time of the pope's visit. It is possible that Father O'Malley knew the Apparition never happened. Except that Leo wanted it to have happened."

"He did," said Pino.

"He wanted his crusade."

"He did," added Bailey.

"The lawyer said that Humberto Venavić knows where the body of the priest is buried."

"Dear God!" sang the chorus.

Carelli got up with an effort and opened the French doors leading to his garden. "The worst thing about this awful mess is that I have no doubt it was Brother Ronnoco who put O'Malley on the plane to Rome." And Cardinal Carelli turned to face his guests.

"You're not suggesting—" began Numa, only to have his voice falter.

"It is very possible, Brother, regardless of our personal feelings for the people involved, that the man sitting on the apostolic throne is an accomplice to murder."

Numa, Pino and Bailey crossed themselves and poured themselves more brandy.

Tomaso put down his glass, stood up and said, "My dear brothers, I refuse to sit here and speculate on matters that can cause the Holy See irreparable harm. It is our duty to immediately investigate to see if the allegations are true before we confront the pope."

"But he will not be back for a week," said Pino.

"In 1542," said Cardinal Carelli, "Saint Robert Bellarmine, a prince and doctor of the Church, said—and I quote—*'it is lawful to resist the pope when he attacks souls or troubles the state, and, above all, when he appears to be causing harm to the Church. It is lawful to resist him by not doing what he commands and by hindering the execution of his will.'* I ask, what are we to do?"

"Is the man sitting on Peter's throne a usurper?" asked Bailey of his brothers.

"Could he be considered an antipope?" added Pino.

"Please!" Tomaso was flushed. "Stop it. This is most unbecoming." Tomaso looked first at Pino and then stared sternly at Carelli. "Think, for the love of Mary! This entire incident could be nothing more than a conspiracy to slander the Holy See with lies and fabrications. It has happened before. Are we to quietly take the word of a criminal over that of the Holy Father? I say, please reflect before you speak!"

"But what if it's true?" Carelli was vehement. "Think about it! Murder, venality, corruption—it will destroy the Church!"

"The pope can be impeached if it can be proven that he falls into heresy," suggested Pino timidly.

"Heresy!?" This goes beyond heresy!" said Carelli loudly. "I want to know what we are going to do about it."

✠

Inspector Nestor Picol was at home enjoying a quiet Saturday afternoon with his wife when the telephone rang.

"Yes?" answered Lucia. She was three times the size of her husband, and weighed almost as much as a piano, but she was pretty, sweet, younger than Picol by ten years and loved to cook. Since Picol loved to eat (although he did not show it), it was a marriage made in heaven, or rather in heaven's kitchen. "One moment, please." Lucia covered the telephone and called out to her husband, who was sitting watching a western in the family room, "Nestor, it's the Vatican!"

"My dear, there is no reason to yell." It always astounded the little detective that his wife behaved as if she were in an opera, when she was only in a modest three-room apartment. "Picol, here—" The inspector pulled up a chair. "Yes, of course. Yes. I'll be right over." And without saying anything else, Inspector Picol hung up, picked up his hat and coat, kissed his bride and went to work.

"But what about your lasagna?"

✠

"Eminence," said Picol, kissing the ring and sitting down on the sofa, next to Tomaso.

"First, Inspector, I want to thank you for taking time out on your weekend. I am very grateful."

Picol nodded. "What is the problem?" The Vatican never called him unless someone (usually a priest) was in trouble. Picol listened carefully to Cardinal Tomaso while sipping espresso and munching on vanilla wafers.

"I know the man," said Picol of Humberto Venavić.

"Is there anything you can do to find out whether these charges are true?" asked Tomaso, looking very worried.

"A lot, but it will have to be done carefully. We certainly don't want this to leak out, and, second, we must not do anything to jeopardize whatever case the prosecutor has against Venavić."

Thus it was decided. Picol would do a little private snooping on behalf of Cardinal Tomaso.

The first thing the inspector did (against rules and regulations) was to place a small, undetectable microphone under the table used by Humberto Venavić whenever he met with his lawyer. It was a simple procedure, and one that two days later produced an interesting piece of information: the location where the body of the murdered man was buried.

The next day, Picol and his assistants found a body, but one without a head or hands, and one that had fed a legion of worms, parasites and insects for some time. Telling if the poor fellow had been a priest was difficult; proving that he was American was impossible.

"No, it's not," said Inspector Picol to his assistant. "We can find out by testing his DNA."

Not quite. To match DNA samples Inspector Picol needed the collaboration of a blood relative of the American priest. Because Father O'Malley had no family when he vanished, and since nobody thought that exhuming the bodies of his mother and father was a good idea (no one knew where they were buried anyway, and they died when the priest was a boy), the detective had no choice but to send the headless and handless corpse to the morgue, and to charge Humberto Venavić with another murder. As far as the police were concerned, there was no evidence that anyone except Venavić was involved in the killing. Without evidence to the contrary, the Vatican had nothing to worry about.

28

"Get him out of the country. I cannot guarantee his safety, nor yours, in fact."

Felix looked carefully at the captain of police, picked up his belongings, then put out his hand. The captain hesitated, looked at the outstretched hand, looked up at Felix and left the room.

Felix waited across the street from the police station for over half an hour. At last, Felix saw an old man walk out of the building.

He was in his late sixties, but he was tall. His hair had turned white, but there was a great deal of it, and what a tangle it was in! He was wearing blue jeans that could have fitted a heftier fellow, and had on a pair of glasses, slightly askew. Damir was clearly having trouble walking. Felix guessed he had not eaten since his arrest and had been tortured.

Damir stopped at the door of the building. He shaded his eyes against the glare of the sun, when a policeman tapped him on the shoulder and pointed at Felix.

Damir squinted, trying to get a better look, when he noticed the fellow walking toward him. They approached each other slowly, quietly, until they stood face to face. Didi frowned, smiled and put his hand to Felix's face. "Saša—"

After almost fifty years, Felix embraced his friend.

The trip back to the orphanage was thankfully uneventful. Felix inquired if Damir had been mistreated and Damir replied with a shrug. "I thought they were going to kill me."

"They were," said Felix, never taking his eyes off the road.

Someone in the orphanage must have seen the car making its way down the hill because the moment it pulled up, everyone ran out to welcome back Don Miguel.

"Get them inside! Now!" yelled Damir to his assistants. Then, he turned to Felix. "Last month snipers killed three of my children. I can't understand how anyone can take aim at a child."

Eventually, the children were rounded up and returned inside—except for one determined toddler who refused to leave Damir's side. Didi grabbed the boy, tucked him under his arm, tousled his hair and handed him to his aide. "Do you know," said Damir to the little boy, "you are a pain in the ass!"

Felix laughed. He remembered.

As soon as Damir released his grip on the little boy, the child wiggled himself free and started going around and around Didi, yelling for Didi to chase him. "I think I've done this before!" said Damir laughing.

Felix laughed again as his friend ran after the child, much as he had done with a baby he called Saša.

That evening, Damir and Felix had dinner with the children, before Damir retired to nurse the bruises and lacerations he had suffered at the hands of his captors. He took a bath and changed clothing. Even though he was not feeling well, Damir insisted on spending as much time with Felix as he could.

They met in the playroom, after the children had gone to bed. "I can't offer you anything to drink except water," said Damir. "How long can you stay?"

"I leave tomorrow morning."

"I searched for you for a very long time," said Damir.

"I was told you were dead," said Felix.

Damir smiled sadly. "And how is the pope?"

"Dead." Felix studied Damir's face, his eyes, his nose, trying to conjure the image of the young face, the young eyes he had tried so hard and for so long to remember.

"He took you from me, and lied," said Didi without anger. "He never answered my letters. There hasn't been a day I did not think about you. I didn't know what happened to you, and I missed you so much—" his voice trailed off.

"I—" Felix started to speak, but instead he looked into Didi's eyes, pressing his lips into a smile to hold back the tears. "Didi, why do you call me Saša?"

"That was your name. What name did he give you?" Didi did not have to explain he meant Draganović.

"Felix."

"Draganović?"

"Ronnoco." Felix sighed. He prayed that Damir could fill in the blanks.

And that in a way is what happened. Damir told Felix about little Saša's murder and about the angel that became Didi's friend when he fell sick.

Felix sprang to his feet and just as quickly sat down again. "It was you! You were the little boy!"

"I was there," said Didi.

"And—and you were standing by that dark man who shot me in the head!" Felix became very anxious and suddenly felt the same pain he had felt at the police station.

"That was the poglavnik," said Didi.

Felix told Damir about the captain of police.

Damir buried his face in his hands and sobbed. "You should have let him kill me."

"No! This—feast of gore, this pageant of bloodshed has to stop!"

"Stepinac was there too," added Damir.

"Stepinac! Aloysius Stepinac?"

Damir nodded.

Finally Felix understood why he had always been terrified of the black and white photograph Draganović had kept in the living room in Trastevere. "How did you find me?"

"We escaped from Zagreb just ahead of the Reds. On the way to Travnik, we had an accident. It was dark, raining very hard and poor Nikola—my father's secretary who was driving us—he hit something and we almost crashed. I left the car and saw the bodies of two men—dead. Then I heard you crying by the side of the road."

"Two men? You mean I was not alone?"

Damir shook his head.

"And these two men—"

"Keep in mind we were on the run, we didn't stop to find out if they had papers or anything else to identify them—or if you did. It was a miracle I heard you crying. The wind was howling, you were covered with mud—but, the moment I saw you I knew I had found Saša. I grabbed you, ran back to the car and we left. That's when I gave you the svirala."

Felix put his hand in his jacket and pulled out the little flute.

"You kept it all these years?" asked Didi. "I'm surprised the priest let you keep it."

"Tell me—please," said Felix. "When we were together at the farm—I know I was a baby—but things do stay with you." Felix looked up at the ceiling. "Did you ever, ever talk to me or mention in my presence what happened to the little shepherd in Glina?" Damir shook his head. "Never?"

"You were a baby!"

"It doesn't matter. Did you, or did anyone else, your mother, your sister—"

"I never told them what happened in Glina."

"I'm haunted by a recurring nightmare of that murder, Damir."

"You *are* Saša," said Damir softly.

Felix paused, shrugged and told Damir he had been baptized Catholic.

"Oh, no!" Damir was disappointed.

"Not only that. I am a priest."

"I'm not surprised. I am surprised your name is Felix."

"Why?"

"You said you would come back as Peter."

Felix smiled. "I am Peter."

And so Damir learned the man he thought was Felix, who as a baby he called Saša, was Felix V, Vicar of Rome, or, as popes call themselves, Peter. "Don't hold it against me," said Felix.

Damir recognized the same cheerful eyes that belonged to the little baby in his loving memories. "You can't be any worse than those we've had so far. And you can do a lot of good for a change."

"You—you don't have children—of your own, I mean?" asked Felix.

Damir smiled sadly and shook his head.

☦

Two days after Damir declared his love for Isabella at the Teatro Colón, the Giglis sailed home. The Pavelićs, without the poglavnik, enjoyed Beniamino's hospitality for the last time in his cabin on board the *Queen Mary*. The compartment suited the discriminating affluence of the great tenor better than its counterpart on the *Afortunato*. Damir and Isabella spent their last moments together holding hands by the railing and looking out to sea. They said very little and tried not to cry. They knew too well how much they would miss each other. When it was time to say good-bye, Damir and Isabella embraced and kissed—kisses sweetened by wet cheeks and vows of love and devotion. Marija and Katarina had to drag the boy off the boat, but not before he announced to the world—with a rare display of bravado and a sudden flight of inspiration—that there was no one more beloved than his adored Isabella. In return, the girl threw kisses at him from above, laughed, waved and, in the end, broke down and cried. Damir remained on the pier, looking terribly sad until the ocean liner vanished in the distance. Isabella did not leave the railing until the coast of Argentina faded into the blue-green mist of the horizon. The only Pavelić who was not sad that the Giglis had left the city, the country, the continent—and who would not have minded if they had been cast off the earth itself and banished from the solar system—was the patriarch of the family. The poglavnik had had about enough of brooding adolescents, infantile tantrums and insolent wives. Perhaps, thought Ante, without the interference of a brazen, meddling troubadour and his oversolicitous daughter, life in his household could assume the quiet, dignified pace he had planned for the family all along.

At long last, his children began to attend a regular school (for the first time in their lives). They did so under their counterfeit identities and, at first, the other children at the Academia Americana thought that Miguel and Sara Bianchi were slightly distracted, perhaps snobs, possibly deaf, or just plain stupid, because Miguel and Sara never seemed to notice when someone called them by name. It would be weeks before Damir and Kati got used to being called Miguel and Sara.

Marija was thankful that, when Isabella left for Rome, Didi did not surrender again to melancholy. Instead, the boy spent his time catching up on his studies, listening to music and writing to his beloved long letters, letters that crossed the Atlantic laden with sighs and plans for a future life together (he used his alias for this international correspondence). He learned the hybrid of Spanish, Italianisms and local inventions that make up the vernacular spoken in Argentina, and longed for spring, when Isabella would return to Buenos Aires.

So, Marija stopped worrying about Didi and began to worry about Kati. The girl, delighted with the company of the other children in school (particularly the boys), amassed half a dozen admirers and developed a fondness for debutante balls and polo that led her mother to distraction. Life was not perfect, but then, it never had been.

Ante also kept himself busier than usual. Although he had been in Argentina for years, he still lived in fear of reprisals from the Yugoslav government. That, however, did not keep him from now coming out of his deep freeze. He established a social club for Croats whose members were, for the most part, expatriates like himself, though none as notorious. For a while, things began to look like the old days except that, while it was true that some of the faces in those secret gatherings in Buenos Aires reminded Pavelić of the backroom plots and conspiracies hatched in Milan and Zagreb before the war, it was also true that, amongst the poglavnik's confederates, Death was counting heads.

When the Soviet Union exploded its first atomic bomb in 1949, many of the fascist autocrats around the globe were transformed almost overnight from murderous tyrants into anticommunist prophets and patriots. In the late 1940s and early 50s South America had an impressive list of strongmen, among them Trujillo, Somoza, Dornelles, Pérez Jiménez, Batista and Perón. Ante Pavelić's legacy, however, outscored the collective Latin American contingent by hundreds of thousands; the poglavnik was in a league of his own.

One morning, while Rubén was driving Miguel and Sara to school, Ante informed his wife that he had agreed to be interviewed by the Italian publication *Epoca*. The interview was supposed to detail Ante's life-long struggle against communism, and show him at home in the company of his wife and children, making plans to return one day to an independent and Catholic Croatia. The banished Croat community around the world could take hope.

A few things came to mind as Marija listened to her husband. First, how had the publication contacted Ante, since he kept his identity and whereabouts a secret. Second, was it necessary to take pictures? With his inimitable laconic charm, the poglavnik explained that the magazine had not contacted him, it was he who had contacted the magazine. "Ah—" Ante had gotten tired of living in the anonymous and shadowy world of an outcast, while others, less deserving to be sure, were basking in the glory of the struggle against international communism. Egotism, that half-brother of inferiority, still thrived in Ante Pavelić. Marija turned from the door and, in a casual way, said that she would ask Damir and Katarina if they had any objections to being photographed. Ante approached his wife and explained that the matter was not up for debate, the decision had been made. "I will ask them anyway," she said.

Katarina loved the idea, but Damir found the prospect of standing next to Ante Pavelić in a portrait of family bliss revolting. The relationship between father and son had not worsened since Damir had recovered from his bout with depression, but it had not improved, either. Marija kept her son's opinion to herself, hoping that the interview would not take place and the matter would be quietly dropped.

Not likely. Several weeks later, on a clear warm Saturday morning, Ante announced that the family should be ready that same afternoon to receive the interviewer. Upon hearing the news, Damir asked the Fritz for a plate of meat pies and a pitcher of grapefruit juice, carried the food to his room, shut his door and turned on his music, with no intention of coming out for the rest of the day. Marija knocked on his door, but received no answer beyond the opening bars of *Tosca*. At precisely two forty-five, the Fritz, wearing a maid's uniform that included a white cap and matching apron, served coffee, tea and sandwiches in the library. Marija, who had changed from her ordinary housecoat into a dark green cotton blouse and skirt, arranged her hair, added a little makeup and returned to the study with a bouncing Katarina—wearing a blue and yellow polka dot dress and black patent leather shoes, but—no Damir. The poglavnik, in a dark grey suit and black tie—sure to impress the interviewer with its sobriety—urged his wife to go back upstairs and demand that Damir present himself to the study without delay. Again, Marija tried to persuade her son to join the family. Her second attempt took a bit longer, but the outcome was the same—no Damir.

Time to get Damir to change his mind ran out at three o'clock, when Rubén helped the hooded reporter out of the car (it was the poglavnik's way of making sure that his residence was kept secret) and led him to the library where he was greeted by Ante Pavelić, the exiled president of the Independent Nation of Croatia, and by his wife and daughter.

The reporter's name was Rodolfo Cracci. He was somewhere in his late forties, not too tall, with curly hair that at one time was black but was now turning grey, and the look of someone who enjoyed not knowing what would happen next. He had bags under his half-shut eyes and sagging jowls. Cracci's brown sports jacket, white shirt and brown tie were as inoffensive as his line of inquiry. He was a simple, friendly chap sent to ask the right questions and get the right answers. He took pictures of Ante, Marija and Katarina with their incredibly big and dangerous dogs walking beside them in the backyard, and never noticed the boy looking out the window from above.

The scene reminded Damir of the times when his father was always being followed by such men around the courtyards of Florence, Milan, Zagreb and Banja Luka. They snapped pictures, wrote praiseworthy articles and disseminated lies.

"I was told you have a son," asked the reporter as the interview came to its predictable conclusion.

"Yes," answered the poglavnik, turning very red, and left the matter at that.

The interviewer was already on his way back to town when Ante sent for Damir. "If you don't mind," said Ante to his wife, "I need to talk to Damir in private." Marija hesitated for a moment before she took Kati by the hand and went into the kitchen to watch the Fritz prepare the Argentinean version of Mexican chimichanga.

"I think you better understand something," said Ante softly to his son. "This is my house. If you wish to live in my house, you will respect my wishes and obey my orders. I don't think that is too much to ask, is it?"

As always when he met with his father, Damir stood in front of the desk looking sullen and bored. "Anything else, sir?"

"Answer my question, Damir. Do you think it is too much to ask?"

"Sir, I cannot respect your wishes because I do not respect you. I cannot obey your orders because I will not yield to your standards. If, in order to live in this house with my mother and sister," Damir continued, "I have to do as you fancy, I will move out at once." Didi looked at his father with the same scrutinizing stare that made many other people uncomfortable. "Anything else, sir?"

Ante stood up suddenly, planted both hands on the desk and leaned toward his son. The poglavnik's face glowed with contempt. "You are a sniveling, spoiled brat—a useless, spineless, soft-bellied disappointment of a son!"

"And you, sir, have never been a good judge of character." Damir turned and left. Now, instead of going up to his room to start packing, he went into the kitchen. Instead of addressing his mother or his sister, who were sitting, as they say, "on pins and needles," Didi asked the Fritz if she knew someone who could put him up for a few days. The question surprised not only Juana but Marija and Kati as well; no one knew what he was talking about. To find out they had to follow the boy upstairs, where he explained in a sad but determined voice that he was moving out.

Kati cried and tried to convince Damir to change his mind. Marija rushed downstairs and confronted her husband. "Damir is not, I repeat, is not moving out!"

"Madame," said Ante with self-righteous dignity, "Damir is free do whatever he wants to do, is he not?"

Damir, in fact, did not move out, at least not right away. Even after the Fritz volunteered to give him shelter in her mother's home in Córdoba, or have him stay with her old flame who ran a tango bar on the other side of Buenos Aires, there were several reasons—

quite practical ones, in fact—why Damir thought better of his decision, and did not go anywhere. Reason number one was money. He had no money of his own and would not think of asking his mother for money because she would only ask his father. What good would it have been to move out of his father's house if he was still going to live on his father's money? Reason number two was his music collection. Moving over twenty thousand records required planning and, more than that, a lot of room. Didi was eighteen years old but sensible for his age.

Late one night, so late in fact that it was close to two in the morning, Didi woke up in a sweat. He stared at the ceiling and thought of how he could go look for Saša and how he could marry Isabella; or marry Isabella and then go find Saša. He needed a lot of money to travel and even more to get married, especially to a girl like Isabella. He did not want to be lawyer, as his father had been; he did not want to be a doctor, or an architect. He wanted to—what? He wanted to work in opera. As a singer? No, he was too shy. So, do what in opera?

Didi tossed and turned until he sat up in bed and decided to ask someone for advice. In a long letter drafted at four in the morning, Damir explained his concerns to Isabella. Her reply came in the mail a month later in a postscript to her regular dispatch. It was short and to the point: *"Go see Don Fulgencio de Jesús, at the Teatro Colón."*

Don Fulgencio de Jesús, the Artistic Director of the Teatro Colón, stood looking sideways at Didi. The director wore a white shirt with the sleeves rolled up to the elbows, a red bow tie, dark pants and reading glasses. "No, no, no—no bowing, please. I would have to bow in return and I'm too short as it is. It puts me at a disadvantage. A handshake will do. Come in, come in—" the artistic director waved him into his office, pointed to a chair, closed the door and went behind a little table that served as his desk. The table had a telephone and piles of papers on it. The office had wooden floors, tall ceilings, one very large window with red drapes that at one time must have been part of a theater curtain, redbrick walls and three bookshelves replete with books and countless musical scores. "Your face is familiar."

Damir explained that they had met at the opening night of *Turandot*.

"Of course!" And Don Fulgencio chastised Didi for almost ruining the opening night with his calling and screaming backstage for Isabella. The artistic director then waved a telegram at Damir. "From the great Gigli. It is about you." At that point the interrogation began in earnest. Damir was asked, first of all, if Damir was his real name, how old he was, where was he from—

"Cr—Yugoslavia."

"Cr—Yugoslavia. Is that like Yugoslavia?"

"I'm sorry, yes, Yugoslavia."

And why did he want to work in opera. Was he a singer?

Didi shook his head and smiled.

"Why do you smile?"

"Because I imagine that most people who come here are singers looking for work."

"Wrong," replied Don Fulgencio. "The people who walk through that door already have work. I'm not running an employment agency. The fact that you're sitting here, young man, is because Beniamino Gigli—who is a good friend but, like all great tenors, a great pain in the rear—asked me to see you. I am—seeing you, that is—and I do not like what I see!"

Didi blinked several times. He didn't know what he was doing to make the artistic director dislike him. Perhaps the artistic director had found out about his father.

"You're too good-looking, and my experience with good-looking people is that their brains are full of chimichurri." Without pausing for breath he asked Damir what could he do? Could he work full time? Did Damir mind not making much money, because he was not going to make a lot at the Teatro Colón? Could he work at night? What did Damir's family have to say about his taking a job at the Teatro Colón? And, did Damir know that by Don Fulgencio's giving him a job Beniamino Gigli would be compromised? Beniamino, of course, was well aware of that, because the great Gigli was not an idiot. Beniamino must have liked Damir a lot, which was very lucky for Damir, and he should accordingly report next Monday afternoon at four o'clock, ready to work.

"Y-y-yes sir," stammered Damir, "but sir—"

"What?" Don Fulgencio was holding the door for Damir.

"What am I supposed to do?"

"Well, you don't sing. Do you conduct?" inquired the artistic director.

"No, sir."

"Of course not, you seem to be a nice boy." Don Fulgencio did not like conductors. "Can you direct?"

"No, sir."

"I didn't think so. Stage directors have a flair for the impossible and small brains. So, what can you do?"

"I—I don't know, sir."

"Well, if you don't, how do you expect me to? But don't worry, I'll think of something." Don Fulgencio smiled, closed the door and left Damir staring at the grain in the wood.

✜

It took Beniamino six years to consent to the marriage of Isabella and Damir. The great Gigli had to make sure that, in spite of everything that was said, in spite of the despondent tears that were shed and in spite of the scenes reminiscent of the best of Puccini, Verdi and Bellini, the young couple's love was not a transient infatuation of adolescence, but a passion that would endure the harsh truths of married life. He also wanted to give Damir time to settle down in a vocation that promised advancement. For the two young people, six years was already nearly half a lifetime; because they were in love, it was an eternity.

They saw each other once a year, in the spring, when the great Gigli arrived in Argentina with his usual fanfare for another series of performances. It was during those greatly anticipated, nerve-racking get-togethers, lasting a couple of weeks, that Damir and Isabella learned more than to love each other. She took it upon herself to show Didi the world he had missed while hiding from his father's enemies. She taught him to play tennis, to dance (Didi could cha-cha and rumba but would not tango), and—thinking that Didi perhaps needed a little gaiety in his life—Isabella introduced him to American film comedies. Young Pavelić became an ardent fan of the Marx brothers' *Duck Soup*.

Isabella could not have turned out more beautiful. She was a woman of noble bearing and a slender, statuesque figure. Her hair was a little darker than when she was a girl, the blond waves of childhood shading into amber, but her eyes—her eyes retained the joy, the excitement and the hope of a child's spirit.

Damir grew tall. His once ungraceful, gangling ways gave way to a smooth, elegant deportment. He was also quite an independent young man. He finished secondary school, withdrew his savings and moved out of his father's house to a one-room flat in a six-story walk-up, in a working class neighborhood of little shops and tenements. It was not much, but such as it was Damir decorated the room with pictures of Isabella, his mother and sister. He took from his father's house only his bed, a small table, a desk and two chairs, his phonograph and his records. The kitchen in Didi's apartment was a hot plate that rested on top of an old stained sink, which remained unused while he lived there. The phonograph and records sat on the cracked, dull wooden floors, alongside the walls.

Soon after moving out of his father's house, Damir enrolled at the University of Buenos Aires. He divided his time between class (in business management) and the Teatro Colón. His passion for opera, in addition to the skills he was learning at the university, allowed him to be promoted often, faster, in fact, than most. He amazed everyone with his knowledge of and respect for the craft. Didi gained almost universal admiration among the artists and staff who worked and struggled at the opera house. Many, in fact, were so impressed with the good-looking young Croat they offered both their hearts and other, more succulent parts of themselves—regularly. As a result, Didi spent many nights anxiously debating with himself whether he should acquire a measure of sexual expertise before joining Isabella in marriage. In the end, he decided that it would be unfair to expect from his bride that which he could not deliver himself. It was difficult at times, even excruciating, but Didi harnessed his libido, tempering it with long hours of work, study, music and lots of—meditation. And so Damir reached the age of twenty-two. At twenty-two and a half, he graduated from the university, and three days later he was promoted to assistant artistic director of the Teatro Colón. That same week, he received an offer from the Teatro dell'Opera in Rome. The position of production supervisor paid three times what he was earning in Argentina. Things were looking up for Damir. The Teatro dell'Opera was but three blocks from the apartments that Beniamino had bequeathed his daughter as a wedding gift; just a few hours drive from Yugoslavia—and Saša.

✠

"Ladies and gentlemen!" The great Gigli raised his glass with typical Gigli flair, just as he had done many times in *Traviata*. "I wish to invite everyone here tonight to join me in celebrating the wedding of my daughter—this beautiful princess on my right—to this handsome prince sitting at her side!" Isabella was absolutely radiant in a long-sleeved, blue silk dress adorned with yellow gemstones in the shape of half-moons. Next to the Giglis, Didi was positively a pillar of conservatism in his dark grey suit, resplendent white shirt and red silk tie. Of course, the entire room expressed their congratulations, embarrassing Damir and Isabella with their applause, followed by a call for the groom to kiss the bride. The wish was granted. Immediately, the pops from the champagne bottles turned into a fusillade.

Lepanto was the finest, most exclusive and most expensive restaurant in Buenos Aires, maybe in all of Argentina. It was there that the great Gigli, wearing a maroon jacket, white silk shirt and ascot, and looking a little more plump, a bit more grey but a great deal happier (he had retired recently from the operatic stage), had decided to go for a sample of authentic Spanish cuisine. It was not a large restaurant. It held only ten tables and a few booths, each set with shining silverware, glasses and perfectly pressed white linen, in a room of red brick and stucco. The dining area was capped by a glass roof that allowed the natural sunlight to caress the lush, refreshing greenery that contrasted exquisitely with the sober Mediterranean decor.

"*Libiam!*" cried the great Gigli. Everyone in Lepanto drank in honor of Damir and Isabella.

Once people had again reverted to their own affairs, Beniamino kissed his daughter, turned to his future son-in-law and said, "Now, Didi, what's this I hear you don't want your father at the wedding?"

Damir had been expecting the question since he sat to dinner. The poglavnik had never been consulted, never been told about and never been expected to attend the wedding; that was Damir's wish.

"Oh, oh, I think I'd better go powder—whatever I have that needs powdering," said Isabella, getting up.

"No, no, stay." Damir took Isabella's hand to keep her from leaving the table.

Isabella shrugged and sat down again. She rarely talked about Ante Pavelić to his son. She had read almost everything there was on the Balkans, its bloody history of manipulation by foreign powers and the Catholic Church, and had learned about Ante Pavelić from Croatian dissidents and Serbian exiles whom she met in Rome. The repugnance she felt for Ante Pavelić was only increased by the love she had for his son.

"Maestro," said Didi, "I want the wedding to be a celebration of life. Having Ante Pavelić there would deny that." Beniamino looked at the glass of wine in front of him and listened to the quiet words spoken without hate or anger, just regret. "I wanted to get married in Rome," continued Damir, "but my mother and sister are still afraid to go to Europe. I don't have to explain why."

A momentary and uncharacteristic silence crept over the *camarones al ajillo*. "There was a time," said Beniamino, "when your father was considered a great man."

"There was a time," observed Damir, "when people thought the world was flat."

Isabella chuckled and Beniamino tweaked her nose playfully, then turned to her betrothed. "It is your wedding and your decision. I promised your mother that I would talk to you about it, and I have. Now—Scarfino!" Scarfino was the maitre d', a spindly man with a wide forehead, a snub nose, curly brown hair, a thin mustache, bulging eyes and perfect poise who, right on cue, led three waiters from the kitchen with trays of lobster and veal prepared with special care by the chef for Damir and Isabella.

Ante Pavelić was not mentioned again that evening. He was dismissed for the time being to those cracks of the subconscious where the human spirit stows its unpleasantness. Unfortunately, the poglavnik was like a pogo stick; the moment he hit the ground, he bounced back. With two days remaining before the wedding, Damir was summoned by his mother to the house—alone. It was going to be a three-pronged attack. Marija was, in fact, in charge of the wedding arrangements, because living in Italy Isabella could not do anything, and because Damir had no clue about what was needed. Marija decided in what church the ceremony would take place, booked the ballroom at the Alvear Palace Hotel, hired a theatrical set designer to decorate and imbue it with the proper wedding mood, chose the menu, collected names and addresses for the exclusive guest list of very close friends and government ministers, had the invitations printed and sent out by courier, hired the musical group that was to provide entertainment, offered counsel (via telephone) on the wedding gown, and asked Beniamino to pay for everything. A whole year planning and buying, making changes to the plans and the buying, and then changing the changes; Marija even procured an Argentinean passport for Damir, so he could travel to New York for his honeymoon, before going to Rome. Finally, Marija went out of her way to calm and reassure the two sweethearts who, as the date of their wedding approached, became more and more relaxed.

29

"Good morning, Juana. I must say, I hope you are as happy as you look today," said Damir, closing the door behind him. "You look as cheerful as a sunflower!"

"Didi!" The Fritz threw her arms around Damir and kissed him on both cheeks. *"Señora, llegó Didi!"*

"I think I can still find my way." Damir walked through the kitchen and into the study where his mother and sister were waiting. The window curtains were open, a sign of the family's lessening apprehension that someone might take aim at them from outside.

Marija rushed to meet her son and embraced and kissed him affectionately. The years had been kind to Marija, although she had gained a little weight, a few lines and more than her share of grey hair; after all, she was closing in on sixty. "I'm *so* glad you could make it," she said with a dash of sarcasm preceding her smile.

"I don't know if I share your enthusiasm," answered Damir.

Katarina kissed her brother. She was dressed in a peculiar American fashion that was just beginning to take hold among upper-class Argentinos: blue jeans, a white polo shirt and tennis shoes. "I love the apartment!" Kati meant the one in the photographs her brother had shown her, where he and Isabella were going to live after their honeymoon. "I hope Papa is that generous when I get married." Katarina stepped back, looked at her brother and added, "I see you're acquiring a sense of—adventure in your dress, Didi." Damir wore a pair of khaki slacks, a navy blazer over a white cotton tennis shirt and chocolate colored, suede shoes. "I love the shoes. Isabella picked them out for you, right?" Katarina smiled and turned to her mother. "Wait until they're married!"

"Enough, please," said Marija.

"Oh, dear!" cried Kati.

"What is it?" asked her mother.

"I don't know if Cedric knows the mambo." Cedric, whose last name was Fogstrand, was the son of the British ambassador and Kati's most fervent admirer.

"He's English, dear, they don't dance," replied Marija, sitting down next to Damir. She took his hand and said, "We have to talk about your father."

They did not talk; they argued for two hours. Katarina was his most formidable adversary. Their sister and brother relationship had changed in the last years. Didi still loved Katarina dearly, but before the boy moved out, Pavelić and son had quarreled constantly. The poglavnik never raised his voice or threatened Damir. He merely stated his position, one that was inevitably based on common sense, a call for discipline and obedience. Damir, on the other hand, would explode in anger and frustration. Instead of falling into depression as before, he became aggressive and confrontational. Katarina was convinced that the change in her brother had to do less with Damir than with Isabella's determined temperament. Kati suspected that Isabella was instilling Damir with a bit too much self-confidence. She began to see her brother as irrational and abusive and to see Isabella as the instigator. It was not long before lines of loyalty were drawn, and Kati ended up on the side of the poglavnik.

"Didi," said Marija, "not to have your father at the wedding is unacceptable. It's humiliating. What do you think people will say when they find out the father of the bridegroom has been banned from the wedding by his son?"

"I don't care what people think."

"You've turned into a selfish boor. You have no regard for anyone except your precious Isabella!" declared Katarina, louder than necessary. She walked over to Damir and looked down at her brother. "You're not being fair, not to Mama, who's busted her ass for this wedding—I mean, your father-in-law has done nothing but tell us to spend his money, thank you—and you're not being fair to Papa, either. Since we arrived in this country he's done nothing but go out of his way for us. But you—why do you hate him so much? Is it that bullshit—"

"Katarina!" Marija demanded the discussion be kept within the bounds of civility.

"But that's all it is, Mama, bullshit! It's that propaganda from Belgrade—the show trials!" Katarina alluded to the trials of Archbishop Stepinac and others that were going on at the time in Yugoslavia. "Is that what's bothering you, Didi? If it is, it's time you grew up!" Damir looked up at his mother. He seemed irritated but not surprised; the morning was turning out just as he had expected. "Papa was a great leader who unfortunately was caught on the losing end of a hopeless war!" Kati turned away from the window and sat down. "I'm telling you now—Papa stays home, I stay home." Katarina folded her arms and waited for Damir to answer.

Damir got up and walked to the door.

"Didi!" Marija ran to her son. "Meet with him, do that for me, please, I beg you!"

Damir stared at his mother for a moment, then sighed. The poglavnik would have his say after all.

That same afternoon, Damir and Isabella could be seen from outside, sitting by the window of El Cuchillo, a hangout for beatniks and starving artists. Isabella rested her elbows on the narrow marble square that stood for a table, and kept her eyes on Damir. Nothing in the dark, smoke-filled bohemian café distracted her— not the imitation Renaissance portraits of princes and dukes peering down from their massive, ornate and very old (but not, properly speaking, antique) frames; not the loud political debate going on two tables away; not the rhythm of jazz from the loudspeakers; not the espresso machine hissing incessantly above the babel and the music; not even the short, round waiter with an attitude who bounced up and down the room like a beach ball with a mustache, and who was told to bring two coffees, two glasses of water, one piece of chocolate cake and two forks.

"You have time to change your mind," said Damir at long last.

"Do I?" returned Isabella, feigning indifference, as she brought the cup to her lips.

"Be warned, if you do, *me caso con Juana.*" Damir imitated Isabella's coolness by taking a piece of the chocolate frosting and dipping it in his coffee.

Isabella quickly put the cup down on the table, took a napkin and covered her mouth to avoid spitting out her drink. Her eyes filled with tears and she held her breath. As soon as she swallowed, she laughed and coughed until Damir got out of his chair and slapped her a couple of times on the back. The thought of Damir marrying the Fritz was as outrageous as *Animal Crackers*.

"She's older, but Juana is a great cook!" said Isabella with great difficulty, unable to stop laughing.

"Yes, I know."

As soon as she regained her composure Isabella got up, leaned forward, took Damir's face in her hands and gave him one of those kisses that are almost never seen except on the silver screen—in close-up, with the music of a thousand strings filling the air, bursting every living cell with sensation.

In a different establishment the shameless display of affection might have raised an eyebrow or two, it might have even brought out a smile among the older gentlemen and ladies who still had fond memories of when they were young and in love. But in a dive where Argentinean beatniks debated what it meant for a third-rate cabaret singer to lead one of the most male chauvinist nations in the world, then to die and become a martyr, nothing was sacred, certainly not love.

"I adore you," said Damir.

As Beniamino had observed one night aboard a steamship called *Afortunato*, they indeed made a handsome couple.

"I better go, it's a quarter to." Isabella grabbed her purse and got up, but Didi took her hand.

"He's never on time, he likes to make people wait."

"Well, I don't want to risk it." Isabella prepared to leave. "I'll be at the hotel." Isabella could not visualize a man like Ante Pavelić sitting among radicals, some intellectuals, some with secret leftist leanings.

Damir got up and walked Isabella to the narrow door with its dark green flakes of paint peeling off every time someone went in or out of the place. Once outside, he flagged a taxi, held the door for Isabella, kissed her good-bye, shut the door, waited for the cab to drive off and went back inside to wait for his father.

The streetlights were coming on. Buenos Aires was getting ready for its nightly revelry, as twilight gave way to evening. It also began to rain, not hard but enough to make people quicken their steps. The drops on the window diffused the headlights and turned the street lamps into miniature, haloed suns against the darkening skies. Slowly, the drizzle turned to a heavy rain. Cars splashed the sidewalk, people covered their heads and scurried. Didi was looking out into the street when he saw a little boy standing on the sidewalk with his back to the window. Didi noticed he was thin and was getting wet, but not much else. The dim lights and the rain made it difficult to get a good look at the child. It was unusual, though, for a kid that age to be walking around by himself. Suddenly, the boy turned around, fixed his eyes on Didi, cupped his hands and yelled loud enough so he could be heard from outside, *"Are you a Jew?"*

A Jew? From the corner of his eye, Damir saw the black limousine turn the corner. He saw Rubén at the wheel. He could not see his father, but he knew Ante Pavelić was sitting in the back seat wondering what type of place his son had lured him to. When Didi looked again, the boy was gone. Odd, thought Didi; what is he doing asking people if they are Jews or not? The limousine went around the block once. Finally, it stopped in front of the café door, attracting its share of attention from a neighborhood not used to limousines driving by, let alone stopping to let off passengers. Rubén went around with an umbrella for el jefe; the little hood had grown a comfortable paunch. Ante Pavelić got out of the car carefully. He was wearing a black suit, a hat, dark glasses and a mustache. The poglavnik looked like any other Argentinean businessman or member of the Junta. Damir had to smile.

Rubén opened the door to El Cuchillo, allowing the poglavnik inside. Ante removed his glasses and looked for his son. Damir did not beckon him to the table but waited for his father to find the way.

"You come here often?" Ante stood looking down at his son. Rubén waited at another table nearby.

"Yes." Damir looked up.

Ante pulled up a chair, took off his hat, hung it on the back of the chair and sat down. It had been almost eight years since he had arrived in Argentina, and his jowls now hung down further, his long flabby ears stuck out a little more, and his flesh had taken on a grey and pasty look, though his hair remained as black as his soul.

"Mother said you wanted to see me."

Ante looked around, inspecting the room, then brought his eyes back to his son. His manner had not changed. "They tell me you're getting married." It was the same indifferent monotone, seasoned with arrogance, that Damir remembered.

Damir did not answer.

Ante reached inside his breast pocket and took out a thick brown envelope. He put the envelope on the table and without a word passed it across to his son. Damir pushed it back toward his father. "Why don't you at least see what's inside?"

"I know what's inside and I thank you, but I cannot accept it."

"That is your choice, but have the courtesy to at least open the envelope." Ante pushed the envelope back toward his son.

The exchange did not go unnoticed by the debaters a little distance away. Although they could not hear the conversation between the handsome young man and the stately older gentleman—with all the music and the hissing contraptions—they speculated that either the older man was making a sexual proposition for which the price was not acceptable, or the younger man was a hired thug, assassin, or police informant turning down a piece of business.

One of the debaters caught Rubén's eye and was compelled to shift his interest back to politics in Argentina—or the lack thereof.

Damir did not pick up the envelope but lifted its flap and saw the large stack of bills inside.

"It's a lot of money," said Ante.

"Yes, it is," confirmed Damir, letting go of the envelope.

"You're going to need it."

"No, I won't," Damir replied without hesitation. "And even if I did, I still would not take it."

"Why?" Ante asked matter-of-factly, his hands clasped in priestly fashion. "What is the difference between the money in that envelope and other money? It's worth the same, buys the same, costs the same—"

Damir knew Ante was trying to keep him from leaving. "May I ask you, sir," Damir leaned forward and looked at his father sternly, "how much the fascist government of this country pays you for whatever it is you do for them?"

Ante smiled.

"Let me guess," said Damir. "However much they pay you, it is not enough for you to live the way you do, for my mother and sister to wear the fancy dresses and expensive jewels they do, and for you to make gifts such as this." Damir pointed at the envelope still in the center of the table. "Which says to me you have another source of money, a vast source, as vast as a treasure. Like the treasure I found in a cave in the mountains above Travnik—six chests all together, full of gold in the form of human teeth from your victims at Jasenovac. The treasure you left in care of Stepinac and which is being guarded and kept for you with Catholic efficiency by your pal Draganović." If Ante Pavelić's complexion had turned a sickly grey in the last years, his son's words made him turn as white as the foam on a cup of cappuccino—without the cinnamon flakes—that was making its way to another table. "I've never told anyone. I love my mother, my sister and Isabella far too much to burden them further with your—indecency." Father and son looked at each other. It was a good minute or so before Ante shifted his weight. "Do you remember the little boy you murdered in front of me? Do you remember his name?" Damir did not wait for a reply. "His name was Aleksandar—Saša he was called." Ante looked away and stared at the white marble tiles dark with grime. "Why did you do it? I've never figured it out. He was pathetically poor, starving—in rags. Did you feel good afterwards? Did it make you a better leader, a better soldier, a better Croat, a better Catholic—a better man to kill a child? Did you think that killing little Saša would help realize your grand vision of Croatia?" Damir's voice was soft, monotone and spellbinding. "You have caused great suffering." Damir stopped and stared at his father for a moment. "Why?" Damir thought he caught a glimpse of a tear forming in the poglavnik's left eye, a mere wisp of a glint. He turned to look out the window. "I had a friend years ago—"

"Damir—"

"—back in Travnik." Damir did not care what his father had to say. "His name was Pero, he was a very old man who worked for Draganović—a shepherd and a Serb." Damir sighed. "I'm sure he's dead now." Damir paused, remembering the sad, sad look on Pero's face just before they said good-bye. "Pero said that people are not evil, that it is in our nature to do good, and it is ignorance that makes us do evil things. I've often wondered about that—wondered, if you had known little Saša like you knew Katarina and me, whether you would have put a bullet in his head." Damir pushed back his chair. "I don't hate you—you have to thank Pero for that—I just find it impossible to forget."

Ante looked up and was going to get up as if he wanted to say something else, but the meeting was over.

"The wedding ceremony will be simple enough. The church, I believe, is open to the public." The son took out two bills, placed them under the sugar bowl and left, leaving the poglavnik by himself.

✢

It was a perfect afternoon for two to become one. The May sun could not have been more radiant if Botticelli had graced it with his singular magic. A crowd was gathered on the sidewalk, and a small crew of attendants did their best to keep it away from the notables pulling up in front of the Iglesia de San Andrés. The small church where Damir and Isabella were to be married was, as churches go, an attractive though not imposing building, standing in front of a park full of fountains, iron lamps and marble statuettes. The church had been built a hundred years before and had a narrow campanile and a façade that was conspicuously plain because the local bishop, at the time the little church was built, decided to devote the diocese's money to a magnificent altar, an altar that, being much higher than those in most other houses of worship, forced the faithful to look upwards at all times during the service, stressing the point that the priest was closer to God than those sitting in the pews.

The groom arrived first. Damir, Marija, Kati and the Fritz stepped out of the limousine and stood outside the church, welcoming the guests. Minutes later, the British ambassador and his family arrived. Sir Malcolm and Lady Fogstrand, along with their son Cedric, guests of the groom's family, were extremely charming and all smiles as they congratulated Damir on his wedding day. Sir Malcolm and young Cedric were perfect examples of British propriety and dress, although Lady Fogstrand might have lost points for her tepid red gown and dead mink stole (not that a live mink would have been any better). The Fogstrands waved at a few people in the crowd, who clapped for some unknown reason. Finally, Kati escorted the Fogstrands inside San Andrés, and an usher showed them to their seats.

An official government limousine pulled up containing Don Anastasio Gómez, the minister of culture and his wife Belinda, good friends of the father of the bride. The minister—his chest full of medals and ribbons—was in formal attire. His wife wore a dress much better suited for the occasion than that of the British ambassador's wife. In a gesture that would be repeated throughout the afternoon, Don Anastasio and Doña Belinda congratulated the groom and kissed the groom's mother; then they waited outside for Don Fulgencio de Jesús, artistic director of the Teatro Colón and the best man, who arrived in his long black American car.

And so, after the wedding party had assembled, after countless repetitions of "Hello!" and "So nice to see you again!" and "My, you've put on weight!" Damir went into the church, took his place and waited for his bride. The young groom, who not long before had been a nervous, shy, insecure, bewildered and sometimes stuttering Damir, remained nervous, shy and somewhat bewildered, but was less insecure, no longer stuttered and was indeed quite a happy Damir. It was in his eyes, thought his mother, in his smile and in his gracious and gentle ways. He was talking to the priest who would marry him to Isabella when a loud cheer went up outside.

"*Gigli*! *Gigli*! *Gigli*!"

Beniamino waved and threw kisses at the crowd at the same time as he helped Isabella get out of the car. If someone had asked

Beniamino how he felt at that moment, the great tenor would have raised his arms to the heavens and praised God, for he was the happiest, proudest father on the face of the earth.

Isabella was the spirit of light. Six beautiful little girls in white dresses with gold lace, and three pretty little boys dressed in blue and gold, each child the essence of innocence, appeared from the church. The little girls scattered rose petals before the bride and the little boys carried Isabella's train.

"*Gigli! Gigli! Gigli!*"

It was the first time Damir had seen his bride that day, as she stood for a moment on the threshold of happiness. The dazzling sunlight cast its radiant halo upon Isabella, and the congregation stood while Verdi's exultant march from *Aida* filled the chamber. Finally, Isabella and Damir stood side by side, waiting for the moment when they would vow their eternal love for one another.

While the wedding ceremony was going on inside, another limousine pulled up to the curb quietly, without anyone taking notice. El jefe arrived with two bodyguards and Rubén. They made their way through the crowd and into San Andrés, where they were forced to remain standing in the back.

In the front pew, Marija was visibly affected; so was Kati, although every so often she would glance at Cedric Fogstrand, hoping that one day, before too long, another wedding would take place. The Fritz was dabbing her eyes with a handkerchief. Elvira, on the other hand, who had known many dramatic moments in life, never allowed herself to display undue sentimentality—never, that is, until Father Macero Roca, a placid little man with big eyes, a small mouth and arms that seemed too big for the rest of his body, introduced Beniamino Gigli.

The great Gigli was more nervous than he had ever been in his life. This was the most important moment in the life of his daughter, the daughter who was his reason for living. The great Gigli walked to the altar, cleared his throat and with a smile that betrayed his nerves said, "To my daughter Isabella and my new son, Damir." No sooner did he stop talking than the great Gigli transported the assembly to the gates of heaven with "Ave Maria".

"*Bravo Gigli!*" came the shouts from outside. After three other musical selections, which included operatic favorites of the bride and groom, Beniamino stepped down from the altar, embraced Isabella and Damir, and the ceremony continued.

Father Roca beckoned Damir and Isabella. "We are here today," began the priest, "to witness Damir take Isabella's hand in holy matrimony."

Katarina finally broke down. She had tried to maintain a cool, detached demeanor, but now, as she saw Damir hold Isabella's hand, she remembered all the wonderful as well as the horrible moments she and Damir had shared in their life together. Her big brother, Damir, whom she worshiped, now belonged to someone else. She was happy for Damir, yes, but she was also aware of her own most profound loss. Marija held Kati's hand tightly, as if to assert the unique bond between herself and her daughter. She felt sorry for her husband, wondering if Ante had made it to the church after all. If she had been able to see him just then, she would have felt even greater pity for the poglavnik. Completely disconnected from the love that imbued the ceremony, Ante Pavelić felt as wretched as when—ten years before, in another life—he had boarded a freighter en route to Argentina.

Damir could not take his eyes from Isabella, not even to look at the priest. At one point, Father Roca had to call his name three times. A page brought forth a red velvet cushion on which sat two gold rings. Damir placed one on Isabella's hand and Isabella placed one on Damir's.

"Do you Damir take Isabella as your wife in sickness and in health, for better or worse?"

"Yes, of course I do," he said, earning an admonishing look from the priest.

"And do you Isabella, take Damir—"

"Yes."

The priest stopped, cleared his throat, decided it was useless to go on, ran through the essentials needed to make the wedding legitimate, and pronounced Damir and Isabella man and wife. "You may—do whatever you want to do, such as—why don't you kiss her now?" Father Roca shrugged and moved to one side.

Damir did just that—except that, to everyone's surprise, Damir did not kiss his new wife on the lips, or make any other such dramatic gesture. Instead, he held Isabella's face in his hands and gave her—on the cheek—the sweetest, purest kiss ever seen, then took her in his arms and lovingly embraced her. In one remarkable moment, Damir showed the world just how much, and in how many ways, he loved Isabella. She was not only his spouse, she was his closest friend. Later, they would exchange the passion of lovers, of husband and wife.

The music began once more, and a chorus of children sang hallelujah or something like it, and friends and family gathered about to congratulate and kiss the newlyweds. Marija had to go and sit with Beniamino for a minute because the tenor would not stop laughing, singing and crying. Marija was afraid that the strain of the wedding had finally taken its toll on the great tenor.

It was about ten minutes before Damir was able to take Isabella by the hand and pull her away from the well-wishers, leading a procession of friends and family out of the church amidst applause, cheers and showers of rice. He did not see his father standing against the wall inside the door; the poglavnik remained hidden in the shadows.

When the newlyweds came out into the open they found themselves going around and shaking people's hands, embracing some, kissing a few and thanking everybody. The bells rang out and suddenly a thousand doves were turned loose from behind the bell tower, white against the blue backdrop. They circled above the throng, a white winged swirl on its climb to happiness—one last spectacular touch from the great Gigli.

"Oh, Papa!" Isabella and Damir lavished Beniamino with kisses and hugs.

"Thank you!" yelled Damir in the midst of the commotion. "Thank you for everything! Thank you for Isabella!"

Ante Pavelić finally left the church. He had taken off his dark glasses and, for an instant, his eyes met Didi's. The poglavnik hesitated, not sure whether to approach and congratulate his son. He did not have a chance to. Rubén tumbled forward and fell dead with a bullet in the head. The other bodyguards pulled out their weapons and returned fire; two men were shooting at Ante Pavelić from the sidewalk. Ante was hit in the shoulder and screamed. People scattered and threw themselves on the ground. The bride and groom were caught in the crossfire. Damir turned in a panic, and for an instant, one so brief that it could only be measured in rage, he hesitated. He had one body, one body that he could protect someone with. His mother? His sister? His Isabella?

Death reached out. Isabella fell into her husband's arms—a trace of blood staining her immaculate wedding dress. She smiled the saddest smile, whispered his name one last time, gently closed her eyes, took wings and became an angel.

30

A truckload of soldiers armed with machine guns arrived and cleared the area. The great Gigli ran into the middle of the street looking crazed and wild. He cursed God, the Devil and himself, all the while spinning like a top, his short arms lashing out at anyone who tried to go near him. Elvira watched in horror from the side. She covered her mouth with her long spider-leg fingers and wept quietly: the great Gigli was mad with grief. Marija fell to the ground, overwhelmed by remorse. She protested the inconceivable with a thousand apologies, but the look in Damir's eyes was enough to maker her understand that none of it mattered anymore. Didi wept, even as his shrieks subsided to long, drawn-out woeful laments. He knelt on the sidewalk holding the lifeless Isabella in his arms, his face, hands and clothes baptized with her blood. Father Roca offered the dead bride her last rites while her husband caressed and kissed the waxen cheeks of his beloved. "I told you! I warned you, oh, my sweet love!" The girl's death confirmed the irreversible misfortune of his damned existence. Love had blinded them both and, in the end, that love was as guilty of her death as the evil that was so much a part of him.

El jefe was rushed to the hospital in the company of his daughter; there the poglavnik was treated for a superficial wound to the shoulder and released. Rubén's body was dispatched to the local morgue, where it waited for weeks in cold storage before an old aunt claimed it, cremated it and scattered the ashes in a cattle field.

A perfunctory investigation of the assassination attempt that had claimed two unintended victims resolved nothing. Because Gigli was incapacitated, Damir, in the midst of his unbearable loss, used what little influence his father-in-law's name wielded and made arrangements to leave Argentina. In a way, it was lucky that he was kept busy trying to untangle the web of red tape because he never had time to sit, reflect and succumb to despair. A week after Isabella's death, Damir said a solemn and tearful good-bye to his mother and sister, and traveled with Beniamino to Rome. There, at the family mausoleum on the outskirts of the city, father and husband looked on in disbelief as they returned daughter and wife to the bosom of her mother. Shortly after, Beniamino moved to his villa in Recanati and went into seclusion. Damir was left by himself and, even while he grieved, had little choice but to call on every ounce of strength Isabella had instilled in him, and stand resolute against the overwhelming sorrow that threatened to end his reason.

He lived in the apartments he was supposed to have shared with his wife. The large rooms, furnished with Gigli family heirlooms, were a constant reminder of Isabella. She was born and raised in those rooms; she played below the vaulted ceilings and learned to skate on floors of black and white marble tiles; learned to draw with crayons on the blue velvets and silk wallpaper (for which she was punished by her nanny); and played hide-and-seek behind the little green forest of potted dwarf trees, plants and flowers. There were gigantic lamps with broad, ornate porcelain bases set on top of handmade antique tables; a gigantic fireplace with a marble mantelpiece that held all one hundred and twenty-five of Isabella's music boxes. The rugs were so fine and beautiful it was almost a crime to step on them. Before the wedding Isabella had replaced the old dark curtains with lighter ones that brightened and cheered each room. Damir loved the music study, of course. It had a grand piano that hugged the wall, dark wood paneling and two large windows framed in thick, cream-colored drapes whose purpose was to keep the music in the room and out of the neighborhood. There were three bookcases with every operatic score ever published, and a hi-fi with a pair of Klipsch corner speakers that offered Damir the extraordinary magic of opera while he gazed at the full-sized portrait of Isabella as a little girl over the fireplace. Everywhere he turned Damir felt his Isabella, smelled her fragrance and even, yes, sometimes heard her laughing—a laugh so happy it had to be real. And there was one other picture frame, on his bedside table. It was small, silver and empty. When Damir, however, glanced at the white piece of cardboard, he remembered Saša, and saw the baby's eyes bright with laughter and happiness. Saša would have loved Isabella.

Damir hired a housekeeper who went by the name of Avelina Simpolina. Avelina was a squarely built woman who had brought into the world ten round children. She kept her auburn hair tied back, giving her a sober demeanor. Avelina looked exactly her age, which was fifty-five years old. No one ever accused her of looking a day older or a day younger. Remarkably, each year on her birthday another wrinkle, another fold would suddenly appear in her face.

Avelina arrived at the apartments every day around midmorning when Didi was already at work. She left in the late afternoon when he was still away. As she rarely saw her employer, Avelina was obliged to leave Didi's supper in the refrigerator.

Damir never arrived home from the Teatro dell'Opera before midnight. His work helped him waste away the countless hours, hours that turned into days, weeks and months; it was time that smothered his suffering with budgets, meetings and reports. When he finally made it home, Didi stood in the hallway, closed his eyes and prayed that Isabella would come running out and leap into his arms. Many nights, when cats lined the rooftops to stare at the great clusters of stars that gathered about the half-moon, a sad and terrifying wail was heard from the dark floors above the street.

Now, instead of Avelina's asking Signor Damir why he left the meals she prepared for him untouched in the refrigerator, instead of her trying to find out if perhaps the pastas were a little too *al dente*, or the sauces a little too spicy, or if the assorted samples of regional Italian cuisine were not to his liking, Avelina simply took the food home, to her own husband and children. As time went on, Avelina's daily menu became less and less what she thought Damir might enjoy, and more and more what her family liked to eat. This gave her great freedom in the preparation of the meals, since there was very little her family would not, in fact, eat.

One day, on the last Friday in November, Damir forgot to leave Avelina's dues in the empty sugar bowl which was empty just for that purpose. The good woman was thus forced to wait until he got home that night. Unfortunately for Avelina, a new production of *Cosi Fan Tutte* was opening that night at the Teatro dell'Opera and Damir did not insert his key in the keyhole until one in the morning. By then, Avelina, who thought of herself as a most patient and understanding woman, was tired and irritable. She was thinking of giving her employer a piece of her mind when the sight of him drew a *"Gran Dio!"* According to Avelina, Signor Damir was emaciated. She was so horrified that she was unable to do anything but take her money, go home and promise herself to improve her cooking. After Avelina had left, Damir put down his briefcase and, without removing his raincoat, sat by Isabella's picture and closed his eyes. He was so weak and tired he thought he had fallen asleep when he felt the softest, sweetest kiss brush against his lips.

"Isabella—"

That night the neighbors did not hear any cries in the middle of the night, and next day, Damir's black suit and grey tie were exchanged for others that reflected a more positive and colorful change of mood. Suddenly, he was greeting and talking to people he had never greeted or talked to before. No one at the Teatro dell'Opera could imagine why. For months they had witnessed his slow capitulation to depression, but it seemed to them this was natural, since Didi was mourning the death of his wife. Besides, he still managed to function and carry out his duties in an efficient and professional manner. His colleagues were sympathetic to his sullen, quiet ways and accepted his lack of affability as a consequence of his loss, a loss that he bore with dignity but in private, because Damir, they understood, was not a friendly man.

Some speculated that the sudden change was due to another woman, others that he had simply terminated his grieving period and decided to get on with his life. Those who made discreet inquiries received a smile and a reply that raised more questions than it answered. "Isabella is back."

Avelina did not find any more of her meals left in the refrigerator and was surprised one day to find a note in the empty sugar bowl asking her to double the amount of food she made for supper. "But I'm already making plenty for two!"

✟

Since the death of Isabella, Damir had made a point of calling on Beniamino at his villa in Recanati every other week, if for no other reason than to inquire about the great Gigli's health. Most times Didi was greeted by Elvira, sometimes by a butler and once even by a maid, but never by Beniamino himself. On his last visit, Elvira was surprised that Didi's mood and clothing had acquired a lighter touch, although, she felt, he was still too thin. She invited Damir to have tea in the garden and later take a walk in the vineyard, but would not consider allowing him meet the tenor. "He never leaves his room. He calls me if he needs anything but we don't talk much anymore." Her voice faded but quickly regained its vitality. "He knows you come visit. He can see you from his window when you arrive."

"He blames me—"

"No, no, no," Elvira put out her hand. "He doesn't, I'm sure of it." Elvira stopped, turned and looked at Damir. "You see, Beniamino is trying to understand why after a life so full of good things, happy things—centered on Isabella—why the Father, the Son, the Blessed Mother and everyone who's supposed to look after us—why they would allow his wonderful, sweet and gorgeous child to be taken from him in such an awful, awful way. He wants to know what he did to deserve such a cruel punishment." Didi and Elvira walked side by side along the straight and dusty path that led to the main gate, which was rusty and covered with weeds. Just on the other side, the taxi was already revving its engine.

From his room, Beniamino opened the wooden shutters enough to allow a little sunlight inside and saw, far off in the distance, Damir get in the taxi and drive off to the train station.

Gigli remained by the window for ten minutes before he called for his secretary. Elvira found him in a red silk robe. He looked tired, and his hair had turned completely white.

"Yes, Maestro?"

"Who was the woman with Damir?" asked the great Gigli.

☩

December has always been a terrible month for those without family or friends. The anticipation of the Christmas holidays can turn holiday cheer into acute anxiety. Maestro Luigi Tarazzini, the artistic director of the Teatro dell'Opera, was concerned enough about Damir that he decided to invite the young man to his Christmas party. Among the guests would be members of the board of directors of the Teatro dell'Opera and their respective spouses, one or two singers, the musical director of the company and other important guests. Damir did not want to go to the party and had spent hours inventing all sorts of reasons to justify not going, when he received a telephone call from the artistic director.

"But I have so much to do," argued Damir.

"Do it for me, Didi, please," said the voice at the other end, in such a way that Damir understood he had to go after all. No one could remember the last time the artistic director of the Teatro dell'Opera had invited the company's production supervisor to his home. Then again, no one could remember when the production supervisor was related to Beniamino Gigli, who was still so popular that the city was considering naming the piazza where the opera theater was located after the great tenor.

Damir took the bus; everyone else arrived at the party in a limousine—Mercedes, Rolls Royces and a single American Cadillac. Tarazzini's residence in the Via Veneto was decked in as many colored lights as were available in the scene shop of the Teatro dell'Opera. The guests first assembled in the drawing room with its grand piano and wall-to-wall portraits of famous singers dating back two centuries, before being shown into the dinning room. It was a simple affair in the eyes of Maestro Tarazzini, who was a large man in every respect. He entered the salon dressed not, indeed, as Saint

Nicholas, but in a black caftan with a white sash and a white silk turban adorned with sequins and black pearls sitting atop his totally hairless head. The maestro was accompanied by a slim, blond, androgynous-looking creature of indeterminate age, who was also dressed in oriental fashion, answered to the name of Vito, and whom the artistic director, with a flick of his wrist and a thrust of his finger, introduced as his wife.

Maestro Tarazzini Christmas decorations included a Christmas tree that was hung upside down from the ceiling. It remained the topic of conversation all night because everybody wondered how the lights, the little dolls, candy, and angel hair, in addition to one translucent archangel impaled at the top—which in the case of the Tarazzini tree meant it was at the bottom—were all kept in place without falling victim to gravity.

Damir thought the spectacle both irreverent and very funny. Even Monsignor Tarazzini, the artistic director's brother, had a good laugh. People gathered in little groups where they talked about, replied to and pondered assorted nonsense. In the background, the Teatro's musical director played the piano, while two of the company's less-renowned singers sang medleys appropriate for the season.

Typical Damir. He kept to himself in a corner sipping a glass of wine, not saying much except greeting this one and that one as they passed by, until the artistic director bounced over and said, "Do you know, my dear, that this is the first year Gigli has not been to my Christmas party? Ever since I took over the company—and it's been a long, long time—he would come and bring Isabella with him. I remember her at six or seven running after her papa. She was so dear! I know you miss her very much and if there is anything I can do—" and Maestro Tarazzini stopped. He saw that Damir had tears in his eyes. Tarazzini grabbed Didi's face and kissed him on the cheeks, ordered champagne for his production supervisor, did a pirouette and went to look after the other guests.

An extremely beautiful girl tapped Didi on the shoulder, giving him such a start that he spilled his drink. "Oh, dear, I'm sorry!" she said with a laugh. She wore a tight blue dress and high heels that were clearly intended to make here look older than she really was.

"It's nothing." Damir wiped his hands with his handkerchief.

"I saw you by yourself and thought perhaps you needed a little company."

"No, I'm fine, thank you." Damir saw the girl had stopped smiling. "I'm sorry," he added quickly. "I didn't mean it that way. I meant—"

"I'm Eleonora Rezzoneti, and your name is Damir Pavelić—Maestro Tarazzini told me. Are you Russian?" Eleonora put out her hand and Damir took it, at the same time darting looks left and right.

"No, from—from Yugoslavia."

"What's wrong?" asked the girl.

"Wrong?"

"Why are you so nervous? I won't bite you."

"He did it on purpose," screamed Damir, throwing his jacket on the chair and yanking off his tie. It was three o'clock in the morning and he had just returned home from the Christmas party. Damir was furious. Tarazzini had seated the young, beautiful Eleonora next to him at the dinner table. It was a terrible disappointment to the other young men because after that Eleonora never left Damir's side. She had the most beautiful green eyes and the sweetest, most perfect mouth, with a pair of lips so sensual they promised romance. Her body was slim but not skinny, full but not hefty, small but not petite, and utterly appetizing. She had an aristocratic nose and long, soft, light brown curls that framed her doll's face like a portrait of a Renaissance princess—which, of course, she was not. She was just the daughter of Ludovico Rezzoneti, a shipping tycoon whose family and fortune had moved to Switzerland during the war. "What do I care!" yelled Damir. "I'll never go to one of his parties again. I'll quit first!"

One morning, while still on his holiday break, Damir decided to get out of the house and go for a walk. It was just after the New Year and it was cold. Damir wandered the city about with his usual unawareness of everything around him. He crossed the Tiber, stopping for a moment to look down on a small barge slowly making its way under the bridge, and continued walking aimlessly among the small shops in narrow streets, until he heard someone call his name. He turned but did not see anyone he recognized. At first, he thought that perhaps it was a colleague from the opera house, but the voice was a thin, high voice, like a child's. No one came forward and Damir went on his way, only to hear his name called again. Damir stopped and looked through the window of a bakery and saw it was full of people. No one caught his eye and the only thing he could see were the backs of a lot of heads and arms with pointing fingers. Damir had turned and faced the street when suddenly, the door to the shop swung open and slammed into Damir from behind so hard it knocked him to the ground. *"Didi!"* he heard the voice call out, this time he thought from the alleyway next to the store. Damir got up, looked at the sign on the storefront and realized he was in Trastevere.

He walked around the old neighborhood, ending up in a small bistro for lunch. Then, instead of going home, he decided to stop at the opera house to pick up a few papers he needed for work. It was almost seven o'clock at night when he arrived at the apartment. It seemed that Avelina had forgotten to turn off the light in the hall. But there was more than a light in the hall, there was the trace of perfume as well. Damir first entered the music room. "Isabella?" He continued to the kitchen and found a note in the empty sugar bowl. It was from the cook and it read, "Your sister asked me to let her in."

"My sister!" Damir rushed out of the kitchen. "Kati!" Damir had not seen his sister since leaving Argentina. "Katarina?" and Damir went from room to room until he reached the bedroom and there she was—not Katarina—but Eleonora. Damir was shocked; the girl was naked and lying on his bed, smiling.

"What are you doing?" said Damir softly, all but speechless.

"I think it's obvious. I—hope you don't mind," she said, thinking that he would not mind at all. Unfortunately for Eleonora, Didi did mind and minded a lot.

"Get out," he said trying to hold back his anger.

"W-what?"

"Get out of that bed! Get out of this room! It belongs to Isabella, you stupid, stupid girl!" screamed Didi.

Eleonora stumbled out of bed, confused and scared, and quickly picked up her clothes.

"This," and Damir waved his arms to include the room, "belongs to my wife!" Damir was not able to say anything else. He sat down next to the bed and sobbed. "My wife, my wife—" he was crying so hard Eleonora put her clothes on and rushed to his side.

"Damir, please forgive me. I had no idea—I heard she died a long time ago. I didn't know—I'm sorry—" Eleonora tried to take his hand but Damir pulled away. After a moment, Eleonora left the room. She was at the front door, embarrassed and angry with herself when Damir called her back.

"Wait, don't go." Didi was standing between the living room and the hall, his eyes red from crying. "I need someone to—I don't—I don't have anyone to—" and his voice faltered. Eleonora turned, closed the door and walked back to Damir. She gently put her arms around him and waited for him to do the same.

He didn't. Didi took Eleonora by the hand and into the kitchen, sat her down at the table and asked her if she had been following him during the day.

"No, why?"

He did not answer, and Eleonora waited for a moment before trying to bridge the uncomfortable silence between them. "Maestro Tarazzini said Isabella was very beautiful, and that you were very much in love."

Didi nodded.

"Sometimes it's impossible to forget, isn't it? You love someone so much you wonder if you can ever love again. And if you do, if it will be as wonderful." Eleonora knew that Damir was not listening, that he was thinking of Isabella. "That's what they say, but I wouldn't know; I've never been in love and don't know if I ever will be. It's too complicated, too involved," continued Eleonora, pushing back her chair and getting ready to leave.

Damir looked down at the floor one last time before getting up, walking to the living room and picking up the phone. "I'll get you a taxi."

"Don't. My car is downstairs." Eleonora found a pen, wrote down her telephone number, gave it to Didi, and kissed him on the cheek. "Call me. Don't wait too long, though, or I'll have to find someone else." Before Didi could even think of a reply, Eleonora opened the door and left.

He looked out the window and saw the red Ferrari drive off. He went into the music room, looked at the picture of Isabella, put on *Tosca* and fell asleep on the sofa.

The next day an irresistible urge compelled Damir to return to Trastevere; he went every day after that as well, for months, always expecting, in a way hoping he would hear someone call his name, though why this should happen or who he expected to step out from the shadows, Damir could not have said. He walked around looking in the shops, going in and buying a bottle of wine here, a newspaper there, but he did not hear his name again. In time, Damir forgot about Trastevere and kept busy on the other side of the Tiber.

On Rome's very festive and sacred Easter Sunday, Damir stood outside on his balcony and watched a crush of the faithful on their way to Vatican City. They traveled by foot, bicycles and bus; thousands upon thousands of men, women and children, priests and nuns.

"Didi!" It was the same voice! *"Didi!"* it called again.

From two stories up, Damir stared down at the crowd hoping to pick out the person yelling his name, but he never did, and whoever was calling out *"Didi!"* stopped. Damir waited until the last straggling novice vanished around the corner and the street was clear. He went inside, locked the French doors leading to the balcony, walked to the library and stood in the center of the room scratching his head.

✠

"Didi, Didi, I need to talk to you!
Let's see what we can do!"

It was Maestro Tarazzini. He popped into the little space Didi called his office. The artistic director looked quite elegant in a dark blue suit and red tie; his head, without a turban, looked as shiny as if it had been buffed by a shoe-shine boy (and it probably had been). "Good morning," he intoned, as if he were going to continue singing.

"Good morning."

The artistic director pulled up the only other chair in the cubicle that was not occupied by hundreds of books, librettos, reports and boxes of papers still to be filed. "I tried to be a singer once, did you know that?"

"I had no idea." Didi smiled.

"I had a most extraordinary voice. I could reach as many high C's as I wanted, and considering that I am not a tenor this was an incredible feat. My only problem was—and is—that aside from hitting high C, I can't do anything else. I'm tone deaf."

Damir laughed, put down the pen, leaned back on his chair and waited to see what his boss needed or wanted, which usually turned out to be the same thing.

"I have a surprise for you."

Didi raised an eyebrow, skeptical of anything Tarazzini might consider a surprise.

"I am giving you another office; I mean, look around, you can't even offer your guests coffee, soda—"

"I don't have guests. Those who come in here do so at their own peril—present company excepted, of course," said Didi.

"Ah, but, if I don't give you a bigger office, where are you going to put your assistant?" It was Tarazzini's turn to smile.

"I don't have an assistant," explained Damir.

"You do now." The answer forced Damir to sit straight and look very serious. "Oh, don't look at me that way, Didi, you'll get used to it."

"What are you saying, Maestro?"

"I am saying that my biggest contributor, my largest donor, the man responsible for paying the full production costs of this season's *Aida* and *Vespri* and—one more." The maestro scratched his chin and snapped his fingers. "*Manon Lescaut*. Yes, this most generous of men asked me in the nicest way if I could place his daughter at the Teatro dell'Opera."

"I don't need an assistant, and if I did I certainly wouldn't hire Eleonora Rezzoneti!"

"Why, Didi, you read the mind!"

"Maestro, that girl—" Didi began, but was cut short.

"That girl likes you. That girl wants you, that girl will do whatever she can to crawl between your legs. Now, I know you're a sensible young man, besides being a great producer. It reeks of politics, I know; we're selling our artistic integrity, I know that too. It's particularly offensive to you, of course! I'd be shocked if it wasn't! After all, you're the most honest and straightforward person—man or woman—I've ever met," and the artistic director sighed. "To you, it may not mean much. To me, it means a great deal. I've never met another honest and straightforward person in my life, certainly not in this business!"

"But Maestro!"

"So, my advice to you is—make her happy; by making her happy you'll make her papa happy, which in turn will make me very happy." Maestro Tarazzini bounced from his chair, smiled and added, "Everyone should always be happy. Any questions?"

Maestro Tarazzini was not being insensitive. Almost two years had passed since Isabella had been laid to rest, and Tarazzini thought that even if Didi had not gotten over the trauma he certainly should have been getting lonely by then.

"If she wants a job—" Damir began to protest. Again, he was not allowed to finish.

"You're not listening." Once more Maestro Tarazzini resorted to singsong. "She doesn't want a job, she doesn't need a job, she wants you!" He pointed at the production supervisor. "Is that so difficult to understand? You're a very good-looking young man—I wouldn't mind having you myself, to be perfectly honest, but that's beside the point. I can always find a lover," Maestro Tarazzini continued, almost as an aside, "a good producer, on the other hand—" He turned his attention back to Damir. "The point is, I don't care what you do. Keep her busy, that's all. How you keep her busy is your business."

"I can't believe this! I feel like a whore!"

"But, darling, that's opera!"

Damir was not a puritanical extremist. That he was a bit scared of sex, however, was understandable. After all, he was as inexperienced and as chaste as the dear girl who had died in his arms. But more than that, he had sworn to remain faithful to that same girl and nothing, but absolutely nothing was going to make him change his mind. On the other hand, temptations like Eleonora made keeping such resolutions more difficult and caused him great consternation, and that translated into impatience and petulance. And since life does not wait around for anyone to pick up the pieces of their disappointments, Damir had to deal with the mandates of the artistic director in the best possible way.

Three months after she began working for Damir, after a very long day running up and down the stairs, carrying boxes of papers, memos and reports to and from the stage, Eleonora sat with her boss in his office. "We've talked about opera all day and all night. Can't we talk about something else, please?"

"For instance?"

"Isabella."

"No."

"Why?"

"Because!"

"Look," said Eleonora softly, "I don't know what you're trying to prove, but you've proved it, all right? You can tell me to mind my own business—"

"Mind your own business."

Eleonora threw an angry look at Damir, not because she was in fact, angry, but because she was used to getting her way. Damir knew the difference. He leaned forward, took her hand and slowly began to tell the story of his love for Isabella.

Two hours later, having dropped Damir off at his house, Eleonora was convinced that seducing Damir would not only be impossible, but it would also be a shame. Damir's love for Isabella ought to remain a recollection of what it was and of what it could have been.

✚

"It was you in the bakery, it was you under my window! You were calling out to me!" said Didi, jumping to his feet and slapping the side of his head.

Felix smiled. He had been living in Trastevere at the time. Yes, it had to have been him; his soul, his spirit reaching out to someone he loved. Unbeknownst to Damir or Saša, their lives had again crossed paths, even though they did so in a foreign land.

"Did you ever go to the opera?" Damir asked Felix.

The pope shook his head. "I led a sheltered life."

"I can tell." Damir laughed and held his friend's face in his hands and kissed him. "You don't know what you mean to me. I know this sounds crazy, but you saved my life, Saša. I was dying when you showed up outside my window." Damir stopped talking and studied his Felix's face. "You know who pays for this orphanage? My sister. She sends me money, lots of it, to keep the place running. You know where she gets it? From a safe in Switzerland. You know who put it there? Draganović. You know where he got it? From a treasure my father's henchmen left behind after the war, a murderer's booty—lots of gold teeth and stuff. Pero and I found it in a cave near the farm. It's Irony dancing the tango with Fate. You remember Pero?"

"The shepherd?" Felix bit his lip. "No, he was—he died just after you left the farm." Felix did not say anything else lest he violate his sacred trust. But speech was not necessary; the deep sadness in Felix's eyes revealed the truth.

Damir sighed and slowly shook his head. "My father's legacy haunts this land. There are too many ghosts with too many scores to settle. But people have to learn to forgive." Damir got up and walked a little distance from Felix. "We have to look at the children and mark the future," he added, "or the killing will start again and never end. The Vatican—it has to stop thinking of the Balkans as its line in the sand. How can the Church justify killing children in the name of Christ? It is an outrage."

"I swear to you, it will change," said Felix.

"You can take some responsibility for what's happened here," suggested Didi. He walked back to Felix and messed up his hair, as he had been fond of doing to Saša. "There is hope for the Church after all." Damir walked slowly around the room because the bruises in his body made it uncomfortable for him to sit down. "I take it I should not ask why the Serbs let me go?"

"You can't stay here," was Felix's answer. "The captain—he let you go, but he'll be replaced by someone else, I know."

"I'm not leaving the children."

"Bring them with you," said Felix. He saw that Damir did not quite understand what he was suggesting, so he mentioned the mountain.

"You mean—to Travnik?"

"Nobody will bother you there, nobody will know where you are."

Damir thought about it for almost ten minutes before he smiled.

It was two in the morning when Felix and Damir decided to get some rest. A cot was brought out and set up in Damir's room, which was large and had its own bathroom. As soon as the lights were turned off, Felix heard the low rumble of jets flying far away. Even as he succumbed to fatigue, though, he could not get the captain of police from his mind.

Damir also heard the jets, and he too was thinking of the officer who had him arrested when he closed his eyes and fell asleep.

Two hours later, Felix opened his eyes, looked at his watch, saw it was four in the morning, and was amazed at the light coming in through the windows. It was brilliant, almost blinding. Then, Felix saw the boy standing by his cot.

"Saša," said the boy. He was about nine years old and very well dressed in breeches and a tweed jacket. "You won't forget me, will you, Saša? I know I'll never forget you, and I'll be waiting for you."

Felix sat up and rubbed his eyes. He realized the little boy was Damir, Damir as Felix remembered him from so long ago when they had met for the first time in that most unfortunate of towns called Glina. "Didi!" Felix turned and looked at the bed where, a few hours earlier, Damir the old man had gone to bed. He was still lying there, his eyes closed and his face serene and at peace.

"Damir, please—no!" cried Felix, kneeling by his friend's side and weeping. Slowly, the ceiling opened to the sky, heavenly music filled the room and there, in the center of that blessed miracle, in the midst of a thousand celestial beings, little Damir was led to heaven by a beautiful angel that Felix recognized as Isabella.

PETER'S CHOICE

31

Rostas was at the door. He looked out into the open. The dew on the grass glistened like drops of crystal beneath the thin layer of mist. The sun peered from the peak of Mt. Vlašić and he felt the eternal tranquility of the mountains that made up his personal haven, a haven that not even war could disrupt, and that made life bearable for the old man. The world, it seemed, had greater concerns and was content to leave him alone. Olga was dead, had been dead for seven years; Draganović never returned to Yugoslavia after becoming pope; and Felix had not visited the farm since Olga's death. It was too long to be by yourself; too long to sit in a tavern until curfew forced you to go home, home to the mountain. Esmeralda was kicked out of town along with every other Croat and Serb, but, for some reason, they—the ones who sit in grey little rooms and decide the fate of others—they forgot Rostas. He was not sure if anyone in town remembered that he had been a member of the Ustaše and a friend of the priest Draganović. He doubted anyone cared. Rostas had become insignificant.

He had the house to himself, of course. There were stacks of magazines and old newspapers everywhere, and every time he went to town he brought back new ones, to help him keep up with what was happening elsewhere.

The barn was empty now, the last sheep having died the year before. That was all right, though; he had never liked tending sheep.

And so, there he was in a bright morning late in summer, just out of bed enjoying the view and wondering if he should boil water for tea, when he heard a strange rumbling from the other side of the range. The civil war that had devastated most of Bosnia had been over for more than a year, though in the Balkans peace never lasted very long. Rostas hoped that whatever was making the rumbling noise would stay away from his mountain. It did not. The rumbling became louder and the old man saw black spots on the sun. It was a good five minutes before the black spots turned into helicopters, and three minutes before Rostas was able to count eight of them flying side by side and heading for the farm. Soon, the helicopters were circling the house, flying low and making so much noise that if he had had chickens, sheep or cattle they would have run off in a panic. The white helicopters with United Nations markings were looking for a place to land. This made Rostas a little nervous because the house was set against the back of a cliff, and there was not a flat stretch anywhere except out where the sheep used to graze, at least two kilometers from the house. It was not long before the whirlybirds disappeared and the rumbling on the mountain stopped. It was as good a time as any for Rostas to go into the house and have his tea.

He had been sitting in the kitchen, reading up on the latest scores from the World Cup when Rostas heard a much different sound to that of helicopters.

"Kids!"

He ran to the window and saw a bunch of kids running up the hill, screaming. "Kids!?" Lots and lots of kids! They were accompanied by men in uniforms and blue berets, one or two other civilians and—Felix!? Yes, that was Felix out in front!

It took the UN six hours to load the children into the helicopters and move them from the orphanage in Srebrenica to the farm. NATO provided air cover—just in case. It was an ideal place for Damir's dream, a dream that Felix was going to help preserve. The farm was isolated enough to be of no interest to anyone, including the Muslims running Travnik. A third of the children in the orphanage had been born to Muslims anyway.

PETER'S CHOICE

To Felix, Rostas looked as big and strong as ever, though his head was all white and some of his teeth were missing.

"Felix! What is this?"

"Time you had company!" said Felix embracing his friend.

"How's the pope?"

Felix stepped back. "Dead."

"The pope—Draganović is dead?"

Felix nodded.

Rostas dropped his arms to his side, and for a second Felix thought the old man was going to cry. He frowned, sadly cast his eyes to the ground then shook his head in disbelief. "What's going on?" he asked at last, following Felix into the house.

"My friend," said Felix after they were sitting down in the living room. "Do you know that once I thought you were my father? You were very kind to me—all those years before I went to Rome. I owe you the fond memories I have of this place. This is and will always be your home. But now, in the same way that I came here long ago as an orphan, these children also need a place to live. You'll be in charge, don't worry. I'm having the place fixed up, and there will be people to help you—no priests or nuns, just folks willing to give of themselves to help the children. I'm having a solar panel installed with a generator so you can have electricity; also I think it's time we had a telephone in the house and, who knows, maybe even—even have a television."

"A television!" Rostas laughed.

"Rostas, I am so disappointed," said Felix changing the subject, the words spoken slowly and sadly. "I was nothing to Draganović."

"What was that?"

"I was a tool, an instrument he used for his own gain, a puppet he manipulated to help him become pope and then to help him bully the Church to do his bidding. I loved him, Rostas, I was devoted to him. I never lied to him, never! I did everything he told me and I never betrayed my vows. But he—he lied to me." Felix shook his head. "I thought he loved me. He didn't. He used me, that's all." Felix sighed. "I mean, just think of this. What would you do if you found your son in bed with another boy, eh? Tell me, what would you do?"

"I'd beat the crap out of him."

"Right."

"Well, you know what I mean," said Rostas softly, feeling that perhaps his answer might have been too harsh.

"Listen, regardless of what you would do, whether you actually 'beat the crap out of him' or not, you would feel let down. It's part of your culture and you can't help it." Felix walked back to the table. "Remember the time he told you to take me to Paradise? Why did he do that? Do you think he might have been worried that I was hurting inside? No! He didn't give a damn about that. Draganović just wanted to know if I would be a liability instead of an asset; he wanted to find out if I was a weak and passive, emasculated freak unable to crack heads." Felix put his hands on the table. "When your child hurts you hurt more than him, tears blind you and the pain wipes out your ability to reason; you certainly would never throw your son in the arms of a whore to prove a point, then mask the shame and embarrassment with a biblical quote! I was nothing to him, I was just one of the little animals from the barn; one he branded with intolerance. He used me, Rostas, the same way he used everyone, including you and Olga."

"Me?"

"How many times did you risk your life for him? Do you have any idea what would have happened to you, to Olga, if the government had found out you were smuggling Pavelić's treasure out of the country?"

"Who told you that?" asked Rostas, the color drained from his face.

"It must have taken you years to bring it all out of the cave and for Draganović to take it to Rome piecemeal in his diplomatic pouch," added Felix.

"Are—are you sure he's dead?" asked Rostas looking worried.

"Yes, Draganović is dead," answered Felix. "He was a sinful, wicked, and despicable fanatic. You have no idea how evil he was."

Rostas sat quietly for five minutes while Felix walked back and forth, a restless and very angry Felix. Rostas guessed Felix must have found out something he was not supposed to. Yes, Felix was disappointed, and that disappointment, thought Rostas, had turned to bitterness. It was to be expected, but, said Rostas, it was wrong.

"Wrong?" Felix turned from the window.

"Wrong, bullshit—you call it what you want," said Rostas. "I knew Draganović better than most, I knew him better than you did. We did a lot of things that were not right, yes we did, and I'm not proud of what I did. I don't know if he was—proud, I mean—but it doesn't make a difference. The man is dead now." Rostas paused, nodded slowly, and stared at his hands, which were resting on the table. Then Rostas at last garnered enough courage to look up at Felix. "Yes, he was a tough fellow; hard as nails, a fanatic, as you said. He was driven, yes, that's it, driven. You know he was tortured by the partisans, right? He was almost killed. I saw him when he got back from the hospital and let me tell you it was not a pretty sight. Maybe he should not have held a grudge for so long, I agree that maybe wanting to get even, to get back at the Serbs for what they did to him was not a very Christian thing to do, but you know, Felix, Draganović was just a man doing the best he could. And—" Rostas pushed back his chair and walked over to Felix. "—and maybe, maybe that wasn't good enough, who knows?" Rostas hesitated for a second before he continued. "I wouldn't be surprised if Draganović did some terrible things. I did, though I never killed anyone—at least I don't think I did. But I know many who did. We were soldiers then, even Draganović. Oh, he might have worn a priest's collar, but he was a soldier, a soldier fighting everybody, the Reds, the Serbs, and the Muslims. Now, don't misunderstand me, I'm not saying we should now justify acting like beasts because say—my grandfather was shot by the partisans in '41. No, I'm not saying that. But who is going to protect my family, my country, my Church if I don't—especially when I believe in my heart that we're all going to be murdered? And Draganović believed that, too! That's what Draganović thought would happen sooner or later. You say Draganović was a liar? I guess he must have lied sometime. But he never lied to me. He always told me the truth, even—even when it was dangerous. You say he was a hypocrite? He was never a hypocrite with me. He didn't have to be. Was he wicked and despicable? I am sure there are some who believe he was, probably with good reason, too." Rostas shook his head. "But I have news for you, Felix, no matter what you say, no matter what he was to others, and regardless of how you feel, Draganović loved you. He loved you more than anything in his life. You were the one person in the whole world who could make that man you call wicked, and a hypocrite, smile. The sound of your name, Felix, it was magic to Draganović. And he was proud of you, of everything you did! You never heard him brag about you—of course not. I did. When he wrote to me his letters were three pages long talking about you. You were his son, period. Before you went to Rome, those couple of years when you were here with me and Olga, he used to drive me crazy with telegrams and letters asking how you were. He had me go to town and call him twice a week to let him know if there was anything you needed; if he could send you this or why I couldn't get you that, and did you have enough clothes, and to make sure to take you to see a dentist, and to see a doctor, and even—" Rostas laughed, and the tears finally rolled down his face, "—he even warned me never to spank you. That was not easy, you know."

Felix sat down on the sofa. He buried his face in his hands and wept. Rostas put his hand on his shoulder. "Felix, you are a priest. You are supposed to forgive. Forgive him—for your sake, and never again say he did not love you. That is just not true."

Felix reached up for the old man's hand and kissed it. Then he stood up and embraced his friend as he had not done since that time when he was expelled from school. "Thank you," said Felix at last.

"Come with me," said Rostas seizing Felix by the arm. "Come!" He led him to the basement while kids, UN personnel, and Didi's assistants went in and out of the house.

"What is it?"

Once in the cellar, Rostas locked the door to keep everyone else outside. He rushed down the stairs and grabbed a hammer from a toolbox that lay on the floor beside the furnace. Then, with the help of a chisel, he removed two bricks from the wall next to a pile of firewood, reached into the hole and pulled out a book and a shawl. "I found them the night you were brought here—as a baby."

Felix looked at the blood-stained Koran, at the paisley shawl. His hands trembled.

"The night you arrived with the Pavelićs, we went back out—Draganović, the little man that came here with the Pavelićs, and me. Draganović wanted to make sure there was no trace of anything that could lead the Reds to the farm. We found two men dead on the road. They didn't have anything on them, no papers or nothing. But when I searched around with a flashlight I found that!" Rostas pointed to the Koran. "Draganović told me to get rid of them."

"You didn't. Why?"

Rostas shrugged.

Felix slowly turned the pages of the sacred book. "Let's go!"

"Where?"

"To Komar!"

"But Felix," said Rostas chasing Felix up the stairs, "it's—it's not safe!"

Rostas and Felix left the cellar and bumped into Damir's freckly aide. "Oh, I'm sorry! I was looking for more rooms."

"This is Rostas," said Felix. "He owns the place. Now, there are rooms downstairs and upstairs—and there's the barn, it's big enough for a dozen cots at least. See what you can do. In any case, we'll just build a new wing or two—something, I'll think of something!"

And while the young woman went outside to help organize the relocation of the children, while children played outside without fear of getting shot by snipers, Felix and Rostas got in the old Citroën and drove down the mountain, and through the town of Travnik. No one stopped them. Some of the locals recognized Rostas as he waved at them, and some remembered Felix.

They reached Komar in twenty minutes, and just beyond the village Rostas found the collective farm where Enes and his clan used to live, and where the shepherd was sure to be living still if he had managed to survive the civil war. "Nothing is changed," said Rostas. "Enes!" he yelled. Then, he turned to a boy about ten years old who had come out of one of the huts. "Hey, kid, do you know Enes?"

"I hope so! He's my father! Hello, Ady! What are you—" The boy stopped and took a closer look at Felix. "You're not Ady!"

"You're right. Do you know where I can find him?"

Rostas and Felix were led inside the shack where Hamdai and his family lived. The family still had only one light bulb, but Ady had built another room in the back, bigger than the one that had held the stove they used to sit around. Adnan had become a teacher and—it soon became apparent—had never stopped looking like Felix, except that the life of a peasant is more difficult than the life of a pampered city boy, and the difference showed in the added lines on his face and his rough hands. He had once traveled as far as Sarajevo in order to practice his profession, but that was before the civil war. He had since moved back home to care for his aging father and mother.

Ady was standing behind his mother. Elma and Hamdai looked remarkably well for their age. Their eyes were not as sad as Felix remembered. And Enes was called and he too joined the group. He had grown taller, and fatter. Enes saw Felix lay the Koran and paisley shawl in front of Elma, who looked at it matter-of-factly. She caressed the book, then kissed it. "My mother's," was all she said, and cried a little.

The sunlight streaked through the windows, allowing extra brightness in a room that was always too dark. Felix took Elma's hand and whispered, "I am your son."

Elma turned and touched his face. "Nermin."

Felix embraced and kissed his mother, his father and his brother, Ady. One by one, Felix greeted every cousin, nephew and niece—most of whom, upon hearing they had a priest in the family, ran to meet him in Hamdai's house. Some were alarmed, but Felix met and hugged them all. It was inevitable that the family should try now to compress a lifetime into a few hours. Felix, finally, would no longer have to answer people that he was "about" eight, twenty, thirty, and so on; he learned he had been born on the fourteenth day of March, 1947.

Slowly, Felix put the pieces of his life together. Once, there had been a little Serbian shepherd, who was murdered and then reincarnated into a Muslim family, only for fate to snatch him and place him in Catholic hands. He was baptized Roman Catholic and christened Felix Ronnoco—O'Connor spelled backwards. It was poetic justice with a local twist: Serb-Muslim-Croat, a Balkan trinity.

32

Rome was covered with a heavy blanket of fog that made air travel dangerous. Felix challenged the elements and, three hours after leaving the mountain, the Italian Air Force helicopter touched down at the Vatican.

The pope was met at the tarmac by Cardinal Tomaso and Father d'Stesi, who accompanied him in a brisk walk across the grounds of the Holy See, to the Apostolic Palace.

"Is that so?" said His Holiness as Tomaso related the events of the past week. "Father d'Stesi, please call Cardinal Carelli and Cardinal Pino. Tell them we wish to see them at eight, tomorrow morning—sharp."

Next morning, Cardinal Carelli arrived at his office with his usual aplomb, threw down his briefcase, but remained standing by his desk. "Good morning, Marcello."

"Good morning, Eminence."

"Are these my messages? Thank you."

"And Cardinal Pino called five minutes ago to remind you of your appointment with the Holy Father in exactly one hour."

"Thank you. Ah, Marcello, the Church is in the hands of the Beast, my son! Did I tell you they found the body?"

Marcello stared at his mentor in disbelief.

"Bring me coffee, will you please. I need something strong to calm my nerves."

The secretary left the room, returning a minute later with a cup of black coffee and a tray of jam sandwiches.

"I don't know what I would do without you, Marcello. You are the only man in the Holy See who understands what I am going through. You are the only man who knows Felix Ronnoco for what he is."

Marcello said nothing, but stood by in case His Eminence needed anything else.

"There, look what I brought you. I know you like history. I think you'll find these books interesting reading."

Marcello picked up the two small volumes from the cardinal's desk. One was a crisp copy of a seventeenth-century booklet by Juan de Mariana entitled *De rege*, in which the author justified tyrannicide. The other book was about François Ravaillac, the assassin of King Henry IV of France (the king had been considered an enemy of Rome). "Ah, my dear boy," said the cardinal. "I warned them, I tried to open their eyes to the danger. What do they do? They run and hide like frightened rabbits. Our Mother Church is in great danger, and no one, not a soul is doing anything about it!"

Forty-five minutes later, Cardinal Carelli arrived at the vestibule to the pope's chambers and found Cardinals Pino and Tomaso waiting for him. If someone had taken Pino's blood pressure at that moment, they would have had His Eminence hospitalized. Cardinal Carelli, on the other hand, was as cool as the breeze caressing the papal curtains. The cardinals were greeted by Father d'Stesi, who led them in to see the pope. The Holy Father was sitting behind his computer. The moment he saw the red hats, he logged off, got up and met them halfway. After the formalities, Felix showed Carelli, Tomaso and Pino to their seats. "Brother Carelli, how are you? It has been a long time since we shared your company."

Carelli nodded, thinking of the thousands of times he had asked himself why.

"What is it you have to tell me?"

"The Holy See is being blackmailed," said Carelli.

"We know all about it. His Eminence Tomaso filled me in last night." The pope stared at the floor for a moment, his eyes profoundly sad, then walked slowly behind his desk. "Do you know the name of our legal counsel?"

"Yes, Holiness."

"Call him at once. Tell him what you know, and that he should contact the authorities. We will not fall prey to blackmail."

Carelli darted a look at Pino (who looked at Tomaso) before he turned once more to the pope. "Yes, of course; after all, the charge is devastating."

"No, it's not. No one will take the accusation seriously; they will think it is the product of a diseased mind, unless we pay or bargain for silence." The pope looked sternly at Carelli. "The answer is no, never."

"They found the body, Holiness," added Carelli.

"We know," returned the pope quickly.

"Holiness—"

"Yes, Brother?"

"Is it—true?" Carelli almost whispered the words. He accompanied the query with a crease in his forehead and a casting of his eyes to the ground, all meant to reflect his humility and deep concern.

"All we will say is this," began the pope. "What we know we cannot divulge, but—we had nothing to do with Father O'Malley's death. We told you what has to be done. We never want to hear of this again."

"But, Holiness—"

"Never!'"

"I beg your pardon, Holy Father, but how did the American priest get to Rome?" asked Carelli.

It was, perhaps, five seconds before the pope turned to Carelli. "Brother Carelli, bureaucrats should never be so reckless. They should know how to camouflage their ambition." And the pope turned to Cardinal Tomaso. "It seems to us that our dear brother Carelli has been working too hard. Please find a worthy candidate to relieve His Eminence from his many responsibilities. Anything else?"

"Holiness!" said Carelli in a tone that was not only loud but openly disrespectful.

"You have your instructions." And the pope rang for Father d'Stesi.

Carelli was as red as his zucchetto. He mumbled something on the way out. He had suffered the worst indignity possible from a man he considered a usurper. He had been publicly humiliated and he was out of a job.

As soon as the cardinals had left the room, Pope Felix sat down at his computer and wrote a secret memorandum to the Curia detailing what he knew about Father O'Malley. He included copies of his correspondence—to and from Pope Leo XIV—during the time that, as Bishop Felix Ronnoco, he had organized the pope's visit to the United States. Felix V went on to detail his opposition to any dealings with the extortionists. The pope threatened to deal harshly with anyone violating his orders.

☩

Marcello left the Vatican at eight o'clock that night. He had spent the day consoling Cardinal Carelli and helping His Eminence pack his belongings. Then, Marcello drove around for another couple of hours in an attempt to put his thoughts in order. He was, to put it mildly, discomposed.

He arrived at his apartment around eleven-thirty, lit candles to his father and mother, picked up a branch of thorns, knelt, prayed and flagellated himself with such devotion that, in a few minutes, he was covered in blood and sweat.

His one-room flat was in a five-story tenement in the center of town. The walls and the ceiling needed a new coat of paint, as the green that had been applied when Noah built the Ark was now peeling. The dull, hardwood floor was covered with an area rug that had seen better days. There were a few amenities in the room: a small but willing trestle table (it never complained when the dishes were removed and it became an escritoire), a sofa bed, two wooden chairs, a tiny refrigerator that along with a hot plate stood in for a kitchen, a sink that along with a toilet and shower stall played the part of a bathroom, and a shaded floor lamp that matched the thick and dreary brown curtains. There were a few pictures of the Holy Family on the walls; a crucifix, a watercolor of a Nordic-looking Jesus, a small blue and white figurine of the Virgin and pictures of Father Subraggi's parents. His devotional books cluttered the room. There was a nightstand by the sofa bed with an alarm clock, a black telephone and a Bible given to Marcello by his mother the day he took his vows.

He recalled his mother's struggle to send him clothes and money for food while he was at Saint Pius; his father had been shot by the fascists during the war and was an invalid. Marcello's father and mother had lived long enough to see their son become a priest. There was no one else.

It was two in the morning when Marcello went to bed. He tossed and turned for an hour but could not fall asleep. He was about to seek comfort in the scriptures when, for some unexplained reason, he thought of a photograph he kept in a cardboard box with his papers. It was a class picture taken two years before he left Saint Pius. The photograph was big and in black and white. Marcello brought the lamp a little closer and carefully studied the faces in the picture. It did not matter that the photograph was not in color because Marcello could remember the vivid hazy blue of the sky and the bright, hot sun of that midafternoon in September. He felt the jostling and the horseplay, heard the banter and the exasperated cries of the priests and nuns calling the boys to order.

There were three rows of boys, teachers, priests and nuns standing on the steps just outside the front entrance to the school. All the boys were smiling (except Marcello), as they waited patiently to have their picture taken. The altar boys looked smart in their freshly ironed surplices and red cassocks, their hair slicked back and perfumed with brilliantine. Their smug self-assurance was evidence that they did not have a care in the world.

Felix Ronnoco was in the back row, on the right of the picture. Young Felix was not looking at the camera, because his attention was on the boy next to him. Felix had a wide grin on his face and was playfully elbowing his friend in the ribs. What was the other boy's name? Marcello did not remember, but was sure it was the same boy that Father Uncelli had wanted to move in with Marcello. Ah, and there was the eagle-eyed priest himself, looking with contemptuous distaste at the antics of Felix Ronnoco. It was interesting that, after so many years, the old picture continued to reveal its little secrets. The photograph captured in time and space the precious, fleeting exuberance of the altar boys. How could Marcello have known that Ronnoco was the anointed one, and that he would rise above all others to become Vicar of Christ? Maybe if Marcello had been a little less arrogant, less of a bore and had behaved more in line with Christian sentiment his life would have turned out differently. Of the boys in the picture, only Marcello looked unhappy. Did he have a premonition, then, that many, many years later, he would look back on the time he spent at Saint Pius and realize that those were the best days of his life?

☦

The princes of the Catholic Church arrived in twos and threes. Cardinal Carelli, although relieved of his obligations, arrived with Cardinal Pino. It was an occasion for all members of the Curia, many from around the world, to meet with Pope Felix V prior to the coronation. Most of the cardinals had never met the pontiff, although Cardinal Bailey's office had prepared a fine four-color brochure that included Felix's biography (even though it did not include a recent photograph).

"Brother Pino, why don't we have an agenda? This is quite extraordinary." The complaint was issued by a thin red stick under a zucchetto at the very end of the line who was archbishop of Pretoria.

"We don't have an agenda because His Holiness did not think it was appropriate. The Holy Father will arrive shortly and I'm sure he will explain everything." Pino wondered when.

"We should address the problems triggered by that ill-advised crusade of Pope Leo!" The suggestion was volunteered by a flat-faced prelate who did not bother to stand. His brothers reacted by making snide remarks and showing solemn frowns.

"That is important, yes," answered Pino, yawning.

"We are coming apart at the seams," said Eleuterio Cardinal Calderón, from Bogotá.

The cardinals mumbled, shuffled their feet and became restless. It was almost lunchtime.

Suddenly, the doors opened quickly and Pope Felix V walked in at a pace described by some as between a quickstep and a jog. He was followed closely by Father d'Stesi. The pope was easily the youngest man in the room. There was an energy emanating from the pope, a vivacity of spirit, a sharpness of the senses that contrasted dramatically with the manner of the men in red.

"My brothers," began the pontiff after a quick look around the room. "It is time we got ready for the next thousand years." The Church, declared the pope, was about to enter a new millennium, and it had to embrace all mankind without reservations. His mandate for the Holy Church would be to make the Catholic Church the seat of divine justice and moral perfection on earth.

After a careful study of the Church's history, its teachings and its sacred traditions; after a dutiful analysis of the times; and with the unequivocal certainty of his reverent responsibility, the pope had decided upon the following reforms, to take place immediately: It would be the policy of the Holy See to mediate conflicts as an impartial arbiter between nations, to try to prevent wars.

It would be the policy of the Holy See to employ its resources to further education and to eliminate ignorance and superstition from the earth.

It would be the policy of the Holy See to combat hunger, poverty and want everywhere.

It would be the policy of the Holy See to struggle against the illegal drugs decimating the children of the world.

Felix took off his glasses, had a sip of water and continued. "These are lofty aims. There will be many who will feel threatened by our new assertiveness and will do anything to see that we fail. But we will not fail! Instead, with utmost humility but firm resolution, we will open our parochial schools to any child, free of charge and regardless of creed or ethnicity."

Jews, Protestants, Muslims, and—free! The emphasis was on "free." The word floated back and forth among the pope's audience like a soap bubble.

"We will contribute to the well-being of the communities where we live and worship by paying property taxes.

"In keeping with our apostolic embrace, we will abrogate all restrictions—except that of abortion—that were promulgated in *Humanae Vitae*." (*Humanae Vitae* was the encyclical put out by Pope Paul VI reaffirming a ban on contraception.)

"Holiness! The sanctity of life!" cried the sanctimonious men in red; half of them were on their feet.

"We are not talking about the sanctity of life!" The pope raised his voice just enough to be heard over the shouting, and cast a long and hard stare at the cardinals. "We are talking about contraception. Abortion is wrong, but contraception is not abortion. Contraception is the intentional prevention of impregnation. The key word is *prevention*. Who are we to tell a woman she should not avoid getting pregnant? It defies common sense. If we can do that, we might just as well argue that people should not inoculate themselves, since inoculation is also a means of preventing a natural condition of the human body—contracting disease." Pope Felix took a deep breath— one that Cardinal Pino thought was close to a sigh. "*Humanae Vitae* is flawed. We are sure you remember that our venerated brother Pope Paul organized a group of experts to counsel him on the subject, only to end up discarding their advice. We think it is arrogant for men who have taken a vow of celibacy, men who know nothing or very little about bearing children, to tell a woman when she should or should not get pregnant. Let me ask you, dear brothers, who in this reverent group has ever seen a prophylactic?"

Well, the cardinals were not making snide remarks anymore; they were not shuffling their feet or grumbling because they were hungry. They were stunned. Pope Felix V had just declared a revolution that would be felt by every man, woman and child on the face of the earth.

✠

"Marcello, Marcello, Marcello! It's the end! We are undone!"

The secretary heard with disbelief the pope's agenda for the Church.

"He is mad, the pope has lost his mind!" His Eminence paced the office, which he had not vacated yet, having been given two

PETER'S CHOICE 451

weeks to clear out his papers and personal belongings. He held a rosary in one hand and a cigar in the other, and was so upset that Marcello worried his boss might suffer a stroke. "All is lost, all is lost!" And Carelli threw himself in his favorite chair, extinguished his cigar, buried his face in his hands and began to cry.

"Eminence, what about the Curia?"

"It's up in arms, it is a scandal!"

And indeed, shortly thereafter, five cardinals, among them Pino and Bailey, arrived in Carelli's vestibule and humbly inquired for their eminent brother.

Carelli received them with a long face and tears in his eyes. Marcello left the room after making sure to leave on the intercom so he could hear everything discussed behind closed doors.

The cardinals met for three hours. They discussed, argued and debated what to do to save the Church from Pope Felix. Pino suggested they draft a document humbly requesting His Holiness to rescind the changes, followed by a motion to impeach the Holy Father. Four of the Eminences in the room agreed this would be the best way to proceed. Carelli did not. He knew the rest of the Curia would be too frightened and would probably never go along with their plans. "And, let me remind you, I am sure we have not heard the last of that abominable criminal Venavić."

Indeed. Against orders from Pope Felix, Cardinal Carelli had contacted the man's attorney, told the lawyer that the Vatican was not going to negotiate a settlement, and suggested they sell the story to the tabloids. Carelli thought an exposé on the day of Felix V's coronation would force the Curia to impeach the Holy Father. Only then would the Church be saved. (The ten newspapers and television networks approached by Counselor Ponti, however, turned down the story, citing legal repercussions if they published it without corroborating evidence.)

"Beware, my brothers, we are standing on the edge of a precipice," said Carelli, fixing his glance on his brothers in red.

That night, Marcello accompanied Cardinal Carelli to his home and stayed for dinner. In the course of a lively discussion on absolution and salvation, Marcello pondered whether it was possible for a man to reach heaven after taking a life.

"You mean killing someone? Well, nothing in life is absolute," replied His Eminence. "There are exceptions to every rule." Carelli meant that all deeds were measured and balanced against universal truths. Killing a human being who was causing irreparable harm and who was the cause of great injustice was, therefore, both permissible and justified.

"I read those books you gave me, Eminence," said Marcello.

"Oh, really?" said Carelli, with a tone of surprise too pointed to be genuine.

"He was a man of great courage," added Marcello.

"Who was that?" asked the cardinal, sipping his wine.

"Ravaillac."

"Yes, he was," answered Carelli. "But, you must remember, Henry IV was an enemy of the Holy See."

Cardinal Carelli was kind enough to have his chauffeur drive Marcello back to Rome. It was past one in the morning, and Marcello expected to rise early and meet Cardinal Carelli at the Vatican at seven and join him in attending Pope Felix V's coronation.

After prayers to his parents, Father Subraggi spent the night, again, not sleeping. He had so many things in his mind, all revolving around the man he once knew as Felix Ronnoco, and around his mentor, Cardinal Carelli. If Pope Felix was forced to give up the apostolic throne, who would take his place? Cardinal Pino? Cardinal Tomaso? Cardinal Bailey? Or was there the remotest possibility that Cardinal Carelli would be chosen? Anything was possible. Still, speculation was unnecessary while Felix V remained on the throne.

It has been documented many times that people contemplating homicide are rarely clearheaded, and that most pass their days in a fog of dread and horror, their thoughts suffocated by nightmares.

Marcello was already up and about at five in the morning. He looked haggard—the circles under his eyes spoke clearly of a sleepless night—and felt just as miserable. He knelt before the pictures of his father and mother, said another prayer, ate a little toast and drank a lot of coffee. He took a quick shower, shaved, pressed his cassock, pants and collar, then opened a drawer in the kitchen and

PETER'S CHOICE 453

took out a long, glimmering and very sharp butcher knife, guaranteed to penetrate deeply and cut through the heart without any trouble. Father Subraggi tucked the knife inside the cassock, practiced a few times the act of taking it and stabbing quickly, prayed some more, and, at exactly at eight o'clock—an hour late—he left for the Vatican.

"My dear, you look positively wretched," said Cardinal Carelli. "Are you ill? Why didn't you stay home?"

"I am feeling fine, Eminence," lied the priest. He apologized for being late, and soon began filling up cardboard boxes with His Eminence's belongings. The Holy See might have been crowning a pope, but Carelli still had to move out.

It was midmorning when Carelli suggested they leave for Saint Peter's. Carelli would sit with the Curia, while his secretary would be on his own.

A hundred thousand people assembled in Saint Peter's square; by eleven in the morning, even the pigeons were displaced. Ten different bands marched and played under the bright blue Roman sky, including that of the Swiss Guards, who looked incredibly spruce in their glittering uniforms and pointy helmets. The atmosphere was of the sort found in large fairs. There were banners and flags and vendors selling just about everything for the occasion, from figurines of the Blessed Mother to figurines of the Blessed Pope (though the little dolls bore little resemblance to Felix because no one knew what he looked like).

Inside Saint Peter's, the dignitaries—ambassadors and representatives of the civilized governments of the world—had gathered and were seated according to their rank and their countries' importance. Three different choruses, including one made up of altar boys from Saint Pius X (the pope's alma mater) entertained the crowd, as thousands of priests, bishops, nuns and Swiss Guards lined the long, wide marble staircase leading down from the Apostolic Palace, waiting for Pope Felix V to appear. The pope, dressed in his coronation robes, was to descend the staircase flanked by ranking members of the Curia, while a small detachment of Swiss Guards led the procession. Once he reached the bottom of the stairs, His Holiness would climb atop a platform that bore a gilded throne upholstered in red velvet, seat himself, and be carried like a Roman emperor on the shoulders of robed acolytes through a multitude of well-wishers until he reached the pulpit in the large cathedral, where Pope Felix V would receive the pontifical miter on his head.

It was, according to many who had witnessed such spectacles before, always an impressive show, one steeped in mysticism and magic.

Ten minutes before Felix V left his chambers, Father d'Stesi entered the room looking very shaken and whispered something in the pope's ear. Immediately, Pope Felix asked everyone to leave the room. He changed quickly into a plain white cassock, left the Apostolic Palace through a rear door, and ran to the Government Palace, followed closely by Father d'Stesi and ten security men. Felix knew the building better than anyone else. He climbed the steps two by two and quickly reached Cardinal Carelli's door. He found the entire floor cordoned off by plainclothes security men.

"What's going on?" asked Felix.

"We don't know," answered a tall brawny fellow guarding the hall leading to Carelli's vestibule. They had heard a scream, rushed to investigate and found the door to Cardinal Carelli's chambers locked. The man inside was the cardinal's secretary, but he would not allow anyone to enter the room, and he kept calling for the pope. "Holiness, it's not safe for you to be out here. Please leave; return to the Apostolic Palace."

"Where is His Eminence Carelli?" asked Felix.

No one had seen Cardinal Carelli since he arrived at the Vatican early that morning.

"What's the man's name?" asked the pope.

"You mean inside?" The security man pointed to Carelli's door. "Father Subraggi, Father Marcello Subraggi."

For a moment Felix said nothing. The name brought back painful memories. He had not known Carelli's secretary was his old nemesis. "What does he want?" No one knew. "Call him."

One of the security men put his face against the locked door and called to Father Subraggi. "Father, His Holiness is out here. He begs you to come out. Please, open the door." The man turned to the pope. "Holiness, please. Don't make this more difficult for us. The man may be armed."

The door was unlocked from inside. Five security men surrounded Pope Felix, while two others opened the door and walked slowly into the room. The narrow hall between the vestibule and Carelli's office was empty. The men proceeded inside and saw, at the far end of the room, Father Subraggi standing against the wall, a rosary in one hand, praying. Across from Father Subraggi, sprawled on the sofa, was His Eminence Cardinal Carelli, the handle of the butcher knife sticking out from his chest.

Marcello looked up and smiled at the security men entering the room. The men made sure there was no one else in the room before they allowed the pope to enter.

Felix, in his white cassock and zucchetto, walked in and stood at the door. He was horrified. He slowly approached Carelli's body and administered the last rites. Then he turned and looked at Marcello.

"He was going to destroy you, Holy Father!" said Marcello, weeping. Marcello tried to advance toward Felix, but was held back by the pope's bodyguards. Felix waved them aside, and Marcello fell to his knees, grabbed the pope's hand and kissed it. "I am your devoted disciple." Marcello turned and pointed to the dead Carelli. "He was an ambitious, evil man, Holiness! He was plotting to overthrow Peter's successor! He was determined to destroy the Holy See! How could I let that happen? But who could I turn to? No one would have believed me. I am just an insignificant peasant. No one would have listened to me. I—I had to do something! I had to save you from him. Will you forgive me, Father? Please forgive me, and pray, pray for my soul."

The pope stared at the deranged, miserable wretch and was overcome with pity; he knew that as a boy, Marcello once had as many dreams in his head, as young Felix Ronnoco.

✠

Hours later, feeling the jeweled, pointed miter on his head, Felix remembered Roger Bacon, a Franciscan and one of the great minds of the Middle Ages who, in the year 1271, wrote the following:

". . . The Holy See is torn by the deceit and fraud of unjust men. Pride reigns, covetousness burns, envy gnaws upon all; the Curia is disgraced . . . Let us see the prelates, how they run after money, neglect the care of souls, promote their nephews and other carnal friends, and crafty lawyers who ruin all by their counsel. The ancient philosophers, though without that quickening grace which makes men worthy of eternal life, lived beyond all comparison better than we, both in decency and in contempt of the world with all its delights and riches and honors, as all men may read in the works of Aristotle, Seneca, Tully, Avicenna, al-Farabi, Plato, Socrates and others; and so it was that they attained to the secrets of wisdom and found out all knowledge. But we Christians have discovered nothing worthy of those philosophers, nor can we even understand their wisdom; which ignorance of ours springs from this cause, that our morals are worse than theirs. There is no doubt whatever among wise men but that the Church must be purged."

It was a slow and painstaking process that took Felix V longer than he expected. Two years after his coronation, the pope had instituted most of his reforms. Many bishops complained, some protested. Felix allowed no dissent; the bishops were replaced.

On the twenty-fifth of December, 2000, with a little more grey at the temples, and wearing reading glasses, Pope Felix V addressed the world from the loggia of Saint Peter's basilica. "On this day we celebrate the birth of our Lord Jesus Christ. In six days we will enter a new millennium. We welcome this new era of understanding and love among men, and embrace all mankind without reservation.

"We beg forgiveness for the unprecedented bloodbaths of the crusades; repent the thousands upon thousands of murders perpetrated by the Holy Roman Inquisition in its pursuit of policies stained with hatred, ignorance and bigotry; atone for our misguided policies of appeasement during World War II; and confess setting brother against brother in Northern Ireland and in the former Yugoslavia.

"We confess our sins and most humbly repent. May the love of God the Father, the Son and the Holy Spirit enlighten your lives as it has enlightened ours. Amen."

✠

Given that he was almost twenty years younger than the youngest bishop or cardinal, Felix V sat back, held fast to his reforms and allowed time to run its course. He never appointed another bishop, never created another cardinal, and so, by the year 2015, only lower-ranking priests and their pope remained as members of the clergy; all others had passed on to glory. The monastic orders too, deprived of apostolic sponsorship, slowly dwindled into nonexistence. By 2020 the Vatican City State was run by a secular Italian bureaucracy and, in the year 2022, Felix V returned the lands of the Vatican to the Italian government. In 2028, at the age of eighty-one, Pope Felix V left the Apostolic Palace for the mountain above Travnik, and once again became Felix Ronnoco, the shepherd.

And so it happened that in the year 2028, the Roman Catholic Church, like its predecessor the Roman Empire, like so many empires before that, became history and the legacy of Peter finally came to an end.